# THE BLOODING

# JAMES McGEE

# *The Blooding*

HarperCollins*Publishers*

HarperCollins*Publishers*
77–85 Fulham Palace Road,
Hammersmith, London W6 8JB

www.harpercollins.co.uk

Published by HarperCollins*Publishers* 2014
1

A catalogue record for this book
is available from the British Library

ISBN: 978-0-00-739459-3

Set in Sabon LT Std by Palimpsest Book Production Limited,
Falkirk, Stirlingshire

Printed and bound in Great Britain by
Clays Ltd, St Ives plc

FSC™ is a non-profit international organisation established to promote the
responsible management of the world's forests. Products carrying the FSC
label are independently certified to assure consumers that they come
from forests that are managed to meet the social, economic and
ecological needs of present and future generations,
and other controlled sources.

Find out more about HarperCollins and the environment at
**www.harpercollins.co.uk/green**

This one is for my cousin, Mark.
Flying free . . .
O:nen Ontiaten:ro

NEW YORK STATE
*1812*

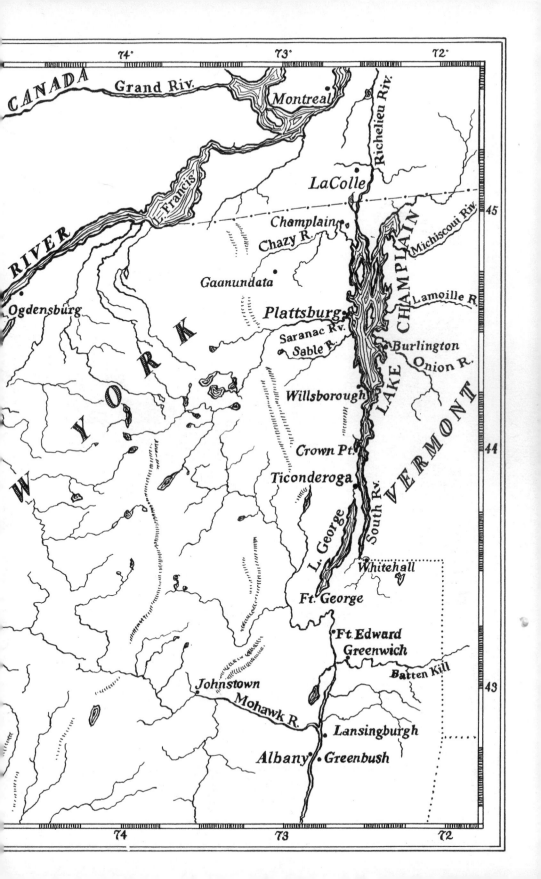

# MOHAWK NAMES

The Mohawk at the time the novel is set had no written language. Iroquois vocabulary was originally transcribed by Jesuit missionaries and therefore, even today, there are discrepancies in the origins, spelling and meaning of certain words. I'm indebted to Thomas Deer of the Kanien'kehá:ka Onkwawén:na Raotitióhkwa Language & Cultural Center in Kahnawá:ke, Montreal, for his guidance.

Rotinonshón:ni: "People of the Longhouse" – the Six Nations – Iroquois Confederacy
Kanien'kehá:ka: "People of the Place of the Flint" – the Mohawk
Kaion'kehá:ka: "People of the Marsh" – the Cayuga
Oneniote'á:ka: "People of the Standing Stone" – the Oneida
Ononta'kehá:ka: "People of the Hills" – the Onondaga
Shotinontowane'á:ka: "People of the Great Mountain" – the Seneca
Tehatiskaró:ros: "People of the Shirt" – the Tuscarora
Kaianere'kó:wa: "The Great Law of Peace" – the Constitution of the Six Nations
Oyata'ge'ronóñ: "People of the Cave Country" – the Cherokee
Wendat: "People of the Island" – the Huron

Ahkwesáhsne: "Where the partridge drums" – Mohawk village near St Regis

Kahnawá:ke: "On the rapids" – Mohawk village near Montreal

Kanièn:keh: "Land of the Flint" – Traditional homeland of the Mohawk

Kenhtè:ke: "Place of the Bay" – Mohawk village on the Bay of Quinte, Canada

Anówarakowa Kawennote: "Great Turtle Island" – North America

Atirú:taks: Adirondacks

Kaniatarowanénhne: "Big Waterway" – the St Lawrence River

Ne-ah-ga: Niagara

Oiqué: Hudson River

Senhahlone: Plattsburg

Tanasi: Tennessee

*If they are to fight, they are too few;*
*If they are to be killed, they are too many.*

Theyanoguin
Wolf Clan, Kanien'kehá:ka
Warrior, sachem, diplomat, orator

# PROLOGUE

*Mohawk Valley, New York State, May 1780*

Reaching the edge of the forest, Lieutenant Gil Wyatt halted and dropped to one knee. Cradling his rifle, he gazed down at the scene spread below him, his expression calm and watchful.

From his elevated position the ground sloped away gently, gradually widening out into a swathe of rich green meadow-grass speckled with blue violets, through which ran a shallow stream bordered by stands of scarlet oak and white willow. Tree stumps dotted the incline, evidence of the labour that had gone into converting the land and raising the single-storey, timber-built cabin that nestled in the centre of the clearing.

A small cornfield and a well-stocked vegetable patch occupied one side of the dwelling. On the other, there was a paddock containing two horses and beyond that a fenced-in pasture where three dun-coloured milk cows grazed placidly, tails swishing to deter the summer flies. Half a dozen chickens competed for scratchings in the shade of the cabin's slanted porch.

A barn and a hen house made up the rest of the homestead, along with a clapboard privy and a lean-to that had been affixed to the cabin wall as a storage shelter for winter fuel. A pile of untrimmed branches lay nearby, next to a large oak stump. Driven into the stump were a hatchet and a long-handled wood-man's axe.

1

There was no sign of the farm's occupants.

*Looks quiet enough,* Wyatt thought as he admired the stillness of the setting. Dawn had broken more than an hour earlier but across the surface of the meadow, dew drops shone like diamonds in the soft morning haze.

It was as the lieutenant's gaze shifted to the plume of woodsmoke rising in a lazy spiral above the cabin's shingle roof that a shadow moved within the trees on the far side of the clearing. Wyatt tensed and then watched as a young female white-tail stepped out from behind a clump of silver birch.

Releasing his breath, Wyatt remained still. His sun-weathered face, forage cap, moss-green tunic, buckskin leggings and tan moccasin boots blended perfectly with the surrounding foliage. The direction of the smoke had already told him he was down-wind so he knew the doe had not picked up his scent. If she had she would have stayed hidden and Wyatt and the four men with him would have been oblivious to her passing; with the possible exception of the individual on Wyatt's right flank.

Unlike the Rangers, he wore neither shirt nor jacket nor any vestige of a uniform, though his appearance would have left even a casual observer with little doubt as to his calling.

His red-brown torso was bare save for two hempen straps that criss-crossed his chest, from which were slung a powder horn and a buckskin ammunition pouch. A quilled knife sheath hung on a leather cord around his neck. His lower half was clad in a blue trade-cloth breechclout and thigh-length leggings. Leg ties beneath each knee held the legging in place. Like the others, he wore deer hide moccasins.

His head, while shaven, was not unadorned, for at the back of his scalp was a ring of long black hair. Braided into the hair were three black-and-white eagle feathers. As if his hairstyle and dress were not striking enough, there was one more affectation that separated him from his companions. His face, from brow to chin, was concealed behind a rectangle of black paint. Not an inch of his natural colour was visible save for a crescent of white muscle set deep in the corner of each unblinking eye.

His right hand gripped a shortened musket. His left rested on

2

the head of a tomahawk tucked into his waist sash. A maple-wood war club in the shape of a gunstock lay in a sling across his back.

The Indian, whose name was Tewanias, kept his gaze fixed on the doe. He did not flinch as a large yellow-jacket, lured by the smell of bear grease and paint, landed on the back of his left wrist, folded its wings and began to explore his exposed forearm.

The white-tail hovered nervously at the edge of the wood, clearly apprehensive at the thought of venturing into the open, though the fact that she was there at all indicated that she was probably a regular visitor to the clearing and therefore not averse to using the stream to satisfy her thirst, despite its proximity to human habitation.

For a moment it looked as though she might overcome her fear, but at a sudden stream of excited bird chatter erupting from within the forest, the doe froze. With a lightning-fast turn, one swift bound and a flash of pale rump she was gone, swallowed by the dense underbrush.

The Indian's attention switched immediately towards a point on the opposite side of the stream. Wyatt followed his companion's gaze to where a natural break in the trees and the beginning of a rough track could just be seen and watched as half a dozen riders cantered into view. They were in civilian dress and each of them carried a musket, resting either across his thigh or strapped across his back.

A sharp hiss came from the man on Wyatt's left. "Militia!"

"God damn!" another nearby voice spat forcefully. Then, more speculatively, "You think they're after *us*, Lieutenant?"

The words were dispensed in a distinctive Scottish brogue.

Without taking his eyes from the riders, Wyatt shook his head, frowned and said softly, "How would they know?"

"Some of their scouts will have got through. They'll have reported in," the second speaker, whose name was Donaldson, responded, murmuring, as though to himself, "They must have gotten wind of us by now. They'd have to be blind, otherwise . . . or bluidy deaf."

Wyatt pursed his lips. "They'd be coming from Albany in force if that was the case. Our own scouts would have warned us."

It was a wonder, Wyatt reflected as he watched the horsemen draw closer to the stream, that the expedition had made it this far without being discovered. Though Colonel Johnson had been very careful in his preparations, periodically sending out skirmishers along Champlain's wooded shoreline in order to fool enemy scouts into thinking the final incursion was merely one in a number of reconnaissance missions and therefore of no specific interest.

Only when the force had finally assembled at Lachine had war bands from the Lake of Two Mountains been dispatched to search for and capture rebel patrols to prevent them from spreading word of the impending raid, thus clearing the path for the main body of troops to come in behind them undetected.

And, incredibly, the plan had worked. More than five hundred men – over three hundred whites and nearly two hundred native allies – had successfully negotiated the landing at Crown Point and completed the nine-day march through enemy territory without a shot being fired.

This morning was the first time Wyatt and his group had sighted a rebel force – either regular or militia. *If that's what this lot were*, Wyatt thought. Their dress and weaponry certainly suggested the latter, but then every man who lived in this part of the state, close to what could loosely be termed the frontier, had a gun, for protection as well as a means of providing food for the table. It was possible they were just a group of friends out for a morning's hunt.

But Wyatt didn't think so. There was something in the way the riders held themselves that smacked of grim authority. They looked like men with a purpose.

As he watched them walk their horses across the stream in single file, Wyatt began to experience an uneasy feeling deep in the pit of his stomach.

When Tam started towards the door, ears pricked and grumbling at the back of his throat, Will Archer's first thought was

4

that it was more than likely a deer. The animals often came to drink at the creek, particularly at this hour, when the sun was just showing over the treetops and the farm was at its most peaceful.

He looked through the window but there was nothing to see, save for the view of the stream and the forest; the same view that greeted him every morning.

Behind him, the dog emitted another low, more menacing growl.

*Not a deer then,* Archer thought, alerted – though he wasn't sure why – by the continuing gruffness in Tam's voice. The hound was extremely good natured as a rule and signs of aggression were rare.

As the first of the riders came into sight Archer's stomach knotted.

"Will? What is it?"

Archer turned to his wife, who was standing by the table in a flour-dusted linen apron. Her hands were bound in a damp cloth, holding a loaf she'd just removed from the oven. Turning the hot bread on to the board in front of her, she put down the cloth and tucked a stray lock of dark hair behind her ear, leaving a fresh smudge of flour on her right cheek.

"Stay here," Archer instructed.

She frowned, concerned by the warning note.

"We have visitors," Archer said.

Curious as to whom they might be, his wife walked towards him, wiping her hands on her apron, and looked past his shoulder. By now, all six horsemen had forded the stream and were nearing the cabin. Her face went pale.

Archer reached for the loaded musket that was leaning against the wall by the door. Beth Archer laid a hand on his arm.

"It's all right," Archer said. "I'll deal with them." Gently removing his wife's hand, he nudged Tam away from the door with his knee. "Good lad, stay."

Before his wife could offer a protest or the dog follow, Archer cocked the musket and stepped outside, closing the door behind him. The hens clucked indignantly as they were forced to step out of his path.

Musket held loosely across his arms, he waited.

The riders slowed their mounts and fanned out, finally stopping in a rough line abreast in front of the cabin's porch. One of them, a lean man in his forties with sallow features and the stain from an old powder burn on his right cheek, eased his horse forward. He was dressed in a long blue riding coat and a slouch hat. With his right hand resting on the musket laid across his saddle horn, he addressed the man on the ground.

"Morning, William! A fine day, wouldn't you agree?"

"It was," Archer said, without warmth.

The rider acknowledged the slight with a thin smile. He considered Archer for several long moments and then said, "You'll know why we're here."

Archer met his gaze. "And you know my answer. You've had a wasted journey, Deacon. I've already told you; my loyalty's to the King."

"I'm sorry to hear that," the rider said.

Archer's eyes moved along the line of horsemen. They were dressed in a similar fashion to Deacon and all, save one, carried the same cold expression on his face. Archer was acquainted with each of them. Four were fellow homesteaders: Deacon, Isaac Meeker – the florid-faced man to Deacon's right, who farmed land two valleys over – and the surly-looking pair on Deacon's immediate left, Levi and Ephraim Smede.

The Smede brothers were seldom seen apart. Rumour had it that was the only way the pair could muster one functioning brain between them. When they weren't helping their father on the family farm, they hired themselves out as labourers to anyone who wanted a wall built or a stream dammed – or someone intimidated.

Axel Shaw, the dour individual on Ephraim Smede's left, was postmaster over at the settler village near Caughnawaga. Archer turned his attention to the rider at the other end of the line. Curly-haired, with angular features, he was the youngest of the group. Archer could see by the way his hands were fidgeting with his reins that he was more ill at ease than the others, as if he would rather have been someplace else.

"That you, Jeremiah?" Archer enquired pleasantly. "Haven't seen you for a while. How've you been? How's Maggie? Beth was hoping to call in on her the next time we picked up supplies at the store."

The horseman shifted uncomfortably, embarrassed at being singled out. "She's well, thank you." Refusing to meet Archer's eye, his gaze slid away.

"Enough," the man called Deacon cut in. "We're not here for a neighbourly chat. This is business." He looked at Archer. "So, you won't reconsider?"

"Not now," Archer said; his tone emphatic. "Not ever."

The horseman considered the reply then said, "Maybe you should have left with the others."

Archer shook his head. "I've too much sweat and blood invested in this place to walk away." He stared fixedly at the man on the horse. "Or see it purloined by the likes of you."

The rider coloured. Recovering quickly, he assumed a look of mock hurt. "You wound me, William. What sort of man d'you take me for?"

"A goddamn traitor," Archer said flatly.

The humour leached from Deacon's face. "Not a traitor, Archer. A *patriot*. Like these men with me; men who've had their fill of paying unfair taxes to a country on the other side of the world and not having a thing to show for it."

"A country *you* fought for, Seth," Archer responded, "as I recall. You took the King's shilling then. Was it so long ago, you've forgotten which side you were on?"

"I've not forgotten, but a little more remuneration wouldn't have gone amiss."

Archer's eyebrows lifted. "What were you expecting? We defeated our enemies; the King's enemies; *and* we lived through it. That should have been reward enough."

"Not for me," Deacon snapped. His grip on the musket tightened and then, as if having come to a decision, he intoned solemnly, "William Archer, by the authority vested in me by the Tryon County Committee, you are hereby called to attend the County Board in Albany. There to appear before the Commissioners for

Detecting and Defeating Conspiracies, in order that you may swear an Oath of Allegiance to the State of New York and the Congress of the United States of America."

"No." Archer shook his head. "I've told you: my allegiance is to the Crown, not your damned Congress. Besides, I've better things to do than make a wasted journey all the way to Albany and back. I've a farm to run; stock to care for."

Deacon looked out towards the pasture and sneered. "Three milk cows? Not what *I'd* call a herd."

Archer stiffened. When he spoke, his voice was brittle. "And you'd know all about that, wouldn't you?"

Deacon's head turned quickly. "What's that supposed to mean?"

Archer stared coldly back at him. "Don't play the innocent, Seth. I know damned well that losing my other two cows was your doing. Wouldn't be surprised if you paid those two to do your dirty work, either." Archer indicated the Smedes. "I hear breaking the legs of livestock is one of their specialities."

Deacon's eyes darkened. "You need to curb that tongue, my friend. That's slander. Men have died for less."

"You'd know about that, too, I expect. And pretty soon, Deacon, you're going to realize I'm not your friend. So you'd best ride on. There's naught for you here."

Archer heard the cabin door open behind him.

Deacon rose in his saddle and tipped his hat. His expression lightened. "Oh, I wouldn't say that. Morning to you, Mrs Archer."

Beth Archer did not reply. She stood in the doorway, the checked cloth in her hands, staring at the line of riders. The flour smudge on her cheek had disappeared, Archer noticed.

Unfazed, Deacon lowered his rump and adjusted his grip on the musket. "Thing is, the Commissioners want reassurance that you're not passing information to enemy forces."

Archer sighed. "I'm a farmer. I don't have any information to pass, not unless they'd like to know how many eggs my bantams have been laying."

"Anyone refusing to swear allegiance to the Patriot government *will* be presumed guilty of endeavouring to subvert it."

Archer's eyebrows rose. "Commissioners tell you to say that, did they? Must be difficult trying to remember all those long words. Good thing you're the spokesman and not either of those two." Archer threw another look towards the brothers.

"There's still time to recant," Deacon said.

"Recant? Now you're sounding like Pastor Slocum. Maybe his sermons are starting to have an effect after all. He'll be pleased about that."

"If you renounce Toryism you'll be permitted to stay with no blemish attached to your character."

"Well, that's a comfort. And if I refuse?"

"Then you'll be subject to the full penalty of the law."

"Which means what?"

"Anyone who refuses to take the oath will be removed."

"Removed?" Archer felt the first stirrings of genuine concern. "To where?"

"A place where they're no longer in a position to do damage. Either to another part of the state, or else to a place of confinement."

"You mean prison."

"If necessary. It's my duty to inform you that unless you're prepared to take the oath, this land becomes forfeit, as do all goods and chattels, which will be sold off for the benefit of the Continental Congress."

"*Sold?*" Archer shot back. "The hell you say! Stolen, more like! And how do you propose to do that? You going to hitch it all to a wagon? Or roll everything up and deliver it to Albany in your saddle bags? *That*, I'd like to see."

"'T'ain't the farm that'll be heading Albany way, Archer. It'll be you. You *and* your family."

It was Levi Smede who'd spoken. A thin smile played across his sharp-edged face.

Archer stared at him. His finger slid inside the musket's trigger guard. "You're threatening my *family*, now?"

Deacon threw the brother a sharp look before turning back. "I've orders to deliver you to the Board, under guard if necessary. It's up to you."

"Well, I suppose that answers *that* question," Archer said.

"Question?" Deacon frowned.

"Why there's six of you."

He looked along the line. Deacon was riding point, but based on their reputations, the Smedes were undoubtedly the more significant threat, though Ephraim was the only one of the two holding a musket. Levi's was still strapped across his shoulders. Of the other three, Shaw and Meeker, although they had their weapons to hand, would probably hesitate. Jeremiah Kidd, Archer sensed, would be too scared to do anything, even if he did manage to un-sling his musket in time.

Throughout the exchange, Archer had become increasingly and uncomfortably aware that Beth was standing behind him. He knew that it would be no use telling her to go inside. Her independent streak was part of what had attracted him to her in the first place. He was surprised it had taken her this long to come out to see what was happening.

"There's just you and me," Deacon said, his voice adopting a more conciliatory tone. "No reason why this can't be settled amicably. All you're required to do is ride with us to Johnstown and place your signature on the document. Small price to pay for all of this."

His eyes shifted to the porch where Beth Archer was framed in the doorway. The inference was clear.

Archer stepped forward. "Go home, Deacon. You're trespassing. This is my land. I fought for it once. Don't make the mistake of thinking I won't do so again."

Deacon turned his attention away from the house and stared down at him in silence, eyeing the musket. Finally, he nodded. "Very well, if that's your decision; so be it. Ephraim, Levi . . ."

*So much for "just you and me"*, Archer thought.

"Will!" Beth cried, as Levi Smede grinned and drew a pistol from his belt.

Archer threw the musket to his shoulder.

"Inside, Beth!" he yelled, as Deacon brought his gun up.

Archer fired.

The ball struck Levi Smede in the chest, lifting him over the

10

back of his saddle and down into the dust. The pistol flew from Smede's hand.

Archer was already twisting away when Deacon's musket went off, but he wasn't quick enough. The ball punched into his side with the force of a mule kick. Pain exploded through him. Dropping his musket as he fell, he heard another sharp yet strangely distant report and saw Deacon's head snap back, enveloped in a crimson mist of blood and brain matter. Hitting the ground, he saw Beth draw the pistol from beneath the checked cloth, aim and fire.

Axel Shaw shrieked and clamped a hand to his thigh. Dark blood sprayed across his horse's flank.

Ephraim Smede, bellowing with rage at his brother's plight, flinched as another shot rang out and stared aghast as Isaac Meeker's mount crashed on to its side, legs kicking. Searching frantically for the source of the attack, his eyes were drawn to a puff of powder smoke dissipating in the space between the barn and the hen house.

"Bitch!" Spitting out the obscenity, Smede aimed his musket at Beth Archer. The gun belched flame. Without waiting to see if the ball had struck, he tossed the discharged weapon aside and clawed for his pistol.

Meeker, meanwhile, had managed to scramble clear of his horse. Retrieving his musket, he turned to see where the shot had come from, only to check as a ball took him in the right shoulder, spinning him like a top.

Archer, on the ground, venting blood and trying to make sense of what was happening, found Jeremiah Kidd staring at him in puzzlement and fear. And then Archer realized that Kidd wasn't staring *at* him he was staring *past* him. Archer squirmed and looked over his shoulder. Through eyes blurring with tears he could see four men in uniform, hard-looking men, each carrying a long gun. Two of them were drawing pistols as they ran towards the house.

Another crack sounded. This time it was Kidd who yelped as a ball grazed his arm. Wheeling his horse about, he dug his heels into the mare's flanks and galloped full pelt in the direction of the stream.

Only to haul back on the reins, the cry rising in his throat, as a vision from hell rose up to meet him.

Wyatt, discharged rifle in hand, stepped out from the side of the barn. He'd been surprised when Archer had shot Smede, assuming that Deacon would be the farmer's first target. It had taken only a split second to alter his aim, but he'd not been quick enough to prevent Deacon's retaliation. As a result, Archer was already on his back by the time Deacon met his emphatic demise, courtesy of Wyatt's formidable, albeit belated, marksmanship.

It had been Jem Beddowes, Wyatt's fellow Ranger, who'd shot Meeker's horse from under him. Beddowes had been aiming at the rider, but the horse had shied at the last moment, startled by the volley of gunshots, and the ball had struck the animal instead, much to Beddowes' annoyance. His companion, Donaldson, had compensated for the miss by shooting Meeker in the shoulder, which had left the fourth Ranger – Billy Drew – and Tewanias with loaded guns, along with two functioning rebels, the younger of whom, to judge by the way he was urging his horse towards the stream, was fully prepared to leave his companions to their respective fates.

Isaac Meeker, meanwhile, having lost his musket for the second time, pushed himself to his knees. Wounded and disoriented, he stared around him. His horse had ceased its death throes and lay a few feet away, its belly stained with blood from the deep wound in its side. Deacon and Levi Smede were sprawled like empty sacks in the dirt, their mounts having bolted. Half of Deacon's face was missing.

He looked for Shaw and saw that the postmaster had fallen from his horse and was on the ground, trying to crawl away from the carnage. The musket looped across Shaw's back was dragging in the dirt and acting like a sea anchor, hampering his progress. He was whimpering in agony. An uneven trail of blood followed behind him.

A fresh shot sounded from close by. Not a long gun this time, but a pistol. Meeker ducked and then saw it was Ephraim

Smede, still in the saddle, who had fired at their attackers. Meeker looked around desperately for a means by which to defend himself and discovered his musket lying less than a yard away. Reaching for it, he managed to haul back on the hammer and looked for someone to shoot. He wasn't given the chance. Ranger Donaldson fired his pistol on the run. The ball struck the distracted Meeker between the eyes, killing him instantly.

Ephraim Smede felt his horse shudder. He'd been about to make his own run for the stream when Billy Drew, having finally decided which of the two surviving riders was the most dangerous, took his shot.

The impact was so sudden it seemed to Smede as if his horse had run into an invisible wall. One second he was hunkered low in the saddle, leaning across his mount's neck, the next the beast had pitched forward and Smede found himself catapulted over its head like a rock from a trebuchet. He smashed to the ground, missing Shaw's prostrate body by inches. Winded and shaken, he clambered to his knees.

He was too engrossed in steadying himself to see Ranger Beddowes take aim with his pistol. Nor did he hear the crack nor see the spurt of muzzle flame, but he felt the heat of the ball as it struck his right temple. Ephraim Smede's final vision before he fell was of his brother's lifeless eyes staring skywards and the dark stain that covered Levi's chest. Stretching out his fingers, he only had time to touch his brother's grubby coat sleeve before the blackness swooped down to claim him.

Determining the rebels' likely escape route had not been difficult and Wyatt, in anticipation, had dispatched Tewanias to cover the stream's crossing place.

It was the Mohawk warrior's sudden appearance, springing from the ground almost beneath his horse's feet, that had forced the cry of terror from Jeremiah Kidd's throat. The mare, unnerved as much by her rider's reaction as by the obstacle in her path, reared in fright. Poor horsemanship and gravity did the rest.

The earth rose so quickly to meet him, there was not enough time to take evasive action. Putting out an arm to break his fall didn't help. The snap of breaking bone as Kidd's wrist took the full weight of his body was almost as audible as the gunshots that had accompanied his dash for freedom.

As he watched his horse gallop away, Kidd became aware of a lithe shape running in. He turned. His eyes widened in shock, the pain in his wrist forgotten as the war club scythed towards his head.

The world went dark, rendering the second blow a mere formality, which, while brutal in its execution, at least saved Kidd the agony of hearing Tewanias howl with triumph as he dug his knife into flesh and ripped the scalp from his victim's fractured skull. Brandishing his prize, the Mohawk returned the blade to its sheath and looked for his next trophy.

Archer knew from his years of soldiering and by the way the blood was seeping between his fingers that his condition was critical. He looked towards the porch, where a still form lay crumpled by the cabin door. A cold fist gripped his heart and began to squeeze.

*Beth.*

Hand clasped against his side, Archer dragged himself towards his wife's body. He tried to call out to her but the effort of drawing air into his lungs proved too much; all he could manage was a rasping croak.

*Why hadn't she done as she was told?* he thought bleakly. *Why hadn't she stayed inside?* His slow crawl through the dirt came to a halt as a shadow fell across him.

"Don't move," a voice said gently.

He looked up and found himself face to face with one of the uniformed rifle bearers.

A firm hand touched his shoulder. "Lieutenant Gil Wyatt, Ranger Company."

"*Rangers?*" Archer blinked in confusion and then, as the significance of the word hit him, he made a desperate grab for Wyatt's arm. "My wife; she's hurt!"

"My men will see to her," Wyatt said. He flicked a glance at Donaldson, who crossed swiftly to the cabin. "Let me take a look at your wound."

"No!" Archer thrust away Wyatt's hand. "She needs me!"

He tried to push himself off the ground, but the effort proved too much and he sank down. "Help her," he urged. "*Please.*"

Wyatt looked off to where Donaldson was crouched over the fallen woman. A grim expression on his gaunt face, the Ranger shook his head. Laying his hand on Archer's shoulder once more, Wyatt helped him sit up. "I'm so very sorry. I'm afraid we're too late. She's gone."

The wounded man let out a cry of despair. Knowing that nothing he could say would help, Wyatt scanned the clearing. Twenty minutes ago, he had been up on the hill, admiring the tranquillity. Now the ground seemed to be strewn with bodies. As Donaldson covered the woman's face with a cloth, Wyatt turned back to her husband.

Archer made no protest as Wyatt prised his hand from the wound, but he could not suppress a gasp of pain as the Ranger opened the bloodied shirt.

One glance told Wyatt all he needed to know. "We must get you to a surgeon."

The nearest practitioner was in Johnstown, but to deliver the wounded man there would be asking for trouble. An army surgeon and a brace of medical assistants had accompanied the invasion force. They were the farmer's best chance.

Although, given his current condition, Wyatt doubted whether the wounded man would survive the first eight yards, let alone the eight miles they'd need to traverse across what was, in effect, hostile country.

He looked off towards the paddock, where the horses were staring back at him, ears pricked. Wyatt could tell they were skittish, no doubt agitated by the recent skirmish, but it gave him an idea.

"Is there a cart or a wagon?" he asked.

"The barn," Archer replied weakly. He tried to point but found he couldn't lift his arm.

"Easy," Wyatt said. Cupping the farmer's shoulder, he called to his men. "Jem! Billy! There's transport in the barn! Hitch up the horses! Smartly now!"

As he watched them go, he heard a murmur and realized the farmer was speaking to him. He lowered his head to catch the words.

"You're Rangers?" Archer enquired hoarsely as his lips tried to form the question. "What are you doing here?"

"We came for you," Wyatt said.

"*Me?*" Puzzlement clouded the farmer's face.

"You and others like you. We're here under the orders of Governor-General Haldimand. When he learned that Congress was threatening to intern all Loyalists, he directed Colonel Johnson to lead a force across the border to rescue as many families as he could and escort them back to British soil."

Archer stared at him blankly. "Sir John's returned?"

"Two nights ago. With five hundred fighting men, and a score to settle. Scouting units have been gathering up all those who wish to leave, from Tribe's Hill to as far west as the Nose."

"There's not many of us left." Archer spoke through gritted teeth. "Most have already sold up and gone north after having their barns burned down and their homes looted, or their cattle maimed or poisoned." Sweat coating his forehead, he winced and pressed his hand to his side until the wave of pain subsided enough for him to continue. "All for refusing to serve in home defence units. This wasn't the first visit I'd had but this time they were threatening to throw me in prison *and* take my farm."

"Those men were militia?"

"Citizens' Committee. They were under orders to take me to Johnstown to pledge allegiance to the flag. I told them to ride on." The farmer bowed his head. "I should have gone with them." He looked towards the cabin and his face crumpled.

"You weren't to know it would end like this," Wyatt said softly. "If I'd realized who they were, I'd have given the order to intercede sooner."

His face pinched with pain and grief, Archer looked up. "How many have you gathered so far?"

"A hundred perhaps, including wives and children and some Negro slaves. They're all at the Hall. It's the rendezvous point."

There was no response. Wyatt thought the farmer had passed out until he saw his eyelids flutter open, the eyes casting about in confusion before suddenly opening wide. As Wyatt followed his gaze in search of the cause, the breath caught like a hook in his throat.

Ephraim Smede came to with blood pooling along the rim of his right eye socket. He blinked and the world took on a pinkish sheen. He blinked again and his vision began to clear. He was aware that the gunfire had ceased but an inner voice, allied to the pain from the open gash across his forehead, told him it would be better to remain where he was so he lay unmoving, listening; alert to the sounds around him.

A few more seconds passed before he raised himself up. He did so slowly. His first view was of his brother's corpse. Beyond Levi, he could see the bodies of their companions, along with the two dead horses. Pools of blood were soaking into the ground, darkening the soil. Flies were starting to swarm.

He could hear voices but they were low and indistinct. He couldn't see who was speaking because the rump of Isaac Meeker's dead nag blocked his line of sight.

It occurred to Smede that he was probably the only one of Deacon's party left alive. From the looks of Axel Shaw, he must have bled to death. There was no sign of Kidd, but Smede doubted the youth would have survived the ambush – or stuck around if he had.

Which meant he was on his own, with a decision to make. Inevitably, his eyes were drawn to his brother's glassy stare and a fresh spark of anger flared within him.

As his gaze alighted on Levi's pistol.

A low moan came from close by. Smede dropped down quickly. He held his breath, waiting until the sound trailed off before cautiously raising his head once. Will Archer was propped some twenty paces away. One of the green-clad men was with him;

he shouted something and two of the attackers ran immediately towards the barn.

Another movement drew Ephraim's attention. A second pair was rounding up the horses. One of them, Ephraim saw to his consternation, was an Indian. His startled gaze took in the face paint and the weapons that the dark-skinned warrior carried about him. There was also what appeared to be a lock of hair hanging from his breechclout.

Bile rose into the back of Ephraim's throat. Escape, he now realized, wasn't only advisable; it was essential.

He watched through narrowed eyes, nerves taut, as the two Rangers pulled open the barn door and disappeared inside. Quickly, his gaze turned back to the pistol lying a few feet away. He looked over his shoulder.

*Now*, he thought.

Concealed by Meeker's horse, Smede inched his way towards the unguarded firearm until he was able to close his fingers around the gun's smooth walnut grip.

He took another deep breath, gathering himself, waiting until the Indian's attention was averted. One chance at a clear shot; that's all he would get.

And then he would run.

He knew the woods like the back of his hand; if he could just make it to the trees, the forest would hide him.

Maybe.

His main fear was the Mohawk, because the pistol, with its single load, was all he had. But his brother's killer came first. An eye for an eye, so that Levi could go to the grave knowing that his brother had exacted revenge. So . . .

In one fluid motion, Smede snatched up the gun, rose to his feet, took aim, and fired.

As the blood-smeared figure tilted towards them, Wyatt, caught between supporting the wounded Archer and reaching for his weapon, let out a yell. Alerted by his cry, Tewanias and Donaldson both turned.

Too late.

The ball thudded into Archer's chest and he collapsed back into Wyatt's arms with a muffled grunt.

Whereupon Ephraim Smede, who was about to launch himself in the direction of the woods, paused, his features suddenly distorting in a combination of shock, pain and disbelief. Mouth open, he uttered no sound as his body arched and spasmed in mid-air.

As Wyatt and the others looked on in astonishment, Smede's legs buckled and, one hand clutching the spent pistol, he pitched forward on to his face.

It wasn't until the body struck the ground that Wyatt saw the stem of the hatchet that protruded from the base of Smede's skull and the slim figure that, until then, had been blocked from view by Smede's temporarily resurrected form.

"No!" Coming out of his trance, Wyatt threw out his arm.

Tewanias, whose finger was already tightening on the trigger, paused and then slowly lowered his musket. A frown of puzzlement flickered across the war-painted face.

Wyatt felt a tremor move through Archer's body. It was obvious from the uneven rise and fall of the wounded man's chest that death was imminent.

The eyes fluttered open one last time and focused on Smede's killer with a look that might have been part relief and part wonderment. Then his expression broke and he grabbed Wyatt's sleeve and pulled him close.

Wyatt had to bow his head to catch the words:

*"Keep him safe."*

The farmer's head fell against Wyatt's arm. Wyatt felt for a pulse but there was none. He looked up.

The boy, though tall, couldn't be much more than eleven or twelve years old. For all that, the expression on his face was one that Wyatt had seen mirrored by much older men when the battle was over and the scent of blood and death hung in the air.

A shock of dark hair flopped over the boy's forehead as his eyes took in the scene of devastation, his jaw clenching when he saw the body on the porch. Running across the clearing to where Wyatt was crouched over the farmer's body, he fell to his knees.

Close to, Wyatt could see tear tracks glistening amid the grime on the boy's face. A trembling hand reached out and gently touched the dead man's arm.

"Aunt Beth told me to hide in the cellar, but I came back up." The boy looked to where Ephraim Smede's corpse lay in the dirt. "I saw that man shoot her. Then he fell off his horse and I thought he was dead. But he was only pretending."

The boy's voice shook. "I wanted to warn you, but there was shooting out front, so I went round the back by the woodpile. I saw the man pick up the gun. I was too scared to call out in case he saw me. I picked up the axe thinking I might scare *him*. Only I was too late. He . . ." The boy paused. "He shot Uncle Will, so I hit him as hard as I could."

The boy's voice gave way. Fresh tears welled. Letting go of the farmer's arm, he lifted a hand to wipe the wetness from his cheeks and looked over his shoulder, his jaw suddenly set firm. "He won't hurt anyone again, will he?"

"No," Wyatt said, staring at the axe handle. "No, lad, he won't."

An equine snort sounded from close by. Wyatt, glad of the distraction, saw it was Tewanias and Donaldson returning with the captured mounts. Behind them, Billy Drew, flanked by Jem Beddowes, was leading one of the two farm horses, harnessed to a low-slung, flat-bed cart.

As they caught his eye, Wyatt gently released the farmer's body, stood up and shook his head. "Sorry, Billy. We won't be needing it after all."

"He's gone?" Drew asked.

"Aye."

"Son?" Drew indicated the boy.

"Nephew," Wyatt said heavily. "Far as I can tell."

"Poor wee devil," Drew said. Then he caught sight of the axe. "Jesus," he muttered softly.

"What'll we do with *them*?" Donaldson enquired, indicating Deacon and the other dead Committee members.

"Not a damned thing," Wyatt snapped. "They can lay there and rot as far as I'm concerned."

"Seems fair." Donaldson agreed, before adding quietly, "And the other two?"

"Them we do take care of. They deserve a decent burial, if nothing else. See if you can find a shovel. It's a farm. There'll be one around somewhere."

"And then?" Beddowes said.

"And then we report back."

"The boy?"

"He comes with us," Wyatt said. "We might as well take advantage of the horses, too." He turned. "Can you ride, lad?"

The boy looked up. "Yes, sir. That one's mine. He's called Jonah." He indicated the horse that Billy Drew had left in the paddock. It was the smaller one of the two.

"There was tack in the barn," Beddowes offered.

Wyatt turned. "Very well, saddle him up and take this one back. Make sure he's got plenty of feed and water. We'll see to the rest." Wyatt addressed the boy. "You go with Jem; show him where you keep Jonah's blanket and bridle."

Hesitantly, the boy rose to his feet. Wyatt waited until he was out of earshot, then turned to the others.

"All right, we'd best get it over with."

They buried Archer and his wife in the shade of a tall oak tree that grew behind the cabin, marking the graves with a pair of wooden crosses made from pieces of discarded fence post. Neither one bore an inscription. There wasn't time, Wyatt told them.

Donaldson, whose father had been a minister, was familiar with the scriptures and carried a small bible in his shoulder pouch. He chose the twenty-third psalm, reading it aloud as his fellow Rangers bowed their heads, caps in hand, while the Indian held the horses and looked on stoically.

The scalp had disappeared from the Mohawk's breechclout. When he'd spotted it, Wyatt had reminded Tewanias of the colonel's orders: no enemy corpses were to be mutilated. It was with some reluctance that Tewanias returned to the river and laid the scalp across the body of its original owner.

"Let it act as a warning to those who would think to pursue

us," Wyatt told him. "Knowing we are joined with our Mohawk brothers will make our enemies fearful. They will hide in their homes and lock their doors and tremble in the darkness."

Wyatt wasn't sure that Tewanias was entirely convinced by that argument, but the Mohawk nodded sagely as if he agreed with the words. In any case, both of them knew there were likely to be other battles and therefore other scalps for the taking, so, for the time being at least, honour was satisfied.

The boy stood gazing down at the graves with Wyatt's hand resting on his shoulder. The dog, Tam, lay at his side, having been released from the cabin when, under Wyatt's direction, the boy had returned to the house to gather up his possessions for the journey.

Donaldson ended the reading and closed the bible. The Rangers raised their heads and put on their caps.

"Time to go," Wyatt said. "Saddle up." He addressed the boy. "You have everything? You won't be coming back." The words carried a hard finality.

Tear tracks showing on his cheeks, the boy pointed at the canvas bag slung over his saddle.

Wyatt surveyed the yard – littered with the bodies of Deacon and his men – and the blood-drenched soil now carpeted with bloated flies. It was a world away from the serene, sun-dappled vision that had greeted the Rangers' arrival earlier that morning.

He glanced towards the three cows in the paddock and the chickens pecking around the henhouse; the livestock would have to fend for themselves. There was enough food and water to sustain them until someone came to see why Archer and his wife hadn't been to town for a while. There would be others along, too, wondering why the members of the Citizens' Committee hadn't returned to the fold.

*Let them come*, Wyatt thought. *Let them see.*

The Mohawk warrior handed the boy the reins of his horse and watched critically as he climbed up. Satisfied that the boy knew what he was doing, he wheeled his mount and took up position at the head of the line. With Tewanias riding point, the five men and the boy rode into the stream, towards the track leading into the forest. The dog padded silently behind them.

Halfway across the creek, the Indian turned to the boy and spoke. "Naho:ten iesa:iats?"

The boy looked to Wyatt for guidance.

"He asked you your name," Wyatt said.

It occurred to Wyatt that in the time they'd spent in the boy's company, neither he nor any of his men had bothered to ask that question. They'd simply addressed him as "lad" or "son" or, in Donaldson's case, "young 'un". Though they all knew the name of the damned dog.

The boy stared at Tewanias and then at each of the Rangers in turn. It was then that Wyatt saw the true colour appear in the boy's eyes. Blue-grey, the shade of rain clouds after a storm.

The boy drew himself up.

"My name is Matthew," he said.

# 1

*Albany, New York State, December 1812*

**BEWARE FOREIGN SPIES & AGITATORS!**

The words were printed across the top of the poster, the warning writ large for all to see.

Hawkwood ran his eye down the rest of the deposition. Not much had been left to the imagination. The nation was at war, the country was under threat and the people were urged to remain vigilant at all times.

He glanced over his shoulder. There were no crowds brandishing pitchforks or torches so he assumed he was safe for the time being. He recalled there had been similar pamphlets on display around the quayside in Boston, presumably the preferred port of entry for an enemy bent on subverting the republic. He wondered how many people read the bills and took note of their content; probably not as many as the government wished.

Fortunately for him.

The bill was stuck on the inside of a hatter's shop window. Under pretence of casting an eye over the merchandise on display, he studied his reflection in the glass, wondering what a subversive might look like and if he fitted the bill. From what he'd seen of the country and its citizens so far, he thought it unlikely that he'd be stopped and asked for his papers, though in the event he was, the problem would not have been insurmountable.

He was about to walk on when movement in the window caught his attention: another reflection, this time of the scene behind him. A man, dressed in an army greatcoat similar to his own was making his way along the opposite side of the street. He was walking with a cane and Hawkwood could see that he was favouring his right leg.

There had been a rainstorm during the night, which had transformed Albany's thoroughfares into something of a quagmire. The fact that the capital was built on an incline didn't help matters and even though the rain had stopped, trying to negotiate the sloping streets on foot was, in some areas, as precarious as wading through a Connemara bog. Quite a few folk were having difficulty maintaining their balance. Though not the two characters walking on firmer feet some fifteen paces or so behind the man with the cane.

Over the years, his duties as a Bow Street officer had brought Hawkwood into contact with criminals of every persuasion and his ability to spot miscreants had been honed to a fine edge. From the way the two men were concentrating on the figure in front, Hawkwood was left in no doubt they were intent on mischief.

A small voice inside his head began to whisper.

*Not here, not now. Let them go. It's not your city. It's not your problem.*

Hawkwood looked around him. There was plenty of traffic about, both vehicular and pedestrian and the street was far from deserted, but everyone else was too intent upon their own business to have noticed anything amiss, including the man in the greatcoat who appeared oblivious to the pair on his tail, despite two sets of eyes burning into his back.

Hawkwood watched as the men's target turned into a narrow side lane. Immediately, the pair quickened their pace. As they disappeared into the lane after him, Hawkwood sighed.

*Damn it*, he thought, as he crossed the street, narrowly avoiding being run down by an oncoming carriage. *Why me?*

Twenty paces into the alley, the man in the greatcoat was down on one knee, with his back to the wall. The cane was in his right hand and he was trying to rise while wielding the stick like a sword to ward off his attackers.

It was a pound to a penny the man's disability was the reason he'd been singled out. A cripple would be considered easy pickings for a couple of rogues. Hawkwood could see that one of the attackers held a knife, while his companion was brandishing a short cudgel.

There wasn't as much mud here as there had been on the street so the traction was better and Hawkwood's boots gave him the grip he needed. He felt disinclined to give the pair fair warning.

Only when they saw their victim's eyes flicker to one side did they turn. Their eyes were still widening as Hawkwood slammed the heel of his right boot against the cudgel man's left knee cap. The man yelped and went down, the cudgel slipping from his grasp as he clutched his injured limb. His companion immediately dropped into a crouch, the knife held in front of him. He scythed the blade towards Hawkwood's throat.

Throwing up his right hand, Hawkwood caught the knife man's wrist and twisted it to lock the arm before slamming the heel of his left hand against the braced elbow. The man yelled as the bone broke and the knife joined the cudgel on the ground. Hawkwood released the arm and stepped back.

"Your choice, gentlemen," he said calmly, already knowing the answer. "What'll it be?"

The two men turned tail. *At least they've one good arm and one good leg between them*, Hawkwood thought as he watched them hobble away. He kicked the discarded weapons into the shadows and reached down to the kneeling man who stared back at him with a mixture of shock and disbelief. Gripping Hawkwood's hand and using his cane as support he rose to his feet and brushed himself down, allowing Hawkwood a glimpse of a uniform jacket beneath the coat.

"Well I don't know who you are, friend, but I'm damned glad you were in the neighbourhood. The name's Quade. Major Harlan Quade, Thirteenth Regiment of Infantry."

The major held on to Hawkwood's hand.

"Hooper," Hawkwood said. "Captain Matthew Hooper."

"I'll be damned. Well, in that case, Captain Hooper, I hope you'll allow a major to buy a captain a drink."

Hawkwood ran a quick eye over what he could see of the major's tunic and smiled. "Happy to accept, sir. It's the best offer I've had all day."

Major Quade was currently on medical furlough from wounds sustained on the Niagara Frontier. Watching him stare into the depths of his whiskey glass, Hawkwood wondered if the major's invitation might not have been born out of a desire for companionship rather than as a gesture to thank him for coming to the man's rescue.

Not that it wasn't gratifying to be appreciated every now and again, but Hawkwood suspected it was the rye that was doing most of the talking and he'd already asked himself: if the major had been in civilian dress and had he not identified himself as a ranking officer, would he still have accepted the offer of a drink?

Probably not, but the greatcoat and a glimpse of the uniform beneath it had made Hawkwood's decision for him. A military man would likely have information about the disposition of local troops, and given Hawkwood's current status as a foreign combatant on enemy soil it could prove useful to know which areas were best avoided.

They were seated at a table in the Eagle Tavern, less than a stone's toss from the Hudson River. It was a comfortable enough establishment, with a generous selection of liquors, a moderately civil staff and, more importantly, a welcoming fire in the hearth.

The major had ordered whiskey and stuck to that throughout. Hawkwood had chosen brandy. The breeze that was coming off the water and eddying up the city's streets was a bracing reminder that it was already winter. A stack of blazing logs and a warming drink were as good a way as any of keeping the chill at bay.

The taproom was enveloped in warmth. With the combined smells of ale, tobacco and victuals and the subdued murmur of conversation permeating the tavern Hawkwood could easily have shut his eyes and imagined, if only for a few brief seconds, that he was back in London, enjoying a wet at the Blackbird Inn.

Only he wasn't. He was in Albany, New York, half a world away from Bow Street, trying to find some means of getting home.

Still, he thought, at least there was one advantage to being here.

He didn't have to speak French.

The voyage from Nantes to Boston had taken thirty-two days, one more than *Larkspur*'s skipper, Jack Larsson, had forecast and thirty-two days too many, as far as Hawkwood was concerned.

Getting out of Paris in the wake of his last assignment had been achieved without too much difficulty but there had always been a weakness in the plan's second stage, which had been reliant on *Larkspur* being intercepted and boarded by a British vessel on blockade duty, whereupon Hawkwood would have revealed his identity and secured safe passage back to England.

Regrettably, no one had allowed for the formidable seamanship of *Larkspur*'s wily skipper. During the five years the blockade had been in place – which required all neutral ships to submit to a cargo inspection at a British port or be seized as an enemy vessel – Jack Larsson had accrued valuable experience in the art of outwitting the Royal Navy's squadrons. Now that Britain was actually at war with America, he had become even more adept at avoiding detection.

Thus *Larkspur* had slipped past the British patrols with ease, presenting Hawkwood with the uncomfortable realization that he was America bound.

The one advantage of the month-long voyage was that it had given him time to gather as much information as he could on the fluctuating state of British–American hostilities.

In Paris, up-to-date intelligence had been impossible to glean. Even though European newspapers carried accounts of skirmishes between the two sides, by the time news from the other side of the Atlantic reached the French newspapers or English ones smuggled in from London, it had to be at least six weeks out of date, if not more; which had left Hawkwood with no option but to tap Captain Larsson and his crew without arousing their suspicions.

First he had to gain their confidence. Aided by fraudulently obtained boarding papers which confirmed his identity as one Captain Hooper – an alias he'd used to good effect on previous missions – Hawkwood had been able to pass himself off as an officer in the First Regiment, United States Riflemen, on recent detachment as an observer to a French Regiment of the Line in Spain.

To his relief, Larsson had accepted 'Captain Hooper's' patchy knowledge of the war as a legacy of his months serving with Bonaparte's army in the Peninsula; which had left them, at least as far as *Larkspur*'s skipper was concerned, as fellow Americans, united in their patriotism, desirous of fresh news and looking forward to a safe return home from foreign climes.

But while Larsson was cognisant with American naval exploits, he knew little of the land campaign; what meagre information he had on military activity on the western and northern fronts lacked credible detail. The last dispatch he'd been privy to had been dated mid-September, a week before *Larkspur* had sailed from Boston.

And anything could have happened since then.

And so, on the cold, misty morning when the dark smudge of the Massachusetts coast finally materialized over *Larkspur*'s larboard bow, while Hawkwood felt the relief surge through him at having made landfall, he knew he was still a long way from salvation.

He'd accepted from the outset that another sea voyage would be an inevitable consequence of his arrival in America, but the thought of trawling the docks in search of a berth on an east-bound merchantman in the vain hope that this time the vessel would be stopped and boarded by the Royal Navy was not an option he'd been prepared to consider; once bitten, twice shy in that regard.

The only viable alternative was to try to reach the British

lines. If he could manage that, he would surely be able to secure passage to England.

To achieve that goal, however, he'd first needed to confirm the whereabouts of the most convenient battlefront; short of enlisting, the easiest way of obtaining that information without drawing undue attention to himself was to consult the newspapers. Thus after disembarking and spending a night in a dockside tavern recommended by Larsson, his first objective had been to find the nearest reading room.

At the Exchange Coffee House, arming himself with a selection of journals – archive copies as well as the latest editions – and securing a seat in a corner with his back to the wall, he'd spent the morning familiarizing himself with the state of the nation. The *Boston Patriot* and the *Washington Intelligencer* had both carried a variety of dispatches, ranging from accounts of skirmishes and copies of letters from front-line commanders to the Department of War, to lists of the dead and wounded, notifications of promotions, requests for militia volunteers and even reward notices for deserters. More informative, by far, however, had been *The War*, the aptly titled New York broadsheet, published specifically in order to cover the conflict.

Concentrating on the latter's editorial, the first thing that struck him was that the tide of war had taken a much grimmer turn since he'd left France, resulting in grave consequences for both sides of the divide.

The main build-up of forces had been along the borderland between the United States and the Province of Upper Canada, down the line of the Great Lakes, Ontario and Erie, with British and American combatants facing each other along opposite shores of the Niagara and Detroit Rivers.

It had been the British who'd seized the initiative when, back in August, General Isaac Brock crossed the Canadian border and laid siege to Detroit, capturing the town and taking his opposite number, General William Hull, prisoner. There had been several cut-and-thrust sorties since then, with the British continuing to have the edge, culminating in the defeat of a recent American counter-invasion attempt into Canada near Queenston, during which the aforementioned General Brock had lost his life to a sniper's bullet. But, so far, it looked as though neither side had been able to summon the troops or equipment to wage a decisive land battle.

While the red-coated regiments had shown their superiority in the land war, the same could not be said for the waterborne operations of the Provincial Marine, the Royal Navy force that patrolled the waterways of the St Lawrence River and the northern lakes. The Americans, against all odds, had managed to seal the Marine inside its main base of operations, the port of Kingston at the eastern end of Lake Ontario.

In sifting events into chronological order, it had soon become clear to Hawkwood that in the weeks since the debacles at Detroit and Queenston the Americans had been regrouping with a vengeance, strengthening their troop numbers along the St Lawrence and bolstering their main naval base at Sackets Harbor – across the water from Kingston – where a number of newly acquired merchant vessels had been converted into war ships and transports.

Emboldened by their new-found confidence, the Americans had also undertaken several small but telling raids against British supply convoys and fortifications along the various river routes. Rumours had even been revived which spoke of another possible invasion attempt on Canada.

Two maps displayed in a four-day-old edition of *The War* had eventually provided the information he'd been searching for: the disposition of British and American forces. One covered the operations around the Detroit River; the other reflected events that had taken place further east in New York State along the northern Canadian border and the Niagara Frontier. Studying the maps carefully while referring to the corresponding dispatches, it hadn't taken long to deduce that if he was to try to reach the British lines, three escape routes were available to him – none of which looked in the least inviting. There was no need to make a decision there and then, however, because no matter which route he ended up taking, all roads led to one inevitable transit point:

Albany.

What had made him hesitate, though only for a moment, had been the fact that Albany had recently been designated the headquarters of the American Army's Northern Command.

Deciding that was a bridge he'd have to cross when he came to it, Hawkwood had surreptitiously extracted the New York map page from the newspaper and folded it into his pocket. As he'd left the Exchange, one thought remained uppermost in his mind.

No one had said it was going to be easy.

The coach had left Boston at the ungodly hour of two in the morning. His seaman's bag having been swapped for a more convenient knapsack, Hawkwood had alighted from the coach at Albany's State Street terminus at eight o'clock in the evening of the following day, a mere three days after his arrival on to American soil.

And more than twenty years since his departure.

The major caught the pot-man's eye and raised his empty glass.

"I'll have the same again and another brandy for my friend." As the order was borne away, Quade began to massage his right thigh.

"How's the leg?" Hawkwood asked.

"Stiff as a board and aching like the devil, but the surgeon told me I can probably return to duty by the end of the week."

Quade didn't look or sound that enthused by the prospect. From the exchanges they'd had so far, Hawkwood could understand why.

The drinks arrived.

"Whiskey for you, Major," the pot-man said. "Brandy for the gentleman."

*If you only knew*, Hawkwood thought. He took a swallow, savouring the warmth of the alcohol as it passed down his throat, and watched as Quade downed half the contents of the whiskey glass in one go.

"You were telling me about Queenston," Hawkwood said.

Queenston was where the major had received his wounds. Not that Hawkwood was that curious as to how Quade had come by his injuries. He was more interested in what information the major might have regarding American and British troop emplacements.

The hamlet lay on the Canadian side of the Niagara River, as Hawkwood had discovered from his visit to the reading room. It was also home to a British garrison, one of a string of Crown fortifications that stretched from Niagara in the north, down to Fort Erie in the south, where the river began its spectacular journey to Lake Ontario. It was this length of frontier that formed the apogee to one of Hawkwood's three possible escape routes.

"Goddamned militia!" Quade's knuckles gleamed white as he gripped his glass. "Citizen soldiers? Useless bastards, more like! If there'd been a regular in command instead of that fool Van Rensselaer, it would've been different. That's the trouble with political appointees, they're easily pressured. He was told he had to attack Canada before winter. He should have stood his ground, told them it was too soon. It was the same with his officers. The idiots were demanding he either launch the invasion or let their men go home for Christmas! God save us! Is that any way to run an army? Well, is it?" The major took another swig. "D'you know there weren't even enough boats for the crossing?"

Beads of perspiration clung to the major's brow. Whether they were a result of his proximity to the hearth or due to the pain in his leg or the effects of the whiskey, it was hard to tell. Quade wasn't slurring his words, so the sweat oozing from his pores could just as easily have been a physical manifestation of the resentment he was giving voice to – with scant regard for discretion. Though no one in the vicinity seemed to be paying either of them any attention.

"Is that so?" Hawkwood said.

"And half the vessels had lost their oars!"

From the tone of his voice, Quade sounded as if he was just getting started. Hawkwood braced himself to endure a lengthy rant about the inadequacies of the General Staff before any useful nuggets of information could be gleaned.

But as Quade's story unfolded, it was difficult not to sympathize, even if he was the enemy. The newspaper accounts of the battle had made much of General Brock's death, but now it emerged that much of the story had gone unreported. American losses had been considerable.

"I was in the second wave," Quade continued, the edge in his voice as sharp as a blade. "We used a fisherman's path to gain the Heights and take their battery – though not before they'd spiked their guns, which we could have done without. Victory should have been ours. With Brock dead, we thought they'd cut and run. What we hadn't allowed for was his aide-de-camp, Sheaffe, bringing up reinforcements from Fort George or the arrival of his advance party – that breed, Norton, and his damned savages!"

Quade's face twisted. "They're what did for us. They occupied the woods at the summit; kept us pinned down with musket fire. All this while Van Rensselaer was still trying to rally his troops into crossing the river. Trouble was, the cowards had seen the redcoats advancing and they could hear the screams."

"Screams?" Hawkwood said.

"Of the wounded . . ." Quade lifted his glass and took a swallow, ". . . and the natives. That's when the militia told Rensselaer they weren't prepared to fight on foreign soil! It was their cowardice that left us stranded. Once the rest of Sheaffe's men arrived, we never stood a chance. Marched towards us as calm as you like. Stopped a hundred and fifty yards out. At that range our muskets were useless. When they fired their volley, we couldn't see them for the smoke. It was only when it cleared that we realized they'd used it to hide their approach. That's when they fixed bayonets and charged."

The American grimaced. "And we ran; every man of us, like frightened jack rabbits. Only there was nowhere to go. We had the drop from the Heights at our backs and the British in front. We tried sending two men out with a white flag, but the savages cut them to pieces. By that time, most of our side were trying to climb down to the river, hoping they'd be able to swim across. You could hear their bodies hitting the rocks, even above the sound of the guns."

Quade shook his head, as if to rid himself of the memory. "I don't know how the hell I made it. Truth is, I was more fearful of what those savages would do if they caught me than I was of falling over the damned cliff. I thought the Mullahs were inventive when it came to torture, but they're nothing compared to the Iroquois."

The major cradled his glass in silence for a moment then his eyes met Hawkwood's. "I took a musket ball in the side and that sent me tumbling. Broke the bone when I landed. One of my sergeants hauled me into the water. Funny thing is, it was one of those missing oars that saved us. We found it adrift on the current and used it to float back to our own shore."

Quade extended his injured limb and resumed kneading the muscle above his knee. "We left a thousand men behind. It wasn't a retreat, it was a rout, plain and simple. No other word for it."

The major had long legs. He was equal to Hawkwood in height and about the same age, give or take a year, though his dark hair was shorter, cut back from a widow's peak and greying at a faster rate. There was also a gaunt aspect to his features, which, Hawkwood thought, could have been due to his injury. Or it could have been from the trauma of reliving his ordeal. That might also have accounted for the haunted look in his eyes.

It occurred to Hawkwood that the more the major drank, the more his looks matched his mood. For while the alcohol appeared to be having little effect on either his balance or his vocabulary, it grew apparent that he was becoming more morose with each sip. Hawkwood suspected that if Quade were to drink to excess he would not be a happy drunk.

Men like Quade were nothing new; officers unwilling to accept their own failings while finding constant fault with others, usually men of a more senior rank. Though if half of what Quade had told him was true, it was small wonder the man was feeling bloody. The American army appeared to be in a sorry state, with a lack of experienced soldiers of all ranks, not to mention supplies and weaponry and even horses for their recently created dragoon regiments.

According to Quade, some enlisted men were having to fight in bare feet because there was a shortage of boots. The major's own uniform jacket was brown and not the regulation blue because there was a dearth of indigo cloth.

Hawkwood tried to imagine what the British army would do if there wasn't enough scarlet weave. It didn't bear thinking about. But then, until this latest conflict, the Americans hadn't been involved in a war on home soil since gaining their independence. Little wonder they were at a disadvantage when they were trying to rebuild their army.

The major was from Virginian military stock. It had been the young Quade's intention to study artillery and engineering at Fort Clinton, until his father advised him that a new professional army was being formed to combat the threat from the northwestern Indian tribes who, a year previously in a bloody battle on the Wabash River, had inflicted the greatest defeat upon the United States Army by a native foe. Quade had been one of the United States Legion's first recruits.

"We got our revenge at Fallen Timbers," he told Hawkwood. "They had no option after that. They had to sign the damned peace treaty."

Hawkwood presumed that Fallen Timbers was a battle the Indians had lost. Quade obviously expected him to know about it. Probably best, Hawkwood thought, to remain silent and not disabuse the major of that particular notion.

The Mullahs Quade had referred to were the Berber Muslims. Hawkwood didn't know much about them either, though he did recall *Larkspur*'s skipper referring to a war the Americans had fought in the Mediterranean some seven or eight years before against North African pirates.

Following the Legion's disbanding, Quade had switched his allegiance to the newly resurrected Marine Corps. The Corps had been looking for officers and with the Legion's mission against the tribes fulfilled, Quade had seen an opportunity for advancement. Since then, by his own admission, the variety of enemy he'd fought against had exceeded that of his father and grandfather.

37

The major shook his head wearily. "If I'd had any sense, I'd have ignored the call. My ship was in Boston when I heard they were in need of serving officers. Men with experience of engaging with irregulars were especially in demand. I guessed that with my time in the Legion and fighting the Berbers, I had what they were looking for, so I offered my services."

He gave a rueful smile. "Saw it as the lesser of two evils, my chance to get back to dry land. I'm no sailor, damn it. I always was prone to sea-sickness. Not so good for a Marine, as I'm sure you'll agree." He massaged his knee once more. "And look where it got me. That damned river was freezing; it's a wonder I didn't come down with pneumonia."

After his wounds had been treated, Quade was transferred to the hospital at Buffalo, where he'd spent the bulk of his recuperation. With the Americans' push to invade Canada along the Niagara having stalled, Major Quade had received orders summoning him back to Albany.

"The fact is; I can't say that I'm looking forward to reporting in," Quade said quietly, his voice dropping to a whisper, as though he'd suddenly become aware, following his previous indiscretions, that walls could have ears.

"I'm not sure Dearborn's cut out for command any more than Van Rensselaer was. He's as old as Methuselah, for a start!" He looked into the fire, staring into the flames for several seconds before pulling back and favouring Hawkwood with a wintry smile. "But you didn't hear me say that. Forgive me; I've a tendency to ramble when I've had a few. I meant nothing by it. I dare say you'll be making your own judgement when the time comes."

As far as the major was concerned, Captain Hooper was newly arrived from the continent where he'd been on extended service, most recently in Nantes, France, there having undertaken a number of unspecified duties on behalf of a grateful United States Government. Now he was in Albany, awaiting orders from the War Department, on the understanding that he was likely to be assigned to General Dearborn's Northern Command Headquarters, where his intimate knowledge of British military tactics could be put to strategic use in the current hostilities.

Hawkwood knew that, as masquerades went, it was tenuous at best and downright dangerous at worst, but as his liaison with Quade was only scheduled to last as long as a couple of drinks, hopefully it would suffice.

"It sounds," Hawkwood said, in an attempt to move the conversation on, "as though the bastards have that part of the frontier sealed up tight. What about Ontario and the St Lawrence? I hear we've given a good account of ourselves there."

Quade's eyes flashed as he nodded in agreement. "Thanks to Chauncey! About time the bastards got a taste of their own medicine! Now they know what it's like to be bottled up with nowhere to go!"

From his reading, Hawkwood knew that Commodore Isaac Chauncey, former Officer-in-Charge of the New York navy yard, was the newly appointed Commander-in-Chief of the Great Lakes Navy. Since his transfer to Sackets Harbor in October, the Americans had taken the war to the British with a vengeance. With their successful blockade of Kingston, it was now the United States who ruled the waves on Lake Ontario and the upper reaches of the St Lawrence, and not the Provincial Marine as had previously been the case.

"The Limeys need the Marine to help keep their supply routes open." Quade said. "We sever those and hopefully we can wear the sons of bitches down. We've made a good start. They're already having difficulty supplying their southern outposts. Once winter sets in, it'll be impossible to move anywhere. Not that either side will want to, so both armies are going to be snowbound until March, which means we'll be ready for them come the thaw."

Hawkwood manufactured a smile in support of Quade's rekindled optimism. From the major's point of view, the reversal of fortune following the Queenston and Detroit defeats was a much-needed boost to national morale, but all Hawkwood could see was the shutting down of his second prospective escape route.

Not that either option had held much appeal, due more to their geography than their military significance. It was four hundred miles to the Niagara frontier and at least two hundred to the St Lawrence, with each route involving a heavily defended river crossing at the end of it.

The third option was looking more inviting by the minute. But then it always had. Quade's disclosures had merely confirmed what Hawkwood had already decided. If he was to have any chance of reaching safety, he should discount the western paths and take the shortest of the three routes: north, up through New York State. If he made for the closest point on the Canadian border, his journey would still involve the negotiation of a river but, unlike the Niagara and St Lawrence, the Hudson, because of its course, had the potential to be an ally rather than an enemy. Winter was approaching fast, however. If he was going to start his run, he'd need to do it quickly.

Though it wasn't as if he'd be heading into unknown territory.

The flames in the hearth danced as a new batch of customers entered the tavern, bringing with them a heavy draught of cold air from the street outside. Hawkwood looked towards the door. The new arrivals were in uniform; grey jackets, as opposed to the tan of Quade's tunic. As they took a table in the corner of the taproom, Quade eyed them balefully over the rim of his now-empty glass.

"Pikemen," he murmured scornfully. "God save us. It'll be battleaxes next."

Hawkwood knew his puzzlement must have shown, for Quade said, "My apologies; a weak jest. They're Zebulon Pike's boys. Fifteenth Infantry. He's had them in training across the river."

"Across the river" meant the town of Greenbush. Hawkwood had been surprised and not a little thankful to discover that Albany wasn't awash with military personnel. It had turned out that General Dearborn had set up his headquarters not in the town but in a new, specially constructed compound on the opposite side of the Hudson. This was much to the relief of the locals, who, while mindful of the economic advantages of having an army camped on their doorstep, didn't want the inconvenience of several thousand troops living in their midst. It was a compromise that suited all parties.

"Battleaxes?" Hawkwood said, confused.

"Pike has this notion to equip his men with pole-arms. He's introduced a new set of drills: a three-rank formation. First two ranks armed with muskets, the third with pike staffs. He reckons it'll enable a battalion to deploy more men in a bayonet charge."

"It does sound medieval," Hawkwood agreed warily.

Quade grunted. "That was my thinking, though there could be some sense in it, I suppose. Most third ranks are next to useless when it comes to attacking in line. Even with bayonets fixed, their muskets are too short to be effective. A line of twelve-foot pikes would certainly do the trick. Would you face a line of men armed with twelve-foot pikes?"

"Only if I had fifteen-foot pikes," Hawkwood said. "Or lots of guns."

"So, maybe I stand corrected," Quade said. "I'm sure they'll give a good account of themselves when it's required." He eyed the recent arrivals. "They'll be enjoying their last drink before heading north to join the rest."

"The rest?" Hawkwood said.

There was a pause.

"They did tell you that Dearborn's in Plattsburg," Quade said. "Didn't they?"

Hawkwood raised his glass and took a swallow to give himself time to think and plan his response.

"I only landed in Boston a few days ago. No one's told me a damned thing."

Quade shook his head and made the sort of face that indicated he despaired of all senior staff.

"Typical. Just as well we met then, though you'd have found out eventually. He's been there since the middle of last month. Winter quarters. Pike's up there with him. I've no doubt my orders will be to join them, which is why I'm in no hurry to return to the bosom. I've a day or two of freedom left and I intend to make the most of them."

He sighed, stared into his glass and then, clearly making a decision, stood it on the table between them.

"Another?" Hawkwood asked.

To Hawkwood's relief, the major shook his head. "Thank you, that's most generous, but on this occasion I'll decline. I've a prior appointment and, no disrespect, Captain, but she's a damned sight prettier than you are!" Quade grinned as he reached for his coat and cane. "A tad more expensive, but definitely prettier."

"In that case, Major," Hawkwood said, "don't let me detain you." He waited until Quade had gained his feet and then accompanied the major as he tapped his way towards the door.

On the street, the major paused while buttoning his coat. "If you're free, why don't you join me?"

"Another time, perhaps," Hawkwood said.

Quade, not in the least put out, smiled amiably. "As you wish. If you should change your mind, you'll find us on Church Street – the house with the weathercock on the roof. The door's at the side. There's a small brass plate to the right of it: Hoare's Gaming Club. It—"

Seeing the expression on Hawkwood's face, the major chuckled and spelt out the name. "Yes, I know, but what would you have it say – the Albany Emporium? Anyway, as I was saying, it caters for the more – how shall I put it? – discerning gentleman, so you'd be in excellent company. A lot of the senior officers from Greenbush take their pleasure there."

*Another reason for giving the place a wide berth*, Hawkwood thought. "Well, I'll certainly bear that in mind, Major, if I find myself at a loose end."

"Ha! That's the spirit! All work and no play makes Jack a dull boy, eh? Besides, we're at war. Who's to say we shouldn't enjoy what could be our last day on earth before we head to the front?"

"I thought everyone was going to be snowed in for winter," Hawkwood said. "There won't be a front until March."

"Ah, but the ladies don't know that, do they?"

*God save us*, Hawkwood thought.

As an ear-splitting shriek shattered the surrounding calm.

Hawkwood pivoted. Heart in mouth, he paused as a broad grin of delight opened up across the major's face.

"Ha!" Quade exclaimed gleefully. "Had the same effect on

me, the first time I heard it. Thought it was the cry of the banshee come to carry me off! They do say it's caused seizures in at least half a dozen of the city's older female folk. Not seen her before? Quite a sight, ain't she?"

The major pointed with his cane.

As his pulse slowed to its normal rate, Hawkwood, embarrassingly aware that other passers-by had not reacted as he had, looked off to where Quade was indicating. They had come to a halt adjacent to the river. Only the width of the street and a patch of open ground separated them from the quayside and the vessels moored alongside it.

The Hudson was Albany's umbilical. It was from the busy wharves and slipways crowding the mile-long shoreline that goods from the city's granaries, breweries and timber yards were transported downriver to the markets of New York, one hundred and fifty miles to the south.

Scores of cargo sloops and passenger schooners competed for mooring space with smaller barges and hoys. It could have been a scene lifted from the Thames or the Seine, had it not been for the tree-clad hillsides rising from the water on the opposite shore and the extraordinary-looking vessel that was churning into view beyond the intermediary forest of masts and rigging. The throbbing sounds that enveloped the craft as it manoeuvred towards the jetty were as curious as its appearance and like nothing Hawkwood had heard before.

There was no grace in either its movement or its contours. Compared to the other craft on the river, it occurred to Hawkwood that the clanking behemoth, with its wedged bow and wall-sided hull had all the elegance of an elongated canal boat, while the thin, black, smoke-belching stove-pipe poking up from the boat's mid-section wouldn't have looked out of place on the roof of a Cheapside tenement.

The threshing sound was explained by what appeared to be two large mill wheels, their top halves set behind wooden housings on either side of the hull, forward of the smoke-stack. They were, Hawkwood saw, revolving paddles; it was their rotation that gave the vessel its momentum through the water.

Another drawn-out screech rent the air, sending a flock of herring gulls, already displaced by the first whistle, wheeling and diving above the nearby rooftops in raucous protest.

Quade moved to Hawkwood's side. "She's the *Paragon*, up from New York. She can do six and a half knots at a push. Seven dollars a ticket, I'm told, and it only takes thirty-six hours. It takes the schooners four days. You've not seen any of them in action?"

Hawkwood shook his head and watched as the steamboat shuddered and slowed. For a few seconds the clattering from her paddles seemed to diminish before suddenly increasing in volume once more. Hawkwood realized the wheels were now revolving in the opposite direction and that the vessel was travelling in reverse.

"Takes ninety passengers," Quade said matter-of-factly as the boat's stern started to come round. "Fulton used to swear they could turn on a dollar – the boats, that is, not the passengers. Don't know if that's strictly true. No one's thrown a dollar in to find out." He chuckled.

For a moment Hawkwood thought he might have misheard.

"Fulton?" he repeated cautiously, trying to keep his tone even.

"Robert Fulton," Quade said. He looked at Hawkwood askance. "Good God, man, you must have heard of him! How long did you say you'd been away?"

Hawkwood said nothing. His mind was too busy spinning.

Fulton?

It had to be the same man. Robert Fulton, American designer of the submersible, *Narwhale*, in which Hawkwood had fought hand to hand with Fulton's associate, William Lee, beneath the dark waters of the Thames, following Lee's failed attack on the newly launched frigate, *Thetis*.

Hawkwood had killed Lee and left his body entombed at the bottom of the river, inside *Narwhale*'s shattered hull. It seemed like an age ago, yet memory of a discourse he'd had with the Admiralty Board members and the scientist, Colonel William Congreve, prior to the discovery of Lee's plan, slid into his mind. Hawkwood heard an echo of Congreve's voice telling him that

44

at the same time as Fulton had been petitioning the French government to support his advances in undersea warfare, he'd also been experimenting with steam as a means of propulsion.

Hawkwood stared at the vessel, which was now side on to the quay, and watched as mooring lines were cast fore and aft. While Fulton's dream of liberty of the seas and the establishment of free trade through the destruction of the world's navies might lie in tatters at the bottom of the Thames, it appeared that his plans for steam navigation had achieved spectacular success.

"Can't say the schooner skippers are best pleased," Quade said. "They've lost a deal of passenger trade since the steamboats started running."

"How many are there?" Hawkwood asked.

"I believe it's five or six at the last count. I do know that two of them operate alternating schedules up and downriver. Others are used as ferries around New York harbour."

"I'll be damned," Hawkwood said, nodding as if impressed. "Y'know, the time's gone so quickly . . . I'm blessed if I can remember when they did start."

"Back in '07." Quade leaned on his stick and gazed admiringly at the boat as the gangplank was extended. "If you recall, *Clermont* was the first. It made its maiden run that August."

The year after Fulton had left London to return home. The British government had thought that his departure meant they would hear no more of the American and his torpedoes – until Lee's appearance five years later.

"Of course," Hawkwood said. "How could I forget?"

"Not the most amenable fellow, I'm told," Quade murmured. "Arrogant, and not much liked, by all accounts, though you can't deny he's a clever son of a bitch. There've been rumours he's trying to design some kind of military version, but last I heard, he's not in the best of health, so I wouldn't know how that's proceeding."

With the steamship now berthed and its passengers disembarking, Hawkwood was able to take stock of her. She was, he guessed, about one hundred and fifty feet in length, with the top of the smoke-stack rising a good thirty feet above the deck.

There were two masts: one set forward and equipped for a square sail, the other at the stern, supporting a fore and aft rig. The sails, Hawkwood presumed, were to provide her with additional impetus if her engine failed. The paddle wheels had to be at least fifteen feet in diameter. There was no bowsprit and no figurehead. Even to an untrained eye, with no attempt having been made to soften her lines, it was plain the vessel had been constructed entirely for purpose. As if to emphasize the steamboat's stark functionality, the top of the cylindrical copper boiler, set into a rectangular well in the centre of the deck and from which the smoke-stack jutted, was fully exposed, not unlike the protruding intestines of a dissected corpse.

"They say the machine that controls her wheels has the power of thirty horses," Quade offered admiringly. "I've no idea how they work that out. I can only assume they tied them to her bow and held a tug of war. Your guess is as good as mine." The major shook his head in wonder. "Y'know, there's also a story that Fulton tried to interest Emperor Bonaparte in an undersea boat, and when that didn't work he changed his allegiance and approached the Limeys for funding. Sounds a bit far-fetched, if you ask me. Not sure I believe it, frankly."

"It does sound unlikely," Hawkwood agreed.

"Well, he's on our side now, and that's the main thing," Quade said. He reached into his coat and dug out a pocket watch. Flipping the catch, he consulted the dial and tutted. "Damn, I should go – wouldn't like young Lavinia to start without me. If they do insist on sending me up into the wilds, this could be our last ah . . . consummation for a while." Snapping the watch shut, he looked at Hawkwood and cocked an eyebrow. "You're sure you won't . . .?" He left the suggestion hanging open.

Hawkwood shook his head. "Enjoy yourself, Major."

Quade tucked the watch away and grinned. "Oh, I intend to, don't you worry." He extended his hand. "My thanks for your intervention, Captain. It was good to meet you. We'll likely run into each other again, I expect, after we've taken up our duties; either here or at Greenbush. They're small towns, when all's

46

said and done. That's if they don't send us to Plattsburg, of course. Or if you'd like to meet for a libation before then, you'll likely find me at the Eagle or Berment's. I've taken a room there."

"That's most kind, Major. Thank you."

"Excellent, then I'll bid you good day."

And with a final wave of goodbye, Major Quade limped off to his assignation.

Hawkwood watched him go and wondered idly if the major's leg would hold out during his impending exertions.

Coat collar turned up, he gazed out over the water. The sky was the colour of tempered steel. Colder weather was undoubtedly on the way, bringing snow, and it was more than likely the river would eventually freeze over. Could steamboats navigate through ice? Hawkwood wondered. Perhaps, if it wasn't too thick. But, presumably, if the weather really did close in, even they'd be forced to stop running.

Hopefully, he'd be long gone by that time.

Reaching into his pocket, he withdrew the page he'd torn from *The War* in the Exchange's reading room. It wasn't the most comprehensive map, and it was probably safe to assume that the hand-drawn features had been copied from a much more detailed engraving, so the scale was undoubtedly out of proportion as well, yet all the relevant information appeared to be in place.

Most of New York State was outlined, from Vermont in the east across to the St Lawrence River and the Niagara Frontier in the west. Major towns were marked, as were the main rivers and the largest lakes. The front lines were represented by cannons and flags. Small crenellated squares and anchors showed forts and naval bases. Crudely drawn arrows indicated advances and retreats. The symbols were at their most prolific around the western borderlands, confirming what Major Quade had told him.

Albany, rather than Greenbush, was shown due to its significance as the state capital. It was surmounted by a drawing of a fort topped by the stars and stripes. The next nearest American military presence deserving of capital letters and distinguishable by another tiny fort, was Plattsburg, where Dearborn had set up his winter camp.

Hawkwood shifted his gaze north, at the river and the landscape that lay beyond. He'd been fresh from a return visit to the State Street coach office and mulling over the choices that had been presented to him by the ticket clerk when he'd encountered the major. Now that Quade had confirmed his suspicions over which was the most advantageous route to Canada, there was still the mode of transport to consider. Hawkwood had no intention of walking all the way to the border.

Albany had received its capital status due to it having become the centre of commerce for the north-eastern states. Post roads ran through the city like spokes on a wheel. The most important one – referred to by the clerk as the Mohawk Turnpike – which led directly eastwards through Schenectady to Utica and on to Sackets Harbor, Hawkwood had already dismissed. It was only when the clerk had listed the intermediate halts along the route, that a cold hand had clamped itself around his heart at the mention of one particular name.

Johnstown.

It was a name from a life time ago and one he'd not thought of for many years. Knowing that his reaction must have shown and aware that the clerk was giving him an odd look, Hawkwood had forced his mind to return to the present.

There was an alternative route, the clerk told him. The northern turnpike, which formed part of the New York to Montreal post road. Though, unfortunately, it was also prone to flooding after heavy rain. In fact, the clerk had warned, stretches of it between Albany and Saratoga had already become impassable due to the recent torrents.

What about the river? Hawkwood had enquired, his mind half occupied with trying to shut out the echo from his past.

The clerk had shaken his head. The Hudson was only navigable as far as Troy, six miles upstream. There might be batteaux travelling further north, but Hawkwood would have to investigate that possibility himself by talking to one of the local boat captains.

Hawkwood had been on the point of turning away when the

clerk said, "Might I suggest the *ferry* to Troy, sir? You could pick up the eastern post road there. It runs all the way to Kingsbury and from there along the old wagon road to Fort George, where it links on to the turnpike you would have taken. See here . . ."

The clerk had referred Hawkwood to the wall behind his counter, upon which was suspended, to use the clerk's own description, 'this most excellent map by Mr Samuel Lewis of Philadelphia'. Following the clerk's finger, Hawkwood had seen that both roads were clearly defined.

Two choices, then, Hawkwood thought as he folded his own map away. Remain in Albany until the northern post road was passable, which could turn out to be a very long wait; or try the ferry route. If he chose the latter, at least he'd be on the move and heading in the right direction.

Johnstown.

The name continued to hover at the corner of his mind, like an uninvited guest hidden behind a half-opened door. Hawkwood pushed the memories away, back into the shadows, forcing himself to concentrate on the more pressing task in hand.

The jetty for the local ferries lay at the end of the steamboat quay. It struck Hawkwood as he set off that the clerk had failed to mention the steamboat when giving him his directions. Hawkwood assumed that was because Albany and not Troy was the vessel's terminus. Either that or the clerk had a questionable sense of humour and had wanted Hawkwood to get the shock of this life if and when the damned thing turned up and he was in the vicinity.

In which case, the plot had worked.

It was a pity Nathaniel Jago wasn't here, Hawkwood reflected. His former sergeant and staunch ally, who'd protected his back from Corunna to the slums of London's Ratcliffe Highway, would certainly have had something to say on the matter, even if it was only to remark that they were both a bloody long way from home.

And even as that thought crossed his mind, there rose within him the reality that the statement would only have been half. For Hawkwood was probably closer to home now than he had been at any time in the last thirty years.

*Johnstown.*

The slow clip-clop of iron-shod hooves and the creak of an ungreased axle came from behind. Hawkwood stepped aside to allow the vehicle room.

It was as he glanced up that he became aware of the expressions on the faces of the people around him. Some appeared curious; others strangely subdued, while a few displayed a more unfathomable expression which could have been interpreted as sympathy. Intrigued, Hawkwood followed their gaze.

It took him a moment to realize what he was seeing.

Of the dozen or so uniformed men seated or slumped in the back of the mud-splattered wagon, more than half wore their tunics in full view while the rest wore theirs beneath shabby greatcoats. All were bare-headed save for a couple sporting black shakos. The ones whose heads were not bowed gazed about listlessly, their pale, unshaven faces reflecting the resignation in their eyes.

It was not the sight of their drawn features that caused Hawkwood's throat to constrict, however. It was the colour of their jackets. Stained with dirt and sweat they may have been, but there was no hiding their scarlet hue.

The men in the wagon were British redcoats.

As if the uniforms weren't sufficient evidence, the mounted officer and the six-man escort marching to the rear of the vehicle and the manacles the red-coated men were wearing left little doubt as to their identity and status.

As prisoners.

A voice called out from the onlookers.

"Who've you got there, Lieutenant?"

The mounted officer ignored the enquiry and kept his eyes rigidly to the front. The last man in the escort line was not so reticent.

"You blind?" he muttered sarcastically from the corner of his mouth. "Who d'you think they are?"

Emboldened, the questioner tried again. "So, where're you taking 'em then? Home for supper?"

Someone laughed.

The wagon halted. The lieutenant rode his horse past the head of the vehicle. As he dismounted and entered the ferry office, the less reclusive trooper, cocky at having been nominated the fount of all knowledge, jerked a thumb at the landing stage. "Ferrying 'em to Greenbush. They'll be quartered in the guard house before we move 'em on to Pittsfield."

"Where've they come from?" a man standing near to Hawkwood asked.

The soldier sniffed and shrugged. "Don't rightly know. I heard they were taken near Ogdensburg. We've only been with 'em since Deerfield. We'd've had to march the bastards if the lieutenant hadn't commandeered the wheels."

"Don't look much, do they?" someone muttered in an aside.

*You wouldn't either*, Hawkwood thought, *if you'd had to march most of the way from Ogdensburg and then been shackled to the back of a bloody prison cart.*

Hawkwood had no idea which British regiments were serving on the American continent and he wasn't close enough to the wagon to get a good view of the insignia, though the green facings on a couple of the tunics suggested their wearers might have been from the 49th, the Hertfordshires, while the red facings could have represented the 41st Regiment of Foot.

The lieutenant returned. "All right, Corporal! Move them down to the landing. You can board the ferry when ready."

As the driver released the brake and flicked the reins to nudge the horses forward, the escort shouldered their muskets.

"Here we go," the talkative one murmured.

The novelty over, the spectators began to drift away and Hawkwood looked towards the men on the wagon. Pittsfield was, presumably, the nearest prison of any note where captured enemy were being held.

His eyes roamed over the tired faces, seeing in them the worn expressions of men who'd come to accept their personal defeat. Two or three looked to be half asleep; either that or they'd chosen to feign exhaustion as a means of avoiding the stares of onlookers and of exhibiting fear in the face of their captors.

The wagon jerked into motion. As it did so, one of the greatcoat-clad soldiers shifted position. Until then, his features had been concealed by the coat's upturned collar. As he turned, his face came more into view.

Had Major Quade not mentioned Fulton by name, causing Hawkwood to revive memories of *Narwhale* and the events surrounding William Lee's assassination plot, the mere turning of the prisoner's head might not have amounted to anything.

Except . . .

It took a second or two and even then Hawkwood didn't really believe it. But as he stared at the wagon's occupants, the man in the greatcoat looked up. At first, there was no reaction; the soldier's gaze moved on. And then stopped. It was then that Hawkwood saw it; the slight moment of hesitation before the prisoner's face turned back. In a movement that would have been imperceptible to those around him, Hawkwood saw the soldier's eyes fix on his and widen in mutual recognition.

And, immediately, Hawkwood knew that every move he'd been planning had just been made redundant.

# 2

Tewanias led the way, with the Rangers and the boy following in single file behind. The dog kept pace, sometimes running on ahead, at other times darting off to the side of the trail, nose to the ground as it investigated interesting new smells, but always returning to the line, tongue lolling happily and tail held high as if the journey were some kind of game.

They walked the horses, letting the beasts set their own pace. Save for the occasional bird call, the woods were dark and silent around them. Talk was kept to a minimum. The only other sounds that marked their progress were the rhythmic plod of hooves on the forest floor and the soft clinking of a metal harness.

Every so often, a rustle in the undergrowth would indicate where a startled animal had broken from cover. At each disturbance the Indian and the Rangers and the boy would rein in their horses and listen intently but thus far there had been no indication that they were being followed.

As they rode, Wyatt thought back to the events that had taken place at the cabin, only too aware of how fortunate they'd all been to have emerged from the fight without suffering so much as a scratch, though it had been clear that the Committee members, having been taken completely by surprise, had possessed neither the discipline nor the instinct to have affected an adequate defence, let alone a counter-attack. Save, that is, for the one who'd somehow come back to life and shot Will Archer. Despite Wyatt's attempts to erase it, the nagging thought persisted:

*If we'd checked the bodies, Archer would be alive. Maybe.*

It was small comfort knowing that by opening fire on the Citizens' Committee, the farmer had been the one who set in motion the gun battle that had left eight people dead in almost as many minutes, having acted intuitively and in self-defence.

Wyatt's mind kept returning to the expression on the boy's face when Ephraim Smede had fallen to the ground, the hatchet embedded in his back. There had been no fear, no contrition or revulsion; no regret at having killed a man. Neither had there been satisfaction or triumph at having exacted restitution for the deaths of his aunt and uncle. Instead, there had been a calm, almost solemn acceptance of the deed, as if the dispatching of another human being had been a task that had to be done.

Only when he'd seen his uncle lying mortally wounded in Wyatt's arms had the boy's expression changed, first to tearful concern, followed swiftly by pain and ending in a deep, infinite sadness when he'd looked towards Beth Archer's body. Even at that tender age he seemed to understand that the balance of his life had, from that moment, been altered beyond all understanding.

Wyatt had accompanied the boy to Beth Archer's corpse. He'd watched as the child had knelt by her side, taking the woman's hand in his own, holding it against his cheek. For a moment Wyatt had stood in silence, waiting for the tears to start again, but that hadn't happened. When he'd laid his hand on the boy's shoulders telling him that they had to leave and that there were graves to be dug, there had been a brief pause followed by a mute nod of understanding. Then the boy had risen to his feet, jaw set, leaving the Rangers to prepare the burials, while he'd returned to the cabin to gather his few belongings and retrieve the dog.

It wasn't the first time Wyatt had seen such stoicism. He had fought alongside men who, having survived the bloodiest of battles, had displayed no emotion either during the fight or in the immediate aftermath, only to be gripped by the most violent of seizures several hours or even days afterwards. Wyatt wondered if the same thing was going to happen to the boy. He would have to watch for the signs and deal with the situation, if or when it happened.

The Rangers, partly out of unease at not knowing what to say but mostly because they were all too preoccupied with their own thoughts, had maintained a disciplined silence in the boy's presence. Wyatt wasn't sure if that was the best thing to do in the circumstances, but as he had no idea what to say either, he had followed suit and kept his own counsel. Without making it obvious what he was doing, he kept a watchful eye on their young charge. Not that the boy seemed to notice; he was too intent on watching Tewanias. Whether it was curiosity or apprehension at the Mohawk's striking appearance, Wyatt couldn't tell. Occasionally, Tewanias would turn in his saddle, and every time he did so the boy would avert his gaze as if he'd suddenly spotted something of profound interest in the scenery they were passing. It might have been amusing under different circumstances, but smiles, on this occasion, were in short supply.

They'd been travelling for an hour before the boy became aware of Wyatt's eyes upon him. He reddened under the Ranger's amused gaze. Tewanias was some thirty yards ahead, concentrating on the trail and when the boy had recovered his composure he nodded towards the warrior, frowned and enquired hesitantly: "Your Indian, which tribe does he belong to?"

Wyatt followed the boy's eyes. "He's Mohawk. And he's not *my* Indian."

The boy flushed, chastened by the emphasis Wyatt had placed on the word "my". "Uncle Will said that the Mohawk were a great tribe."

"The Mohawk *are* a great tribe."

The boy pondered Wyatt's reply for several seconds, wondering how to phrase his next question without incurring another correction.

"Is he a chief?"

"Yes." Wyatt did not elaborate.

The boy glanced up the trail. "Why does he keep staring at me?"

"Same reason you keep staring at him," Wyatt said evenly.

The boy's head turned.

"He finds you interesting," Wyatt said and smiled.

"Why?"

"Why do you find *him* interesting?" Wyatt countered.

The boy thought about his reply. "I've never been this close to an Indian before."

"Well, then," Wyatt said. "There you are. He's never been this close to anyone like you before."

"Me?"

"A white boy," Wyatt said. Thinking, but not voicing out loud: *who killed a man with an axe.*

The boy fell silent. After several seconds had passed he said, "Why does he paint his face black?"

"To frighten his enemies."

The boy frowned. He stared hard at the Ranger.

"I don't need paint," Wyatt said, "if that's what you were thinking. I'm frightening enough as it is."

A small smile played on the boy's lips.

It was a start, Wyatt thought.

It was close to noon when the woods began to thin out, allowing glimpses of a wide landscape through gaps in the trees ahead. Wyatt trotted his horse forward to join Tewanias at the front of the line.

"Stand! Who goes there?"

The riders halted. Two men stepped into view from behind the last clump of undergrowth before the trees gave way to open ground. Wyatt surveyed the red jackets, muddy white breeches, tricorn hats with their black cockades and muskets held at the ready. The uniforms identified the men as Royal Yorkers; the colonel's regiment. Wyatt knew that Tewanias would have detected the duo from a long way back. Indeed, he'd have done so even if the men had been dressed in leaf coats and matching hoods, but there had been no need to give

56

a warning. The Mohawk had known that the soldiers posed no threat.

*Good to know the piquets are doing their job*, Wyatt thought. Though what the troopers would have done if the returning patrol had turned out to be of Continental origin was unclear. Fired warning shots and beaten a hasty retreat, presumably, or stayed hidden until they'd passed and then sounded the alert.

He addressed the soldier who'd given the order. "Lieutenant Wyatt and party, returning from a reconnaissance. Reporting to Captain McDonell."

The corporal ran his eye around the group, noting the hard expressions on the unshaven faces. His gaze did not falter when it passed over Tewanias, but flickered as it took in the boy, who looked decidedly out of place among his fellow riders.

"That your hound, Lieutenant?" The corporal jerked his chin towards the dog, which was sniffing energetically at his companion's gaiters.

"Best tracker in the state," Wyatt said.

"That so?" The corporal regarded the dog with renewed interest. "What's his name?"

"Sergeant Tam."

The corporal gave Wyatt a look. "Well, when the sergeant's stopped sniffing Private Hilton's crotch, sir, you'll find the officers down by the main house."

Wyatt hid a smile at the trooper's temerity. "I'm obliged to you. Carry on, gentlemen."

Raising knuckles to their hats, the two piquets watched as the men and the boy rode on.

Private Hilton hawked up a gobbet of phlegm, spat into the bushes and cocked an eyebrow at his companion's boldness in the face of a senior rank. "*Sergeant* Tam?"

The corporal shrugged. "Wouldn't bloody surprise me. You know what Rangers are like."

Private Hilton sniffed lugubriously. "Scruffy beggars, that's what. If they've given the dog stripes, wonder what rank they've given the Indian?"

The corporal, whose name was Lovell, pursed his lips. "I heard tell some of 'em have been made captains, but if you want to ask him, be my guest."

Private Hilton offered no reply but scratched his thigh absently, his nose wrinkling in disgust as his hand came away damp. Wiping dog slobber from his fingers on to his uniform jacket, he shook his head.

"Bleedin' officers," he muttered.

Quietly.

Emerging from the treeline, Wyatt reined in his horse and stared out at a rolling countryside punctuated with stands of oak, pine and hemlock. The estate was spread across the bottom of the slope. It covered a substantial area, comprising barns, store-houses, workshops, grist and saw mills, a smithy and several cottages, and could easily have been mistaken for a small, peaceful village had it not been for the tents and uniformed troops gathered at its heart.

One building, set apart from the others by virtue of its size and architecture, caught the eye. Sheathed in white clapboard, and with leaf-green shutters, the mansion, which was built on a slight rise, was protected at the front by a circle of yellow locust trees and at the rear by two enormous stone blockhouses.

As they approached the camp perimeter, Wyatt's attention was drawn towards several dark smudges moving slowly across the south-eastern horizon. The plumes of smoke were too black and too dense to be rising from cooking fires. Somewhere, off beyond the pinewoods, buildings were ablaze. As he watched, more drifts began to appear, like lateen sails opening to the wind. The fires were spreading. For a second he thought he could smell the burning but then, when his nose picked out the scent of coffee, he knew the aromas were emanating from the field kitchen that had been set up in the lee of one of the blockhouses.

In the camp itself, all appeared calm. There were no raised voices; no officers yelling orders, putting the men through their drills. There was, however, no hiding the purposeful way the soldiers were going about their business or the sense of readiness that hung in the air. There were no musket or rifle stands. Every man carried his weapon to hand in case of attack. Wyatt glanced towards the boy who, to judge from the way his eyes were darting about, was overawed by the appearance of so many troops.

A peal of girlish laughter came suddenly from Wyatt's right. He turned to where half a dozen children were engaged in a game of chase on the lawn beneath the trees. A knot of adults, all dressed in civilian clothes, was keeping a close watch on the high spirits; families who'd made their own way or who'd been delivered to the Hall by the other patrols. Wyatt wondered if their numbers had swelled much since he'd left.

Standing off to one side was a group of two dozen Negroes, of both sexes, some with children in hand. Servants and farm workers, either collected from the surrounding districts or who'd arrived at the Hall of their own volition in the hope of joining the exodus.

Halting by the first blockhouse, Wyatt and the others dismounted and secured their mounts to the tether line.

"Wait here," Wyatt told the boy. "Keep your eye on the horses and make sure Tam stays close. Don't let him run off, else he'll end up in one of their stews." He jerked a thumb at a dozen Indian warriors who were gathered around a circular fire pit above which a metal pot was suspended from a tripod of wooden stakes.

The boy's eyes widened.

"It was a jest, lad," Wyatt said quickly, smiling.

Behind him, he thought he heard Tewanias mutter beneath his breath.

"Best keep him near, anyway," Wyatt advised, indicating the dog. "We won't be long."

To Donaldson, Wyatt said quietly, "Look after them. I'm off to report to the captain." He turned away, paused and turned back. "See if one of you can rustle up some victuals. And some coffee. *Strong* coffee."

Leaving the others, Wyatt and Tewanias, long guns draped across their arms, made their way to the group of officers gathered

59

around a table strewn with papers that had been set up on the grass close to the mansion's rear entrance.

As Wyatt and Tewanias approached, a green-coated officer glanced up and frowned.

"Lieutenant?"

"Captain." Wyatt tipped his cap.

As the officer straightened, Tewanias moved to one side, grounded his musket and rested his linked hands on the upturned muzzle. He looked completely at ease and unimpressed by the ranks that were on display.

Captain John McDonell glanced over Wyatt's shoulder towards the tether line. He was a tall man; gangly and narrow-shouldered with a thin face and a long nose to match. A native of Inverness, with pale features and soft Scottish lilt, McDonell always reminded Wyatt of a schoolmaster. The captain's bookish appearance, however, was deceptive. Prior to his transfer to the Rangers he'd seen service with the 84th Regiment of Foot and had survived a number of hard-fought engagements, including St Leger's expedition against Fort Stanwix. He'd also helped defend British maritime provinces from Colonial attacks by sea and on one memorable occasion had led a boarding party on board an American privateer off Lunenburg, Nova Scotia, capturing the ship and crew and delivering them into Halifax in chains.

"Who've you got there?" McDonell asked.

"Name's Matthew," Wyatt said.

The captain nodded as if the information was only of passing interest and then he frowned. Something in the equation was missing, he realized. He turned his attention back to the Ranger. "Where's his family?"

Wyatt's expression told its own story.

McDonell sighed. "All right, let's hear it."

"We ran into some opposition," Wyatt said.

Behind McDonell, the officers gathered around the table paused in their discussion.

Instantly alert, McDonell's chin lifted. "Regulars or militia?"

Wyatt shook his head. "Neither. Citizens' Committee."

60

McDonell's eyebrows rose. "Really? I'd not have taken *them* for a credible threat."

"They weren't," Wyatt said.

Pondering the significance of Wyatt's terse reply, the captain waited expectantly.

"Turns out they were on an incursion of their own. We interrupted them."

"Go on."

"We were at the Archer farm," Wyatt said. "We—"

"Did you say Archer?"

The interjection came from behind McDonell's left shoulder. A bewigged, aristocratic-looking officer dressed in a faded scarlet tunic stepped forward.

Wyatt turned, remembering to salute. "Yes, Sir John. William Archer. We were tasked to bring him to the Hall. His homestead is . . . was . . . on the other side of the Caroga."

Colonel Sir John Johnson matched McDonell for height but where the captain was thin the colonel was well set, with a harder, fuller face. His most prominent features were his dark blue eyes and his beaked nose, which gave him the appearance of a very attentive bird of prey.

"My apologies, Colonel," McDonell said quickly. "Allow me to introduce Lieutenant Wyatt; 4th Ranger Company."

"Lieutenant." The colonel's gaze flickered sideways towards Tewanias before refocusing on the Ranger.

"Colonel," Wyatt said.

"You said you were at what *was* the Archer homestead."

"I regret that both William Archer and his wife were killed in the exchange, Colonel."

A look of pain crossed the colonel's face. His eyes clouded. "Tell me," he said.

The two officers listened in silence as Wyatt recounted the events of the morning.

"Bastards!" McDonell spat as Wyatt concluded his description of the skirmish. "God damned bloody bastards!"

The colonel looked towards the boy.

"He's Archer's nephew," Wyatt said.

Sir John said nothing for several seconds and then turned back. He shook his head wearily and sighed. "No, actually, he isn't."

"He referred to Archer as his uncle," Wyatt said, confused.

The colonel's expression softened. "For the sake of convenience, I dare say. Though, I've no doubt that's how he came to look upon them."

Wyatt looked to McDonell for illumination, but none was forthcoming.

Removing his wig, Sir John ran a calloused hand across his cropped hair. Though not yet forty, flecks of grey were beginning to show through the darker follicles. "The boy and the Archers were not related. They were his guardians. The boy's father entrusted him to them."

"You knew them, sir?" McDonell said, unnecessarily, he realized, as soon as the words were out.

"The father. He was a good man. His name was Hooper. Ellis Hooper."

McDonell frowned. "I know that name." He stared at the colonel, as if seeking confirmation.

"We were comrades in the French and Indian War. He was with me at Lake George and at Niagara when we fought alongside the Iroquois auxiliaries under my father's command, though we were barely old enough to heft a musket."

A rueful smile touched the colonel's face before he added, "Ellis Hooper was a Loyalist through and through. Because of his allegiance to me, the Continentals put a price on his head. He was with me when I made my run in '76 and he was one of my first recruits when Governor Carleton granted me permission to form the Royal Greens."

Wyatt knew the story. There wasn't a man serving under Sir John's command who didn't. It was the stuff of legend, of tales told to raw recruits as they sat huddled around the camp fires at night.

Sir John's father, William, had built the estate. Arriving in the valley in the late 1730s, he'd made his fortune trading furs with the voyageurs and the Six Nations, the Iroquois tribes who'd held dominion over the vast region of forests, lakes and mountains that lay between the Hudson River and the great waters of Ontario and Erie. It had been William who'd supervised the construction of the Hall and founded the settlement that was to bear the name of his eldest son: Johnstown.

Such had been his skill in diplomacy and his standing among the Six Nations that Sir William had persuaded the Iroquois to side with King George against the armies of the French. For his services, the Crown had awarded him a baronetcy and appointed him Superintendent of Indian Affairs for the entire Northern states.

Sir John had inherited the lands and title upon his father's death. He'd also inherited his father's loyalty to the King, to the dismay of the leaders of the burgeoning republic who'd tried to persuade the son to swear allegiance to the new Congress. When persuasion failed, a less subtle approach had been attempted.

The level of intimidation had been so aggressive that in the interest of self-preservation, Sir John had gathered about him a company of Loyalist supporters and Indian allies to act as a protective shield and to defend the interests of the King. Fearing the formation of a private army, the local Committee of Safety, with the Tryon County Militia at its back, had immediately ordered all Loyalists in the county to relinquish their weapons. It had then placed their leader on parole under the order that he would not take up arms against the new government.

Unbowed, Sir John, while agreeing to the demand, had continued to show dissent. An arrest warrant had been issued. Forewarned, Sir John, along with more than one hundred and fifty followers and helped by a trio of Iroquois guides, had evaded capture by fleeing north through the mountains to gain safety across the Canadian border.

It had taken them nearly three weeks, during which time their provisions ran out and they were forced to forage for roots and leaves before they'd eventually stumbled, half starving, into an Iroquois village on the St Lawrence River.

As soon as he reached the safety of Canada, Sir John had petitioned the Governor for permission to raise a force capable of taking the war back to the enemy. With authority granted, the King's Royal Regiment of New York, under their new colonel, had begun recruiting. The first to sign up had been the men who'd accompanied him into exile.

"He was with us at Stanwix," McDonell said, looking contrite.

"He was." The colonel's voice dropped. "He fell at Oriskany."

"Oh, dear God, yes," McDonell said, looking even more crestfallen. "Why did I not remember?"

The operation had formed part of an invasion plan devised by British generals to gain control of the Hudson River Valley and cut off New England from the rest of the American colonies, thus creating a vantage point between the Hudson and Lake Ontario from where Crown forces could direct operations against the Continental army.

The strategy had involved a two-pronged attack, launched from Montreal. The main force, led by General John Burgoyne, had marched south towards Albany by way of Lake Champlain, while a diversionary force under the command of General Barry St Leger, with Sir John Johnson as his second-in-command, had driven through the Mohawk Valley, intending to approach Albany from the west. It had been the Royal Yorkers' first major campaign and it was to have been the opportunity for Sir John to exact revenge on those who'd forced him into exile the year before.

St Leger's force had made it as far as Fort Stanwix, a Patriot outpost controlling a six-mile portage between the Mohawk River and Wood Creek known as the Oneida Carry, where they'd encamped and laid siege to the American garrison. The plan had been to capture the fort and secure Burgoyne's eastern flank.

News of St Leger's advance had spread, however, and a relief column of New York Militia under the command of Major General Nicholas Herkimer was sent to assist the beleaguered garrison. On hearing the column was on its way, St Leger dispatched a force of Royal Yorkers, Jaeger riflemen and native auxiliaries under the command of Sir John Johnson to intercept. The ambush had taken place some six miles from the fort, at the bottom of a narrow ravine through which ran a shallow three-foot-wide dribble of water called the Oriskany Creek.

Even three years after the event no one knew for certain how many men had perished. Some reports said the Patriots lost 450 dead, the British 200, and because of that it had been deemed a British victory. Native losses had been put around 100, but the numbers were speculative. What was not in dispute was the degree of butchery that had been perpetrated in a fight that had lasted more than six hours. When the ammunition ran out, men – both white and Indian – had fought hand to hand with knife and tomahawk. It was said that the rock-strewn waters of the Oriskany had flowed red with the blood of the slain for weeks afterwards, while the stench of the rotting corpses had carried for miles on the warm summer winds. It was also rumoured, though never confirmed, that some prisoners, captured by Indians, had been taken from the field and eaten in ritual sacrifice.

"He was one of the turncoats," McDonell said.

Catching Wyatt's expression upon hearing the term, Johnson said softly, "It's not what you think, Lieutenant."

The colonel stared down at the wig he was holding. A small spiky leaf was trapped in the weave. He picked it out and flicked it away, watching it spiral to the ground. He looked up.

"We learned from rebel prisoners that Herkimer had dispatched messengers to the fort commander requesting that a sortie be sent to meet the relief column. We thought we could use the request to our advantage by passing off our own men as that relief party. The plan was to infiltrate them into the militia's ranks and then, hopefully, create mayhem and in the confusion capture Herkimer's senior officers."

The colonel shook his head. "Regrettably, our ruse was discovered. Given the time we had, our only disguise was to turn our uniforms inside out. When one of the militia saw the green linings to our coats and recognized a former neighbour whom he knew to be a Loyalist, he raised the alarm. We lost more than thirty men in the first volley. Those that didn't perish in the second fusillade were hacked to pieces, mostly by Oneida warriors fighting on the rebel side. Ellis Hooper was one of those slain. We found his body when the Americans withdrew from the field."

The colonel placed the wig back on his head, straightening it with both hands. His face was set tight. "He was an exceptionally brave man." Looking past Wyatt's shoulder towards the tether line, he added softly, "Who never lived to see his son again."

"The mother?" McDonell asked, though his tone suggested that he already knew the answer.

"Died in childbirth, alas, the year before Ellis Hooper and I made our escape to Canada. The boy would have had a sister, had mother and child lived."

Wyatt knew it wasn't his place to broach the subject of why Hooper had not remained in the valley with his son. Some might have accused him of abandonment, but many a good man had found himself facing the same dilemma and made the same choice as Hooper, Sir John Johnson among them.

The colonel's own wife had been pregnant with their third child when he'd received the warning that troops were on their way to transport him to New York. A pregnant woman would never have made the journey through the mountains, certainly not with two young children in tow, so he'd been forced to leave his family behind.

Ellis Hooper and the rest of Sir John's men had prices on their heads; if they had stayed, they would have been subject to the same prospective fate as their colonel – and an imprisoned man could no more provide for his family than a dead one. But for a man who was alive and free there was always hope that his family would remain untouched by the authorities, which meant there was every possibility that they'd be able to affect their own escape in due course, as had been the case with Sir John's wife, whose own subsequent flight to freedom with, by then, three children in hand, had been every bit as dramatic as her husband's.

Sir John sighed. "Hooper and Archer were friends of long standing, as were their wives. It was natural Hooper would choose them to look after the boy. I recall him telling me that Elizabeth Archer had lost a child – a boy – and that she and her husband would look after his son as though he were their own. It was always his intention to return at a later date and take him back to Canada, which is even more heart-breaking when you consider the reason we're here now."

The colonel looked off towards where the children were playing and then he turned to Wyatt. "I'd deem it a personal favour, Lieutenant, if you'd make sure the boy is placed with someone suitable, a good family who'll take him under their wing for the journey north."

"I'll see to it, Colonel."

"Good man." Sir John looked over Wyatt's shoulder at Tewanias, who hadn't moved a muscle during the entire exchange. "Skennenko:wa ken, Tewanias?"

The Mohawk straightened. "Skennenko:wa, Owassighsishon."

Sir John smiled at McDonell's bemused expression. "Don't look so perplexed, Captain. Merely a greeting between old friends."

"Owassighsishon?" McDonell said. "I'm not familiar—"

"It's the name they have for me; it means He-who-made-the-house-to-tremble. Don't ask me which house as I've no damned idea."

McDonell was given no chance to respond for at that moment the colonel's attention was diverted once more, this time by the approach of another lieutenant in the uniform of a Royal Yorker. After acknowledging Wyatt's presence with a nod, he saluted briskly and announced, "We've retrieved the barrels, Colonel."

A smile lit up the colonel's face. "Have you? Splendid! Thank you, Lieutenant. I'll be with you directly." He turned to Wyatt. "You'll see to the boy?"

"Yes, sir," Wyatt said.

*Barrels?* he thought. Movement over by the doorway to the mansion made him turn and watch as four Royal Yorkers in dirt-stained uniforms and an equally dishevelled Negro civilian emerged from the house, carrying between them two large wooden casks.

*Wine?* Wyatt frowned. It seemed unlikely.

"Well done, William!" Sir John clapped the Negro on the back, sending puffs of dirt into the air.

Intrigued, Wyatt hovered as the barrels were deposited on the ground. A bayonet was produced and a lid was levered off. It looked at first glance as if the cask was full of old sacking.

*Odd*, Wyatt thought, until the top layer was removed.

Wyatt had never seen a pirate's treasure trove unearthed but he suspected it probably wouldn't look much different to the sight that met his eyes. The barrel was stuffed to the gunnels with what was clearly a fortune in silver plate. Salvers, decanters, tankards, punch bowls, coffee jugs, gravy boats, condiment shakers, even serving spoons; all individually wrapped. He stared as each object was divested of its Hessian cocoon and placed reverentially on the ground.

"Belongs to my family," the colonel explained. He seemed unconcerned that Wyatt was loitering. "Bequeathed me by my father. We weren't able to take it with us when we went north, so we concealed it beneath the floor in the cellar." Sir John indicated the manservant, who was brushing himself down. "William here was the only person we entrusted with the hiding place. He's kept it safe these past four years. Well, this time, it's coming with me. I'll not have those damned rebels lay their hands on it. I've seen too many friends who've had their inheritance usurped by those scoundrels." He watched as the last piece of silverware was exposed before turning to the lieutenant. "There should be around forty pieces all told. Split the load. One item per man. Full inventory to be taken."

"Yes, sir." The lieutenant turned and waved an arm towards a small detachment of troops waiting by the blockhouse. "Number Two Company, fall in! Quartermaster to me! Sharply now!"

The troops ran across to form a line and began to open their knapsacks. The Quartermaster produced his ledger and licked the point of his pencil. As the plate was distributed, a description of each item was written alongside the name of the soldier to whom it had been entrusted.

Wyatt couldn't help but smile to himself. How, he wondered, would the army function without lists? It didn't matter if they concerned cockades, cannons or the colonel's heirlooms; lists were as integral to military life as marching and muskets.

Having satisfied himself that the inventory was being conducted to the required standard, the colonel turned to McDonell and the other officers who'd been with him around the table and who'd been observing the disinterment with considerable interest.

"Right, gentlemen – back to business. As I recall, we were conducting a situation report. Captain Anderson?"

A dark-haired, thin-faced officer dressed in the uniform of a Grenadier stepped forward.

"Colonel?"

"The patrols that were sent to retrieve our people should have returned by now. How many civilians have we collected?"

"By my count, one hundred and fifty-two, Colonel."

The colonel looked towards Wyatt. "Better amend that, Captain. Make the total one hundred and fifty-three."

"Yes, sir. We've also acquired thirty-two Negro servants."

"Very good. Prisoners?"

Captain Anderson consulted his figures. "Twenty-seven in total, mostly civilians . . ."

There was a pause, then Anderson continued ". . . including Sammons and his brood."

A nerve flickered along the colonel's jawline. "Release those that are too young or infirm. We gain nothing by subjecting them to the rigours of the return march."

"And Sammons?" Anderson enquired tentatively.

Several officers exchanged glances. After the colonel's escape and following his wife's departure from the valley the mansion and grounds had been seized by the Tryon County Commissioners, who'd appointed local Patriots to act as caretakers until the property could be sold. The Sammons clan, former neighbours of the colonel, had been selected for the task. The patriarch, Sampson Sammons, along with his three sons, had been among the first prisoners captured by the raiding party upon its arrival at the Hall, where the colonel, in a deliberate display of bravado, had set up his temporary headquarters.

"You can let the old man go; Thomas, too. Jacob and Frederick aren't going anywhere save to Canada with us." The colonel smiled. "The walk will do them good."

The comment drew satisfied grins all round. Jacob Sammons was the Commissioners' chief overseer at the Hall. His face, when he'd realized who'd come to interrupt his slumbers in the dead of night, had been a picture to behold.

For the family's part in the occupation of the estate, the father would remain free to reflect on his impudence on the understanding that two of his sons were to be marched as prisoners to a Canadian stockade by the very man whose property they had usurped.

Justice had been served.

"Yes, sir . . ." The captain paused once more. "And the militia captain, Veeder?"

"Release him, too. He's given me his word that, if we let him go now, he'll look upon it as the first half of an exchange. He's promised me the Americans will reciprocate and free one of our own: Lieutenant Singleton. You may recall he was wounded and taken prisoner during the Stanwix engagement."

Anderson frowned. "You trust Captain Veeder's word, sir?"

"He gave it as an officer, and I knew the family in happier times so I see no reason to doubt him. He comes from good stock. His brother's a lieutenant colonel in the county militia. I think it's a risk worth taking if we can get Singleton back. Three years' incarceration is enough for any man."

Still looking sceptical, Anderson managed to force a nod. "Very good, sir."

Sir John turned. "It would appear, gentlemen, that in the light of what we've accomplished, our enterprise has been rather successful, though a number of Captain McDonell's raiding parties have yet to report back – correct?"

"Yes, sir," McDonell said.

The colonel looked up to where the smoke clouds were staining the eastern sky. "The evidence would indicate that they've been performing their duties admirably. In which case it's time we started to organize our withdrawal. I'd hate to think we've outstayed our welcome."

The officers smiled dutifully.

The colonel picked up his hat from the table and brushed it down. "Prepare to dismantle the camp. Also, the civilians need to be advised of their responsibilities. It took us nine days to get here from Champlain. We'll need to step up the pace if we're to get back to the rendezvous point without mishap. Our enemies may have slept through our arrival, but they know we're here now and will, I suspect, be most anxious to make our acquaintance. Captain Duncan, how many fresh horses have we acquired?"

"Sixty-seven, Colonel."

"Very good. We can put them to use as baggage animals and as mounts for the elderly and the youngest children. The ablest of the ladies and the older children will have to walk with the men. You'd better tell them they should wear suitable attire. They've been told to travel light, I take it? See to it they adhere to that. Anything they can't carry gets left behind. No exceptions."

He turned to a stocky officer with salt-and-pepper hair. "As to the troops: Captain Scott, your regulars are to act as escort. Captain Leake's Independents and the other irregulars are to deploy as individual commanders see fit. The same goes for your riflemen, Captain Friedrich, if you'd be so kind. We will have use of them, should a delaying tactic be required."

A slim, officious-looking officer, with hair so blond it was almost white, dressed in the uniform of a Hessian Jaeger, inclined his head. "At your command, Colonel."

"Good. Well, unless there's anything else . . .? No? Excellent. In that case, let's get to it. Dismissed." Sir John turned abruptly. "That includes you, Lieutenant."

"Yes, sir," Wyatt said quickly, though there had been drollness in the colonel's tone rather than rebuke. "Leaving now."

He paused, struck by the expression on the colonel's face. Sir John continued to hold the Ranger's gaze before giving a small, almost imperceptible nod. Acknowledging the unspoken message,

Wyatt summoned Tewanias to him. With the Mohawk at his shoulder, he headed back to the tether line.

"Why can't I stay with you?"

The boy was mounted on his horse. The dog lay stretched out on the grass alongside.

The question took the Ranger by surprise, as did the look of apprehension in the blue-grey eyes. It was the first time the boy had shown anything approaching trepidation or doubt.

"Colonel's orders. He wants all civilians to travel together."

A frown creased the boy's face. "Why?"

"He wants to keep you safe."

"Can't *you* do that?"

*Too many damned questions*, Wyatt thought, *for a twelve-year-old*. Though he wasn't sure if that was, in fact, the boy's age. As with the name, he hadn't bothered to enquire. It hadn't seemed relevant. It still didn't, not really, because there had been little doubt the boy was older than his years would suggest. But then, Wyatt thought, taking a man's life could add years to a person; it didn't matter if they were twelve, twenty-five or seventy. He remembered how he'd felt, the first time.

Wyatt shook his head. "My men and I have to scout the trails. We might run into trouble. It's all right, though. You'll be safe with Reverend De Witt." Wyatt turned. "Isn't that so, Reverend?"

The question was greeted with matching smiles from a burly, ruddy-complexioned man in a wide-brimmed black preacher's hat, black breeches and waistcoat, and a sturdy yet homely woman in a navy-blue dress and bonnet. The reverend's hand rested paternally upon the shoulder of a small, auburn-haired girl of around nine years old. A grey mare stood saddled and ready behind them.

The woman laid a proprietorial hand on the pastor's arm before he could respond to Wyatt's question. "The young man will be as safe as houses, Lieutenant. Don't you fret."

The pastor nodded enthusiastically. "Indeed, Mother! The more the merrier! That's what I always say!"

Wyatt wondered if, despite the attempt at humour, the preacher

72

wasn't trying a little too hard to exude a confidence he might not be feeling, in order to reassure his wife and young daughter and perhaps himself that they were about to embark on nothing more arduous than an afternoon stroll through the countryside.

Though, maybe, Wyatt thought, noting again the solid, square shoulders and the brawny muscles along the pastor's upper arms, De Witt wasn't quite the humble shepherd he made himself out to be. In fact, having already elicited details from some of the pastor's fellow travellers, Wyatt knew he couldn't have been.

Wyatt had learned that De Witt was pastor to a small community on the eastern side of the Dadenoscara Creek, who'd come to the attention of the Commissioners for, supposedly, inciting disaffection against the State of New York from his Sunday pulpit. As a consequence, the pastor had been served with an order to appear at the Albany County Sessions to answer charges of sedition. Having seen what had befallen former neighbours and fellow Tories who'd faced the same accusation, and knowing that his calling offered no protection against a charge of treason, the pastor had accepted Sir John's alternative summons to join with other Loyalist families in their flight to the Canadian border.

It had been the sight of the pistol butt protruding from one of the mare's saddle bags as well as De Witt's more obvious credentials that had prompted the Ranger to take the preacher aside and enquire quietly if he and his wife might be willing to look after a couple of strays in the person of a twelve-year-old orphan boy and a racoon hound of a more indeterminate pedigree.

When the pastor had asked after the boy's parents, Wyatt had seen no reason to hold back. Neither, after revealing what he knew of the boy's background, had he spared details in describing how Will and Beth Archer had died. What he had not disclosed was how the boy had dispatched one of his guardians' attackers with a hatchet. The last thing he'd wanted was for either De Witt or his wife to think that they would be taking some delinquent ne'er-do-well under their wing.

The reverend, who'd known of the Archers through mutual

acquaintances within the Loyalist community, had turned pale at the telling. When he'd summoned his wife to apprise her of the situation, the anguish in her face had mirrored that of her husband.

"Oh, my dear Lord – the poor wee boy!" she'd gasped, lifting a hand to her throat in horror.

"Can't argue with that, ma'am, but probably best not to make a fuss over him," Wyatt had advised. "From my dealings with the lad, I'd say he's got true grit and then some. My sense is he's strong enough not to need any reminders. He just needs to sit for a spell. It'll hit him hard eventually and when that happens—"

"You can rest easy on that score, Lieutenant," the pastor had reassured Wyatt firmly. "Esther and I'll not crowd him. War makes orphans of us all in one way or another, and Mrs De Witt and I have seen more than our share of pain in that regard. And if there's one thing I've learnt in ministering to those who've suffered a loss, it's that people vent their sorrow in all sorts of ways. With some, it leaks out a few droplets at a time, while others keep the grief bottled up so tight it's like watching water rising behind a dam, so that when the hurt becomes too much to bear—" The pastor clenched a fist against his chest. "Well, I don't have to tell you. All we can do is offer comfort if and when that happens and place our trust in the Lord."

Not being a particularly religious man, Wyatt wasn't sure if the pastor had been expecting him to say 'Amen' at that point, but he'd made do with a solemn nod, which had evidently sufficed.

"What's his name?"

For a moment, Wyatt thought the girl had directed her question at him, but when he turned he saw that it was the boy who was being addressed. There was an awkward silence.

"His name's Tam," Wyatt said, thinking: *He can kill a man with an axe, but he's lost his tongue to a preacher's daughter?*

At the mention of his name the dog pricked up his ears.

"And that's Matthew," Wyatt added.

"Does he bite?" the girl asked nervously.

"No," Wyatt said. "Leastways, Tam doesn't. Can't say as I can speak for his master."

Wyatt's reply drew a bark of laughter from De Witt.

The girl giggled as she held her hand out to the dog. To her delight, Tam rose to his feet and licked at her outstretched fingers. With his interrogator distracted, the boy caught Wyatt's eye. For the second time he looked awkward and unsure. Shifting in his saddle, he stared off over Wyatt's right shoulder, to where Tewanias was standing.

The war paint was gone. While the effect was not as fearsome, there was no disguising the Mohawk chief's striking features, his calm repose and the strength of his gaze.

Curious as to the boy's obsession with the stern-faced warrior, Wyatt said, "If you want to say 'goodbye', it's O:nen ki' wahi'."

"Interesting-looking fellow," De Witt mused, breaking into Wyatt's thoughts. "He's Mohawk, yes?"

Wyatt hid his surprise. Most civilians took one look at an Indian and thought *heathen savage*. For a preacher to show such equanimity, no matter how enlightened, was unusual.

"Yes," Wyatt said.

"O:nen ki' wahi', Tewanias," the boy called softly.

There was no response. It was as though the Indian had not heard or had chosen not to acknowledge the words. Several seconds went by. Wyatt saw the expectancy on the boy's face give way to confusion and then to disappointment. The slim shoulders drooped. It was at that point that the warrior's expression changed. It was, Wyatt thought, like watching someone awaken from a trance.

When the Mohawk raised his head the pastor's daughter was first to react, letting out a sharp gasp and shrinking back against her mother's skirts, her play with the dog forgotten. Moving with cat-like grace, Tewanias lifted his musket and strode directly towards her.

The pastor tensed.

"No," Wyatt said quickly. "It'll be all right."

Paying no heed to the reaction he'd provoked, Tewanias halted beside the boy's horse. Wordlessly, he reached up with his free

75

hand and removed from around his neck a rawhide thong from which was suspended a small piece of carved yellow bone. He held it out. Finally, he spoke.

"O:nen ki' wahi', Mat-huwa."

"Take it," Wyatt instructed. He realized he'd been holding his breath, though he wasn't sure why.

The boy accepted the offering, turning it over in his hands, examining it closely. He turned to Wyatt. "How do I say—"

"Niá:wen," Wyatt said. There was dried blood, he noticed, and what looked like a matted clump of hair and tissue adhering to the edge of the war club that was strapped across the Mohawk's back; residue from the attack on the horseman at the Archers' farm. He wondered if the pastor or his wife had noticed. Hopefully not; the club face wasn't in their direct line of sight.

"Niá:wen, Tewanias," the boy said, slipping the thong over his head and around his neck. He held the piece of bone in his hand and stared at it once more, slowly massaging its smooth surface with the ball of his thumb.

"Anowara." It was the Indian who spoke.

"It means turtle," Wyatt said. "Tewanias is a war chief of the Turtle clan. That's his totem."

"Well, bless my soul," De Witt murmured softly as the Mohawk stepped back.

*Amen to that, Reverend*, Wyatt thought.

With Tewanias by his side, he looked about him. The preparations for departure were almost complete. Tents had been struck and fires doused. The stolen horses had been formed into a line and troops were checking their packs, settling into ranks, readying themselves for the march. Those Loyalists who'd chosen to remain behind were saying their final goodbyes, hugging and clasping the hands of those about to embark.

Had Wyatt not known differently, the scene might have suggested that some festivity had been taking place and that guests were preparing to wend their way home after a picnic or a barn-raising, instead of stealing away from a homeland that no longer saw them as legitimate citizens. Though, as he'd walked the grounds, he'd seen that there were many who were in tears at the thought of abandoning all that was familiar in exchange for an arduous journey towards an uncertain future.

A faint call sounded from up ahead. As the order was taken up by NCOs stationed down the line, a mood of anticipation ran through the column. The civilians began to gather themselves.

Wyatt held out his hand. "Take care, Matthew."

Fingering the amulet, it took a second for the boy to respond, but when he did his grip was firm.

"We won't be far," Wyatt said. "Don't forget that. You might not see us, but we'll be there."

"Stay safe, Lieutenant," De Witt said.

"You, too, sir." Wyatt shook the pastor's hand, winked at the girl, who had re-emerged from hiding, and tipped his hat to Mrs De Witt. "Ma'am."

De Witt took hold of his daughter's waist, helped her feet find the shortened stirrups and, with his wife holding the bridle, lifted her gently on to the mare's back.

He addressed Wyatt over his shoulder. "How's your knowledge of the scriptures, Lieutenant? Exodus, Chapter 12, Verse 51: 'And it came to pass the selfsame day that the Lord did bring the children of Israel out of the land of Egypt by their armies."

Wyatt shook his head apologetically. "Sorry, Reverend. I'm afraid my knowledge of the good book isn't that good. Though from what I do recall, when the Israelites took their leave they were heading for Canaan not Canada, and it took them forty years. If that's the colonel's plan, we're going to need a few more supplies."

De Witt grinned. "I'm not sure how Colonel Johnson would take to being compared to Moses!"

"Well, if Canada does turn out to be the Promised Land, Reverend, you make sure you put some of that milk and honey aside for Tewanias and me."

"I surely will, Lieutenant. It'll be my pleasure."

A fresh call came from up ahead. De Witt checked his daughter was secure, took hold of the bridle from his wife, adjusted the knapsack that rested across his shoulders and, with a final nod to the Ranger, coaxed the horse into motion.

"Walk on, Nell," he said.

Wyatt presumed the reverend was talking to the mare. He had a feeling the pastor's daughter was called Libby.

As the preacher and his family merged with the rest of the column, the boy summoned his dog and, holding the reins in his right hand and clutching the amulet in his left, he nudged his horse forward to join them. He made no attempt to look back.

"The boy shows courage," Tewanias murmured softly as he stared after the preacher and his party.

"He does that," Wyatt said.

The Mohawk had spoken in English. Wyatt had long become immune to his friend's arbitrary use of language. As well as English, Tewanias was competent in French and the various Iroquois dialects. There never seemed to be a logical reason why he chose to converse in any one of them in particular and Wyatt had come to suspect that Tewanias switched back and forth for no better reason than he enjoyed being contrary.

The two men waited until the remainder of the column was on the move, then made their way to where the rest of the patrol was waiting.

Wyatt immediately registered the grim expression on Donaldson's face.

"What is it?" he asked.

"Scouts have reported back. Seems the local militia's woken up. The call's gone out: all members are to collect their weapons and assemble at Johnstown."

Wyatt shook his head dismissively. "They won't risk attacking us – we outnumber them two to one."

"They've sent messengers to Albany," Donaldson said.

*Reinforcements*, Wyatt thought. He swore softly and looked off to where the last of the column was disappearing into the trees. It was almost ninety miles to Champlain, where the vessels of the Provincial Marine were waiting. Ninety miles of near-virgin forest through which the only means of passage was a labyrinth of old military roads cut during the French-Indian wars, and ancient Iroquois trails, none of which had been adequately mapped.

The colonel had led civilians to safety through a wilderness once before, but that last occasion had involved less than two hundred souls, all of them men, most of whom had been used to living off the land. This current exodus included women and children. Adding their number to the invasion force meant there would be almost seven hundred bodies on the move; the majority of them on foot. Wyatt thought about the pastor and his implicit faith in God and of the forces that would be arrayed against them.

*Better start praying now, Reverend. We're going to need all the help we can get.*

# 3

*December 1812*

It was just after eight o'clock in the evening when Captain Maynard Curtiss of the 11th Regiment of Infantry emerged on to a darkened Church Street. As the door to the club closed softly behind him, he buttoned up his greatcoat, adjusted his hat and awarded himself a wide grin of satisfaction. He had just spent the last hour with a very attractive and, it had to be said, rather energetic young lady by the name of Jessica, and he was feeling not only replete but somewhat over-awed by the dexterity of his own performance.

Admittedly, Jessie was a whore and thus her enthusiasm and the praise she'd lavished upon him for the pleasure he'd provided during their riotous coupling might have had more to do with the fact that she was being paid for her time rather than it being a true reflection of her client's expertise between the sheets. But that knowledge in no way detracted from the captain's sense of well-being as he made his way down the quiet moonlit street.

To counteract the cold breeze that was coming in off the river, he turned up his coat collar. Increasing his stride, he headed for the alleyway and the shortcut between Church Street and Court Street that would lead him to his eventual destination, the South Ferry terminal. There was a hint of rain in the air and he had no desire to be caught out in the wet.

The alley was empty and the tread of the captain's footsteps seemed to echo in the darkness. A few people had been out on the main streets, wrapped up against the cold as they'd hurried off to hearth and home. In this less salubrious part of the town, the citizens most liable to be abroad were either drinkers or parlour-house punters like the captain. Given the distinct nip in the air, even these hardy souls preferred to remain indoors, in the warmth, indulging in their chosen pastime. The only others willing to brave the cold were the prospective passengers heading for the last ferry to Greenbush before the service shut down for the night.

Curtiss had travelled not more than fifty paces when he realized that he might have company. It wasn't any particular sound that had alerted him to the possibility. More a feeling in his bones, a sense that someone was watching.

He paused and stole a quick glance over his shoulder. A stooped figure, clearly the worse for wear, a knapsack across its back, was weaving unsteadily down the alleyway towards him, left hand outstretched, using the wall as guidance. There was a brief silvery glint as a beam of moonlight glanced off an object held in the figure's right hand. Curtiss felt a flash of fear until he saw that the reflection had come not from a blade but from a glass bottle. As he watched, the figure lifted the bottle to its lips and took a hefty swig from the contents, almost overbalancing in the process, despite the fact that one hand was still braced against the brickwork.

Grimacing with distaste at such a pathetic display of drunkenness, the captain turned and continued on his way, keen to return to the comfort of his billet, there to enjoy one last tot of whiskey and to bask in the warm memory of his recent exertions before he finally retired for the night.

Another thirty paces and it occurred to Curtiss that, whoever the drunk was, his footsteps were inaudible. This struck Curtiss as unusual, given the noise his own boots were making as they scuffed their way through the dirt and the occasional puddle. Not unduly concerned, more curious than suspicious, he turned again, half-expecting to see a comatose form sprawled face down in the dirt several yards behind him.

It wasn't the sight of the figure looming two feet away from him that caused the captain to take a quick step back so much as the knowledge that the man had managed to cover the distance between them not only in a matter of seconds but in total silence as well.

There were no street lamps in the alleyway. That convenience had yet to penetrate Albany's narrow dockside lanes. What illumination there was came from the candlelight that spilled weakly from gaps in a few badly fitting shutters and the pale moon that hung, suspended like a pearl, high above the surrounding chimney pots.

As he stared at the shadowy form before him, Curtiss had a fleeting impression of a dark-haired individual as tall as himself. The captain's startled gaze flickered across what he could see of the man's features, to the dark eyes set in a hard face and the two ragged scars that ran in parallel furrows across the upper curve of the man's left cheekbone.

Curtiss never saw the blow that struck him and thus had no chance of defending himself. One second he was standing in the alley, the next he was coming to his senses, face down in the dirt, feeling as if he'd just been run over by a coach and four – several times.

He raised his head cautiously, and then wished he hadn't as a sharp bolt of pain lanced through his jaw and speared its way into the backs of his eyeballs. Letting out a groan, he winced and sank down again. Confused by his situation, he lay still for several seconds until the nausea had subsided and then tried again. This time, he made it as far as his knees. He reached up and felt along the side of his head. His hand came away damp and sticky and he stared blankly at the stain on the tips of his fingers. He realized, with some apprehension, that he was staring at his own blood, as black as pitch in the moonlight.

The nausea overtook him again and he reached out with the same hand, pressing the now-bloodied palm against the wall to keep himself upright. As he did so, he had a sudden vision of a dark-clad figure performing a similar manoeuvre not so long ago. He closed his eyes as a fresh bout of dizziness arrived and then, as the moment passed and his mind began to clear, his memory reasserted itself.

There had been a man, he remembered; a stranger, who, using the shadows of the night and the captain's own footfalls to mask his presence, had followed him into the alleyway; a tall man who had first appeared drunk and whom he had then turned to confront.

After which . . .

Fuzzy as to the exact sequence of events, Curtiss hauled himself up until he had gained his feet, then slumped back against the wall. No sooner had he done so than he let out a gasp as his spine made contact with the cold hard surface of the bricks. It was then he realized that his memory wasn't the only thing he was lacking.

His overcoat and uniform tunic were gone, too; which would explain why he was suddenly so damned cold.

Curtiss looked around fearfully. He was in a narrow passageway leading off the alleyway he'd been walking down. There were no candle-lit windows in the passage, only a couple of murky doorways. Ignoring the throbbing in his head, he thought back to the last thing he remembered and tried to bring the face of the man who'd robbed him to mind.

Though he'd employed considerable stealth to conceal his approach, the stranger hadn't looked like a footpad. Which was not to say there was anything benign about his attacker; those saturnine features – not to mention the scars – had marked him out as the last person you'd want following you into a dark alleyway. And yet Curtiss had allowed him to do precisely that. He should have been more observant from the start. Probably would have been, had his mind not been filled with the memory of his recent entanglement with the nubile Jessica. If only he'd avoided the shortcut and taken a more public route home.

And what kind of footpad was it that stripped a man of his coat and tunic instead of just rifling through his pockets and making off before he regained consciousness? It wasn't as if the man didn't have a greatcoat of his own. Curtiss couldn't recall what his assailant had been wearing under it. That much was a blur.

Groggily Curtiss felt delicately for his head wound, probing the bump. What the devil had the man hit him with? The bottle? Perhaps the scoundrel had used a fist and he'd hit his head when he'd fallen to the ground. Using the wall for support, he began making his way cautiously towards the entrance to the passageway, but had proceeded only a couple of yards when his boot made contact with something lying on the ground. He flinched, the sudden movement sending another shock wave through his skull. Hesitantly, ignoring the pain, he forced himself to look down. In the spectral gloom, the bundle at his feet appeared to be a body. Summoning resolve, he peered closer.

To his immense relief, he saw that he had been mistaken. There was no body. What he was looking at was an empty coat – his own coat, he realized with a start – that had been folded and propped against the wall. His boot had snagged in the sleeve, causing the garment to fall open. Gingerly Curtiss crouched to pick the coat up; head swimming, he waited for the nausea to subside before shaking out the garment and put it on. He let go a thankful sigh as the cloth enveloped him: warm again. Well, almost.

Without thinking, he patted the pockets and frowned when he heard the clink of money. Further investigation revealed he was still in possession of his change. He withdrew the coins and stared down at them. Why would someone steal his jacket and yet leave his finances intact? Curtiss sucked in his cheeks. Not a good idea; the pain was a sharp reminder. Checking further, Curtiss discovered that his pocket watch was there, too. Apparently the only item that had been purloined, apart from his tunic, was a small tin containing some tapers and his flint and steel.

Curtiss, his mind awash with confusion, emerged hesitantly into the alleyway. There was no one around, no faces at any of the windows or doors that might have witnessed the assault. He considered his options. The obvious thing to do was to inform the constables that he'd been the victim of a robbery, but he could imagine the looks on their faces as he told them that the only items stolen were his army tunic and fire-making tools. What kind of thief would leave his coat folded on the ground with his money and watch still inside?

Thoughts of his watch had Curtiss reaching back into his pocket. He lifted the timepiece out, consulted the dial and groaned. He'd missed the damned ferry. There wasn't another one scheduled until the morning. From past experience, Curtiss knew that it was well-nigh impossible to cadge a ride with anyone trustworthy after dark, so he was stuck. Marooned might have been a better description.

But at least he had money, and therefore the means to pay for a room. Things could have been a lot worse. He could have been lying in the dark with his throat slit from ear to ear. That thought sent another shard of pain scooting through the back of his skull.

Burrowing into his coat, Curtiss decided there was no alternative. Cutter's Tavern was just around the corner, and the accommodation there was a sight more comfortable than his billet in the officers' quarters. Galvanized by the thought of a dram and a seat by the tavern's roaring fire, Captain Curtiss quickened his pace.

Maybe, after he'd warmed his insides, he could warm the rest of his person by retracing his steps to Hoare's Gaming Club and revisiting the delectable Jessica. After all, there was nothing more likely to garner sympathy in a young lady's bosom than a gentleman's sorry tale of woe. Mrs Delridge, the club's proprietress, might even be sufficiently touched by his plight to offer a discount.

Cheered by that prospect, Captain Curtiss took new bearings and headed for the first of his goals.

After all, it wasn't as if a missing tunic was the end of the world. The quartermaster would undoubtedly moan about the difficulty of finding a replacement, but that was the way of quartermasters. The loss would be rectified and the militia would survive.

*Like me,* Curtiss reflected thankfully as he continued on his way.

Ten yards further on, though, it suddenly occurred to him that he wasn't wearing his hat.

The thieving bastard had stolen that, too.

Hawkwood cursed under his breath. The captain's uniform chafed like the devil. It didn't help that the tunic was tighter than he'd expected around the chest and underneath the arms, and that the sleeves were on the short side. The hat fitted well enough, though, for which Hawkwood was grateful. Since leaving the army he'd abandoned headwear, unless it was part of some disguise he'd had to adopt in the course of his duties as a peace officer. Thus even though the damned thing was relatively secure on its perch it still felt decidedly unnatural.

He had, however, drawn the line at purloining the captain's breeches. He'd no intention of going back on the self-imposed rule that had stood him in good stead through the years: never wear another man's trousers.

The tunic had been a different proposition. Hawkwood knew he needed it to give him authority. So while the thing might be bloody uncomfortable, it was ideal for his purposes. Hopefully, he wouldn't have to bear the discomfort for too long.

He'd been waiting in the shadows opposite the gaming club entrance for almost an hour when he spotted a suitable candidate: someone of his own height and build, in officer's garb.

He hadn't expected it to go so well. There had been a moment when his intended victim had turned round, but Hawkwood had planned for that eventuality by collecting an empty bottle from the window sill of a nearby tavern to use as a prop. Pretending to be tipsy had given him something to do with his hands, and as most law-abiding citizens were repelled by drunkards the ruse had proved a sound one. The final approach had been tricky, but matching his own footsteps with those of his target had enabled him to get up close. Before his victim had time to react, Hawkwood had launched a blow to the carotid that cut off the blood supply as effectively as a tourniquet.

The strike had been taught to him by Chen, an exiled Shaolin priest Hawkwood had met in London. They sparred together in a cellar beneath the Rope and Anchor public house. Chen had cautioned that, if delivered too robustly, there was a danger such a blow could kill. He had then proceeded to demonstrate the precise speed at which the strike had to be delivered in order to subdue rather than maim or kill, by using the technique against Hawkwood. After being laid out half a dozen times, Hawkwood had got the idea. As the unfortunate Captain Curtiss had discovered to his cost, Chen's former pupil had learned his lesson well.

Suitably attired, Hawkwood was on the ferry by the time the captain stumbled out of the alleyway. The three hundred yard crossing proved uneventful, though the numbing wind that eddied downriver from the northern reaches offered a prophecy of wintry conditions ahead. In the darkness it was difficult to make out the far bank; the high bluffs that dominated the eastern shore cast dark shadows over the Greenbush waterfront. All that could be seen were the lights from the rag-tag collection of houses huddled behind the landing stage, which seemed to be drawing the ferry like a moth to a candle flame.

The vessel – if the flat-bottomed, punt-shaped barge could be called such a thing – was not overladen. There were only half a dozen passengers, all male. Three were in uniform, presumably heading back to barracks after a night out. The others could have been military men in civilian dress or Greenbush residents; Hawkwood had no way of knowing. One of the uniformed men had been drinking heavily, or at least beyond his capacity. He spent the short voyage voiding over the ferry's gunwale, his retching almost matching in volume the wash of water against the hull and the rasp of the ropes as they were hauled through the pulley rings.

Hawkwood was glad of the distraction this provided, for he'd no wish to engage his fellow passengers in conversation. Even the most cursory enquiries would inevitably reveal his ignorance of both his regiment and the cantonment to which he was heading. And the less opportunity anyone had to study and memorize his features, the better. He had, therefore, affected a show of distaste for the vomiting and removed himself from his fellow passengers, gazing out over the rail while immersing himself in the darkness of the night and thoughts of what his next move might be.

It was a fact of war that even the best-laid plans had a tendency to fall apart upon first contact with the enemy. On hostile ground, with limited access to resources, Hawkwood had no alternative but to improvise. And time was running out.

The cantonment lay at the end of a well-trodden dirt road that rose in a steady incline stretching a mile and a half from the landing stage. Hawkwood knew the way. He'd made a dry run that afternoon. Had he not had the benefit of studying the lie of the land in daylight he would have found it impossible to find his way now, with the trees creating deep dense shadows across the path.

Hoisting his knapsack on to his shoulder, he increased his stride and forged up the trail. He kept up the pace for several minutes before halting. His long coat rendering him almost invisible in the blackness, he listened for the other ferry passengers; long seconds passed before his ears picked up the sounds of slow stumbling progress further down the hill. No threat there; he moved on.

Soon the ground began to level off and the trees started to give way. Lights that had hitherto been the size of fireflies grew into patches of candle-glow spilling from windows and from lanterns as the cantonment appeared before him.

The camp was large, probably close to two hundred acres. Even in daylight it had been difficult to determine the exact boundaries, for there were no perimeter walls or fences separating the place from the outside world. Hawkwood could not determine whether this was a monumental dereliction of security or because the army deemed it impractical or unnecessary.

From what he'd seen during his afternoon sortie, the buildings were in good condition. Quade had told him that work on the site had only commenced in March, with the last of the barracks erected in September. Hawkwood doubted the paintwork would look so pristine after the winter snows and the spring thaw had wreaked their havoc.

Courtesy of Major Quade, he also knew that the cantonment could accommodate four to five thousand troops, close to three-quarters of the total complement of the American regular army. As a divisional headquarters, it boasted impressive facilities: living quarters for soldiers and officers of field rank and below: stables; a smithy; a powder magazine, armoury and arsenal; a multitude of storage areas and essential workshops; a guard-house; and a hospital. The dominant feature, however, was the parade ground. It straddled the centre of the camp and was bordered by soldiers' barracks – four blocks on either side – and by officers' quarters at either end. The accommodation wings had been easy to identify by the manner in which the soldiers entered and exited the buildings. Not that there appeared to be that many personnel about, which confirmed Quade's account of General Dearborn having transferred the bulk of his command to Plattsburg. That might also explain why precautions appeared to be so lax.

As part of his reconnaissance, Hawkwood had scanned the approach roads for sentry posts, but like the perimeter safeguards they'd been conspicuous by their absence. Even now, there appeared to be no piquets on duty at the access points. Could the Americans really be that complacent? Were they so confident in their might and their independence that they assumed no one would dare breach their unguarded perimeter? Well, he was about to prove them wrong.

Opening his greatcoat buttons so as to reveal a glimpse of the tunic beneath, he drew himself up, adjusted his hat, and strode confidently into the lions' den.

It had been a few years since Hawkwood had last set foot in an army compound, but even if he'd been delivered into the cantonment blindfolded and in pitch-dark, he would have found his bearings almost immediately. Military camps the world over had an odour and an atmosphere all of their own. And so it was with Greenbush.

Hawkwood's objective was the cantonment's southern corner. He'd already marked the site of the stables but they would have been easy to find by sense of smell alone. The combination of horse piss, shit, leather and straw was unmistakable. The three blocks of stalls formed a U-shape around a yard, with a farrier's hut positioned in the centre. Illuminated by lanterns hanging alongside the stable doors, the place looked to be deserted. It couldn't be that easy, surely?

It wasn't.

Someone laughed, the sound abrasive in the quiet of the evening. Hawkwood paused, looking for the source, and saw a faint beam of light leaking from a door at the end of the left-hand stable block. As he moved towards it, his ears caught the low murmur of voices and another dry, throaty chuckle. The exchange was followed by a rattling sound, as though several small pebbles were being rolled around the inside of a hollow log.

He paused, aware there were two choices now open to him. The first was to continue by stealth alone in the hope that he could achieve his objective without being discovered, which was unrealistic. The second carried an equal amount of risk, but was more overt and would involve a lot more nerve. If he could pull it off, though, he'd undoubtedly save time.

He decided to go with the second option.

Placing his knapsack against the wall, he took a deep breath and pushed open the door.

Three men, coarse-faced and lank-haired, dressed in unbut-toned tunics, were seated at a rough table surrounded by walls festooned with tack. A small pile of coins and a tin mug sat by each man's elbow. In the centre of the table a half-empty bottle of rye whiskey stood next to a lantern and a wooden platter containing a hunk of bread, some sliced ham and a wedge of pale yellow cheese with a small knife stuck in the centre of it.

One of the men was holding a wooden cup. He gave it a shake as Hawkwood walked in; the resulting rattle was the sound that had been audible from the yard. Not pebbles in a log but wooden dice. The dice man's hand stilled and three sets of eyes registered their shock and surprise. Clearly, evening inspection by a ranking officer was not a regular occurrence.

"Good evening, gentlemen."

Hawkwood fixed his attention on the man holding the dice. He waited two seconds, then demanded brusquely: "Your name – remind me."

The dice man scrambled upright. "Corporal J-Jeffard, sir." His gaze flickered nervously to the collar and top half of the tunic, made visible by Hawkwood's unbuttoned greatcoat.

"Ah, yes," Hawkwood said, injecting sufficient disdain into his voice to inform everyone in the room who was in charge. "Of course. Labouring hard, I see."

The corporal reddened. His Adam's apple bobbed. Hawkwood swung towards the other two, both of whom had also risen to their feet. One of them was trying to fasten his collar at the same time. Recognizing a losing battle, he gave up. Whereupon, reasoning that it might be better if he assumed at least some sort of military pose, he dropped his hands to his sides. His companion followed suit. The movement tipped his chair on to its back. All three men flinched at the clatter.

Hawkwood could smell the alcohol on their breath. "And *you* are . . .?" he enquired.

"Private Van Bosen, sir."

"Private Rivers, Captain."

Hawkwood viewed the bottle and the mugs. "Care to explain, Corporal?"

Jeffard flicked a nervous glance towards his companions.

"Don't look at them!" Hawkwood snapped. "Look at me!"

The trooper swallowed and found his voice. "Taking a break between duties, Captain. We were about to return to our posts when you arrived."

"Of course you were," Hawkwood said witheringly. "Nice try. Shame you've been rumbled. If I were you, I'd practise those excuses. You can put down the dice; I've a job for you."

He paused, watching as a chastened Jeffard did as he was told, allowing the silence to stretch to breaking point before adding, "I'm here because I have urgent dispatches for both General Dearborn and Colonel Pike. I need two good mounts, saddled, fully equipped and ready to depart in ten minutes.

Manage it quicker than that and you can finish your game." He turned to the others. "Anyone else on duty here, or is this it?"

A flustered nod from Van Bosen. "No, sir. I mean, yes, sir. Just us, sir."

Hawkwood vented a silent sigh of relief as he waved his hand dismissively. "Yes, well, whichever it is, I don't care, frankly. Only, with the three of you, it won't take long, will it? Ten minutes, gentlemen. I'll expect those damned animals to be ready or I'll want to know why. Don't make me put the three of you on a charge. That happens and you'll be shovelling shit till doomsday."

Giving them no chance to respond, Hawkwood turned on his heel and stalked out of the room.

As soon as he was outside and out of sight, he moved swiftly towards the shadows cast by the farrier's hut. Tucking himself against the wall, he waited. A few seconds later, he watched as the three troopers left the tack room and hurried towards the adjacent stable block. The moment they disappeared inside, Hawkwood, his movement concealed by the intervening hut, crossed to the stable block on the opposite side of the yard. Grabbing a lantern from the wall, he hauled back the door. He was immediately assailed by the pungent aroma of hay, horse sweat and fresh droppings.

The stalls were set out along both sides of a central aisle. Beyond the reach of the lantern glow, dark forms stirred restlessly in the shadows. Straw rustled. A soft whickering sound eddied around the walls as the stable's occupants caught his scent. He moved down the aisle, treading carefully. He had no desire to panic the animals. At least not yet.

As he looked for an empty stall, he prayed that Jeffard and his cronies were as inefficient as they had appeared to be. With luck, the brew they'd been drinking would slow them down long enough to allow him the valuable seconds he needed.

Two stalls had been left vacant. Hawkwood picked the one furthest from the door and looked for a supply of dry straw. Bales of it were stacked in a storage area at the end of the aisle. Laying aside the lantern and working quickly, he broke open one of the bales, gathered the contents in his arms and piled the bulk of it loosely against the slatted walls of the empty stall, trailing the rest out into the aisle.

Then he set it alight.

He used the lantern. He'd been planning to use the stolen flint and steel to start the fire, but they weren't needed. The accelerants had been provided for him. He watched anxiously as the first tentative flames scurried along the dry stalks. When he was confident the fire had taken hold, he tossed the lantern to one side and backed away, unlatching the doors to the stalls as he went. By the time he reached the main door, the first of the horses was already stamping the ground and snorting nervously.

Exiting the stable, Hawkwood propped the outer door open as far as it would go and retraced his steps to the farrier's hut. He made it to the tack room just as Corporal Jeffard led the first of the saddled horses into the yard.

Hawkwood counted to five and strode arrogantly into view. His sudden appearance had the desired effect: the troopers started in surprise. The less time they had to think, the less likely they would be to question his orders or, more inconveniently, his identity. Hawkwood wanted them on tenterhooks as to what this supercilious bastard of an officer would do next. From their expressions, the ruse appeared to be working.

"Well done, Corporal," Hawkwood drawled. "There's hope for you yet."

The corporal drew himself up. "They're sound, Captain. They ain't been out for a day or two, so they'll be glad of the exercise."

*Then they won't be disappointed*, Hawkwood thought, running a critical gaze over the animals. "All right, gentlemen. You've redeemed yourselves. You may return to your, ah . . . duties."

A grin of relief spread across the corporal's face. "Yes, sir. Thank you, sir."

At that moment Private Van Bosen lifted his gaze to a point beyond Hawkwood's shoulder and gasped hoarsely, "Oh, Christ!"

The exclamation was accompanied by the unmistakable clatter of hooves coming from the other side of the farrier's hut.

Hawkwood, Corporal Jeffard and Private Rivers spun round in time to see a dark mass of stampeding horses careering noisily towards the open end of the stable yard and the darkness beyond.

"Jesus!" Jeffard stared in horror and disbelief at the vanishing animals.

Hawkwood frowned. "I smell smoke."

"Bloody stable's on fire!" Rivers yelped as the realization hit him.

Turning to Jeffard, who was holding the reins of the two saddled horses, Hawkwood barked, "Wait here! Don't let them go! You two, with me! Move!"

The blaze had spread quicker than he had anticipated. The interior of the stable looked to be well alight, though the fire had yet to reach the roof. From inside, the fizzle of burning straw and the splintering of timber could be plainly heard. It wouldn't be long before flames were dancing around the open door. Smoke was starting to pour through the gaps in the shingles, further darkening the already overcast night sky.

Hawkwood pushed Van Bosen towards the fire. "Don't just stand there, man! Get buckets! We can save it! You, too, Rivers! I'll go for help!"

Leaving them, Hawkwood ran back to where Corporal Jeffard was struggling to hang on to the two mounts. Both were now straining at the reins, having picked up the smell of the fire, and the scent of fear from their fleeing stable mates.

"Give them to me!" Hawkwood stuck out his hand. "Fetch water! I'll alert the camp! If it spreads to the other blocks, we're done for! Go!"

Jeffard, mouth agape, passed the reins over.

"Go!" Hawkwood urged. "Go!"

Jeffard turned tail and ran. Pausing only to snatch up his knapsack, Hawkwood climbed on to the first horse. Coiling the reins of the second in his fist, he dug in his heels and spurred the frightened animals out of the yard. As he did so, he saw from the corner of his eye two figures running frantically with buckets towards the smouldering building.

When he was clear, Hawkwood looked back. There were no flames to be seen as yet, but it could only be a matter of time before they became visible. It was doubtful the corporal and his friends would be able to cope on their own. Soon, they'd have to decide whether to carry on trying to save the stable block, or let it burn while they led the remaining horses to safety. From what Quade had told him about the chronic shortage of horse-flesh available to the American army, they'd be anxious to preserve at all costs the few they did have.

Either way, they had enough to keep them busy for the moment.

Leaving the scene of impending chaos behind him, he urged the horses up the trail and into the trees. It was darker in among the pines and the last thing he wanted was for the animals to stumble, but he was committed now so he prayed that animals accustomed to carrying dispatches at the gallop would be agile enough not to lose their footing on the uneven slope.

Keeping to the higher ground, he could just make out the rectangular shape of the soldiers' barracks below him and the latrine blocks attached to each one. Lights showed dimly behind shuttered windows. From what he could see, most of the garrison was slumbering, oblivious to the drama unfolding at the other end of the camp.

A break appeared in the path. Hawkwood paused and took his bearings before dismounting. The last of the barrack blocks was now in sight. At any moment Corporal Jeffard and the two privates would tire of wondering why no help had arrived and decide to sound the alarm for themselves. When that happened, all hell would surely break loose. Tethering the horses to a tree, he made his way down the slope using the woods as cover.

The camp guardhouse lay at the north-eastern corner of the cantonment at the end of a short path linking it to the parade ground. Two-storeys high and built of brick and stone, its entrance was protected by a wooden porch.

And an armed sentry.

Hawkwood waited until the sentry's back was turned before emerging from the trees at a leisurely pace. He was twenty yards away from the building when the challenge came.

"Halt!" The sentry stepped forward, musket held defensively across his chest. "Who goes there?"

Hawkwood kept walking. "Captain Hooper, with orders from the colonel. Stand down, Private. You've done your job." Hawkwood hardened his gaze, letting it linger on the sentry's face. "Who's the duty sergeant?"

Recognizing the uniform and disconcerted by the clipped authority in Hawkwood's voice, the sentry hesitated then stood to attention. "That'll be Sergeant Dunbar, sir."

"And is he awake?" Hawkwood forged a knowing smile to give the impression that he and Dunbar were old comrades.

"Yes, sir." The sentry relaxed, allowing himself a small curve of the lip.

"Glad to hear it." Hawkwood raised a dismissive hand. "Don't worry. I'll find him. Carry on."

"Sir." Flattered at having been invited to share a joke with an officer, the sentry shouldered arms and resumed his stance.

Hawkwood let out his breath.

*Not far now.*

It didn't matter which army you fought for, guardhouses were always cold, cheerless places, built for purpose and furnished with only the most basic of amenities. So Hawkwood knew what he was going to see even before he passed through the door. There'd be a duty desk, above which would be affixed a list of regulations and the orders of the day; an arms rack; a table and a couple of benches; probably a trestle bed or two; a stove and, maybe, if the occupants were sensible and self-sufficient enough, a simmering pot of over-brewed coffee and a supply of tin mugs.

He wasn't disappointed. The only items he hadn't allowed for were the four leather buckets lined up along the wall just inside the door; fire-fighting for the use of, as the inventory might well have described them.

*Four buckets aren't going to be nearly enough,* was Hawkwood's passing thought as he turned his attention to the man behind the desk, who was already rising to his feet at the unexpected and probably unwelcome arrival of an officer.

"Sergeant Dunbar," Hawkwood said, making it a statement, not a question. "Just the man."

*Always pander to the sergeants. They're the ones who run the army. It's never the bloody officers.*

The sergeant frowned. "Captain?" he said guardedly.

Hawkwood didn't bother to reply, but allowed his gaze to pass arrogantly over the other two men in the room, both of whom were in uniform, muskets slung over their shoulders. Relief sentries, presumably, either just returning from their circuit or about to begin their rounds. They straightened in anticipation of being addressed, but Hawkwood merely viewed them coldly in the time-honoured manner of an officer acknowledging the lower ranks; which is to say that, aside from noting their existence, he paid them no attention whatsoever. Neither man appeared insulted by the slight. If anything, they seemed relieved. Let the sergeant deal with the bastard, in other words.

"Everything in order here?" Hawkwood enquired.

The sergeant continued to look wary. "Yes, sir. All quiet."

"Good. I'm here on the colonel's orders: I need information on the prisoners that were transported from Deerfield earlier today."

Caution flickered in the sergeant's eyes. "Yes, sir." Turning to his desk and the ledger that lay open upon it, he rotated the book so that Hawkwood could view the cramped script. "Names entered as soon as they arrived, Captain. Eleven, all told; one officer; ten other ranks."

"Very good."

Hawkwood ran his eyes down the list. His heart skipped a beat when he saw the name he was looking for. Keeping his expression neutral, he scanned past the name to the prisoner's rank and regiment and place of capture: major, 40th Regiment, Oswegatchie.

"Is there a problem, sir?" The sergeant frowned.

Hawkwood recognized the defensive note in Dunbar's query. Like guardhouses, duty sergeants were the same the world over:

convinced that nothing ran smoothly without their say so and that even the smallest hint of criticism was a direct insult to their rank and responsibility. The other truth about sergeants was that every single one of them worth his salt had the knack of injecting precisely the right amount of scepticism into his voice to imply that any officer unwise enough to suggest there might be the cause for concern was talking out of his arse.

"Not at all, Sergeant. Everything's as I'd expected. Nice to see *someone's* keeping a tight rein on things around here."

Hawkwood allowed the sergeant a moment to preen, then assumed a pensive look. He let his attention drift towards the two privates.

The sergeant waited expectantly.

Hawkwood returned his gaze to the ledger and pursed his lips. "We've received intelligence suggesting there may be an attempt to free the prisoners."

The sergeant's eyebrows took instant flight. "From what quarter, sir?"

Hawkwood didn't look up but continued to stare ruminatively at the ledger while running his finger along the list of names.

"That's the problem: we're not sure. *My* guess is it's some damned Federalist faction that's refused to lie down. Or the Vermonters. This close to the border, it's certain they've been keeping their eyes open and passing on information to their friends in Quebec."

Hawkwood was relying on information he'd siphoned from Major Quade; support for the war was far from universal among those who depended for their livelihood on maritime trade and cross-border commerce with the Canadian provinces.

The sergeant stared at Hawkwood, not quite aghast at the thought but close to it. "You think there'll be an attack on the camp, sir?"

Dunbar had not spoken loudly. Nevertheless the disbelief in his voice must have carried for Hawkwood sensed the two sentries pricking up their ears.

"Not if *I* can help it, Sergeant. Frankly, I doubt the bastards could raise enough of a mob for that to happen. No, if there *is* to be an attempt, they will employ subterfuge – that's what we must guard against."

"Subterfuge, sir?"

"Deception, Sergeant Dunbar. Deception."

"Well, they'll have to be damned quick, sir. We're only holding them for one night. They're off to Pittsfield in the morning."

"True, Sergeant, but that doesn't mean we shouldn't be vigilant. That's the thing about deception: you never know where and when it's going to be used. That's why I'm here."

The sergeant's eye moved towards the heavy wooden door at the back of the room. Then he turned to Hawkwood and frowned. "Sir?"

*That way to the cells, then*, Hawkwood thought.

"I'm to inspect the facilities, to reassure the colonel that we've done everything possible. No criticism implied, Sergeant, but you know how it is: the colonel climbs on my back and I climb on yours. It's the army way."

Hawkwood had no idea who the colonel-in-charge was, but there was bound to be one somewhere and Sergeant Dunbar, he hoped, would come to his own conclusion on which one it might be.

The sergeant gave Hawkwood a look which spoke volumes. "Indeed, sir."

"Let's get it over with then, shall we? Might as well start with the officer. Lead the way."

"Sir."

The sergeant reached for a set of keys hanging from a hook on the wall behind him, then turned to the two privates. "All right, McLeary, make yourself useful. Fall in with the Captain and me while we check the prisoner. Jennings, you stay here and try to look alert. This way, sir."

Sergeant Dunbar had no sooner stepped forward to lead Hawkwood across the room when a distant bell began to clang.

The sergeant paused in mid stride. His head came up. He looked at Hawkwood. "That's an alarm, sir."

Hawkwood turned. "You're right. Find out what's happening, Jennings."

"Sir?"

"At the double, man!"

The private broke into a run. Hawkwood turned back. "It's probably nothing. Carry on."

The sergeant hesitated, then thought better of questioning an officer and unlocked the door.

There weren't as many cells as Hawkwood had been expecting. Just six of them, arranged along a stone-walled corridor lit by a solitary lantern.

Dunbar lifted the lantern off its hook. "He's in the one at the end. Got the place to himself at the moment, as you can see."

Though conscious of Private McLeary hovering at his shoulder, Hawkwood betrayed no concern. "Has he given you any trouble?"

The sergeant shook his head. "Been as good as gold. Can't tell you about the rest. You'll have to check with the provost." Adding as an afterthought: ". . . sir."

It was cold in the corridor, with no stove provided for the prisoner's comfort. As the three men made their way past the empty cells their footsteps echoed off the walls. Halting beside the last door, Dunbar held up the lantern. "Here we are."

Hawkwood peered through the bars. The cell's stark, almost bare interior, just discernible in the gloom, made the main guard-room look positively opulent. A pallet bed and a slop bucket were the only furnishings. An empty set of shackles hung from one wall.

"As you can see, sir, all secure. Only a fool'd try to break in. Plus they'd have me to deal with," the sergeant added darkly.

"Good God, keep the damned noise down, can't you? It's been a bugger of a day and a fellow needs his sleep!"

The request came out of the dark recesses of the cell. Hawkwood could just make out an indistinct shape stretched out upon the bed. As he watched, the shape stirred and materialized into the figure of a man who, after casting aside the single blanket, sat up and swung his feet to the floor.

"My apologies, Major," Hawkwood said drily. "Didn't mean to disturb you."

"A bit late for that. The damage is done. Is this a social visit, by the way? If so, it's a damned strange hour to come calling."

The figure stood and approached the bars. As he did so, his features became visible.

The face wasn't as florid as Hawkwood remembered, though that could have been due to the candlelight. He'd lost some weight, too; a change that hadn't been immediately apparent during the few seconds that their eyes had locked at the ferry terminus. The red hair was now toned down by a sprinkling of grey; the subtle changes, lending him a more distinguished and grittier cast than there had been before. But while circumstance could alter an individual's looks there was no doubt in Hawkwood's mind as to the identity of the man that stood before him.

Major Douglas Lawrence, 1st Battalion of His Majesty's 40th Regiment of Foot. The same officer who, on a misty morning in Hyde Park, close to the Serpentine, had stood by Hawkwood's side and acted as his second in a duel against an arrogant son of the nobility, one John Rutherford Esquire.

"My apologies again, Major," Hawkwood said. "I dare say the accommodation isn't up to the standard you're used to, either. I'm afraid Greenbush can't compete with Knightsbridge."

Which was close to where the pair of them had last parted company. Hawkwood prayed that neither Sergeant Dunbar nor Private McLeary would attach any significance to the exchange – and that the prisoner would.

It was time to find out. Stepping forward, he removed his hat, allowing his face to catch the light.

Shock showed instantly in the prisoner's eyes but only for a second. It was enough. Hawkwood flicked a glance towards McLeary and the musket he was holding.

He was to wonder later if it was the light of recognition that had shown so briefly on Lawrence's face that caused Sergeant Dunbar's sixth sense to suddenly snap to attention.

"Seen enough, Cap—" was as far as the sergeant got before the words died in his throat and he took a quick step backwards, realizing, that the deception referred to by this anonymous officer was no longer a possibility but a terrible reality.

As yet another alarm began to clang; this time a lot louder and much closer to home than the first.

Hawkwood identified the sound immediately. Someone was running the metal striker around the inside of the alarm triangle hanging from the underside of the guardhouse porch.

Spinning his hat towards the sergeant's face, Hawkwood went for the man with the gun first, sweeping the musket barrel aside before driving the heel of his other hand up under the base of the sentry's nose. This time, there was no attempt to pull the punch and he felt the cartilage rupture.

As the trooper went down Hawkwood pulled the musket free, pivoting quickly as the lantern dropped to the floor with a clatter, followed by a muffled grunt.

The sound was all Sergeant Dunbar could manage, given that Lawrence's arm was wrapped tightly around the sergeant's throat. Having dropped the lantern, the sergeant was trying to break free. His feet were scrabbling for purchase as he clawed at the arm, but without success. Ignoring the beseeching look on the man's face, Hawkwood reversed the musket and drove the butt hard into the sergeant's belly.

As the sergeant collapsed to the floor, Hawkwood reached for his key ring.

He was stooping over the prone body when Private Jennings ran in from the guardroom.

"Fire, Sergeant! The stables—"

The sentry skidded to a halt. His jaw went slack as he took in the scene. Had his musket been slung over his shoulder and not held in the port arms position, Hawkwood might have given the man the benefit of the doubt, but there was no time. As Jennings brought his weapon up, Hawkwood reversed the musket he was holding and fired.

The ball slammed into Jennings' shoulder, punching him against the wall. As the musket fell from his grip, Hawkwood scooped up the keys, threw the discharged musket aside and sprang to the cell door.

There was a sudden silence from outside. The sentry who had been sounding the alarm was no doubt on his way to investigate the sound of the shot.

It took two attempts to find the right key before the bars swung open.

"Quick march, Major!" Hawkwood urged.

Lawrence needed no further encouragement. The two men sprinted for the door, reaching the guardroom at the same time as the incoming sentry. Astonishment flooded the trooper's face as it had his colleague's. Recovering more swiftly than his fellow troopers, however, he swung his musket round.

Far too soon.

There was a sharp crack and a flash as Lawrence swept up and fired Trooper Jennings' still primed weapon. The sentry screamed as his jaw blew apart and he went down. With the wounded man's shrieks rising in volume, Hawkwood led the way outside.

The cantonment was now wide awake. Hawkwood looked past the row of soldiers' barracks towards the southern perimeter. Beyond the trees, flames from the burning stables were now licking into the night sky. Men were rushing towards the blaze, many in a state of semi-undress, too distracted to have heard the shots from inside the guardhouse. Hawkwood thought he could hear the sound of hooves over the increasing shouts of panic.

"I take it that's your doing?" Lawrence said, in awe.

"What were you expecting? A guard of honour?" Hawkwood headed towards the trees. "This way, I've horses waiting."

Lawrence grabbed his arm. "What about the others?"

Hawkwood knew Lawrence was referring to the captured redcoats. "Sorry, Major. I can't help them. Not this time."

*Not ever*, he thought.

Indecision showed on Lawrence's face. He stared about him wildly as if some clue to their whereabouts might manifest itself.

"I don't know where they're being held," Hawkwood said. "It's a big camp, the alarm's sounded and we don't have time to search the place. I'm sorry."

Lawrence looked him in the eye, then nodded. "You're right. Forgive me."

"Up there! Come on!" Hawkwood, pointed towards the pine trees.

As the guardhouse alarm started up again, followed by a ferocious yell:

"Prisoners escaping! STOP THEM!"

Sergeant Dunbar – doubled over and apparently still suffering the effects of the blow to his stomach – had made it out on to the porch and was running the striker around the inside of the metal triangle. Pointing and gesticulating frantically, he yelled again. "STOP THOSE MEN!"

Hawkwood glanced to one side and saw that the sergeant was gesturing in his direction. Two men had responded to his call for help; one of them carrying a pistol, the other carrying what looked like . . .

Hawkwood stared.

A pike?

"Should've locked the bugger in the cells!" Lawrence swore. "Where are those damned horses? No wait, I see them!"

"Stop them, God damn it!" Sergeant Dunbar had abandoned the alarm and was stumbling after them.

"He's a game sod, though," Lawrence muttered. "I'll give him that!"

"You men! Halt!" The order came from the pikeman who, along with his companion, was running hard now.

The man with the pistol paused and took aim. A crack sounded, accompanied by a bright powder flash. Hawkwood ducked and felt the wind from the ball as it tugged at his collar. There were only the two pursuers, as far as he could see. Three, including the sergeant. Everyone else was mesmerized by the fire.

Lawrence had reached the horses. Untying them, he hooked the musket strap over his shoulder, grabbed the reins of the nearest one and vaulted into the saddle. "Hurry!" he called.

The pikeman had made up ground and drawn ahead of the second trooper. As his attacker ran in, it struck Hawkwood that

105

the pike looked ridiculously long and unwieldy and not the ideal weapon to grab in the heat of the moment. Presumably this was one of Colonel Pike's men, and he'd been trained to reach for his pike the same way a rifleman was drilled: when reveille or the alarm sounded, it wasn't your breeches or your boots or even your cock you reached for. It was your "BLOODY RIFLE, you idle bugger!"

That would certainly explain why this particular trooper had on his breeches and his boots and an under-vest, but no shirt or tunic. Not that his attire was of any interest to Hawkwood, who had his hands full trying to avoid being spitted like a hog on boar hunt.

In a three-rank advance and as a defence against cavalry, the pike was moderately effective. But when it came to close combat, if you didn't incapacitate your target with your first thrust, you might as well be armed with a warming pan. As his enemy rushed at him, pike held in both hands, Hawkwood did the one thing his opponent didn't expect. He attacked.

The trooper was already committed and it was the pike's length that was his undoing; that and the fact that Hawkwood had reached the trees. The closeness of the trunks left no space to manoeuvre such a cumbersome weapon. As the pike-head jabbed towards him, Hawkwood darted inside his attacker's reach, clasped the weapon with two hands – one either side of the trooper's leading grip – and rotated the shaft downwards, away from his opponent's hips. Caught off balance, the pike-man's only recourse was for his left hand to let go, allowing Hawkwood to gain control of the weapon, twist the shaft out of the pikeman's right hand and drive it back up into the trooper's throat.

As the pikeman went down, Hawkwood heard Lawrence yell. He turned to see the second man had caught up and was charging in, his pistol raised as a club.

He was less than ten paces away when Hawkwood hurled the pike.

It had been an instinctive act, but the consequences proved catastrophic for his attacker. The length of the pike meant it did not have far to travel. The running man stopped dead, his face frozen into a mask of disbelief as the steel tip sank into his chest. Dropping the pistol, he fell to the ground, hands clasped around the wooden shaft protruding from his body.

There was a scream of rage as Sergeant Dunbar saw his men dealt with so comprehensively. And then Lawrence was there with the horses.

"Move your arse, Captain!"

Grabbing the dead man's pistol and thrusting it into his coat pocket, Hawkwood threw himself into the saddle.

Behind them, Dunbar, fighting for breath after his exertions, had fallen to his knees.

Lawrence turned as Hawkwood found the stirrups and brought his mount under control. "Which way?"

Hawkwood quickly surveyed the bodies of the two troopers and the dark figures running about the parade ground like demented termites. The cantonment appeared to be in total disarray.

"North. We head north."

Lawrence grinned. "Excellent! After you!"

"Yes, sir, Major!"

As they dug their heels into the horses' sides, Hawkwood couldn't help but grin in return. Relief at having accomplished what he had set out to do was surging through him. And the only cost had been a hat. A more than fair exchange for the freedom of one British officer, in anyone's book.

Especially as he'd hated wearing the bloody thing anyway.

# 4

*May 1780*

From his vantage point at the head of the column, Sir John Johnson turned to view the ranks of uniformed men marching in file behind him. They were a formidable fighting force, as good as any he'd served alongside; tough, fearless and loyal, he was proud of each and every one of them. When the right men fought for a cause, he thought as he gazed at their gritty, determined faces, they were well nigh unstoppable.

It was approaching midday and though the forest canopy provided a welcome shade, it was still oppressively warm. Ignoring the sweat trickling down the inside of his tunic, he addressed the man riding by his side. "How are they faring, Thomas?"

Captain Thomas Scott turned and looked over his shoulder, beyond the first phalanx of troops, to where a string of tired-looking civilians could be seen emerging slowly from around a bend in the trail.

"A few more blisters, a sprained ankle or two; nothing too calamitous."

"The surgeon's taken a look?"

Scott turned back. "He has. He tells me we won't have to put any of them out of their misery just yet."

"And the prisoners?"

109

"Cursing your name with every breath, sir."

Johnson smiled. He'd become used to his second-in-command's dry sense of humour. Scott, a former lieutenant in the Company of Select Marksmen, had been assigned to the expedition by Governor Haldimand. Even though their time together had been short, the two officers had formed a strong bond.

"Splendid! I'd feel insulted if they weren't."

Scott returned the smile, shifted in his saddle and winced. The colonel and he were the only officers on horseback; their mounts had been donated by a Loyalist sympathizer whose farm lay adjacent to the invasion route. Neither of the animals had taken kindly to having a new rider and it showed in their skittishness. To add to his discomfort, Scott, unlike his colonel, was not a natural horseman.

"We'll take a rest," Johnson said, reining in. "Thirty minutes. It'll give the stragglers a chance to catch up. Pass the word. Deploy piquets. The men may smoke if they wish."

"Yes, sir." Hoping his relief didn't show, Scott turned his horse about and trotted back down the column to relay the order.

The colonel rested his hands on the pommel. Taking a deep lungful of air, he let it out slowly and gazed about him, first at the forest and then at the trail running through the trees ahead of them. Though it was referred to as a road, the description was a misnomer. In reality it was no more than a rough dirt track; for the most part wide enough to accommodate a heavy wagon or half a dozen men marching abreast, but here and there, in short stretches where the path had become overgrown, there was hardly room for two men to walk side by side.

Every four or five miles the trail would open on to a clearing where two or more paths converged. Usually, the wider trail was the correct one, but in some instances it was only by referring to the compass that the column had been able to maintain its course. That and by following ancient wheel ruts which, although worn shallow with age and crumbling at the edges, were still visible beneath the layer of pine needles and the animal tracks that decorated the forest floor.

Often, the indentations would give a clue as to who and what might have gone before, with some of the deeper impressions hinting at army ordnance, further proof that the roads were of military manufacture or had been utilized by troops over the years. A quarter of a century before, Johnson's own father would have made use of such pathways to move soldiers and equipment against the armies of the French general, Montcalm.

The plaintive call of a whip-poor-will rang out from the woods to Johnson's right. His gaze switched as he attempted to trace the bird's location, but with the shadows among the trees constantly shifting, it was an impossible task.

As he looked away he caught sight of a broken trunk at the edge of the track. Carved into the bark was a single letter: "H". It signified "Highway", a sign that the road had been widened by army engineers. They had passed several similar markers during the time they had been travelling and at each one Johnson had sensed the ghost of his father peering over his shoulder.

The column had come to a halt. Soldiers and civilians alike had taken up temporary residence along the wayside. Canteens had been broached and pipes lit and plumes of tobacco smoke began to drift into the air.

Consigning thoughts of his father to the back of his mind, Johnson walked his horse slowly down the line. From what he could see and from the grins and respectful nods he was getting, all the men appeared to be in good spirits. With just cause, he thought to himself. Having visited the wrath of God upon a succession of rebel homesteads and Continental supply lines, not to mention escaping without suffering a single casualty, a celebratory pipe was the very least they were owed.

The calibre of Johnson's men was not the only factor in the raid's success; good intelligence and forward planning had played their part too. The colonel had chosen harvest time to strike because the bulk of the local militia regiments were made up of farmers who would be released from duty to attend their crops at this time of year. Long before the raiders landed at Crown

Point they had been confident that their presence would go unhindered.

And so it had proved. As a result, a substantial number of Loyalists had been rescued and prisoners taken without opposition, and a not inconsiderable amount of damage had been inflicted upon an unsuspecting enemy. By his officers' reckoning, some one hundred and twenty rebel-owned barns, mills and houses had been destroyed on the north side of the Mohawk River, put to the torch by the colonel's soldiers and their native allies.

Inevitably, blood had been spilled along the way; mostly from livestock, slaughtered during the coordinated attacks, though there had been human fatalities as well. Not that any sleep had been lost over either the cattle or the rebel corpses that had been left on the ground. Every one of them was another nail in Congress's coffin.

As far as could be calculated, the rebels had suffered between fifteen and twenty dead. Not many, considering the acreage and the number of properties that had been laid to waste. Nevertheless, a sufficient quotient to have sent a resounding message to all concerned.

The majority had not died easily, most notably those who'd fallen victim to patrols that had included Mohawks. Despite Johnson's orders, there had been at least half a dozen scalpings, with the mutilated bodies left in full view so as to spread terror among the enemy; the argument being that it was time they had a taste of what it was like to suffer intimidation and the destruction of livelihood.

Disciplinary action had not been taken against those who had carried out the mutilations; nor would it be. Johnson was aware, as were his superiors, that the support of the Six Nations was vital if the Crown forces were to have any chance of defeating the Continental army. To chastise warriors too harshly for engaging in what they considered to be a legitimate form of warfare would be to risk breaking the alliance, and that could not be allowed to happen.

For their part, those tribes of the Six Nations that had allied themselves to the Crown had done so not because they were fiercely loyal to a distant monarch but for more prosaic reasons. Chief among these was Britain's promise to support the Iroquois in their battle to prevent American seizure of their tribal lands.

There were other inducements on offer; plunder being high on the list. By far the most persuasive, however, was the opportunity it gave the tribes to wreak bloody revenge upon the Yan-kees. The previous year, under the personal orders of General George Washington, Continental troops had launched a massive raid against the Iroquois' homeland, in reprisal for joint Indian and Loyalist attacks along the Pennsylvanian and New York frontier. More than forty Iroquois villages had been brutally destroyed. The Iroquois might have had only a nodding acquaintance with the scriptures but they were perfectly familiar with the concept of an eye for an eye and a tooth for a tooth.

Which was why, Johnson knew, that pursuit in one form or another was inevitable. Had the roles been reversed, no power on earth would have prevented him from tracking down the men who had visited such devastation upon *his* valley.

As a further precaution, therefore, he had split his force. Following his earlier orders, an advance party – one company of Royal Yorkers and the warriors from the Lake of the Two Mountains – had been dispatched to Bulwagga Bay at Crown Point to secure the embarkation site. With half the irregulars and the remaining Mohawks assigned as scouts and outriders, that had left the rest of the irregulars and Yorkers, along with the men of the 29th, 34th and 53rd Regiments, to protect the column.

As yet, there had been no noticeable signs of pursuit. The scouts who had reported in had noted some enemy activity to the south, but Johnson's men far outnumbered any mustered force that was likely to be sent after them. For the moment, therefore, the column was safe, but that didn't mean there was room for complacency. Until they boarded the Marine vessels, they would remain at risk.

It was curious, he noted as he made his way down the line, how, after four days on the road, convention within the civilian ranks was being stripped away. With everyone united in flight from a common enemy, the gap between the privileged and the not-so-privileged, that had been so marked before the evacuation had become less defined. The sobering realization that each and every one of them, irrespective of status, was now subject to the same privations – fatigue, hunger, the risk of injury and lack of privacy – had begun to peel back the layers like skin from an onion.

Adversity, the colonel mused, always was the great leveller.

That said, it was clear from the way they were carrying themselves that some civilians were feeling the strain of the trek more than others, which was only to be expected. The colonel knew he'd been pressing them all hard, without fear or favour, and had no qualms about doing so. He'd warned them that was how it was going to be; how it had to be if they were to survive.

The hardier souls were those whose forefathers had cleared the land, built their farms and cultivated the soil. They had found little difficulty in coping with the hazards of the march, secure in the knowledge that every mile traversed brought them ever closer to the rendezvous point and the boats that were waiting to transport them to freedom.

The ones showing less fortitude were those from the more prosperous families; estate owners who'd never needed to swing an axe or push a plough along a muddy furrow. They had workers and slaves to perform those tasks for them. A handful had been heard grumbling at the pace at which they were being shepherded, or, as some put it, herded along.

Not that comfort had ever been a consideration. The day was taken up with marching. With the exception of intermittent rest stops, only at dusk would a complete halt be called, at which point lean-to shelters would be constructed for the women and children and boughs cut for bedding. After snatching a meal and a few hours' sleep the fugitives would rise an hour before first light to dismantle the camp and pick up where they had left off.

The colonel had anticipated a degree of protest, knowing it

would be an inevitable consequence of the requirement to put as much distance as possible between the column and its pursuers. And if that meant that some of them had to suffer sore feet and bloody blisters, then so be it. The alternative would be far worse.

Of all of them, it was the children, curiously, who'd proved to be the most adaptable. There were no babes in arms, a fact for which Johnson was exceedingly grateful, and to the dozen or so youngsters who were on the trail – the youngest being eight, the oldest fourteen – it had become a thrilling escapade; keeping pace with the soldiers, listening wide-eyed to their tall stories and their coarse banter, and camping out with them in the woods beneath the stars.

Just as uncomplaining were the Negro servants. Indentured into a life of domestic servitude and therefore no strangers to hardship, they had proved themselves resilient travellers, stoically accepting the rigours of the journey as a price worth paying for their escorted passage north.

The column, now comprising some three hundred troops, nearly two hundred assorted civilians and more than sixty pack animals, stretched for several hundred yards. As he rode the line, the colonel offered another silent prayer to the men who'd carved out the road. Had it not been there, it would have been impossible for the fugitives to have cut their own path through the woods and maintain the pace, though in this part of the state any witnesses to their presence were more likely to be of the four- rather than the two-legged variety. The mountainous hinterland that stretched between the Hudson and the Great Lakes could not be termed virgin territory, as indicated by the trail they were currently following, but, save for the military and fur trappers, few white men had ventured beyond the forest's eastern rim.

On ancient maps, it was the custom to indicate unexplored regions with representations of winged beasts and the inscription *Here be dragons*. There were no such drawings on the maps of the north-eastern states currently in circulation. The cartographers had made do with a one-word inscription: *Couxsachrage*.

An ancient Indian word; to some, it translated as the Habitation of Winter. To others, the Dismal Wilderness. But these definitions were the white man's interpretation. To the tribes of the Six Nations there was but one name, one meaning:

The Hunting Grounds.

By the time the end of the column came into the colonel's sight, the rest period had drawn to a close. Canteens and pipes had been stowed and packs shouldered. From his stops along the line and the briefings he'd received from his officers, all appeared to be well. There had been some griping from the civilians about the heat and the brevity of the halt and the pace at which they were being forced to walk, but the complainers had been mollified by the news that, all being well, at the speed they were travelling they would reach their destination the following day. With spirits lifted, the overall mood had become one of increased optimism. Or so the colonel thought until he came upon his second-in-command, who was looking anything but cheerful.

Scott was talking with a heavy-set civilian whose face was hidden by a wide-brimmed hat. A grubby, once-white shirt and a pair of mud-stained breeches showed all the evidence of the march. He was one of a small group of similarly attired and weary-looking men and women that had attached itself to the rear of the column, tucked in among the last few horses of the baggage train.

At the colonel's approach, Scott turned, his normally laconic features uncharacteristically tense.

Johnson felt the first flicker of unease. "Captain?"

Taking hold of Johnson's halter Scott steered the horse to one side. "We have a problem, Colonel. It appears we're missing a civilian."

"Who?"

"One of the children."

Johnson steeled himself. A missing adult would have been bad enough. A child was far worse. "Do we have a name?"

"A lad named Hooper, Matthew Hooper." Scott hesitated. "I understand you know him, sir."

"Is he missing or merely mislaid?" Johnson tried to keep his voice calm.

"Sir?" Scott frowned.

"You're certain he's not with us. You've checked the rest of the line?"

"Not yet, not personally. The reverend has."

"Reverend?"

"Reverend De Witt, sir." Scott nodded back towards the civilian with whom he'd been talking. "The boy was travelling with the pastor and his family. It was Lieutenant Wyatt who arranged it. The boy's an orphan. He—"

Johnson held up a hand to belay Scott's explanation. "I'm familiar with the boy's background. It was I who directed Lieutenant Wyatt to find him a suitable guardian." He looked towards the pastor, who'd been joined by an equally stout, apprehensive-looking woman whom he assumed was the pastor's wife.

"Colonel . . ." De Witt stepped forward. He did not extend his hand but indicated the woman. "My wife, Esther."

"Madam." Johnson regarded them both for several seconds before asking, "You're positive the boy's not with the column?"

"We've checked all ways, Colonel. Up *and* down. He's not here."

"When did you see him last?"

The pastor hesitated, took off his hat and wiped the brim. He looked uncomfortably at his wife, who stared back at him help-lessly. "Truth is, Colonel, I can't rightly say. Not to the minute. It would have been a while ago. An hour maybe, possibly two."

*Dear God*, Johnson thought. He stared at the man. "There's a big difference, Reverend. It'd help if you could be more precise. Was it one hour or was it two?"

It was the woman who answered, with a wavering note in her voice. "It's been nearer two, I think."

De Witt shifted awkwardly. "Thing is, Colonel, it'll sound like I'm making excuses, but the boy has a tendency to keep to himself. A lot of the time, he'll ride on ahead; other times he lags a ways behind. We kept our eye on him at the beginning,

117

but then we got used to him drifting off. It was plain he preferred his own company. He'd ease back to us eventually, during rest periods, but mostly during our night stops when we'd be taking supper. Esther and I got to thinking that maybe he was afraid of the dark and was having bad dreams over what had happened and didn't like being alone then . . ." The pastor paused and looked up. "You know about . . .?"

Johnson nodded. "Lieutenant Wyatt informed me."

"A terrible thing for a child to witness," Mrs De Witt said, her voice sounding as if it was about to break. "Just terrible."

"And he's not spoken about it," De Witt said. "Not once."

His wife shook her head. Her eyes were clouded with sorrow. "It's not right, Colonel, him keeping that sort of thing bottled up inside, especially at his age." She looked up. "We thought it would come out, given time. But—"

"So you've no idea when he left the line?" Johnson cut in. "Is that what you're telling me?"

De Witt shook his head. "No, Colonel. I mean, no, we don't know."

"Maybe he broke off to take a squat," Scott suggested, "and got left behind."

It was a possibility, Johnson thought, though on the face of it an unlikely one.

For the civilians, answering calls of nature was just one of the many challenges of the march. Those who felt impelled to relieve themselves had to make do with finding a convenient tree or a clump of underbrush to go behind. The soldiers and the Indians were long used to a lack of amenities but to those less worldly, attending to such a basic need in public was a salutary experience, even though everyone was subject to the same indignity. When the column was on the march it didn't grind to a halt because one person was caught short between rest stops. If you had to go, you moved off the path, found a spot to carry out your business and then you rejoined the line, without taking too long about it. It had become a common sight to see people slip away. It wasn't as if they required an armed escort to accompany them.

But if that's what had happened, Johnson thought to himself, the boy wouldn't have moved *that* far off the trail. It wouldn't have taken him a couple of hours to catch up, surely?

"What do you want to do, sir?" Scott asked, breaking into Johnson's thoughts. "Reverend De Witt tells me the lad has his own horse, which makes it even more curious that he hasn't caught us up, the rate we're moving. Unless he got thrown," he added pensively.

"Oh dear Lord!" Esther De Witt gasped. "The poor child could be lying hurt somewhere!" Mortified, she stared at her husband. "It's our fault, Thaddeus. We should have been more mindful." No longer able to suppress her emotions, her face finally crumpled and she began to sniffle.

*Damned right, you should,* Johnson thought, though his anger was assuaged by the sight of the woman's obvious and genuine distress. And could he place all the blame for the boy's absence at the De Witts' door? From Lieutenant Wyatt's account of the catastrophic events at the Archer farm it was clear that the boy had suffered massive turmoil. Who knew what went through a twelve-year-old's mind at a time like this? Could it be that the lad was trying to return home?

Johnson looked along the line. The troops were forming up, awaiting the order to move out. Even the civilians were looking restless, wondering why the march hadn't resumed.

He turned to Scott. "Pick a search party. Four men, including a tracker. Give them horses; cut out some of the baggage animals or commandeer civilian mounts."

"Yes, sir," Scott said.

"Trouble is it's not just *when*; we don't know *where* he left the damned column, either," Johnson said pensively. "When you checked the line, Reverend, you *did* enquire if anyone had seen him leave – correct?"

"No one noticed, Colonel." De Witt stared bleakly back along the trail, as if by sheer force of will he could make the boy reappear.

"How long should they search for?" Scott asked quietly, with a sideways glance at the pastor's wife who, having controlled her sobs, was now dabbing at her eyes with a handkerchief.

Johnson looked through the trees to the expanse of unbroken blue high above them. There were, he thought maybe six or seven hours before sunset.

"Until it's too dark to see."

"And then? You want them to stay out?"

The inference in Scott's voice echoed the question he'd been about to ask himself.

"Advise them they'll require one night's provisions. I expect to rendezvous with the Marine at noon tomorrow. Tell whomever you assign that's when I want them back with us. They're to give themselves time to repair to Bulwagga for embarkation. We cannot – we *will not* – wait for them. Make that clear."

"Yes, sir." Scott's grim expression said it all. If the search party failed to find the boy in time, they were consigning him to the perils of the forest, which meant his chances of survival were not merely remote, they were non-existent.

For a brief moment Johnson found himself debating the wisdom of sending four trained soldiers to look for one missing child in ten thousand square miles of wilderness, even though he knew that to consider any other course of action was unthinkable. Had it been any one of the other civilians, he'd have given the same order. Be they Loyalist, slave, servant or prisoner, his commitment was to transport every single one of the civilians to safety. No one would be left behind, not if he could help it. Especially not Ellis Hooper's boy. Hooper had been a good man, a loyal soldier who'd given his life for the Crown. Sending out men to look for Hooper's missing son was more than a matter of guardianship or trying to make up for the De Witts' negligence – if that's what it had been. It was about duty. He owed Hooper and his boy that much.

"We've probably traversed at least three crossing places since the lad was last seen," Johnson said. "So make sure the search party marks its trail. We don't want *them* wandering round in bloody circles, too."

"You think that's what happened?" Scott enquired doubtfully. "He found his way back to the road and then took the wrong path?"

120

"If he's not lying injured somewhere, it's a possibility. In these backwoods all it takes is one wrong step and then every damned tree starts to look like every other damned tree. Easy enough for a grown man to lose his way, never mind a twelve-year-old boy with no woodcraft. Put yourself in his shoes."

Scott didn't have to. He was already there.

*A twelve-year-old boy with no family to come back to and no one to miss him*, Johnson thought grimly.

"I'll go and select the men," Scott said.

Johnson did not speak.

"He's not *all* alone," a voice said, as Scott hurried off. "Tam's with him."

Johnson turned.

The speaker was a small girl seated atop a grey mare. Until that moment, Johnson had been too preoccupied to notice her as anything other than background scenery.

"Libby?" the preacher enquired cautiously. He turned to Johnson. "My daughter, Colonel."

"Tam?" Johnson said.

"The boy's dog," De Witt explained.

Johnson cast his mind back to when Lieutenant Wyatt had returned to the Hall. The boy had been over by the tethering line. There had been a dog there with him then, some breed of hound; big, with shaggy fur, a typical farm dog, no doubt used to herd sheep or cattle – children, too, probably.

"Anyone seen the dog?" Johnson asked.

De Witt and his wife shook their heads. "Can't say as we have," the pastor said.

There was a collective shaking of heads from the other civilians in earshot.

Johnson dismounted. Careful not to intimidate the girl, he smiled as he walked towards her. "Hello, Libby. I'm Colonel Johnson. So, you're a friend of Matthew's, then, are you?"

The girl rewarded the question with a shy nod.

Johnson made a slight bow. "Well, I am most honoured to make your acquaintance. Y'know, I've a daughter, too. She's called Mary. She has blonde hair and she's very pretty, just like you. She has a baby brother. He's called William, after his grandfather."

Johnson felt the lump rise in his throat, as it did whenever he thought of his children, for there had been a second boy, christened John, born five months after Johnson's escape from the valley. As a babe in arms when Johnson's wife, aided by friends, made her own escape from the family home, the infant, along with his older brother and sister, had survived the flight from Albany to New York and thence to Montreal, only to succumb to a fever a few months before his second birthday. There wasn't a day that passed when Johnson didn't bring his dead son's face to mind or think of the first time he'd held him in his arms.

"Tell me, Libby," he said, blinking away the memory and speaking softly, "did you see where Matthew went?"

He doubted the child had any concept of time. It made more sense, therefore, to ask her *if* she had seen the boy leave rather than to enquire *when* he had left the column. That's if she'd seen anything in the first place, of course.

The girl regarded him solemnly for several seconds; then her gaze dropped.

"If you know something, Libby," Esther De Witt urged, her eyes red-rimmed, "you tell the colonel. There's a good girl."

The girl hesitated, then, in a smaller voice, she said tentatively, "Tam ran away. Matthew went to look for him."

"You *saw* him go?" Johnson said, maintaining his smile and keeping his tone level.

Dipping her head, the girl regarded Johnson from beneath her eyelashes. "He told me not to tell."

There was a sharp intake of breath from Mrs De Witt.

"Well, you've done exactly the right thing, telling *us*, Libby," Johnson said before either of the girl's parents could respond. Though how far it added to their store of knowledge, he had no idea. Against hope, he asked, "Do you remember *when* he left? Was it a long time ago or was it not so very long? Can you recall?"

"She's not going to know that, Colonel," the pastor cut in, with a note of censure. "She's only nine."

The little girl frowned as if trying to concentrate. "It was near that big old tree we passed," she said eventually, her head lifting. She looked towards her father.

*A tree?* Johnson thought desperately. *In a forest of trees? Well, that's damned helpful. That certainly narrows it down.*

"Which tree was that, Libby?" the pastor enquired gently.

The girl's face brightened. "You remember! You said it was just like the one behind our house. The one without the branches."

Johnson turned, fixing the pastor with a penetrating look. "Branches? Do *you* know what she's talking about, Reverend?"

De Witt was staring at his daughter. "You're sure, Libby? That's where you saw Matthew go to look for Tam?"

The little girl dipped her head vigorously.

"What tree, Reverend?" Johnson sensed the girl start and realized he'd posed the question more sharply than he'd intended. He turned quickly. "That's splendid, Libby. You've been most helpful." Patting her on the knee, he said, "Y'know, when we get to Montreal, I shall take you to meet my Mary. I've a feeling that you and she could become great friends. What do you say to that?"

After giving the suggestion deep consideration, the little girl gave another solemn nod.

"Excellent!" Johnson said. "It's settled then."

As the pastor's wife stepped in to speak to the girl, Johnson pulled De Witt to one side. "*What* tree, Reverend?"

De Witt frowned. "There was a giant oak behind our cabin. It was struck during a lightning storm and I had to saw the branches back. I—"

"Not that bloody tree, man! The one on the damned trail!"

The pastor reddened. Recovering, he said, "It was similar, an old oak tree. It looked as though the branches had been cut away a long time ago, to clear the road."

"How far back?"

The pastor thought about it. "Four, maybe five miles. I seem to recall there was some sort of mark carved into the bark."

"Mark?" Johnson said, pulse quickening. "What kind of mark?"

"It might have been an H, though I could be mistaken."

*God love the Engineers!*

At the sound of hooves approaching, Johnson looked up. It was Scott, accompanied by four men on horseback; irregulars by their dress. One of them, a hard and capable-looking individual, wore a corporal's chevrons.

"Name?" Johnson enquired.

"Stryker, Colonel," the corporal said, saluting.

"Captain Scott's explained the situation? You know what's required?"

"Yes, sir."

"Very good. It appears we have some new information to aid you. Who's the tracker here?"

"We can all follow a trail after a fashion, Colonel, but it's Private Fitch who has the gift." The corporal indicated a lean, sharp-nosed soldier mounted on his right-hand side.

Fitch touched his cap respectfully. "Colonel."

"There's a large oak by the side of the trail; four, maybe five miles back," Johnson said. He turned to the pastor. "East side or west?"

"West," De Witt said, after another moment's consideration.

"It's old," Johnson said, "and it carries the highway mark. You might be able to pick up the boy's spoor from there. You know he's mounted?"

"Yes, sir," Fitch said.

"There'll be paw prints, too, hopefully. His dog. That's why he left the trail – the hound ran off. Needless to say, the boy is your priority, nothing else."

"Colonel Johnson," De Witt said from behind.

Johnson turned and discovered that while he'd been relaying instructions to the soldiers De Witt had taken his daughter's place in the mare's saddle.

"Reverend?" Johnson said, frowning.

"With your permission, Colonel. I'd like to go with them."

Johnson stared at him. "What? No. Out of the question."

The pastor's expression changed. His face took on a hard cast. "In that case, Colonel, I'm afraid I must insist."

It occurred to Johnson that the pastor was on horseback while he was on foot, not a good position to be in when you were trying to assert your authority. Climbing into his saddle, he fixed the pastor with a flinty stare.

"*Insist*, Reverend? Need I remind you who's in command here?"

De Witt shook his head though his expression did not alter. He suddenly looked a different man to the one Johnson had been introduced to; more purposeful, a man whose confidence had been restored. "I assure you that's not necessary, Colonel. If I gave the impression of having suggested anything other than that, I apologize. I certainly meant no disrespect. However, the boy *was* placed in my care. If I may quote the good book: 'What man of you having an hundred sheep, if he lose one of them, doth not leave the ninety and nine in the wilderness and go after that which is lost, until he find it?'" The pastor drew himself up. "I consider the boy to be one of my flock. I am responsible for him, therefore, and he is *lost* in the wilderness, is he not?"

Johnson stared at the pastor. "I'm familiar with the parables, Reverend. So forgive me if I ask whether your motive in wanting to go with my men is to find the boy or to earn absolution for not keeping your eye on him in the first place?"

The pastor flinched. "He's twelve, Colonel. He has no one other than those of us on this march. He was in my care and I neglected him. I intend to make amends. Besides, there is an advantage in my joining the search."

"Really? How so?"

"I may have failed him, but he does know me. He does not know *these* men." The pastor swept a hand to encompass the corporal and his party. "After what he saw happen to his guardians, what do you think he might do if he sees these strangers bearing down upon him?"

There was a silence. Scott leaned in close. "He could have a point, sir. They're fine soldiers, but they do have the look of the ruffian about them. No offence, Corporal," he added, throwing a quick glance over his shoulder.

"None taken, sir," Stryker responded drily.

125

"I'm also another pair of eyes, Colonel," De Witt said. "*And I know the place where he might have left the column. It could save time, and time is of the essence, is it not? I'm assuming your scouts would have advised us if the enemy was in the vicinity. They have not done so. There would appear to be little risk, therefore, in my joining the search.*"

Johnson flicked a glance towards his second-in-command. Scott looked back at him and shrugged.

*What harm could it do?*

Johnson turned, collecting his thoughts. "They'll be out overnight."

"I've a warm blanket and a coat, and I have provisions in my saddlebag. I'm used to the inconvenience, Colonel, believe me."

"And are you armed, Reverend?"

"I am, sir."

*At least you didn't say, "the Lord will protect me"*, Johnson thought. He held the pastor's gaze for several long seconds and then sighed resignedly.

"Very well. While it goes against my better judgement, you may ride along with Corporal Stryker and his men. But know this, sir: they will make no allowances. It will be *your* job to keep up with *them*. And you will obey the corporal at all times. You understand me?"

"Perfectly, Colonel. Thank you."

Johnson turned. "Corporal Stryker, this gentleman will assist you in the search."

"Very good, sir." Stryker's face stayed neutral. Then, with a sideways glance to where the preacher had taken his wife's hand, he enquired in a low voice, "And if we can't find the boy, Colonel?"

Johnson followed Stryker's gaze. "Assuming you've exhausted all avenues, you are to return to the column. You do not have long. As I believe Captain Scott has informed you, I expect to depart Bulwagga at midday tomorrow. You have until then to catch us up. The Marine will not wait. The safety of the remaining civilians is paramount. Much as it pains me to say so, I cannot jeopardize the lives of two hundred for the sake of one, even if he is a child. I cannot. So I'm relying on you and your men, Corporal. Find the boy and bring him home. You hear me?"

"Yes, sir."

"Good man." Johnson stole another glance at the preacher and saw that De Witt and his wife had parted company. Turning back to the corporal, he steered his horse aside. "All right – on your way. We'll see you at Bulwagga."

Stryker touched his cap. "Colonel."

"God go with you, Thaddeus," Mrs De Witt called softly. Clutching her daughter's hand, she watched as the five riders cantered back down the trail. Then, squaring her shoulders, she collected her belongings and with a final glance towards her disappearing husband, she took her place in the line.

"Let's hope God's listening," Scott murmured. "If they don't find him, the lad doesn't have a hope in hell."

Johnson said nothing. With a contemplative Scott by his side, he watched in silence until the search party was out of sight, at which point Scott turned to him. "Awaiting your orders, sir."

Johnson continued to stare down the trail.

"Are you all right, Colonel?" Scott asked.

Realizing he'd been holding his breath, Johnson let it out slowly. "There are times, Thomas, when I wish I was just another bloody ranker. That way I wouldn't have to make such God-awful decisions."

Scott remained silent. After several seconds, Johnson ran his hand through his hair and said heavily. "Let's get them moving."

"Yes, sir."

They'd travelled less than half a mile when Scott stiffened in his saddle as two men appeared suddenly from a gap in the trees ahead of them. Had the men not been bearded, from a distance it would have been hard to tell if they were white or Indian, for they were burnt brown by the sun and dressed in native fashion: blue cotton shirts, buckskin leggings and moccasins. Ammunition and supply pouches hung across their shoulders and both men carried long guns.

"Scouts," Scott announced unnecessarily as the duo jogged effortlessly towards them.

"Mr Boone, Mr Cavett," Johnson said, addressing the men as they drew level. "You have fresh news, I take it?"

Boone, the taller and swarthier of the pair, nodded. "We do, Colonel and it ain't good." Turning his head to one side, he spat a stream of black mucus on to the ground. "Militia's catching up."

"God damn!" Scott said.

"From what direction?" Johnson asked.

"Take your pick, Colonel," Boone said, transferring the tobacco plug from the inside of his left cheek to the inside of his right. "There's a combined force of Continentals and militia coming up round Lake George by way of the Albany road, heading for Champlain. I'm guessing it aims to get there before us. Word is Governor Clinton himself is leading 'em."

"Is he indeed?" Johnson said. "I'm honoured. And there are others, you say?"

"Another division from the New Hampshire Grants headin' out by way of Ticonderoga. It plans to rendezvous with Clinton's men."

"Anyone else?"

"We did hear the Tryon County Militia mustered at Johnstown – Third Battalion," the scout added.

"That's Veeder's battalion," Scott said. "Maybe he's annoyed that we released his brother."

Johnson smiled thinly as Boone said, "Aye, well I don't reckon we'll be hearing from them. They're too far behind. Also, it seems they're being diverted back to the Mohawk."

Boone grinned, showing tobacco-stained teeth. "There's a rumour Brant and his warriors were seen south of the river. Militia thought it prudent to stay and offer a defence if the heathens attempt a crossing."

Johnson awarded himself a pat on the back. During the raid, to draw Patriot attention away from the column's escape route, the scouts had let slip false word that a band of Mohawk auxiliaries was also on the rampage. The decoying tactic appeared to have worked.

"Well, you were right, sir," Scott said brightly. "They fell for it. Should keep the bastards occupied for a while."

"All warfare is based on deception," Johnson murmured.

Scott looked at him and raised an eyebrow. "Your father?"

"Sun Tzu," Johnson said with a smile.

Boone frowned. "He an Iroquois, Colonel?"

"Different tribe, Mr Boone, but as good as. Clinton's militia – how close to us, would you estimate?"

The scout pursed his lips. "Hard to say, seeing as they ain't chasing us, exactly. They're trying to cut us off. Given our current position, maybe a day to intersect."

"Hell fire," Scott swore.

"Then we should pick up the pace," Johnson said. "We *must* get to Champlain before they do. The Marine's waiting, but it can't risk a confrontation. If we don't make it, the boats will leave without us. And it's a bloody long walk to the border – assuming we can avoid a fight."

"The civilians won't take too kindly to the added mileage," Scott said.

"Indeed." Johnson looked back to the scout. "Very well, Mr Boone, I thank you for the intelligence. I'd be obliged if you'd replenish your provisions and return to the field. See what else you can find out. It's clear from your report that the enemy knows or has guessed our intentions. They probably haven't determined our exact route, but they've deduced we're heading for Champlain. That means we're up against it."

Johnson addressed his second-in-command: "Captain Scott, kindly inform the company commanders of the situation. They are to increase the pace, but subtly. We don't want to spread panic among the civilians."

Scott pursed his lips. "What about . . .?"

"If Corporal Stryker and his men fail to find the boy before nightfall and the enemy comes between us, they will have to take their chances. How good *is* Stryker?"

"Better than any damned militia, that's for sure," Scott said.

"Then I've no doubt they will make the rendezvous on time," Johnson responded confidently. He turned to the scout. "How many men would you say Governor Clinton has to hand, Mr Boone?"

"'Bout fifteen hundred, give or take."

"Dear God!" Scott paled and sucked in his breath. "That many?"

"We gave 'em a bloody nose, Colonel. They mean to get their own back," Boone said. "One way or t'other."

Johnson absorbed the comment. "I doubt they'll march at night, which means we may yet have the advantage. So we move now and we move fast." He addressed Scott. "Smartly, Thomas. Smartly."

"Yes, sir."

As his second-in-command cantered away, Johnson looked back down the column, thinking of the boy and the men he'd dispatched to look for him.

*And the Devil take the hindmost,* he thought bleakly.

# 5

"How long before they come after us, do you think?" Lawrence asked, his tone suggesting speculation rather than worry.

Hawkwood shrugged. "Difficult to say. From what I saw, they'd be hard pushed to find their own arses in the dark, so it could be some time. It'll have taken a while for them to round up their damned horses. *And* they had a blaze to put out. My guess is that should keep them busy 'til dawn, so we've a few hours in our favour."

"Ah," Lawrence murmured. "The fire; I'd forgotten about that."

Hawkwood smiled ruefully. "A diversion was all I could think of. I heard they were planning to ship you off to Pittsfield, wherever the hell that is, so I didn't have much time."

Lawrence chuckled. "Well, I'm damned glad you used it wisely, my dear fellow! I could tell you were a resourceful bugger the first time I clapped eyes on you. Good to see you haven't changed."

The major raised his mug and in a lowered voice said, "To brothers-in-arms and confusion to the enemy!"

"Whomever they may be," Hawkwood responded. The two men drank.

There had been no need for Lawrence to speak softly. They

were alone in the taproom. The weathered sign hanging above the door had identified the inn as Peake's Tavern. Anxious to snatch some sleep before daylight, and none too keen on bedding down outdoors in the cold and rain, they'd seen a light on in the window and stopped to enquire whether there might be a room available for what was left of the night.

The landlord had peered at them blearily before shaking his head. What rooms the tavern did possess were already taken, but if they were prepared to invest in a jug and a couple of tankards they were welcome to make use of the settles by the fire. The least he could do, he'd told them, for our brave infantrymen.

Hawkwood was still wearing his stolen tunic while Lawrence's uniform was partially visible at the collar of his greatcoat. As the latter was neither regulation blue nor make-do grey but British scarlet, Hawkwood assumed their host was either colour blind or conveniently unfamiliar with American regimental colours. Whatever his motivation, the offer had been gratefully accepted.

After they'd seen their mounts quartered in the adjoining and equally unprepossessing stable, they had returned to the taproom's warmth. Too late for a hot supper as well, the landlord had advised them apologetically, but there was bread and some cheese and a wedge of beef pie, which they were welcome to if they didn't mind the latter being served cold.

They didn't mind at all, Lawrence had replied, while throwing Hawkwood a broad wink behind the landlord's back.

Having seen to the food, the landlord had bid them a good night. His only instruction upon departing for his own bed had been for them to keep an eye on the fire and to prevent the embers from falling out of the hearth.

Consisting of three houses and the tavern, the hamlet was too small to warrant a name. From what they could tell in the darkness, there wasn't a lot to recommend the place other than its position in relation to the post road and its distance from Greenbush.

It had been after midnight when they arrived. Hawkwood

had been unsure how far they'd travelled until he spotted the mileage marker on the hamlet's outskirts. If the figure was accurate, Albany lay some twenty-five miles behind them. He would have preferred to put a greater distance between them and their pursuers, but there were risks involved in travelling over unfamiliar country in the dark at speed. And even though their horses were army dispatch mounts and thus used to being ridden hard, it was clear they had reached their limit. Had they been domestic nags, he reflected, they'd likely have expired several miles back. The only respite the sweat-caked animals had been given was when they slowed to walking pace upon approaching any village on their route, so as avoid waking the slumbering townsfolk and drawing notice to themselves.

For the most part they had stuck to the main road, maintaining their direction north, up through Troy to Lansingburgh, where Hawkwood had thought about using the bridge to re-cross the river. Realizing that this would entail yet another crossing of the Hudson further upstream, probably at Fort Edward, he had opted to remain on the east bank.

As the warmth of the fire penetrated his bones, he gazed into the flames and thought about the chaos they'd left behind them. By this time Sergeant Dunbar would have been ordered to recount the evening's events to his superiors, as would Corporal Jeffard and his card-playing associates. If there was one thing that Hawkwood knew about military procedure it was that every mother's son involved in the fracas would be trying his level best to plant the blame on someone else. Part of him did wonder if the camp commander might not think it was a waste of his already over-stretched resources sending men to chase the fugitives. With luck, he would deem it an incident best swept under the carpet and his actions would be dictated by fear of high command finding out that one man, acting alone, had managed to breach the cantonment's inner sanctum and break a prisoner out of the guardhouse.

He dismissed the thought as wishful thinking. At least one man, possibly two, had died and several others had been wounded, not to mention the damage to the stables and the loss of two horses. No, the army would be looking for retribution.

Which was all the more reason for Hawkwood and Lawrence to grab what sleep and sustenance they could while they had the opportunity. With a few hours' recuperation under their belts they'd be able to continue their journey at sun-up and still be ahead of any pursuit party.

Lawrence's voice cut into Hawkwood's thoughts.

"So, my dear fellow, I think it's about time you explained what the devil you're doing here, don't you?"

Hawkwood wondered how much he should divulge. Since it really didn't matter in the long run, he smiled. "Would you believe me if I told you I'm trying to get home."

Lawrence frowned over the rim of his mug. "From where?"

"France," Hawkwood said.

The mug almost slipped from Lawrence's grasp. "France! Good God! Well, I hate to cast aspersions, but your navigation leaves a lot to be desired! Shouldn't you be pointing the other way?"

"It's a long story," Hawkwood said with mock weariness.

Lawrence fixed him with a perceptive stare. "Well, we've a fire in the grate, food in our bellies and a drink in our hands – and neither of us has a bed to go to. So, if you've the inclination to regale me, I'm all ears. If I should nod off, though, don't be offended. Just take my drink away and let me sleep."

Stretching out his legs in front of the hearth, the major lifted a hand in a regal salute. "Proceed."

Hawkwood studied him for a moment and then grinned. "All right, Major; you asked for it. Tell me, what do you know about the Alien Office?"

Lawrence blinked. "Not a damned thing. What's that when it's at home?"

Hawkwood told him.


"Good God Almighty!" Lawrence said after the telling was over. He stared at Hawkwood in astonishment. "*Bonaparte*? You actually went to Paris to overthrow *Bonaparte*?"

"It seemed like a good idea at the time," Hawkwood said wistfully.

"Well, of that I have no doubt. And Grant? Colquhoun-bloody-Grant! I'll be double damned! There we were, thinking the Frogs had killed the bugger! I need another drink! Where's that damned jug?"

Lawrence poured himself a fresh mug, from which he took a deep swallow before shaking his head in wonderment as if he couldn't quite believe what he'd just been told. "Bonaparte! Good God!"

"So, what about you, Major?" Hawkwood said. "What's your story? I saw in the guardhouse ledger that you were captured at Oswegatchie. That's up on the St Lawrence, correct?"

"Which carries a certain irony, don't you think?" Lawrence made a face. "But you're right about the location. Though there's some who call it Ogdensburg. That's the trouble with the Americans – they can't seem to make their bloody minds up."

"What happened? Where's the rest of the Fortieth? Did you get separated?"

"Separated?" Lawrence looked surprised by the question. "Ah, yes, well, you could say that, seeing as the rest of the regiment is in Spain."

Hawkwood frowned, mystified. "Then, what the hell are you doing *here*?"

A fresh smile broke out across Lawrence's face. "Unlike you, I'm here on purpose. Or at any rate, the Army's purpose. I was assigned."

"On your *own*? To do what?"

"Recruit the natives."

Hawkwood stared at him, dumbstruck.

"Ha!" Lawrence chuckled at Hawkwood's expression. "Thought that'd strike a chord!"

*Just as well we've eaten,* Hawkwood thought as he watched Lawrence take another sip, *or else we'd both be in our cups.*

Not that he was feeling particularly fatigued. And Lawrence was showing no signs of flagging either. He suspected it was the excitement of the night that was keeping them awake. Sleep was never going to come easy after being shot at and spearing a man through the guts with a twelve-foot pike – no matter how tired you thought you might be.

"Can I just begin by saying that, although my being here is in part your fault, I bear you no ill will," said Lawrence. "And the same goes for Major Grant."

"Me?" Hawkwood said, recovering and wondering if he'd misjudged Lawrence's capacity for absorbing alcohol, though the major's comment had been delivered in a tongue-in-cheek tone. "What did I do? And what on earth does Col Grant have to do with it?"

"He inherited your contacts with the *guerrilleros* when you returned to London, yes? Ended up as Wellington's chief exploring officer?"

"That's right," Hawkwood said warily, wondering where this was leading.

"So who do you think took over Grant's liaison duties after he was captured by the Frogs?"

Hawkwood was about to plead ignorance when the answer dawned on him.

"You're not serious?"

"Damned right, I'm serious. If it wasn't for me taking on his mantle, they wouldn't have posted me to the Canadas and I wouldn't have been captured and *we* wouldn't be having this chinwag. If I were a God-fearing man, I'd say that your coming to my rescue was a clear case of Divine intervention." Lawrence shook his head. "Since I'm not, let's put it down to happy coincidence."

"Bloody hell!" Hawkwood said.

"Quite so," Lawrence responded. "Strange how chance takes a hand, ain't it? I felt sure I was imagining things when I saw you back at the ferry landing."

"That makes two of us," Hawkwood said. "How did you end up taking over Grant's role?"

Lawrence put down his tankard and picked up a poker. After steering a couple of glowing log ends away from the edge of the hearth, he replaced the poker, reclaimed his drink and sat

136

back. "It was following our last adventure, when you and I said our goodbyes and I returned to Spain. There was a lot of bad feeling after the Badajoz affair, and Wellington—"

"Badajoz?" Hawkwood said.

Lawrence fixed Hawkwood with a questioning gaze. "You *know* about the victory, obviously?"

"I read about it."

"Aye, well it wasn't near as glorious as the journals might have made out. In fact, it was anything but. Our losses were appalling. And when our troops did finally take the city, they went on a three-day killing spree. Men, women, even children, were put to the sword. It was ghastly, a bloody massacre." He gave a shudder at the thought of it. "You can imagine what it did to our relations with the Spanish. Naturally, Wellington wanted bridges rebuilt as soon as possible, and one way to achieve that was to have British officers working with their Spanish counterparts to try and smooth things over.

"My colonel volunteered me for the role; he knew my Spanish was good. One thing led to another and before I knew it I was spending more time delivering dispatches to the local guerrilla commanders than I was marching with my regiment.

"In the course of all this, I worked with Grant, got to know him a little. After he was captured, and because I was already entrenched with the *guerrilleros*, I was tasked to take over the running of some of his courier routes."

"But how did you end up here?"

Lawrence eyed Hawkwood over the rim of his mug. "When you were in Spain, did you ever come across Lieutenant-Colonel Pearson?"

"Can't say the name means anything."

"A hell of a soldier; wounded at Aldea de Ponte and sent home, unfit for active service. Not good for a man of his calibre. Anyone else would probably have drunk himself into a stupor. Luckily, a friend came to his rescue." Lawrence paused to let Hawkwood take the bait.

"And this friend just happened to be . . .?"

"General Prevost, Governor-General of Canada."

"That's impressive."

"Ain't it just. They served together in Martinique. Rather than see him put out to grass, Prevost offered him a staff position as Inspecting Field Officer of Militia in Canada. He was already en route when hostilities broke out. Didn't take him long to see that improvements were needed. Came up with quite a few, one of which was establishing a web of paid informants. To liaise with them, he recruited special, ah . . . correspondents, I suppose you'd call 'em – like the ones employed by your Alien Office – to gather intelligence from behind the American lines. That got him to thinking about the way Grant had recruited the *guerrilleros* in Spain and Portugal. He thought it might be possible to try the same tactic with the indigenous tribes. It worked during the Revolution – why not now?"

"So they sent for you," Hawkwood said.

"Grant wasn't available, on account of he'd been captured, so the generals decided I was the man for the job. I received my marching orders in October. Hardly drew breath before they had me on a packet out of Lisbon."

Lawrence smiled thinly. "Put the Indian Department's nose out of joint, of course: Pearson bringing in his own man. There's a rift deep between the department and the military. The army reckons most of the department's officials are corrupt and only out to feather their own nests. There's a fair number who've married into the tribes, so they've a vested interest in the Nations remaining neutral. It protects their positions.

"Now that we're at war, as far as the army's concerned, those who ain't with us are agin us. It wants the Nations to take a positive stance. If we're to defend the Canadas, as we must, we need the tribes on our side.

"For that to happen, we have to convince the leaders that their best interests lie with us and not the Americans." Lawrence sighed. "And there's the rub. The Indian Department would prefer the peace chiefs to be in charge. The army, for obvious reasons, wants the war chiefs to hold the reins. Up until a month or so ago, it was what the Frogs call *impasse*."

"What changed?"

"His Majesty's government realized war was imminent so the army got its way. When the civil governor went back to England for a spot of leave, he was replaced by General Brock. When he was killed at Queenston Sheaffe took over. He was on the Niagara too, along with a fellow called John Norton. I won't even attempt to pronounce his Indian name. He has a Cherokee father and a Scottish mother and he's the son-in-law of Joseph Brant, the chap who led the Nations and fought alongside us in the Revolution."

"Thayendanega," Hawkwood said softly.

Lawrence paused. "I do believe that was his Mohawk name, yes. You've *heard* of him?"

"A long time ago."

Lawrence paused for Hawkwood to elaborate, but when he saw that wasn't going to happen, he went on: "Soon as Sheaffe became Commander, he rewarded Norton with a title: Captain of the Indian Confederation, in recognition for his action at Queenston."

A memory of one of Quade's outbursts entered Hawkwood's mind.

*"That breed, Norton, and his damned savages!"*

"That sealed it," Lawrence said. "They might as well have crowned him King of the Iroquois, because as far as the army's concerned that's what he is. So now they have a war chief – *their* war chief – as leader of the Nations. Norton can use his influence to persuade the tribes to fight for *us*. The Indian Department's hopping mad, of course. It's worried that with a war chief as leader, if the tribes ever decide to turn against His Majesty's government they'll wreak havoc among the whites."

"There's a risk of that?"

"Not if we keep them sweet."

"You think that will work?"

Lawrence shrugged. "So long as we have Norton in our corner. There are other inducements. The main one being that if Canada falls to the Americans it won't only be the British who'll lose, but the Nations, too. There'll be nothing to stop the Yankees from taking everything, including Indian land. Not that there's

139

much left of it, mind you, but they'll have even less if we lose.
We can't let that happen.

"Norton's doing a good job persuading the Indians on the
Canadian side of the line to join us but it's the ones in residence
on this side of the border I was sent to convince. We know
they're veering towards neutrality and that some have been in
secret correspondence with their Canadian brothers advocating
that. We want them to see things differently. Pearson believes
the Iroquois to be a pragmatic people who'll side with the nation
most likely to emerge victorious. Our successes at Detroit and
Queenston will show them we have the resources and the skill
to defeat the Americans.

"I wasn't here more than five minutes before Pearson called
me in. He's not a man who believes in prevarication. And he's
no diplomat! The Canadians have taken to calling him 'Tartar'
Pearson behind his back. Well deserved, too – I can vouch for
that!

"Anyway, he decided there was no time to lose. I was sent
across the river on the back end of a raiding party."

"So what went wrong?"

"We wound up in the wrong place at the wrong time. Sheer
bad luck, simple as that; not helped by the fact there were more
of them than there were of us. I was supposed to slip through
the lines while the raid was taking place, but I never made it.
My guide was killed and I was taken prisoner – the mackerel
caught in a net full of haddock, you might say.

"So much for Pearson's plan. He'll be fuming, I expect.
Probably just as well I'm here rather than there." The corner of
his mouth twitched. "Y'know, back in London, when I said that
I hoped we'd meet again, this wasn't at all what I had in mind.
But, by God, I'm glad to see you!"

"Likewise, Major," Hawkwood said.

Lawrence's brow creased. "That reminds me – wasn't there a
lady? Rather exotic, too, as I recall. Whatever became of her?
Did you and she . . .?"

"She died," Hawkwood said.

"Oh, my dear fellow, I'm so sorry!"

"Don't be," Hawkwood said. "She was a murderous bitch."

Lawrence's eyebrows took off again.

"She was a French spy. Killed at least two people and came close to assassinating the Prince Regent. She got what she deserved. Justice was dispensed."

Lawrence stared at him. After a pause, he enquired cautiously, "Er . . . by your hand?"

"And a bullet from a Baker rifle, yes."

"My God," Lawrence said again, though his voice was muted this time. He took a sip from his mug, grimaced at the taste and laid it down on the table in front of him. Then he reached into his pocket and took out a watch. "Remember this?"

It was the watch that had brought the two of them together. A pickpocket had lifted it from Lawrence's sash while the major was watching a bare-knuckle bout. Hawkwood, who'd been involved with a criminal case nearby, had witnessed the theft, retrieved the timepiece and returned it to its grateful owner. There was an inscription on the back of the casing:

*Lieutenant D.C. Lawrence, 40th Regiment.*
*A gallant officer.*
*With grateful thanks, Auchmuty.*
*February 1807*

The watch had been given to Lawrence by his commanding officer, as a mark of respect and in honour of his lieutenant's bravery during the attack on Montevideo. As a result of which Lawrence had received his captaincy.

"Only a couple of hours until dawn," Lawrence observed. "We should probably make use of the accommodation while we can." He laid back on the settle, stretched out his legs and drew his coat about him. "So what's our next move?"

"Continue north; head for Canada. With luck, we'll make it before the weather turns."

Lawrence tucked his head on to his chest. "Splendid. And did you have a particular route planned?"

Hawkwood summoned the Lewis map to mind. "Maybe. It'll

141

depend on the state of the roads. There's been heavy flooding along some stretches of highway. We might have to make it up as we go."

Lawrence folded his arms, snuggled down and let out a low chuckle. "Ha, nothing new there, eh?"

"Story of my life, Major," Hawkwood said.

But he was talking to himself. Lawrence was already asleep.

It had been four days since the old man's passing.

The entire village had turned out for the feast in honour of their departed brother and prophet, Ayonhwathah. Now, in the pale light of morning, they gathered to watch as the deceased's relatives accompanied the body from the long-house to the waiting scaffold.

With great solemnity, the corpse bearers carried the litter through the village and out to the place that had been chosen at the edge of the forest. The mourners followed closely behind, many weeping openly as the procession made its way towards the ten-foot-high elm-bark platform. The scaffold timbers creaked as the blanket-wrapped bundle was laid to rest and his weapons – hunting knife, tomahawk, war club and carbine – were placed alongside him. When the final items had been added – a pipe and a full tobacco pouch – a black bear skin was drawn across the corpse to protect it from the wind, rain and snow.

Perched in the surrounding trees, a flock of crows fixed their gimlet-bright eyes upon the small baskets of food that hung from the scaffold; left there to sustain the deceased's spirit on its journey into the afterlife.

When all the baskets and the water pots had been secured, the ladder was taken down and the funeral fire was lit. The fire was neither large nor fierce enough to consume the corpse, for that was not its purpose. It was there to deter scavengers and to help the dead man's spirit prepare the food.

When the flames had been reduced to small flickering tongues, the mourners turned and with heavy hearts began to wend their way back towards the village, their lamentations gradually fading in volume as they re-entered their houses, where the grieving would continue.

On the evening of the ninth day Kodjeote left his bed to tend the funeral fire. The night was dark and clear and bitterly cold, and the ground, already veneered with a thin frost, crackled beneath his feet.

He paused as a low pale shape padded soundlessly through a patch of moonlight in front of him; letting out his breath when he recognized it as one of the village dogs. The animal stopped and stared at him through yellow eyes before it moved on, into the night.

As Kodjeote approached the fire, the robed figure standing guard there rose to its feet.

"Was it not Deskaheh's turn to tend the flames?" Cageaga said, frowning.

"I could not sleep, Uncle," Kodjeote said. "I told Deskaheh I would take his place."

"He did not ask it of you?" the older man enquired suspiciously.

Kodjeote shook his head. "The choice was mine." His gaze turned from his uncle to the scaffold's slender framework, outlined against the stars. "Deskaheh says he cannot remember the last sky burial."

Deskaheh was Kodjeote's brother and his senior by five years.

"He's too young," Cageaga grunted. "It took place before he was born."

"Did *you* see it?" Kodjeote asked. "Do *you* remember?"

"I remember it was a long time ago."

"Why have we not placed him in the ground?"

"Because this was his wish."

"For the flesh to fall from his bones for all to see and for the birds to peck at his eyes?" Kodjeote said doubtfully.

The response was curt: "No, it is so his journey from the earth to the sky world will be a short one."

"The Christian fathers say the dead should be buried below the earth and—"

143

"The Christian fathers say a lot of things," Cageaga sniffed dismissively. "Just because the white man tells us something does not mean we have to take their word for it." Cageaga's face darkened. "*That* is how our lands were stolen from us."

"So you believe in the Great Spirit?"

"More than golden idols and wooden crosses."

Kodjeote looked pensive.

"When the time comes, we will bury him. Not because the Black Robes say so, but because that has always been our custom."

The Black Robes were the Jesuit missionaries – *les prêtres français* – who had come to the land of the Iroquois to spread the word of their god. Their first converts had been the Huron, enemies of the Mohawk. When Kodjeote's ancestors had launched raids against Huron villages, they had returned with Black Robe prisoners. Many of the priests had died under torture, while others had been ransomed to the authorities. Some, however, had forged bonds with their captors and had remained, hoping to persuade the Iroquois to abandon their beliefs. Over the years, they had won many converts, until the Christian god had as many followers as the old religion.

Kodjeote stared down at the flames. Tomorrow would be the tenth day, when the fire would be extinguished and the old man's spirit would begin its journey westwards along the spirit world path and on into the afterlife. There would be another feast, during which the deceased's possessions would be distributed among his friends and relatives.

"I will leave you now," Cageaga said, breaking into Kodjeote's thoughts. "Keep your eyes about you – I heard noises earlier; a bear, perhaps. Most will have retired to their dens, but if any are around and they smell food . . ." Cageaga left the sentence hanging.

Kodjeote surveyed the dark outline of the trees with trepidation. Any bear in the vicinity would be unable to resist the odours arising from the decomposing corpse and from the food offerings hanging alongside it.

"I will be vigilant," he said firmly.

Satisfied, his uncle turned away. Kodjeote watched him go. Cageaga was tall and lithe and walked with a warrior's bearing, even though he was edging towards his fiftieth year. He was a man of few words, but when he chose to speak, people listened. The younger members of the tribe held him in awe, for he had taken many scalps. Anyone foolish enough to doubt his prowess had only to count the number of tattoos stitched across his thighs, each one a testament to an enemy slain in combat.

The fire was popping and spitting as bubbles of resin trapped in the bark exploded with the heat. As he gazed down at the flames, glad of their warmth and protection after the cold of the long-house, it occurred to Kodjeote that his uncle may have been toying with him when he mentioned the bear. Cageaga's sombre demeanour hid an unexpected and very dry sense of humour.

Kodjeote sat down by the fire. He was drawing the blanket around his shoulders when a long drawn-out howl sounded from deep within the woods. The hairs along Kodjeote's arms prickled as the call was answered by the rest of the pack. Sound travelled further at night and Kodjeote knew the wolves were some way off, most likely well beyond the northern ridge and over in the next valley, but nevertheless he moved himself closer to the flames.

He looked up at the platform, at the dark shape resting upon it. The old man used to tell stories of skin walkers – warriors who would take on animal form to wreak havoc. Disguised as wolves, hawks or eagles, they could cover vast distances at speed. Kodjeote wasn't sure he believed the stories, but he knew there were many who did. Especially older members of the tribe, like Cageaga. The old man must have believed the stories, too. Why else would he have chosen this particular means of burial?

A log cracked, jolting him from his reverie. For one moment he thought he saw the body twitch. A stray gust of wind, exploring the edge of the bear pelt, he reassured himself. But then a groan came from the scaffold, followed by a low keening. The wind again, trying to find a path through the gaps in the bark, he reasoned.

That was when he noticed a dark object resembling a bird's wing outlined at one edge of the platform. The crows had been eyeing the old man's body ever since it was raised aloft. Were they now feasting on the remains? But crows did not feed at night, so it must be the bear's hide, loosened by the wind.

Kodjeote looked for the ladder. If the wind picked up, there was a danger the entire skin might be dislodged. He daren't allow that to happen. It was his responsibility not only to attend the fire but to protect the remains, for according to the old beliefs a body that was damaged or rendered incomplete would prevent the spirit from entering the afterlife.

The ladder lay a few feet away. Picking it up, Kodjeote rested it against the scaffold, dropped his blanket to the ground, wincing as the cold bit into his exposed skin, and began to climb. The timbers groaned again as his weight shifted. As he drew closer he could see where the bear skin had come adrift. When he was waist high to the platform he braced himself against it and reached for the edge of the hide.

A dry rustling sound came from the trees behind him. Kodjeote turned to look. The tops of the branches were swaying from side to side as though an invisible force was trying to fight its way through the leaves. He shivered and turned back. His hand closed around the corner of the hide. Its suppleness had almost disappeared because of the cold. Taking a firm grip, he steadied himself, preparing to pull it taut. His hand paused in mid-air as his attention was caught by the play of moonlight on the dark, emaciated shape beneath the fur covering. In the gap between the hide and the bark strips, Kodjeote could see part of a tomahawk blade and the curved head of the old man's war club. He hesitated and looked over his shoulder towards the village. All was quiet.

Cautiously, Kodjeote drew back the hide, revealing the weapons. He ran his hand across the hatchet blade, tracing the pitted metal with his fingertips. The grip, bound with rawhide, was blackened by age and wear. His eye moved to the war club, its stock worn smooth with use. What must it be like to wield such a weapon in anger? By the time the old man was his age, Kodjeote thought enviously, he was already a seasoned warrior, fighting for the King across the Great Water against a mutual foe – les français. Twenty years later, he had taken up his hatchet and war club for another English king, this time against the Yan-kees.

But the British had lost that war and their Iroquois allies had been driven out of their traditional strongholds into smaller land tracts, the Nations reduced to little more than a disparate collection of nomads.

Nearly two decades had passed since the Kanien'kehá:ka last took to the war path. As he listened to his father and uncle, and the other older men sitting around the council fires, trading stories of brave deeds and battles fought and of scalps taken, Kodjeote was filled with envy. But it would not be long before they, too, were called to take the spirit world path. *Soon*, Kodjeote thought sadly, *there will be no more warriors save for those mentioned in stories around the camp fires. By the time my children's children are born, there will only be half-forgotten memories and graves filled with dry bones and dust.*

He moved his hand from the war club and laid his palm gently upon the blanket above his grandfather's chest. It was the custom to talk to the dead; to gaze upon them one last time and to tell them they were not forgotten.

Kodjeote wanted to tell the old man how much he missed him and to ask forgiveness for disturbing his final rest. He took a deep breath and then hesitated. He did not know how to begin. He thought then about Cageaga's comment and wondered if anyone in the tribe had said a Christian prayer over his grandfather's remains. Those who followed the long-house teachings believed that no white man could enter the sky world. It made Kodjeote wonder if that meant a chief of the Kanien'kehá:ka was unable to enter the white man's heaven.

What if, despite his uncle's scepticism, the Catholic fathers were right and the true Creator was not the Great Spirit but the white man's god? That would mean the only afterworld was the one promised by the white man's deity. If that was so, in order for his grandfather to gain admittance, should not a white man's prayer be spoken over him?

In his mind's eye Kodjeote saw the ancient features that were hidden beneath the blanket: the lined face, the eyes that had remained bright almost until the moment of death and the mane of silver hair that had reached to the old man's shoulders. Keeping his hand in place above the stilled heart he began to intone softly, "Shoegwaniha karonhyakonh teghsideronh . . . *Our father, who art in heaven . . .*"

Kodjeote closed his eyes.

". . . neoni toghsa tagwaghsharinet . . ."

From the forest there came the skittering sounds of leaves rustling in the wind. Beneath the scaffold, the flames began to gutter and dance.

". . . *ne-aewese-aghtshera tsiniyeaheawe neoni tsiniyeaheawe.*"

As he uttered the final words, Kodjeote began to sense that he was not alone. Someone was standing close by, watching him. The sensation was not unpleasant and he did not feel afraid, yet it was intense enough to make him open his eyes with a gasp.

He looked about him. The trees were still swaying restlessly and the fire was glowing brightly; he could feel its heat upon his legs. Feeling vaguely foolish, he bowed his head in respect, drew the bear skin back over the remains and secured it to the platform with the rawhide strip that had come loose. He was preparing to descend the ladder when he heard his name spoken.

"*Kodjeote.*"

It had been no more than a whisper. Hardly daring to breathe, he waited for the sound to be repeated but all he could hear was the beating of his own heart.

It was the wind, he told himself. Nothing more than that; his ears playing tricks. He thought of the skin walkers and the noises that his uncle claimed to have heard. His eyes darted about, trying to locate whoever was watching him. He felt a sudden, desperate need to return to the fire.

"*Kodjeote.*"

His breath caught once more. Swallowing nervously, he stared down at the dark contours of his grandfather's corpse.

"Tota?" he enquired hesitantly. "Is that you?"

A soft sigh reached his ears. It was hard to tell its origin. Was it the wind . . . or something else?

"Tota?" he said again; the word came out as a cracked whisper.

His ears picked up what sounded like a low murmur, as if someone was talking softly while holding a hand over their mouth. As Kodjeote's eyes fell upon the bear hide, the muffled sound came again.

Hesitantly, Kodjeote leaned forward and placed his ear against the contours of his grandfather's body.

"Tota? It is Kodjeote," he called softly. "I am here. I hear you."

There was nothing. For several long seconds he did not move. Then, unsure as to whether to be disappointed or relieved at the silence, he raised his head.

*"Tell them."*

He gasped. The words, though spoken quietly, had sounded so clear and so close. He lowered his head. "Tell who, Tota?"

Several more seconds passed.

*"Tell them all."*

"What should I tell them?"

This time, the silence seemed to stretch for ever. Kodjeote was on the point of repeating the question when the response came. It emerged as a dry-throated rasp, like the skittering of autumn leaves as they were blown across a dry forest floor.

Spoken in his grandfather's voice. Three words.

*"He is coming."*

# 6

May 1780

The boy stared down at the sorry-looking bundle of blood and fur before turning to Tam, who looked very pleased with himself, in the way that dogs do when they think they've performed a clever feat and are seeking a reward.

"I don't know what you're looking so happy about, Tam Hooper. You had me chasing you all over the woods for a cottontail? You could at least have found a decent mouthful! Wait till I get you home!"

Detecting the admonishing tone in his master's voice, Tam stared ruefully at the carcass and wagged his tail tentatively before sinking down and placing his head on his front paws.

When he'd seen Tam pad off into the trees during the morning rest stop, the boy hadn't been that concerned. In the days since they'd left the big house, Tam had often wandered away from the march to follow an interesting scent or explore a mysterious rustle in the bushes.

A few times, he'd returned bearing gifts; either a plump rabbit or a squirrel held fast in his jaws. The kills had been handed to the cook, who'd accepted them with due reverence because when there was no guarantee where your next meal was coming from you never turned down rations, no matter how meagre. Not that anyone was likely to starve on the march as game was plentiful and the hunting parties invariably returned to camp with food for the pot.

On this last occasion, however, when the end of the column came into sight and there was no sign of the hound, the boy had decided to go and look for him. In doing so he knew he had to be careful.

It had reached the stage where no one paid much attention when people left the trail; it was something everyone did when they needed to take a piss or a shit, and the edges of the woods were usually close enough that no one would notice him leave anyway. Even if they were to see him go, they'd likely assume that he'd been given permission to leave the line on his own. After all, it wasn't as if he was a child who needed someone to take his breeches down and wipe his backside for him.

But it paid to take precautions.

As far as he knew, the only person who'd seen him leave had been Libby. The two of them had been riding a few yards behind the reverend and his wife when he'd told the girl that he hadn't seen Tam for a while and he was going to look for him.

He'd not exchanged many words with the pastor's daughter during the march and because of that he suspected she would probably tell on him if he did not take her into his confidence.

The obvious solution, therefore, had been to involve her in his plan by asking her if she could keep a secret. He knew all small children liked to keep secrets, especially from grown-ups, even if their father was a reverend. Her shy grin and nod of acquiescence had sealed the bargain. Whereupon he'd hung back, letting the column wend its way past while he waited anxiously for the dog to reappear. And when that didn't happen, he'd left.

Libby obviously hadn't told on him, else someone would have called out or tried to stop him. Not that there had been any reason for concern; as soon as he'd caught up with Tam the two of them would simply rejoin the line and no one, other than his partner in crime, would be any the wiser.

Only it hadn't worked out that way. After twenty minutes or so of searching and calling Tam's name, the dog was nowhere to be seen. That's when he'd begun to worry that something had happened and that Tam might not be coming back. But instead of returning to the column, he'd continued in his search.

It had been sheer luck that he'd chanced upon the deer trail. He'd not been following it long when he heard snapping and snuffling from patch of wood ahead of him. Taking it for granted that Tam was involved in the altercation, he'd called out the dog's name but there had been no answering bark in response. With mounting trepidation he'd crept towards the source of the disturbance, softly repeating the dog's name over and over, conscious that Tam wasn't the only sharp-toothed beast at large in the woods.

And then came the response he'd been hoping for: a single excited bark. This was followed immediately by a series of yaps and a muffled grunting sound that swelled suddenly into a ferocious snarl, causing the short hairs to prickle like stalks along the boy's forearms. Jonah, who until that point had been content to proceed along the trail, immediately planted all four hooves firmly into the ground and stopped dead, ears flattened, before backing away, snorting with fear.

As he tried to calm his frightened mount, Tam came into view. He had positioned himself, head thrust low and forward, hackles raised and teeth bared, at the edge of the path about fifty paces further on, his attention focused on whatever was thrashing about in the thicket. Deep growls reverberated at the back of the dog's throat.

Swallowing his fear, he called out, "Here, Tam! Here, boy!"

Tam's ears pricked up, showing that he'd heard, but he stayed put. Unable to persuade Jonah to move any closer, the boy called again, sharply this time.

"Tam, you get back here! You get back here RIGHT NOW!"

This time Tam responded, albeit with reluctance. There was none of his customary tail-wagging and no grin. If there was a message in his brown eyes it was relief that reinforcements had finally arrived.

All eyes turned back to the undergrowth as the grunting grew louder, then came a humphing sound and a breaking of branches followed by a flash of dark matted fur as something large and ponderous crashed through the far side of the thicket and headed for an even deeper part of the wood.

The boy and his companions stood transfixed, afraid to move. A strong, musty odour lingered in the air, confirming that the interloper had indeed been a bear, and a large one too. Bears weren't prone to attack, being more likely to back away in the face of danger – unless they felt cornered. Had that been the case, a boy and dog would have been no match for it.

He climbed down from his horse and called the dog to him.

And that was when Tam padded back to where he'd faced off the bear and retrieved the dead rabbit, which he then deposited with great aplomb at his master's feet.

He knew he'd been too quick to scold Tam. He knew that although the hound was bright, he wouldn't have understood the worry his master had felt at his disappearance. In any case, it was always better to reward a dog for doing something right than to chastise it for doing something wrong. So he ruffled Tam's fur and hoped the animal had learned a lesson which would make him less likely to run off in future.

"It's all right, boy. I didn't really mean it."

His eyes moved to the rabbit's corpse.

Seeing it there, he was suddenly reminded of the times he and Will Archer had hunted for game in the woods around the farm. Sometimes, they'd camp out, skinning and cooking what they'd trapped over an open fire: rabbits, squirrels or, if they were lucky, wild turkey. Mix in a little salt, a dash of pepper, some wild onions and herbs and you had a supper fit for a king. Thinking of Will Archer brought the prick of tears to his eyes as he thought back to the events at the farm. Inevitably, that brought on a memory of the day he'd learned that his father would not be coming home.

It had been three years ago, late on a summer's evening, when a messenger had arrived at the cabin. The looks on the Archers' faces as the rider had galloped away had told him immediately that something terrible had happened. Just how terrible he was to discover when they walked with him out into the soft green meadow and under the shade of the oak tree that grew behind the cabin broke the news of his father's death at a place called Oriskany.

From that first day when his father had left him in their care, the Archers had treated him as though he was their own kin and it had seemed perfectly natural for him to refer to them as Uncle Will and Aunt Beth. The moment he knew he was an orphan the affection he felt for them had taken on an even greater resonance. The couple had come to mean as much to him as if they'd been his own parents, and for their part Will and Beth Archer could not have loved him any more than if he'd been their own son.

And now they had been taken from him, too, by evil men. He'd been made an orphan twice over.

Blinking back the tears, he picked up the dead rabbit and put it in his saddle bag; as he did so his thoughts turned to the family into whose care he'd been placed. He knew he should have told the pastor and his wife where he was going, but had he done so they'd have forbidden it. No doubt the reverend would have said that Tam was a dog who could fend for himself. He'd have left regardless, but it would have caused bad feeling.

In his search for Tam, he'd mislaid all sense of time. From the position of the sun, he reckoned it must be mid afternoon, so he'd been away for at least an hour, perhaps two. He wondered if anyone other than Libby realized that he was not with the column. If they stopped for a rest they'd notice; he usually joined them then. But they probably wouldn't be too worried – unless he wasn't back by the time it got dark.

Calling Tam to him, he turned Jonah around and the trio set off along the deer trail at a brisk pace. They had not gone far when it began to dawn on him that they might be heading the wrong way. There had been a number of places where the trail had merged with other paths and as he looked about him, he realized that nothing seemed familiar.

He stared up through the trees. The colonel was leading the column north; Will Archer had taught him that the way to find north was to position yourself so that the sun was behind your left shoulder. But when he found the sun, it wasn't where it was supposed to be. It was over his right shoulder.

He did not panic. He suddenly remembered that he had another way of working out his bearings. Twisting in his saddle he reached for the bag he'd taken from the cabin and drew out a small tobacco tin. He gazed down at it, running his fingers across the pitted lid. How could he have forgotten it? The tin had belonged to Uncle Will.

He opened it carefully. Resting inside were several objects: a spool of twine, two fish hooks, a stub of candle, a needle and thread and, wedged into a corner, a circular brass box. Closing the tin, he lifted up the box lid to reveal a two-inch diameter compass. He placed the compass in the palm of his hand, stared down at the dial and waited for the needle to settle; which it refused to do. It just kept moving back and forth, as though it couldn't make up its mind where to stop.

Frowning, he turned to his right, extended his arm and tried again, with the same result. He turned to his left. There was no change. The needle kept revolving.

*What's happening?* he wondered. *Is it broken?*

Only then did he feel the first stirrings of apprehension. He tried to recall the last time the compass had been used. It had been when he'd gone hunting with Uncle Will. There had been nothing wrong with it then, he was sure of that. He looked about him. If the compass *was* damaged, how was he going to find his way? What would Uncle Will do if *he* was here?

Will Archer had known how to navigate through the woods, using skills he'd acquired when he'd been in the army. He'd tried to pass on that knowledge. There were plants, the boy remembered, that grew on certain sides of trees. The habits of animals and birds were also useful. Spiders chose the south side to build their webs because it was the warmest, while woodpeckers dug their holes on the east side of the tree. The boy tried to recall these tips, but to his shame he was unable to. He looked at the dense forest around him, the fear growing inside him as he pictured himself frantically looking for woodpeckers and spiders as darkness fell, leaving him all alone out here with only Tam and Jonah for company.

He tried the compass again. The needle continued to gyrate rapidly. It was no use. Trying to stay calm, he placed the instrument back in the tin and returned the tin to his bag. He looked for the sun again and steered Jonah on to what he hoped was the right heading. There was path of sorts, he saw, leading off in the direction he thought he should take, but was it the right one? Would it lead him to where he needed to go?

He wondered if he should give Jonah his head, but there was no guarantee the horse would take him back to the column. Indeed, there was a strong possibility he'd head south, back to the farm, and that was the last place they should go. That was where the men had come out of the woods and killed Uncle Will and Aunt Beth.

He thought about the lieutenant and his men and how they'd helped to bury the Archers beneath the tree in the meadow, and how they'd taken care of him during the ride to the big house, treating him not as a child but as an equal. He wondered if that was because he'd killed Ephraim Smede. Would they have respected him otherwise? He didn't know the answer to that.

He remembered the smell of the man he'd hit with the axe: a combination of soiled clothing, sweat, piss and tobacco.

He thought then about Tewanias. He lifted a hand to his throat and the bone turtle that hung there on its leather cord. Lieutenant Wyatt had said it was a totem. The Mohawk chief had called it *Anowara*.

The gift had been a token of respect. The boy understood that and liked the way it made him feel inside. As he rubbed the amulet between his finger and thumb he wished Tewanias was with him, to guide him through the woods.

As he turned to check that Tam was keeping up, it occurred to him that maybe Tam could find Tewanias. What was it that Lieutenant Wyatt had said?

*You might not see us, but we'll be there.*

Maybe they were here now, close by.

He stared about him, at the trees and the late afternoon

sunlight filtering down through the gaps in the branches and the shadows that lay beyond. If he shouted, would they hear him? No sooner had the thought suggested itself than he dismissed it; there was a danger that someone or some*thing* else might hear. That bear, for instance. Will Archer had told him about the dangerous animals that roamed the forests – as well as bears, there were panthers and wildcats and wolves. A pack of wolves had killed a dog on a neighbour's farm and it had not been pretty. He didn't want to run into any of those.

And what about Indians? Archer had told him stories of the savages who'd lived in the valley before the arrival of the white men, before they had built the towns and the big Hall. They were tales told to disobedient children. Be good, or else the Indians will steal you away and turn you into slaves.

Not all Indians, he thought.

He stroked the amulet. Removing it from around his neck, he held it tightly in his hand and dismounted.

"Here, Tam," he called. "Come here, boy."

He waited as the hound trotted towards him. Squatting down, he held the totem to the dog's nose.

"Find, boy! Find Tewanias!"

The dog looked at him and wagged his tail, sniffing at the object in his fingers.

"Go seek!" he said. He cupped his hand, enclosing the amulet, pressing it to the dog's cold muzzle. "Tewanias! Go find!"

He took his hand away and waited.

The dog gazed up at him expectantly.

*It's not going to work*, he thought bleakly. *It's up to me.*

And then, as he got to his feet, Tam let out a bark and bounded away, only to stop twenty yards further down the path. Looking back, he barked again.

The boy's pulse began to race. Quickly, he remounted Jonah.

"Go, Tam!" he urged. "Go find!"

Tam turned. Nose to the ground, tail held high, he set off once more. This time it was fifty yards before he looked back. This time he did not bark, but waited patiently until the boy caught up. Then he trotted ahead again.

Hope flared in the boy when he saw that the sun was where it should be. Provided they stayed on this heading, they would be moving in the right direction.

Northwards.

"This is it," De Witt said, reining in the mare. "This is the place. There's the tree and there's the mark. You see?" He was unable to prevent the relief creeping into his voice.

Corporal Stryker looked to where the pastor was indicating.

Even with its lower branches lopped off, the oak was massive. It would have taken too much work to uproot it completely or reduce it to a stump, so judicious pruning had been the order of the day. Carved into the trunk at eye level were three gouges arranged to form the letter H. So even was the symmetry that Stryker suspected they were as much a symbol of the engineers' respect for such a worthy and indomitable specimen as they were a recognition sign for those who followed in the footsteps of the men who'd made the road. He wondered why he hadn't taken note of it the first time he'd marched past.

The search party dismounted.

Stryker tapped Fitch on the arm: "Jubal, you and Hector take the west side. Me and Dan'll take the east." Then he addressed De Witt: "You stay with the horses, Reverend. The rest of us'll see if we can pick up the boy's trail. Don't you go wanderin' off now, you hear?"

De Witt nodded solemnly.

Stryker turned to his men. "We'll split up at fifty paces; one heads north, the other south. That way, if the lad did leave the road hereabouts, we've four chances of crossin' his trail."

De Witt removed his hat and wiped his brow with a handkerchief as each pair of soldiers took their respective side of the road and stepped into the trees. As he watched them vanish, the pastor was struck by the scale of the task facing them. What if Libby had been wrong, he thought apprehensively, what if the boy hadn't left the road here but somewhere else? How would they pick up his trail then?

So his heart leapt when, after only a few minutes, he heard a whistle from within the forest over on the west side of the road. He barely had time to register the sound before he was rejoined by three of the four soldiers. Trooper Fitch, he saw, was not among them.

"Looks like Jubal's struck lucky," Stryker announced confidently. "All right, let's move."

Taking the reins of Fitch's horse along with his own, Stryker led the way. De Witt walked behind him. The other two troopers brought up the rear. They found Fitch seated on the ground with his back resting against a silver birch. His musket lay across his knees. He stood as the others drew near.

"What've you got, Jubal?" Stryker asked, his voice couched low.

Fitch indicated a set of indentations on the forest floor. "Hoof prints."

"Recent?"

Fitch pursed his lips. "Well, they ain't that old. There's been other critters through here; some of 'em came before, some of 'em after. But edges are sharp and there's not many leaves in the tracks yet, so a couple of hours, maybe."

De Witt stared down at the ground. All he could see were patches of scuffed earth amid a carpet of forest litter. "It has to be him, hasn't it?"

Stryker looked at Fitch who gave a curt nod and said, "Whoever it was, his horse was shod. I'd say it's a good chance." Fitch lifted his chin to indicate a spot a little way off. "Found some paw prints, too."

"Hound?" Stryker said.

"Aye. They ain't in a straight line neither. I'd say he was chasing something, followin' a scent most likely."

"Saw something in the bushes and left the trail to give chase," Stryker said. "That fits with what we know. All right, we'll stick with the hoof marks. They're all yours, Jubal. I'll hold your horse while you take point. Reverend, you're behind me; no talkin'."

They set off on foot, Fitch walking ahead with his eyes fixed on the trail, cradling his musket. The others followed in single file, leading the horses.

The men kept up a steady pace in pursuit of Fitch as he quartered the ground, sometimes indicating for the others to wait while he examined the path ahead, then calling them on.

After forty minutes, Fitch, who was some fifteen paces in the lead, held up his hand. They stopped.

"We've got bear scat," Fitch said.

"Oh, dear Lord," De Witt said softly. He searched the trees anxiously.

"Don't worry, Reverend," Fitch said. "It ain't that fresh."

Fitch pointed towards the splintered stump at the side of the track. To the pastor, it looked as if someone had taken an axe or a hammer to it, for it had been split open to reveal the rotten wood within. "She stopped a while; broke the stump open to get at the innards."

"She?" De Witt said.

"There's cub prints over yonder. Cubs travel with the mother. Once Papa Bear plants his seed, he don't give a shit. Leaves the sow to bring up the youngsters." Fitch studied the disembowelled tree stump, sifting through the slivers of bark that lay alongside it. "Berries ain't ripe enough to eat. She was after grubs." The tracker's expression hardened. "I got broken grass and paw prints over there an' all." Fitch indicated the ground. "Hoof marks, too."

De Witt sucked in his breath.

"No signs of a set-to, though," Fitch murmured. "The boy was damned lucky. Either she knew he was no threat to her cubs or else she wasn't in a mood for a fight because of the dog. She headed off that way." The tracker lifted his chin to indicate the direction.

"And the hoof prints?" De Witt said.

Fitch frowned. "They stopped. I'd say the horse caught her scent and decided he weren't goin' no further."

"At least one of them showed good sense," Stryker murmured.

This drew an accusing look from De Witt.

"If the boy had brains, he'd be with the column," Stryker said.

"He's twelve," De Witt said. "He was worried about his dog."

Stryker gave a shrug. "Dog would've found its way back eventually. Boy's a fool. He should've known better."

"He got off his horse," Fitch interjected, before De Witt could think of a reply. "Walked around a spell. Their tracks are mixed in, so I reckon the boy and the hound found each other." Fitch dropped on to his haunches and laid his palm across a small area of flattened leaves. "Here's where the dog lay down."

"So it *was* injured?" De Witt asked.

Fitch shook his head. "Don't reckon so. Like I said; tracks are too clean. No sign of slippin' or slidin', and there's no damage round about. If'n there was a scrap here, the ground'd be all mussed up. Ain't nothing like that. No blood trail, neither. I'd say the boy found his dog and took a rest. Stopped to get his bearings, maybe."

"Then which way'd they go?" Stryker asked.

Fitch pursed his lips. "Back."

"Back?" De Witt echoed.

"The boy got what he came for," Stryker said. "He found his dog. Now he's trying to find his way to the column."

The pastor frowned. "Wouldn't we have come across them?"

Stryker looked at Fitch.

The private shrugged and spat into the dirt. "Easy enough to take the wrong path. Shouldn't be too hard to track 'em, though."

"Sun's goin' down," Stryker observed. "Be dusk in a couple hours, dark in three."

"Best get a move on then."

They set off once more, Fitch in the lead, following the new trail.

De Witt wasn't sure how long they'd been walking or how far they had come since discovering the bear tracks when Fitch, who'd been studying the forest floor, paused, straightened and held up a hand for them to halt.

They were strung out in a line in a steep gulley, the walls of which were plaited with roots and boulders. Ferns grew thickly around them while the leafy canopy high above gave the illusion they'd entered some kind of vaulted nave. It reminded the pastor

162

of his church back on the bank of the Dadenoscara, even more so when he realized how still the woods had become. Before, he'd been aware of bird calls and the occasional clatter of wings, but when Fitch raised his hand it was as if the woods were obeying the order to be silent, too. Had a single leaf fallen, De Witt felt sure he would have heard it land.

The pastor's skin began to prickle. It was not a pleasurable sensation. He stole a glance over his shoulder. Private Hector Lyle, a lightly built man with pale blue eyes and a day's growth of beard, was directly behind him. The fourth soldier, taller with darker features, whom Stryker had called Dan, and whose last name De Witt had learnt was York, was bringing up the rear. Both troopers were looking about them warily.

"Is it the boy?" De Witt hissed. "Have we found them?"

Stryker did not reply. His eyes were on the tracker.

Wondering if Stryker had heard him, and made uneasy by the new-found alertness of the men on either side of him, the pastor was about to repeat the question when the stillness was broken by two loud clicks as Corporal Stryker and Privates Lyle and York cocked their muskets, and by the rusty-pump call of a blue jay which came suddenly from the woods to their right.

Fitch spun towards the sound.

With a whoop that turned De Witt's blood cold, a sleek brown shape dropped from the trees in front of them. Fitch did not complete his turn. The warning died in his throat as the toma-hawk blade sliced into his jugular. Blood jetted as the Indian tugged the weapon free. Stryker let go of the horses, brought his musket up and fired from the hip. The Indian fell back with a cry as another wild ululation erupted from the trees behind and a second dark-skinned figure burst into view.

Dropping his reins, Trooper York pivoted towards his attacker. With astonishing speed the Indian hooked the musket barrel away with the head of his war club, ducked and sliced the knife he was carrying in his other hand across the trooper's thigh, severing the artery. As York collapsed with a scream, the musket dropped from his grip and the club curved around again, shattering his skull.

163

Three more breech-clouted figures appeared above them. There was another sharp report and Stryker's horse toppled on to its side, legs kicking. Making a grab for the bridle of Fitch's by now terrified mount, the corporal threw his musket aside and drew a pistol from his belt. Using the horse as a shield he aimed the pistol towards the top of the bank and fired. A body toppled into the gulley.

"Behind me, Reverend!" he shouted.

Trooper Lyle yelled a warning as his friend's killer ran towards him. Ramming his musket one-handed into the Indian's chest, he squeezed the trigger. The Indian threw up his arms as he was catapulted backwards by the force of the shot. But even as Lyle's victim fell, another warrior rose from concealment. Teeth bared, he drew his arm back and with a wild shriek hurled his tomahawk at the trooper, who was frantically trying to reload his weapon.

De Witt heard Lyle grunt and go down. Spinning, he stared in horror as, in a move almost too fast to follow, the Indian sprinted forward, grabbed a knot of hair, scored the knife blade around Trooper Lyle's skull, placed his knee in the dead man's back and ripped away the bleeding scalp. Only then did he wrench the tomahawk from the dead man's chest and turn towards Trooper York's body.

Stryker, meanwhile, having discharged both his weapons, was attempting to control Fitch's horse. "Ride, Reverend! It's our only chance!"

As Stryker vaulted into the saddle, another musket cracked. Stryker's mount reared and the corporal's body pitched to the ground. Freed from restraint, the horse took off, mane flying. It did not get far. There came yet another sharp report and the animal faltered. A second shot sent it crashing to the ground, eyes rolling white in its head, dark blood frothing from its nose.

Fear lent De Witt impetus, but as he hauled himself on to the mare's back two more half-naked figures launched themselves over the lip from the opposite side of the gulley. Terrified, the pastor failed to see the new threat rising towards him.

It was only in the final second that he saw the dull gleam of steel as the sword curved towards the mare's neck. Before he could react, he felt the shock as the blade sank into flesh. Following through with the blow, the attacker darted aside as the mare staggered under the assault. With her strength gone and the artery in her neck severed, she managed only a few faltering strides before her legs gave way and she collapsed to the ground, trapping the pastor beneath her.

A chorus of excited barks greeted the tumble.

De Witt shook his head dazedly. He had lost his hat and he was covered in blood, but not his own, for the mare's heart was still pumping. He tried to move his legs but he could only feel his right one. His left was numb, pinned by the mare's weight. As she convulsed and let go her final breath, the pastor looked for Stryker and saw the corporal's bloodstained and motionless body in the dirt. Four wiry, semi-clad figures were crouched over him.

De Witt watched, helpless and in horror, as a knife rose and fell. The action was followed by a crow of triumph as a remnant of bloody scalp was brandished aloft. The pastor felt his stomach contract and his bowels turned to water when he saw their faces turn towards him.

Desperately, De Witt clawed for the opening to his saddle bag. Thrusting his hand inside, he searched for the pistol. Felt the stock beneath his fingers. His hand, though, was slick with the mare's blood. The weapon slid from his grip. He made another frantic lunge. Curling his hand more firmly around the pistol butt, he pulled the weapon out and drew back the hammer.

Blood was trickling into the corner of his eye. Half-blinded, he tried to blink it away. Through a crimson mist, he saw that the Indians were making their way towards him. They were walking slowly. Taking their time, he realized; knowing full well that he wasn't going anywhere.

One of them was holding a short sword. The blade dripped blood. De Witt knew this had to be the one who'd slit the mare's throat. The sword-holder grinned. His mouth formed a malevolent gash in his sun-darkened face. Another brave extended a finger and mimed the pulling of a trigger; taunting him, playing on his terror. A third drew a long knife from a sheath across his chest.

Raising the pistol, De Witt thought of his wife and daughter.

"Forgive me, Esther," he whispered tearfully.

Before placing the muzzle of the pistol in his mouth and pulling the trigger.

At the sound of the first shot, Wyatt raised his head. He didn't have to ask the others if they'd heard it. He knew they had, even though it was very faint; just as they all heard the succession of reports that followed it.

"Don't sound like a hunting party," Donaldson said, frowning as the firing faded away. "How far do you reckon?"

"Hard to say," Wyatt said. "Could be a mile, could be three."

"Not the column then," Billy Drew said.

Wyatt shook his head. "Too close. Besides, if they were under attack, there'd be more shooting."

"Scouts in trouble?" Jem Beddowes suggested.

"Could be," Wyatt said. "Only one way to find out."

They set off running.

It was the stench of blood that drew them to the place of ambush and the faint whiff of powder that had failed to dissipate, having been trapped by the gulley's walls. They had gauged the distance and then fanned out to cover the ground in a search pattern. Somewhat inevitably it was Tewanias – whose sense of smell had led them to the place – who discovered the first body.

The dead horse lay on its side. The blood from the wounds in its head and chest had congealed upon its hide and pooled on to the ground beneath it. The flies were already clustered thickly around the animal's eyes, nostrils, mouth and hindquarters.

The next corpse was human and was sprawled a yard or so away, a wide slit in its throat and the front part of its scalp removed. The flies were busy there as well.

"Anyone know him?" Wyatt asked, looking down at the ruined features.

The others shook their heads, their expressions grim.

They moved to the next body. The pungent odour of animal grease rose from the corpse and mingled uneasily with the smell of blood. Squatting down, Tewanias drew a finger along the single white feather attached to the corpse's scalp lock and viewed the breech-clouted remains with disgust.

"Oneniote'á:ka!" He stood and spat out the word. "Oneida! Bear clan."

"I know *this* one," Beddowes said, a resigned look on his face as he indicated the chevrons on the dead man's sleeves. "Name's Stryker. A good soldier, I heard."

Tewanias had walked on. He stopped and called softly, "Wy-att."

Wyatt turned.

Tewanias was standing over a blood-soaked corpse which lay trapped beneath one of the horses. There was a lot of injury to the dead man's skull, Wyatt saw, as he approached, which he might have put down to a killing blow from a war club had it not been for the pistol that was held loosely in the corpse's right hand. It wasn't hard to gauge the sequence of events. Then he saw who it was lying there and realized why Tewanias had summoned him over and his throat went dry.

"I got three more," Donaldson said, breaking into his thoughts. "Two white, one Indian. More dead horses, too."

Billy Drew, who'd been examining the perimeter called across, "Got one over here; an Indian. Been gut shot."

"Looks like they put up quite a fight," Donaldson said.

*Maybe not all of them*, Wyatt thought as he stared down at the pastor's corpse. He tried to imagine what he might have done, had he been in the pastor's shoes; unable to free himself and with only one loaded pistol to repel what had quite evidently been a superior number of attackers. Only a fool would have viewed the pastor's decision to take his own life as an act of cowardice. By using his own pistol, De Witt had saved himself the pain of an excruciating death, though his actions had not prevented his scalp from being taken after his demise.

At least Wyatt hoped the man had been dead when the deed had been committed. Scalping was usually carried out after death, though he'd heard of cases where someone came to, having lost consciousness during an attack, and discovered they had been mutilated in this manner.

Sickened, the Ranger turned away.

A body count revealed a total of eight dead, excluding the horses; five white men and three Indians.

*What the hell were they doing here?* Wyatt asked himself.

Had Reverend De Witt's body not been among the dead, he might have assumed, as Jem Beddowes had first supposed, that Stryker and his men were a scouting party. But scouts would have been on foot, as Wyatt and his men were, not on horseback. In the dense forests, horses were at best a hindrance and at worst a liability, requiring food and maintenance. A man on foot could travel fast and light and in a straighter line, using the terrain to his advantage.

Wyatt turned, in search of Tewanias. The Mohawk was squatting over one of the Indian dead and examining a musket he had found nearby.

"Well?" Wyatt asked.

Tewanias stood and held out the gun. "Scouts in the pay of the Yan-kees."

"They were looking for the column," Wyatt said.

Tewanias nodded.

"And their run in with Stryker and his men will have told them they're close."

The Mohawk nodded again and then frowned.

"What is it?" Wyatt asked.

"Five riders dead. But tracks say six horses."

"Six?" Wyatt said, confused. "Someone got away?"

Tewanias shook his head. "One rode through before. These men came later."

There was a pause.

"Tracking the first one, you think?"

The Mohawk shrugged. "Perhaps."

"Or he was riding point and was way in front when these five were brought down," Donaldson suggested.

Maybe, Wyatt thought, though that didn't explain what the pastor was doing there. He looked at Tewanias. "Attackers?"

Tewanias shrugged. "More than six."

"They've lost three," Wyatt indicated the half-naked corpses. "Question is, how many are left and which way did they go?"

He watched as Tewanias dropped the gun to re-examine the ground around the perimeter of the ambush. "Well?" he asked when the Mohawk returned.

"Four go north," Tewanias said, indicating with his chin.

Wyatt followed the Mohawk's gaze.

"And one goes south."

*Damn it*, Wyatt thought. He turned back. "You're sure?"

"Ea. Yes."

"What's that mean?" Billy Drew asked.

Wyatt sighed. "They've sent a runner to tell the main force coming behind that they've picked up the trail."

The Mohawk stayed silent.

"That's why they killed the horses. They didn't want them returning to the column. The colonel sees riderless horses, he knows the enemy's discovered them."

"God damned bastards," Billy Drew said.

Wyatt offered no dissent. "They made a mistake though. If they hadn't killed Stryker's party, we might not have found out they were here. Now we're going to be on their trail, and that gives us the upper hand."

All save Tewanias looked at him.

"Why'd they do this?" Billy Drew asked, staring round at the carnage. "They could've let them ride by, carried on trailing the column. Then no one would be any the wiser."

"Like you said, they're bastards," Wyatt muttered. "Or maybe Stryker picked up their trail and was closing in on *them*. Maybe they saw a way to turn the tables."

*Which still didn't explain the pastor's role.*

Wyatt turned to Tewanias. "The Runner. Can you catch him?"

Tewanias rewarded him with a look, saying nothing.

*Stupid question*, Wyatt thought. "All right. You catch him and you kill him before he can report back."

A gleam shone briefly in the Mohawk's eyes.

"We'll go after the rest," Wyatt told the others. "They know the column is somewhere ahead. They'll be cautious till they have it in sight. That'll give us a chance to make up the ground."

"What about the bodies?" Billy Drew asked. "We going to leave them like this?"

"Have to, Billy," Beddowes said heavily. "Don't have time to do any burying."

"Jem's right," agreed Wyatt. "We've no choice. No telling how close the opposition is, given they've sent their Oneida scouts in here. They find five graves and they're going to figure out that we know they're here. I'd rather we kept the advantage. It might just give us an edge, providing they don't pick up *our* tracks."

"Don't seem right, just leaving them," Donaldson said. He looked at Wyatt. "I'd like to say a few words, Lieutenant, if'n we've got time. I'd feel better about it."

Wyatt read each of their faces in turn and the message in their eyes. They were good men. They knew it could just as easily have been one of them lying there and they were thinking, if that had been the case, they'd have appreciated a prayer to mark their passing. He gave the go ahead.

As Donaldson reached into his pocket for his bible, Wyatt turned to Tewanias. "We'll see you back at the column."

Wordlessly, Tewanias handed Wyatt his musket. By the time Donaldson had his hat off and the bible open in his hand, the Mohawk had already slipped away into the woods.

Weariness was setting in.

It had been hard to judge exactly how much time had elapsed since he'd shown Tam the amulet and asked the dog to follow its nose. He knew only that the late afternoon sun was now well beyond the trees and before long it would be sunset. Soon it would be too dark for him to find his way and he would have to find somewhere to bed down for the night. The last time he'd camped out had been the previous summer and he'd had Will Archer for company. This time he had Tam and Jonah. Neither of them could talk, but it was better than being alone.

And at least it was warm, so there would be no need to build a shelter; he could make do with the blanket beneath Jonah's saddle. He knew how to build a fire; along with the tobacco tin he had a tinderbox, another legacy of the times he and Archer had spent together. Uncle Will had told him that if he was ever in the woods he should always carry the tools to make a flame. Fire provided warmth and a defence against predators. More importantly, when you were lost and alone, it raised the spirits. It meant you'd won your first battle against the wilderness.

So, if he could get a fire lit, it would be a start.

His thoughts were interrupted by the sound of gunfire. Had he been alone, he would have struggled to tell which direction the sounds had come from, but Tam had turned his head half a second before the first shot even sounded, as if he'd anticipated the event. During the series of reports that followed, his focus did not waver.

"You hear that, lad? It's the column! It must be!" Suddenly, he didn't feel so afraid.

Picking up on the excitement in the boy's voice, the dog wagged its tail.

The shots had come from a long way off, but gunfire signified people, which told him, if he discounted his horse and his dog, that he was no longer alone in the woods. That was enough to send a wave of relief coursing through him.

It was most likely a hunting party, he reasoned, sent out by the colonel to secure meat for the evening halt. He looked about him. Despite the density of the forest canopy there was still light beneath the trees. If he let Tam take the lead, there was every chance he'd be able to find his way back to the line, or at least cover most of the distance before it got too dark. With luck, it wouldn't be long before he'd be close enough to see the cooking fires and they would guide him the last few yards.

Encouraged by that possibility, he cast aside all thoughts of finding a place to sleep and instead, with Tam running ahead of him, nose to the trail, he set off towards the source of the gunshots.

\* \* \*

Tewanias had settled into a comfortable loping gait, unencumbered by the weight of his musket; his war club was strapped firmly across his back. He was breathing easily and, save for the soft pad of his moccasin-shod feet on the forest floor and the swish of his ammunition pouch against his hip, he produced no extraneous sounds as he ran.

Tracking a man through dense woodland was notoriously difficult. Fortunately, the Oneida scout was making no attempt to conceal his spoor. Neither, to judge from the length of his stride, was he moving at full stretch. His pace was that of a man hurrying while trying to conserve energy, a rate of progress that suggested he had some distance to cover. Whatever his motive, it made him easy to follow, despite the fact that he was not forging his own path through the brush but retracing the steps he and his scouting party had taken in their outward journey.

Tewanias had gauged the measure of the Oneida's stride at the start. In so doing he was able to calculate where each succeeding footfall would land. He could keep up the chase without pausing constantly to take stock.

Whether the prey was human or animal, unless it was something big and heavy it was rare for a pristine imprint to be left behind, even in the softest soil. If the hunter was chasing a man, there might be the hint of a depression to indicate where his quarry had pushed off to take his next step or, if not that, then perhaps a small patch of flattened earth where the texture of the surface had been altered by a weight pressing down upon it. But it was seldom that convenient. Other peripheral signs therefore took precedence: a crushed flower, or a stone that had been dislodged on the path, or a branch bent back by a careless body moving past. Meaningless to those without the skill to understand what they were seeing, but as prominent as milestones to someone with the required knowledge.

Streams and rivers presented the biggest challenge. Tracking in water was well nigh impossible, so one had to scan the banks for signs: a broken cat-tail, a bent reed or, in the case of the Oneida scout, a muddy palm print that showed where the runner had forded the stream, slipped, and used a hand to steady himself as he emerged from the current and regained his footing.

At the sight of the print, Tewanias halted. The mud was still damp, which told him that he had almost closed the gap. He wondered if the man he was chasing was a stranger to the woods or familiar with them. Though the Oneida lands lay far to the west, beyond Te-non-at-che, the river that flowed through the mountains, it was likely that in the times before the Six Nations had been divided by the war – when the Oneida and the Tuscarora had chosen to side with the Americans – the runner had hunted in these mountains and therefore knew the hidden as well as the main trails.

That was not the only reason Tewanias was cautious. The Stone People – as the Oneida were known by the tribes within the Six Nations – had been given that name by their enemies. Legend had it that if they knew they were being pursued, the Oneida could transform themselves into rocks to escape capture.

Tewanias hoped that wasn't an omen. His hand moved to his neck, only for it to pause when he remembered that he had presented his totem to the boy. *No matter*, he thought. *The Oneida were spineless dogs and no match for a war chief of the Kanien'kehá:ka, the Eaters of Men.*

He remained still, senses alert, listening to the chatter of the forest as the water flowed swift and clear about his feet. Around him, rocks and boulders had formed a pattern of natural bridges and weirs, over which the stream tumbled in a series of shallow, silvery cascades.

Nothing appeared untoward. About to move off, however, his eyes were suddenly drawn to a clump of snakeroot by the side of the path ahead. He paused.

There was a patch of damp earth at the base of the plant. Tewanias sniffed the air. There was something else present, too: the pungent odour of human piss. He slipped the war club from his back, knowing, even as he did so, that he had profoundly underestimated his enemy's guile. The palm print had been placed there not by accident but by design.

Sensing movement at the perimeter of his vision, he pivoted

just in time to see a dark human form rise up on the opposite bank, accompanied by a thrumming sound as a slender metal object whickered across the narrow stream, sunlight glancing off the spinning blade.

Jerking his head aside, he felt the displacement of air across his skin as the hatchet flicked past his cheek and thudded into the tree beside his ear, scattering bark chips like rain.

There was no time to dwell on how or when the Oneida runner had discovered he was being stalked. Just as Tewanias had drawn upon the signs and sounds of the woods to aid him in his tracking, so the Oneida scout must have used the same resources to detect his enemy's presence and bait a trap to ensnare him.

The sound of the musket shot was flat and loud. The ball struck Tewanias on his right side; punching him backwards. The war club fell from his grasp.

Then he was dropping, too.

Not a spineless dog after all, Tewanias thought, as he hit the water. Through a haze of pain he saw the Oneida leap from the bank with a howl and hurtle across the stream towards him. Dressed in cloth kilt and leggings, with a single feather woven into his tufted hair, one half of his face coloured red, the other half black, the Oneida was painted for war. His right hand gripped the hilt of a short, broad-bladed sword; his left, a military-issue carbine.

Ignoring the pain, Tewanias scrabbled vainly for the knife at his waist.

With a savage yell, the Oneida raised his sword above his head and drove it down towards Tewanias's throat. Tewanias rolled, felt the kiss of the blade as it ripped through the skin of his upper arm, heard the clang as the sword glanced off the rock beside his head. He slashed his knife towards his attacker's thigh and heard an exhalation of pain as the blade parted the Oneida's flesh. But the speed of his opponent's reaction told him that he had inflicted only superficial damage. The Oneida twisted aside and slammed the butt of his carbine down towards Tewanias's knife hand, trapping it against the rocks on the bed of the stream. As he raised the sword, his mouth split into a grin of triumph.

Pinned and unable to move his arm, his blood darkening the stream, Tewanias launched a kick towards the Oneida's crotch. He saw the Oneida wince as his moccasined foot made contact, but he knew it had been a pitiful effort. Staring up at his opponent, at the murderous expression on the red-and-black face, he waited for the death blow to fall.

Savouring the moment, the Oneida drew back his sword, grinned again and thrust downwards.

And his right eye exploded.

The sword blade missed Tewanias's throat by a hair's breadth as the Oneida's corpse slumped sideways, the smile still affixed. Released from the weight on his wrist, Tewanias pulled his arm free and stared in disbelief at the body draped across him and at the blood trickling from the ruined eye socket and skull. As the echo of the shot died away, he pushed the dead man from him and raised himself out of the water, blood dripping from his wounds.

*Wy-att*, he thought immediately.

Then he heard the bark. Thinking that the runner had not been alone, he reached for the dropped war club, his eyes searching the bank for the source of the sound. And then his eyes widened in surprise.

Above him on the bank was a large dog. Standing in front of the dog, feet in the water, gazing down at him with a questioning look in his blue-grey eyes was a slim, dark-haired boy holding a discharged army pistol.

# 7

*December 1812*

It was approaching noon and although the day had turned surprisingly mild, a bank of low cloud to the north-west implied that rain was a possibility as Hawkwood and Lawrence rode their tired mounts into Fort Edward.

Located close to marshland on a bend on the east side of the river, there was little to distinguish the settlement from any of the other unprepossessing villages they'd ridden through that morning; a couple of dozen houses, an assortment of clapboard-fronted stores, a brace of scruffy-looking taverns, a livery stable and a small, white-painted church abutting a cemetery fringed by alder bushes.

There was no fort, despite the name, though there had been one once. The coach-office clerk in Albany had drawn attention to its pedigree when he'd referred Hawkwood to his choice of north-bound post roads. Originally a stockade and trading post and strengthened during the French and Indian War, it had been used as a training camp for British irregulars and a base from which to launch cross-border raids against Quebec. Last manned during the Revolution but then vacated, all the military buildings were long gone, worn away by neglect. Now, where stone bastions and gun batteries had once stood guard over river and wetland, there were only grassy mounds and a weed-filled dry moat. From the look of the local architecture, it wasn't hard to guess where most of the foundations had ended up.

They had set off before dawn. Only the landlord and a sleepy stable boy had witnessed their departure. Asking after their destination, the landlord had merely wished them a safe journey when Hawkwood revealed that they were on their way to Bennington, Vermont. Judging by the landlord's manner, the enquiry was merely for the sake of conversation. Hawkwood suspected that any answer would have sufficed; nevertheless he took the opportunity to wrong-foot any pursuers that might turn up at the tavern asking awkward questions with a misdirection.

Mindful that they would be travelling in daylight, they had agreed that it would be best to proceed at a steady, unhurried pace rather than attract attention. But once on the road, they'd discovered that the landlord had been correct in his prediction that they would encounter little traffic at this time of year. Apart from the occasional farm cart, they had the highway to themselves. So wherever the terrain permitted they urged their mounts onward at the gallop.

Eventually the speed they had been maintaining, combined with the state of the roads, began to take its toll. Realizing that the horses needed rest, Hawkwood called a halt at the next settlement they came to. Not that he wasn't glad of the excuse to take a break; it had been six months since he'd last ridden and the past two days had brought into play muscles that he'd forgotten he possessed. Aches were starting to appear in all sorts of inconvenient places.

Lawrence, on the other hand, seemed to be suffering no adverse effects. He'd proved he was at home in the saddle during their escape from the cantonment. When they'd first met back in London, the major hadn't looked the equestrian sort, but appearances were often deceptive. No doubt Lawrence's skills had been well-honed during his time in Spain, negotiating the high winding trails of the Sierra de Guadarrama. Traversing New York State must seem positively sedentary by comparison.

Leaving the horses at a livery stable to be fed and watered, they made their way to the nearest tavern. As he followed Lawrence into the smoky interior, there hovered at the back of Hawkwood's mind the knowledge that, by now, word of the events at Greenbush was sure to be radiating outwards like the ripples in a pool, spread not just by military personnel but by the civilian population as well. In all likelihood, descriptions of the prisoner and the individual who'd aided his escape were already circulating, possibly by poster bill, so the sooner they were on the road again, the better. But while their mounts enjoyed the respite, it made sense for Hawkwood and Lawrence to make use of the facilities as well, providing they kept their wits about them and didn't linger too long.

Ignoring the seats by the fire and the communal dining table, they chose a table on its own, close to the front window, from where they could view the street and at the same time observe the rest of the room.

A waiter, sleeves rolled to the elbow and wiping his hands on a greasy apron, materialized out of the gloom. "What'll it be, gentlemen?"

"Rye," Hawkwood said, "and whatever's on the board."

The slate upon which the daily fare was scrawled was too far away to be read clearly through the dinginess and the tobacco fumes.

"There's venison stew, roast potatoes and carrots."

"So long as it's hot," Hawkwood said.

The response was a dry sniff. "Should be; been on the stove since Tuesday."

As Hawkwood tried to remember what day it was, Lawrence grinned. "With luck, the whiskey'll hide the taste," he murmured as the waiter left with their order. There was no rancour in the remark. Both of them had long experience of making do when food was scarce; on the march, a day-old stew would have been considered a veritable banquet.

Two glasses arrived, along with an earthenware jug from which the waiter poured two liberal measures before leaving them to it. Lawrence took a tentative sip. "Well, it ain't Bowmore's." Adding

179

with a sly wink while raising his glass in a mock toast, "Any port in a storm, though, eh?"

The major rested his drink and unbuttoned his coat. A plain brown jacket, purchased from a general merchandise store in Fort Miller, a village eight miles south of Fort Edward, had replaced his scarlet tunic. The tunic was tucked away in a knapsack similar to Hawkwood's that had been bought at the same establishment. Lawrence planned to re-don the scarlet when they got to the border, as a precaution against being used for target practice by an over-enthusiastic British piquet.

Hawkwood was again clad in his own clothes. While the stolen uniform had served its purpose, now he needed no disguise beyond a mud-splattered coat and boots. With no distinguishing facings to draw the eye, they were just two more road-weary travellers in search of a drink and a meal, and thus no different to anyone else in the room.

The food turned out to be surprisingly good. When they finished, they pushed their empty plates to one side and Hawkwood surveyed the room over the rim of his glass. The tavern was enjoying a brisk trade and no one had given them a second glance. He considered stretching his legs and then decided it was probably best not to get too comfortable.

"Damn it," Lawrence muttered.

Hawkwood followed his gaze. Spots of rain were hitting the window.

The waiter returned for the empty plates. About to bear them away, he paused. "Would you gentlemen be heading north, by any chance?"

Hawkwood tensed. He felt Lawrence do the same. The question, however, had been rhetorical; without waiting for a reply, the waiter indicated the droplets of water running down the window pane. "If'n you are, you're in for a delay. There's no road the far side of Glens Falls. Bridge is down and the mud's axle-deep. There's wagons been stuck there half a day, they say, backed up through to Caldwell. Some folks have been taking the Whitehall road. If the ferry's in service, it'll take you to

180

Ticonderoga. Quicker'n the road, that's fer sure. You'll be able to pick up the highway from there."

The waiter gave another nod in the direction of the window. "Thought I'd mention it, seein' as the rain's settin' in and we've run out of rooms." He allowed himself a crooked grin before adding, "Now, anything else I can get you? 'Nother whiskey or a beverage? Coffee pot's clean – cook scrubbed it this morning."

"We'll take the coffee," Hawkwood told him, digesting the information about the disruption to traffic. That would explain why they'd encountered no south-bound coaches during their ride. "We'll settle the account, too."

"Whitehall?" Lawrence murmured when the waiter had departed. "If that's not an omen, I don't know what is."

It was time to bring out the reading-room map. Waiting until the coffee and the bill had been delivered, Hawkwood pulled the folded page from his pocket. Lawrence drew his chair closer.

Hawkwood found Albany and traced the river north, up the shepherd's-crook squiggle that was the Hudson River. Lake George and Lake Champlain were represented by two parallel, dark-coloured elongated shapes that resembled claw marks.

"There." Hawkwood tapped the paper.

Whitehall lay at the southern tip of Lake Champlain. Above it was a small anchor.

"Ticonderoga's here." Hawkwood indicated a point a quarter of the way up Champlain, where the two bodies of water appeared to touch.

Lawrence stared thoughtfully at the illustration. "It's a risk, it being a naval base but Whitehall *is* close to Vermont."

"On the border, or as near as."

A border which ran north, bisecting Lake Champlain's entire length all the way to the Canadian line.

Lawrence said, "I'm told the good citizens of Vermont don't have quite the same enthusiasm for the war as other easterners. Have you heard that?"

Hawkwood nodded.

"So it could suit us very well."

"You mean if we're discovered they may offer us sanctuary?"

"It's possible. Worth thinking about, anyway."

There was some merit to this, Hawkwood thought, though the idea of throwing themselves upon the mercy of the local populace on the off chance they'd be of a Federalist persuasion wasn't the most sensible reason for a making a detour, the possibility shouldn't be discounted.

"How far is it?" Lawrence asked.

"Hard to tell; this map's bloody useless." Hawkwood tried to bring the coach-office map to mind. "Twenty miles; maybe a bit more."

Lawrence's head lifted. His eyes took on a shine. "If our friend in the apron's right and the road's not in too bad a state, we could be there tonight."

Hawkwood thought about the ferry. Although he'd just spent a month at sea, he'd never felt entirely at ease on water. He preferred solid ground beneath his feet to the rolling of waves. And lake waters could get very choppy. And Lake Champlain was a very big lake.

But Whitehall to Ticonderoga by way of Champlain couldn't be *that* great a distance and, with their intended road now blocked, it made sense to at least consider the alternatives.

After all, there was the first rule of evasion to consider:

Moving targets were harder to hit.

"Well, this is jolly," Lawrence said.

The major was being sarcastic; it wasn't jolly at all. It was anything but.

They were Whitehall-bound. The cloudburst, which had begun as soon as they'd left the tavern, had stopped after just thirty minutes. Unfortunately it had done its damage, turning the already muddy road into a fetlock-deep sludge that threatened not only to suck the shoes from the horses' hooves but the hooves themselves from the horses' legs. The going had not been easy.

There were two ways of getting to Whitehall from Fort Edward, the boy at the livery stable had told them. The first was to stay on the post road as far as Kingsbury then turn east at the Whitehall sign. The alternative route was to take the fork to Fort Ann and join the Kingsbury to Whitehall road there. As the latter promised to shave at least four miles off their journey, it had seemed the sensible option, but Hawkwood was now wondering if the shortcut was worth the bother, because he was staring at the object that had caught Lawrence's attention.

The road between Fort Edward and Fort Ann was military in origin, as evidenced by its construction, which in several stretches consisted of hundreds of cut-down trees laid side by side to form corduroy causeways. It was a means by which vehicles and cannon could be transported over soft soil and marshland and one with which both Hawkwood and Lawrence were very familiar. Unfortunately, these causeways had succumbed to the ravages of time and it didn't take a genius to understand why coaches preferred to take the long way round. Many of the logs had rotted away, leaving chasms wide enough to swallow wheels and break the axles of even the stoutest wagon or gun carriage. And vehicles weren't the only casualties: discoloured bones littered the underbrush at the side of the road, the remains of beasts of burden that had suffered broken legs.

It was a horse's skull, complete with a bullet hole where the animal had been put out of its misery, that had prompted Lawrence's comment. The skull was resting on a shattered wagon wheel and the image was so symmetrical it had obviously been placed there as a warning to others. Both men dismounted.

"Bloody engineers." Lawrence shook his head in mock disgust. "Couldn't build a chicken coop if their lives depended on it, never mind a road."

"It's done well to have lasted this long," Hawkwood said. "It must be sixty years since these logs were laid down."

"You think it's going to be like this all the way to Whitehall?" Lawrence frowned pensively as he surveyed what had started out as a sturdy, solid surface but which now resembled a wooden jetty that had lost an argument with a mud slide.

"We've come too far to turn back. We'll have to walk them."

"It'll slow us down, which is a bugger."

"Can't be helped." Hawkwood patted his horse's neck and eyed the skull. "I'd hate to have to waste a horse *and* a bullet."

"The lad said it was eight miles to Fort Ann," said Lawrence, gazing into the distance. "There can't be more than a couple of miles to go." Drawing himself up, he gave a wry grin. "Ah, well, they do say that exercise is good for the soul."

They led their mounts into the trees, where they were relieved to discover that a secondary trail had already been created, a sign that they weren't the first travellers to have abandoned the log road in favour of a safer course. Although the ground was still exceedingly boggy, it wasn't as treacherous as the causeway. Invigorated by the improved conditions, they set off along the trail, boots and hooves squelching in harmony.

It might have been the familiar scent of the woods or the snatches of remembered birdsong that triggered the recollection, Hawkwood would never know, but it was so sudden and so vivid that he felt his breath catch.

In his mind's eye he saw a twelve-year-old boy lost in a forest wilderness, surrounded by shadows. Whether the shadows were cast by men or beasts, he did not know. He could not make out details. He knew only that some were friend and some were foe and that his life depended on being able to tell the difference.

A nuthatch squawked. Jolted from his reverie, he found that Lawrence was gazing at him with a look of amused enquiry.

"A penny for them," the major said amiably.

Hawkwood forced a smile. Lawrence, sensing his comment had hit a nerve, did not press him, a courtesy for which Hawkwood was grateful.

After a further hour's trudging, the ground grew firmer and the trail widened out. They remounted.

Fort Ann lay beyond the next belt of woodland. Reaching the village, they found there was no fort there either, though a few isolated pine stumps from the original stockade remained. A sprawling farmhouse, a couple of barns and a timber mill occupied the site.

By now it was late afternoon. Keen to make up for lost time, they pressed on. By the time the lights of Whitehall finally appeared it was early evening and Hawkwood felt as if he'd just travelled two hundred miles instead of twenty.

"Well, whoever named this place certainly had a sense of humour," murmured Lawrence as the town took shape before them. "Whitehall, indeed! I'll wager they've never been within a thousand miles of Horse Guards."

Hawkwood couldn't fault Lawrence's pithy observation. Crouched at the bottom of a gorge and dwarfed by the steep slopes that surrounded it, the New York version of Whitehall was as far removed from its London namesake as it was possible to get.

The only similarity was its proximity to a river. Having followed the course of this particular waterway since Fort Edward, where it had begun life as an insignificant tributary of the Hudson, Hawkwood and Lawrence had been well-placed to observe its changing character. In some stretches it had over-reached its banks to create patches of soggy marshland, hence the causeways; from Fort Ann, it had meandered on its way before finally arriving at Whitehall as a sluggish, sixty-yard-wide creek that skirted the village on its eastern flank before emptying into a small harbour basin at the base of a precipitous limestone outcrop.

They tethered the horses and retrieved their knapsacks. Lawrence slipped the musket strap over his shoulder. "Another town, another tavern," he intoned, glancing at the weathered sign creaking a few feet above his head. Sotto voce, he added, "Y'know, for two gentlemen on the run, we seem to be spending an inordinate amount of time in plain sight."

It was hard to disagree. While they were ahead of the hounds, they were far from safe and every time they engaged somebody in conversation they left a trail, placing themselves in jeopardy.

On the other hand, they needed information and taverns were prime sources for that. If they wanted to get home it was a risk they had to take.

"Where will we find the ferry office?" Hawkwood posed the question casually when the pot-man arrived with a brace of whiskies.

"The landing. It's over the bridge; other side of the creek."

*As easy as that.*

"Though it'd be a waste of a walk," the pot-man added as he placed the drinks on the table. "It's closed."

Lawrence reached for his glass. "Would you know when it opens?"

"I would not. An' I doubt anyone else does, either."

*An odd comment*, Hawkwood thought.

"How so?" Lawrence enquired innocently.

"Because there ain't no ferry service, that's how so."

Lawrence's smile remained fixed. "Since when?"

"A month back. Suspended due to the hostilities. The military went and commandeered all large vessels, includin' the *Vermont*. Services required elsewhere, so they said. Whatever that means."

The *Vermont*, Hawkwood assumed, being the name of the ferry.

"And there's nothing else?" Lawrence asked.

"The old schooner ain't due back fer a week."

*As opposed to the new schooner?* Hawkwood thought, but didn't say. Presumably, the new one had ended up under military control along with the other "large" vessels.

"That's our only choice?" Lawrence asked.

The pot-man's face soured "Rumour has it they'll be commandeerin' her as well. Batteaux'll be the only things left, I shouldn't wonder."

Lawrence frowned. "Batteaux?"

"Military took charge of the shipyard, too. Been building fleets of 'em. Workin' day and night. Been hard sleepin' sometimes on account of the hammerin'."

"I can imagine," Lawrence said. He glanced towards Hawkwood and raised an eyebrow over the top of his glass.

Hawkwood knew the major was making a direct translation from the French; after all, what else would they be building in a shipyard if not boats?

The pot-man, his store of relevant information exhausted, took Lawrence's comment as his cue to depart and moved off in search of another table. As soon as he was out of earshot,

Hawkwood explained to the major that an American "batteau" was a shallow-draught craft constructed primarily for river usage. The smallest could be operated by one man, while the largest needed half a dozen oarsmen and could carry up to ten tons of cargo. In the colonies, they had been deployed by the military to transport troops and supplies through the wilderness.

"That's a bugger." Lawrence sighed. "Seems we were sold a pup. Maybe we should retire to Fort Edward and shoot that damned waiter."

"Not until I've finished my drink."

"Looks as though it's the border and the Vermont road, then," Lawrence ventured.

Hawkwood did not reply. Lifting his glass, he rotated it gently, watching as the contents swirled, catching the candle light.

"I know that look – I recognize it from our London adventure." Lawrence lowered his own glass and leaned close. "What's on your mind?"

Hawkwood gazed into the glass. "Jago's first rule of commerce."

"I'm not with you."

"A friend of mine, Nathaniel Jago – first-class sergeant and former member of the smuggling fraternity. He has a saying: 'Never let political differences get in the way of turning a profit.'"

"How does that help us?"

"There may be an alternative to the Vermont road."

Lawrence looked sceptical. "You're not proposing we wait a week for the schooner to return? We can't tarry that long. It'd be asking for trouble."

"I agree. And there's bad weather on the way, too. The last thing we want is to be snowed in here."

Lawrence baulked at the thought. "It'll be that bad?"

"You can count on it."

"So what do you propose?"

Hawkwood smiled. "Finish your drink, Major. I do believe it's time for a refill."

"Oh Lord," Lawrence groaned, as Hawkwood raised his arm to summon the pot-man. "There's that bloody look again."

\*     \*     \*

"Remus Stagg?" Hawkwood said.

The heavy-set man seated alone in the booth at the back of the taproom made no reply. Instead, tearing a crust from the loaf by his elbow, he squeezed the bread between his fingers and dipped it into the small pool of gravy that had settled at the bottom of his otherwise empty plate. When the bread had been soaked to his satisfaction he delivered it to his waiting mouth. Chewing deliberately for several seconds he swallowed, wiped his lips with a none-too-clean napkin and reached for the glass at his elbow. Only then did he look up.

"Who's askin'?"

"I'm Smith," said Hawkwood, before jerking a thumb at Lawrence. "He's Jones."

"That so?" The seated man made no attempt to hide his scepticism.

"Well, it'll do for the time being," Hawkwood said evenly.

Stagg's right eyebrow rose. He stared hard at the two men, calculating whether or not they constituted a threat. Deciding they didn't – at least not immediately – he said in a gravelled voice, "So? You want somethin'?"

"We're looking for a passage north."

"Are you? An' what makes you think I give a rat's ass?"

Hawkwood ignored the riposte. He knew it was Stagg's way of letting them know who was king of the castle.

"We arrived too late for the ferry. When we asked around for any captains preparing to depart who might be willing to take on a couple of passengers, your name was mentioned."

"Was it now?" Stagg's expression changed from irritation at having his supper interrupted to instant suspicion. "An' who by?"

"Sorry, can't help you there; didn't catch the fellow's name. We were in one of the other taverns. Not even sure which one now."

Stagg's gaze flickered past Hawkwood and round the edge of the booth, probing the taproom's darker nooks. His eyes narrowed as they alighted on the pot-man who'd served Hawkwood and Lawrence, and who was moving furtively towards the kitchen with a tray of leftovers and dirty plates. Watching until the pot-man had disappeared from view, he

188

turned back. "Sorry, Mr . . . Smith, was it? 'Fraid you were misinformed."

"That's a pity." Hawkwood shared a glance with Lawrence and shrugged. "Looks like we'll have to take our business elsewhere."

He'd chosen the word on purpose. "Business" suggested there was money to be made. He watched as a spark of interest glowed briefly in the other man's eyes.

Lawrence, who had been watching for it, too, said quickly: "Allow us to stand you a drink anyway, Captain. Call it recompense for disturbing you. It's the least we can do."

Stagg hesitated.

*Come on*, Hawkwood thought. *Come on.*

Stagg considered the offer for all of two more heartbeats before tipping back his head and draining his glass in a single swallow. "I'll take a whiskey."

Catching the eye of a passing servant girl, Lawrence pointed to Stagg's empty glass and held up three fingers.

The girl glanced towards Stagg, as if seeking his approval. Stagg nodded obliquely. As she picked up the glass along with the dirty plate and cutlery, Hawkwood and Lawrence slid into the booth and took their seats.

Hawkwood waited a couple of seconds before leaning forward. "If you can't help us, Captain, is there anyone you can recommend? We'd make it worth their while."

They fell silent as the girl returned. Setting the fresh glasses down, she looked hesitantly in Stagg's direction. "Will there be anything else?"

"Aye," Stagg said. "You can tell Cooter I'll be wanting a word with him later."

Although he'd spoken firmly rather than sharply, the girl blanched. Giving a quick nod, she hurried towards the kitchen.

Cooter must be the pot-man, Hawkwood surmised; he wondered what chastisement would be meted out when the luckless fellow attended Stagg's summons. Evidently the bullish seaman ruled the roost hereabouts, using the tavern as a handy niche from which to conduct business and dispense justice or largesse to his acolytes. He'd probably had his eye on Hawkwood and Lawrence from the moment they'd entered and had seen them engage the pot-man in conversation.

"A toast –" Hawkwood raised his drink – "to private enterprise."

"Ha!" Lawrence grinned. "I'll drink to that!"

Stagg said nothing, though Hawkwood could see the man's mind working as he reached for his whiskey. After taking a swallow, he sat in silence, toying with his glass. His hands were big and strong, well suited to hauling rope or, as was just as likely, dealing out recrimination. Finally he looked up. "How far north?"

There was a cautious silence which stretched for several seconds.

"As far as we can go," Hawkwood replied.

"You do *know* there's a war on?" Stagg said.

"So we've heard. Is that a problem?"

"To some." Stagg took another swig.

*But not to you*, Hawkwood thought.

Stagg put down his drink but kept a hold of it. "It'll cost you."

"We were expecting that," Lawrence said. "But as Mr Smith mentioned; we'd see our pilot was well . . . compensated."

Stagg studied what remained of his whiskey. Then he raised his head. "*How* well?"

"Are we to take it you've changed your mind?" Hawkwood asked.

As if giving the matter further consideration, Stagg continued to stare at his glass, his lips pursed in concentration. Then he said, "Depends. How were you plannin' on payin'?"

"Coin of the realm," Hawkwood said. "Naturally."

"Spanish or American?"

Hawkwood shrugged. "Either. Or guineas. Take your pick."

At the mention of guineas, Stagg began to nibble the inside of his lower lip. Hawkwood knew then that they had him on the hook.

"Could be I'm open to persuasion," Stagg said eventually.

"Wouldn't be a pleasure cruise, mind. *Snake* ain't built to take passengers. We usually deal in . . . dry goods."

"We've no baggage," Lawrence said, "save what we're carrying. We wouldn't take up a lot of room."

"How *much* persuasion?" Hawkwood asked.

"We are talking about the border, yes?"

Prevarication, Hawkwood decided, was pointless. "We are."

Stagg held Hawkwood's gaze. His eyes took on a nefarious glint. "Fifty dollars would cover it."

Lawrence gasped. Fifty dollars was a monstrous sum, an outrageous sum. Hawkwood managed not to betray any reaction, but in his mind's eye he saw a poster at the steamboat landing in Albany advertising fares to New York at seven dollars. Whitehall to the Canadian border was roughly the same distance.

"Good God, man!" Lawrence protested with a smile. "We're not after buying your damned boat. We only want to charter it."

"That'll be each," Stagg said.

The smile slid from Lawrence's face.

Hawkwood shook his head. "Too rich for our blood. We'll leave it. Best if we try elsewhere."

"Good luck with that," Stagg said. "There's not another Whitehall boat'll carry you."

"How come?"

"No one moves cargo out of the basin without my say so, be it human or freight. 'Course, you could always hang around for a week and wait for the schooner to dock, but something tells me you're after an earlier departure. Ain't my place to enquire why that should be. Your reasons are your own." The corner of Stagg's mouth lifted again. "Which is why it'll cost you fifty dollars . . . each."

There was a long pause.

"Twenty-five," Hawkwood said. "Each."

Stagg shook his head in what appeared to be genuine amusement. "By God, I do like a man with a sense of humour, Mr Smith. I surely do. But, please – that's perilously close to a personal insult."

"Really?" Hawkwood said. "And there was I thinking it was

more than generous. After all, it's not as though we'd be your *only* cargo, is it? It's not as though you'd be making a special run, right?"

Stagg stared at him.

"And as this *is* a private transaction, it'd be just between us and you. No other crew involved. That's fifty dollars in your hand. Free and clear."

*Which is what we'll be*, he thought as he left the phrase hanging. *If the bugger agrees.*

There was another, longer silence.

"Seventy," Stagg said eventually.

"Sixty," Hawkwood countered, thinking: *God save us. That's more than three months' salary for a Runner!*

Stagg gazed into his drink as if turning things over in his mind. His fingers played against the side of the glass like a flautist covering the stops. Finally, he looked up and with a show of reluctance that didn't fool anyone, he announced, "All right, Mr . . . Smith. Seeing as you *did* stand me a whiskey, you've just bought yourselves passage."

"Excellent," Hawkwood said. "When?"

Rising, Stagg drained his glass and set it down on the table. "Happens you're in luck. We cast off at midnight. Harbour basin, end jetty. You got the name? She's called *Snake*."

"I remember," Hawkwood confirmed. "We'll be there."

"Best not be late, else you *will* be waitin' for the schooner."

They watched him walk away.

"I'll be damned," Lawrence said, stunned by the speed of the final transaction. He turned to Hawkwood and raised his glass. "Looks as if we *are* on our way home."

Hawkwood smiled. "What did I tell you, Major? First rule of commerce. Works every time."

Thinking, *Nathaniel, this is another one I owe you.*

There were no street lamps. The moon was the only source of illumination. It hung in the sky like a pearl pendant, throwing shadows into the alleyways and casting the hills in coal-black silhouettes as, collars raised, Hawkwood and Lawrence headed for the harbour. There weren't many people around. The few that were paid them no attention. The only moment of apprehension occurred when Lawrence let out a warning hiss: "Eyes right!"

Hawkwood tensed as three men in what were clearly military uniforms emerged from a darkened alleyway and crossed the street a few yards ahead of them. The men glanced briefly in their direction but did not linger. Hawkwood released his breath.

"Well, that just took ten years off my life," Lawrence muttered as he watched the trio fade into the night.

They walked on, their senses heightened, but there were no more surprises. Turning the next corner, they found themselves at the edge of the moonlit basin looking out on to a row of spindly wooden landings against which vessels of various configurations were berthed. A few craft showed lights, but most were in shadow.

The odour coming off the *Snake*'s tar-painted hull was detectable long before she came into view. It was that as much as her appearance that told them they had the right vessel.

A small, single-masted sloop perhaps forty to fifty feet in length and berthed well away from prying eyes, she had, presumably, been deemed too insignificant to be commandeered by the military. Or maybe it was the smell that had put them off.

"Christ!" Lawrence whispered. "I've seen better looking night-soil barges."

Barely discernible in faded lettering across her transom was the legend *Snake*. And indeed there was something undeniably sinister in the way her blackened timbers seemed to overlap like scales.

There didn't appear to be any sign of life aboard, but as Hawkwood and Lawrence drew closer a face appeared over the port gunwale and a sinewy figure rose into view from a hatchway amidships.

"Lookin' for somethin'?" The enquiry carried no warmth.

"Here to see Captain Stagg," Hawkwood said. "We're expected."

The figure stared at them for several seconds before turning and disappearing from view.

A couple of seconds later it was back.

"Best come this way then."

They climbed aboard.

In the course of his research into the best route homeward, Hawkwood had learned that the ban on trade with Canada had led to an increase in cross-border smuggling. Being familiar with the smuggling brotherhood of the Kent coast, he was willing to wager that the free-traders active in Vermont and New York State would be similarly inclined when it came to laying patriotism aside in favour of lining their own pockets.

The variety of goods transported across the border here was as diverse as the shipments of contraband that slipped undetected across the Channel, albeit slightly less exotic. In addition to cattle, leather, butter, salt, corn and glass, the smuggling of tea was big business. The previous month, two sloops had been apprehended close to the Canadian border with more than one hundred chests of the finest Assam leaf hidden in their holds. Hawkwood remembered reading that the sloops in question had sailed from Whitehall, and it was this detail that had suggested the possibility of finding a smuggler willing to transport fugitives.

The derogatory tone in the pot-man's voice when he'd described the commandeering of the ferry and the local shipyard had suggested that his sympathies would lie with the smugglers rather than the authorities. And given the fondness of mariners for taverns, it was natural to assume that the pot-man would have an extensive knowledge of the men that constituted the local smuggling fraternity.

At first the pot-man had been reluctant to release the information – and having met Remus Stagg, Hawkwood could understand the man's reticence – but all information could be bought for a price. Obtaining Stagg's name along with his whereabouts had simply been a matter of negotiation. The fact that he'd been sitting only a couple of booths away had been an unexpected dividend.

Prior to the opening of negotiations, Hawkwood had guessed

that a not insignificant sum might be involved in securing their passage and he'd asked Lawrence how much he was carrying. As an officer, the major had been permitted to retain the cash he'd had on him when seized. He had dipped into this fund to purchase the jacket and knapsack from the Fort Miller store, but Hawkwood knew that Lawrence was also in possession of English guineas. As veterans of the Spanish campaign, both men had adopted the practice of sewing gold coins into their belt in case they needed to recruit help or bribe their way out of a tight spot.

As Stagg's response had demonstrated, the value of gold was universal, even if it came with the King's head stamped on it.

Unsurprisingly, the *Snake* was as scabrous below deck as above. But then, as Stagg had explained so succinctly, she wasn't in the business of pleasure boating.

He was seated at a table in the lantern-lit stern cabin which, Hawkwood presumed, passed for the crew's quarters, along with a tiny galley. Half a dozen cubbyholes ringed the eating area, each one housing a narrow cot and a dubious-looking blanket. There were no concessions to privacy. Along with the pervading smell of the tar that coated her outer hull, the compartment stank of sweat and bilge water.

Hawkwood wasn't sure if it was a trick of the light, but there appeared to be something approaching a smile of welcome on Stagg's face. He did not rise to greet them but remained seated, dismissing his crewman with orders to ready the boat for departure. As soon as they were alone, he came straight to the point.

"You have the fee?" Shadows played across his expectant face.

Hawkwood dug out a bag from his coat pocket. "Sixty dollars. Thirty Spanish, the rest in English guineas. I trust that meets with your approval?"

"It will when I've counted it." Stagg held out his hand.

Hawkwood and Lawrence watched as the coins were emptied out of the bag and tallied. When he'd confirmed the amount, Stagg slid the coins back into the bag, pulled the drawstring tight and slipped the lot inside his waistcoat.

Only then did the smile reach his eyes. "Welcome aboard, gents! Nice to have you with us!"

His eyes switched to the musket slung over Lawrence's shoulder. "Expectin' trouble, Mr Jones?"

"Family heirloom," Lawrence responded blithely. "Belonged to my father. Feel quite naked without it."

Stagg's eyes moved to Hawkwood.

"Oh, he's the marksman," Hawkwood said.

Stagg frowned and then nodded assent. "Aye, well if we need food for the pot, I'll give you a shout. As for the accommodation, if you were expecting your own cabin you're in for a disappointment. Sixty dollars may have bought you passage but it ain't bought any home comforts. You'll be bunking down with the crew. There are six of us and there'll always be at least two on deck, so there's a pit each. As far as your bellies are concerned, you'll eat when we eat. There're no guest privileges here."

"How long's the journey likely to take?" Lawrence asked.

"We won't be callin' in anywhere, so three days, with a fair wind. Four at the outside." Stagg got to his feet. "Remember, gentlemen, *Snake*'s a working boat, so try not to get under our feet," he added drily.

Having launched his parting shot, he left the cabin.

Lawrence turned. "Is it my imagination, or has our captain mellowed since last we spoke?"

"I suspect our sixty dollars has had some influence in that regard," Hawkwood said. "Though I doubt we'll be singing sea shanties together any time soon."

Lawrence smiled. "Ah, well, better a grin than a grimace, eh?"

They stowed the knapsacks and the musket in a couple of the cubbyholes and followed Stagg on deck. By this time *Snake* had slipped her mooring and was being pushed clear of the jetty.

As he stood in the breeze blowing across the harbour basin, Hawkwood pondered the reason for *Snake*'s night-time departure. Perhaps it had something to do with the three men in military gear who'd crossed their path earlier. This far from the border, there'd be no Customs service; it would be up to the local militia to combat smuggling. Presumably they were the ones Stagg was attempting to avoid.

Light showed over the port rail and Hawkwood could just make out a line of slipways ranged along the shoreline. Several vessels were drawn up on them, in various stages of construction, each part-built frame looking like the exposed ribcage of some beached animal. The shipyard, Hawkwood presumed, where the military was assembling its fleet of troop carriers. To starboard, tucked in at the foot of the hill, was the unmanned ferry landing. A line of lights flickered dimly on an adjacent slope, spaced along the vague outline of something solid; a fortification of some kind. It was hard to make out details.

"New blockhouse," Stagg's voice grated behind them. "Case you were wonderin'. Nothing like havin' the army camping out on your doorstep."

"Just as well we're on our way, then," Lawrence whispered.

Stagg growled an order to the crew. To Hawkwood's surprise, they did not raise the sail. Instead, leaving one crew member to man the tiller, the remaining four picked up two sets of oars that had been lying alongside the upturned dinghy secured amidships and, after dropping them into the rowlocks, they began to scull the *Snake* through the ink-black water. There was no rasp of metal, which suggested that all the housings had been well greased.

"Creek's too narrow for us to tack," Stagg said from behind Hawkwood's shoulder. "Rowing's easier an' quicker."

The breeze began to pick up, nipping at Hawkwood's flesh. He heard Lawrence grunt with the shock of it. There were no other moving vessels in sight and Hawkwood wondered if there were more craft out there like the *Snake*, sailing without lights on a clandestine mission. Despite the moonlight, Hawkwood doubted whether anyone on shore would be able to make out much more than a patch of shadow moving silently over the water, there one minute, gone the next; a figment of someone's imagination, hopefully.

The creek extended north in a gradual left-hand dog-leg before narrowing sharply until there were less than fifty yards between

197

the banks. A stone flipped casually from either side of the boat would have struck land. Though he was no sailor, Hawkwood could see the difficulty boat crews would have if they relied solely on the wind to take them into such a tight funnel.

Lawrence nudged Hawkwood's arm and murmured softly, "You want to stand watch or shall I?"

"You don't trust our captain?"

"Let's just say the jury has the matter under consideration."

"In that case, get some rest, Major. I'll take the first stint."

Lawrence turned to go and then paused. "Y'know, I think it's about time we dispensed with rank, don't you? Given our circumstances."

Lawrence had spoken quietly even though Stagg had moved further along the deck and wasn't close enough to overhear. The nearest crew member was the helmsman, whose attention was centred on maintaining their course and awaiting his skipper's instructions.

"It's been a while since I was captain of anything," Hawkwood said. "The name's Matthew."

"Douglas," Lawrence said with a grin.

Hawkwood smiled. "I remember."

Lawrence clapped him on the shoulder. "And it's been a while since *I* slept with a loaded musket. Here's hoping I don't move around and blow my bloody head off."

"If you do," Hawkwood said, "I'll be asking Stagg for a refund."

"Ha! Good man. You do that. You can put it towards the funeral expenses."

With a final chuckle, Lawrence turned and made his way below as Stagg returned aft. Arriving at the stern, he ordered the helmsman to the bow while he took command of the tiller.

It occurred to Hawkwood that, despite his aversion to matters nautical, the movement of the *Snake*'s deck beneath his feet was, as well as being instantly familiar, strangely comforting.

He studied the rowers as they continued their steady pull. A couple were similar to Stagg in stature. The others were not as hefty, but their sinewy frames suggested a tough resilience. Irrespective of the difference in their builds, from the way they handled themselves and drove the oars they all looked to be very fit men. The trim and pace of the boat had not faltered once, suggesting they had worked together for some time.

None of them had acknowledged the arrival of their two passengers. Hawkwood suspected that too had much to do with the chain of command. Stagg was the skipper, the one who made the decisions, who negotiated the jobs, paid the wages, and put food on the table. His word was law. If the rest of his crew were curious about his acceptance of Hawkwood and Lawrence's presence, they were keeping it to themselves.

The Vermont and New York shorelines glided by in eerie silence, save for the soft splash of the oars. Vermont to starboard; New York to port. In the darkness it was just possible to make out some details as the wooded hills began to give way to a skein of marshy backwaters along both sides of the main channel. Moving north, the eastern shore then merged into a series of rocky headlands, while the western shore grew more undulating before giving way to marshland once again. Thin glimmers of light indicated the presence of isolated homesteads.

Hawkwood felt the tension slipping away. As long as he and Lawrence remained on the move, every mile covered was a victory gained. But that didn't mean they could relax. In that regard the cold was an ally, for it prevented sleep. Nevertheless the constant dipping of the oars was beginning to have a hypnotic effect upon his senses. It was something of a relief, therefore, when Lawrence emerged from below a few hours later and said softly, "Your turn."

"Wasn't I supposed to give *you* the tap?" Hawkwood said.

"No need, my dear fellow." Lawrence smiled. "If we may return temporarily to our respective ranks, as a major to a captain, I'm giving you a direct order: get some sleep. You've earned it."

Hawkwood didn't have the energy to argue. He went below, located his cubbyhole and climbed into his cot. He felt something hard strike his knee and realized that Lawrence had transferred guardianship of the musket. Smiling to himself, Hawkwood stretched out, still in his coat, and drew the blanket across his body. Within minutes, he was asleep.

When he awoke, he was aware of two things. It had grown colder and the deck was canted, so they must be under sail. Making his way topside, he found that dawn had broken and that the sky was the colour of wet slate. Stagg was manning the tiller.

"Mr Smith."

"Captain," Hawkwood said.

Lawrence was leaning against the dinghy, gazing out over the starboard gunwale. His coat carried a light coating of spray. He turned and smiled. "You slept well?"

"Strangely, yes. Did I miss anything?"

"Nothing of note. We're out of that damned river at last, and we've just passed Ticonderoga." Lawrence indicated a bleak-looking promontory a mile or so behind them on the port side.

There wasn't a lot to see: a curve of muddy foreshore behind which a bare, tree-denuded slope rose towards a two-hundred-foot-high summit strewn with rocks and clumps of immature woodland and what appeared to be the remains of massive stone ramparts nestling among them like stubs of broken teeth.

"There was a better view from the south," Lawrence said. "Not that there's much left of the place, mind."

Hawkwood had lost count of the abandoned forts they'd passed along their route. Most, like the one occupying the hill behind them, had changed hands so many times it was hard to remember who'd built them in the first place. Their stones were steeped in blood; not just British but French, American and Indian, along with a host of other nationalities. Now there was nothing to show for all that sacrifice of life but these moss-covered ruins. And in their midst, men were at war yet again.

The dawn light revealed sweeping vistas of both shores. Along the Vermont side the woodland was broken up by areas of meadowland – some of it under cultivation – while in the distance a range of dark mountains could be seen crouching beneath heavy skies. It was New York, however, that provided the more dramatic backdrop. There, the land rose sharply from pine-covered bluffs towards a series of misty ridges beyond which a backdrop of rugged, snow-powdered peaks stretched the entire length of the horizon.

"Reminds me of Scotland," Lawrence murmured softly.

"That where your family's from?" Hawkwood asked.

Gazing across the water, Lawrence shook his head. "Not directly. My mother's Scottish. My father was from Carlisle. We used to travel north to visit my mother's family. They were highland stock. I saw something of the country when I was a boy."

"You didn't join a border regiment?"

"Too damned cold." Lawrence mimed a shiver and smiled. "I went south to seek *my* fortune."

"London?"

Lawrence turned and grinned. "No, Chester, where I met up with a very persuasive recruiting sergeant."

"You came up through the ranks?"

"I did indeed. My first posting was to Ireland, then St Vincent, garrison duty in Gibraltar – which was where I picked up my Spanish – Malta, Egypt, and then on to South America."

"Montevideo," Hawkwood said.

Lawrence looked back at him. "Ah, you got that from the watch."

"That, too," Hawkwood said.

Lawrence smiled then. "So you *do* remember? I recall when our paths first crossed in London you denied we'd met before."

"I remember that, too," Hawkwood said. "I apologize. I wasn't on my best behaviour."

Lawrence chuckled. "Apology accepted."

"And then the Peninsula?" Hawkwood said, bringing them back to the present.

"Aye. And now here we are in America. Curious how things turn out. By the way, did you know the Fortieth was formed in the Canadas?"

"I didn't, no."

"Annapolis Royal, Nova Scotia – would you believe? New Scotland. There's irony in there somewhere. They were with Wolfe when he took Quebec. Fought in the Revolution, too. I think it's called coming full circle."

Lawrence shook his head at the mystery of it.

"Heads, gentlemen!" Stagg called from behind them. "Coming about!"

Stagg moved the tiller over and Hawkwood and Lawrence ducked and then stood braced as the deck swayed beneath them. There was a groan as the boom swung across and as the mainsail snapped taut Stagg's crew jumped to haul fast on the sheets. As the sloop righted herself, Stagg eased back on the helm.

*Snake* was not the only vessel plying the lake's white-tipped waters. There were several sails in view; some near, some mere dots in the distance so that it was impossible to judge the size of the craft they were affixed to. There were no large spreads of canvas to suggest any were naval vessels, however, which made Hawkwood wonder what sort of ships might be employed to patrol against smugglers or to stymie encroachments by British ships tempted to raid across the border from Canada. Though it was doubtful the Americans had anything larger than a schooner, even a schooner could carry up to a dozen guns.

He looked to the shore, formed on both sides by small wooded coves and stony beaches. Signs of settlement were few and far between, though occasionally a log-built farmhouse would come into view with a thin wisp of smoke spiralling above its shingle roof. Whenever that occurred, Hawkwood, waylaid by memories, found it almost impossible not to turn away.

There were abandoned homesteads as well, many destroyed by fire; the charred beams and broken walls sad memorials to those who'd tried to eke a living out of what could be a harsh and unforgiving land. Sometimes there would be an overgrown plot of ground close by in which rough wooden crosses jutted from tangles of briar and weed.

*Snake* sailed on.

It was some three hours later when they came to a place where the opposite shores appeared to be converging. On the

Vermont side of the channel Hawkwood could make out the remains of a settlement. A handful of buildings still stood, including a mill and what might have been a tavern, but all that was left of the rest were a few blackened chimneys.

It was the same on the New York side, where clusters of fire-ravaged houses were set back from the shore. Hawkwood looked beyond them, up to where the remnants of another huge abandoned military installation occupied the crown of yet another barren hilltop.

His eye moved on, to a line of hills strung out behind the tops of the ruined blockhouses. A shiver ran down his back. As the *Snake* nudged her way through the narrows, Hawkwood kept his eyes to port, knowing what he was about to see – and recognize.

What had appeared to be a fortified headland was in fact the tip of a peninsula. As *Snake* emerged into the section of the lake that lay beyond it, the bay that had been hidden on the other side of the headland gradually came into view.

"Matthew?" Lawrence said.

He sensed Lawrence was studying him with an expression of bemusement etched with concern; the same look that had been there on the Fort Ann road. Even so, Hawkwood did not answer. He was too busy remembering.

A stretch of driftwood-covered beach, the bark of guns, the roar of a cannon, the screams of men as they fell and died.

And a place called Bulwagga.

# 8

*May 1780*

Tewanias made no sound as the needle pierced his skin nor did he flinch as the thread was pulled through behind it. His brow furrowed slightly only when the two sides of the wound came together.

His fingertips reddened and slippery with blood, the boy paused, adjusting his grip on the needle.

"Why do you stop?" Tewanias asked brusquely. He had posed the question in English.

"I don't want to hurt you," the boy said.

The Indian looked puzzled by the statement. "I am already hurt. Continue."

The boy hesitated. He was trying hard to stop his hands from shaking. With the arrival of dusk, the light had deteriorated considerably. Determined not to let his patient see how nervous he was, he drew in a deep breath and pushed the needle into the swollen flesh. After the initial press of resistance he felt the skin give way and, encouraged by that minor success, he completed the second suture, not daring to look up until he had finished his surgery. It took three more stitches to seal the sword gash in the Mohawk's upper arm. The result was far from neat but other than a line of tiny red bubbles beading along the length of the cut there was no noticeable seepage of blood.

Inspecting the work, Tewanias traced the edges of the wound with his fingers before handing the boy his knife to cut the surplus thread. When that had been done he took the knife back. "Good. Thank you, Mat-huwa. You did well."

The Mohawk held the boy's gaze for several seconds before turning his attention to the wound in his side. An earlier examination had told him that it could have been a great deal worse. The ball from the Oneida's carbine had entered his flesh between his pelvis and his lower ribcage, performing an almost straight trajectory before exiting just above his hip. A couple of inches either side and the ball would have struck bone. It was fortunate that he had not been wearing a shirt, otherwise cloth would have been forced into the wound, increasing the risk of infection.

Taking pulped cat-tail root from his medicine bag and soaking it in water from the stream, Tewanias cleansed the area before pressing a moss poultice to both the entry and exit holes. Beneath the blood, the edges of the wounds appeared unsullied, but it paid to be sure. If any poisons were present the moss would draw them out and reduce the swelling.

The boy looked on in silence, the dog seated by his side. Watching the concentration on the Mohawk's face, the boy's mind went back to the moment he'd shot the Oneida runner. It was strange, he thought, that he'd been unable to stop his hand shaking as he sewed up the wound in the Mohawk's arm, yet he'd acted without hesitation when it came to firing the pistol, or using the hatchet back at the farm. He wondered why that was. The only answer he could come up with was that the men he'd hurt had been bad men. One had been responsible for killing Will Archer, the other had been trying to kill his friend.

Friend? The word had come to him unbidden. Was Tewanias really his friend? In the time since their paths had first crossed, few words had been exchanged between them and yet, curious as it seemed, some sort of bond had been created. As he pondered why this should be, the boy's hand moved unconsciously to the amulet around his throat.

When he'd heard the Oneida's yell and followed the sound to where the two men were fighting in midstream, his hand had automatically reached for the pistol. It was the same one Beth Archer had used to shoot one of the horsemen. He'd retrieved it, unseen, along with Will Archer's powder case and ammunition, when he'd collected his belongings from the cabin. Uncle Will had taught him how to shoot during their hunting trips, and how to load and maintain a firearm. Even so, he feared that if the pastor knew he had a weapon he would confiscate it, so the gun had remained hidden in the bag that he carried on him at all times. Thankfully, he'd taken the precaution of loading it after Tam's encounter with the bear. When the moment came to use it, his grip had not faltered and his aim had been firm and steady.

Tam nuzzled his arm. Stretching out a hand, he ruffled the dog's fur. It had been Tam's nose that had led them to Tewanias. How, the boy had no idea. Despite Tam's eagerness to latch on to a spoor, the likelihood of finding one man in this endless tract of forest had seemed an impossible task. And yet here they were. He wondered if it had been the smell of bear that had set Tam on the right trail. One of the first things he'd noticed about the Mohawk was his scent. Wyatt had explained.

"That's the grease you can smell. Indians use a lot of it. Hell, they kill an animal, don't matter if it's a rabbit or a bear, there's not one part of it they can't find a use for. Fur keeps them warm; meat keeps them fed; grease keeps them slippery. Means an enemy can't grab a hold."

Wyatt had laughed at the boy's expression. "Well, that's not all they use it for. Bear fat's good for cooking. It doesn't turn rancid, so it keeps longer. They smear it on themselves for all sorts of reasons. Keeps mosquitoes away – vermin, too – if they're sleeping outside. It protects their skin from the sun and keeps water out of their moccasins. They use it to mix their war paints and to keep their guns oiled. The women like it because it makes their hair shiny; the men, too. Tewanias might not have much hair, but what he has he looks after – which is more than can be said for most white men!" Wyatt had laughed as he'd said that.

The boy wondered where Lieutenant Wyatt and the other Rangers were now. And who was the Indian he had shot?

Tewanias had as yet offered no explanation and the boy had felt too intimidated to enquire.

Despite his wounds, Tewanias's first action on seeing his enemy slain had been to drag the dead warrior out of the stream and place it on the bank. At first the boy had assumed this was a mark of respect, but then he recalled Will Archer doing something similar once, back at the farm. They had come across a dead buck sprawled in a creek, upstream from the cabin. The deer looked as if it had died of old age. Archer had taken hold of the antlers and pulled the carcass out of the water, telling the boy that if it were left in the water anyone taking a drink downriver might be poisoned.

"How do you know there aren't more dead animals tainting the flow further up?" the boy had asked.

"I don't," Archer had replied. "But that doesn't mean we should leave this one where it is."

After depositing the body on the bank, Tewanias had collected the Oneida's weapons, including the carbine that had fallen in the stream and the tomahawk that had struck the tree. He'd also relieved the body of its ammunition pouch, which he had given to the boy.

Only after he'd gathered the weapons had Tewanias turned his attention to his wounds. It was as he was examining the gash in his shoulder that the boy, without thinking, had blurted, "I have a needle and thread."

When the Mohawk had indicated for him to start sewing, the boy had experienced both alarm and disbelief. It wasn't until he'd completed the last stitch that he wondered if it hadn't been some sort of test. If the Mohawk's expression on examining the results of his surgery was anything to go by, it was a test he had passed.

A feeling of relief had swept through him. For reasons he couldn't fathom, it mattered a great deal what the unsmiling warrior chief thought of him.

"Now we rest," Tewanias told him. "Tomorrow we find Wy-att."

The boy immediately delved in his bag and produced his tinderbox, but Tewanias shook his head. Though he registered the boy's puzzled expression, he offered no explanation. He did not want to alarm the boy by telling him that they dare not risk travelling in the dark or lighting a fire in case there were more Oneida scouting parties abroad. Tewanias did not want to run into them or alert them to his presence; not when he was wounded, and especially not with the boy in tow. Admittedly, the boy had more than proved his mettle, but there were some risks that were not worth running.

Tewanias reached for one of the small leather bags he carried at his waist, wincing slightly as he did so. Reaching inside, he drew out two strips of pemmican and offered one to the boy. The dog's nose twitched at the scent of the dried venison and berries coated in fat. Gnawing off a piece, the boy passed it to Tam who wolfed it down. He remembered the rabbit he'd stowed in his saddlebag. He knew how to skin and cook game, but with no fire, he had no desire to eat the animal raw, though he suspected the Mohawk would not be so squeamish. He took another bite of the pemmican and tried to push the thought of a cooked supper to the back of his mind.

"We will stay here," Tewanias repeated as the boy chewed. "Tomorrow, we will meet with Wy-att and Owassighsishon."

The boy frowned. "Owass . . .?" He stumbled over the rest of the word.

"You call him Col-onel," Tewanias said.

"Colonel Johnson?"

"John-son, yes." The Mohawk nodded towards the blanket the boy had removed from the pony's back. "Now you sleep. I will watch."

"I can watch, too."

Tewanias shook his head. He could see the weariness in the boy's face. "No. Sleep."

As the boy lay down and closed his eyes, Tewanias reached for the Oneida's carbine. Taking the carbine's ramrod and removing a rag and a small brush from his own ammunition pouch, he set about cleaning out the weapon's barrel and lock mechanism. Every so often, he would pause to watch the gentle rise and fall of the boy's chest as he slept. He had listened to the boy's explanation as to why he was alone in the woods with puzzlement. He knew white men had a curious affinity with their animals, but to head into the forest in search of a missing dog seemed foolhardy in the extreme. His people kept dogs, but they came and went as they pleased. A dog was far better equipped to fend for itself in the wild than any human, especially a child. And dogs weren't stupid; they would find their way back to their human companions sooner or later, drawn by the prospect of food and warmth.

Tewanias noted the hand curled around the turtle amulet. The boy was certainly an intriguing mix. While it was said that a man's courage could be judged by the number of enemies he had dispatched, there were other criteria that were more important – chief among these being strength of character. How a man conducted himself in the face of danger was a far better measure of his resolve than the tattoos etched into his skin. Tewanias had learnt of the boy's history from Wyatt. As he gazed upon the figure huddled against the dog's flank, one thought occupied his mind.

*This one carries the blood of a warrior.*

An owl screeched but the boy did not awaken; neither did he stir at the rustling and the accompanying sequence of scuffling grunts that came from the direction of the river, which suggested that something was being dragged through the bushes. Tewanias paused in his task and listened. Gradually, the noises faded. When he looked up he saw that he was under observation. The dog was watching him, eyes bright in the moonlight, its ears pricked. For several seconds man and dog stared at each other, before Tam dropped his head on his paws. As the dog closed its eyes, Tewanias returned to cleaning the gun.

From the direction of the river there came the sounds of crunching bones and of an animal feeding.

"Cut's fresh," Jem Beddowes murmured softly, running his fingers across the edge of the coin-sized blaze. "It means we're closing."

"Eyes peeled, boys," Wyatt whispered, knowing the instruction was unnecessary. The Rangers were versed in forest warfare.

They knew what was expected of them and didn't have to be reminded.

Not that tracking the Oneida scouting party had proved difficult. The enemy had left signs which, although subtle, had been easy to follow. They were intended to be. These signs would guide the main force that was coming up behind; a force which, Wyatt hoped, was now floundering because Tewanias had caught and killed the Oneida runner who had been sent to rendezvous with it.

The blazes were carved into the bark of trees, small so as to be unobtrusive, yet deep enough so that the trained eye would be drawn to the white wood that lay beneath the cut. The combinations of marks – circles and rectangles – indicated which direction to take.

"They're moving north," Donaldson grunted. "They'll know the lake is the colonel's quickest route home."

Billy Drew peered into the forest and fingered the hammer of his rifle. "How far is Bulwagga?"

"Fifteen miles maybe," Wyatt said. "Give or take."

"If they stay on this trail, we've time to get ahead of them," Donaldson mused, throwing Wyatt a speculative look. "We pick our spot, we can cut them out."

"Payback for Stryker," Jem Beddowes muttered.

Wyatt looked towards the sun, which had risen less than half an hour before. Fearful of losing the trail markers in the dark and secure in the knowledge that the men they were tracking would also have sought to rest, the Rangers had spent the night under a hastily built lean-to, without a fire and with each man taking a two-hour watch. They had resumed the chase at first light.

Despite Tewanias's confidence, Wyatt wondered if the Mohawk had caught up with the runner. If he hadn't, how close *was* the enemy? The Rangers had been defacing the markers as they'd come upon them, laying false blazes to obstruct pursuit, which was all well and good, but Wyatt knew that the best way of protecting the colonel's retreat wasn't for the tail of the enemy snake to be cut off, it was the head.

"What are you thinking?" Donaldson asked, cutting into Wyatt's thoughts.

"I'm thinking that you're right. We move fast, we can outflank the buggers."

Billy Drew showed his teeth. It wasn't so much a smile as a feral grin.

"What's keeping us, Lieutenant?" he said.

Exultant at having visited the first blow upon their enemy, the Oneida scouts were moving fast. Travelling in single file and with each man taking it in turns to lead, they knew it could only be a matter of time before their quarry was sighted. They had tasted blood. They wanted more.

The roar could be heard long before the falls came into view. Situated in a wide cleft at the end of a wooded gorge and tumbling in a thundering cascade from a height of seventy feet, it dominated the scenery around it. The narrowing of the gorge forced the track to veer away from the valley floor and up on to the side of the slope where it rose in a steady incline before eventually disappearing from view over the cataract's boulder-strewn rim. Vapour from the falls filled the air and it was not long before the Oneidas' muscled bodies were damp and glistening with spray. As they climbed higher, the noise of the water grew in volume, muting all other sounds.

Including the first gunshot.

The lead warrior was flung backwards as the rifle ball took him in the throat before angling upwards into his brain. The second man was unaware of the strike until he saw the back of his companion's skull blow apart, showering him in blood and bone. As the scout let go a warning yell, Jem Beddowes, concealed among the rocks at the top of the slope, took his shot and grunted in satisfaction as his target clutched at his chest and jerked aside, toppling over the edge of the path into the torrent raging below. The surviving Oneida turned to flee, eyes widening as Wyatt and Billy Drew stepped into view, cutting off their retreat. There was nowhere to run. Both Rangers fired as one. The dual reports were deadened by the deluge of water. The

Oneida went down, limbs splayed. From first shot to last, the culling had taken less than five seconds.

Donaldson and Jem Beddowes were already on their feet and making their way down the path, rifles cradled. Wyatt and Drew met them where the bodies lay in crumpled abandon.

"Bastards," Donaldson swore. His face and hair were beaded with water droplets. Nudging the nearest corpse with the toe of his moccasin, his expression grew even harder. "Ah, sweet Jesus," he murmured.

Wyatt looked down. Attached to the strap of the dead warrior's ammunition pouch was a ragged segment of bloodstained flesh and matted black hair.

Beddowes reached for the knife at his waist.

"Don't do it, Jem," Billy Drew said warningly, taking his companion's arm.

The flesh around Beddowes' jaw tightened. His face a mask, he slid the knife back into its sheath.

Wyatt let go a sigh.

"What?" Donaldson turned.

"We're missing one," Wyatt said.

The others looked at him.

"Tewanias said there were four."

"Could have got it wrong," Billy Drew said.

Donaldson shook his head. "If Tewanias says there's four, that's how many there are." He looked at Wyatt. "You think he passed us?"

"Not since we got here, and their point man wouldn't be that far in front. He must have left a ways back, while we were skirting round them."

"Didn't see any sign that he'd crossed our path," Beddowes said.

"That's because we weren't looking." Wyatt frowned, then swore under his breath as the realization hit him.

"Lieutenant?" Donaldson said.

"They sent another runner."

There was a moment's pause. "They wouldn't send two back the same way," Donaldson said warily. "So which way'd he go?"

213

Wyatt's head lifted. "Ticonderoga'd be my guess. New Hampshire Militia's mustered close by. That's, what, ten miles east of here? From there, Bulwagga'd be less than a morning's march."

"Damn it!" Beddowes' shoulders slumped.

"Colonel needs to know," Wyatt said.

Billy Drew sighed and slung his rifle over his shoulders. "Bloody hell. More runnin'."

Wyatt indicated the two dead Oneida on the trail. "Throw them over; weapons, too. We've enough to carry. Take their ammunition, though. We can always use that."

The Rangers heaved the bodies into the river, not bothering to watch as the current dragged them under. They would undoubtedly bob to the surface and beach either on the rocks below or somewhere further downstream. Concealing evidence of their presence was no longer a priority for Wyatt and his men. If a second Oneida scout had indeed been dispatched to report on the column's progress and destination, the most pressing matter was to make it to the embarkation point and the boats of the Provincial Marine before the enemy got there.

Or, as Billy Drew put it as they set off:

Runnin' like buggery.

Flattened grass and drag marks showed where the Oneida brave's body had been pulled through the underbrush to the spot where it now lay, sprawled on its back and partially concealed beneath a clump of copperleaf, twenty metres from the edge of the stream.

The area around the base of the shrub was crawling with flies and in the middle of the swarm that buzzed around the body the curve of a rib could clearly be seen protruding from the corpse's chest cavity and the torn remnants of a blood-soaked shirt. As the sickly smell drifted towards him, the boy wrinkled his nose and turned his head away, tightening his hold on Jonah's halter.

"No, Tam!" he said sharply as the dog started forward to investigate, snout twitching.

The dog turned and looked up at him, puzzlement on its face.

"Heel!" the boy commanded, patting his thigh.

Reluctantly, the dog returned to the boy's side, head hung low.

The boy's thoughts strayed to the sounds he thought he had heard the night before as he'd drifted off to sleep. At the time, he hadn't been sure if the noises were real or a figment of some descending dream. Now he knew why they had reminded him of the noises Tam made when he was chewing on a bone. Something had been drawn to the riverbank by the stench of death. Something with the strength to move the body to a place where it could feast without being disturbed. From what he'd seen before he'd averted his eyes, there looked to be a substantial amount of flesh still available. No doubt the scavenger would return to finish its meal. The boy scanned the edge of the woodland nervously. He was very glad that Tewanias was with him.

The Mohawk paid no heed to the remains, other than giving them a cursory glance as he led the way past. The Oneida warrior had chosen his path and had paid dearly for it, as decreed by the laws of war. By now, Wyatt and his fellow Rangers would surely have caught up with and passed sentence on the rest of the scouting party, dispatching them into *Ha-ne-go-ate-geh*, the land of eternal darkness, where they would rejoin their companion and, together, reflect upon the wickedness of their deeds. It was not Tewanias's task to dwell on the destiny of others. He had but one duty now and that was to escort the boy to a place of safety. It was a duty he would carry out even if his own life became forfeit in the process.

"Awaiting your orders, sir."

Colonel Johnson, who had been studying his watch, returned the instrument to his pocket. "No word from Stryker, I take it?" he asked his second-in-command pensively.

"No, sir."

Johnson gnawed the inside of his cheek and then sighed. "Damn it. Very well. You may recall the piquets."

Scott touched his cap, turned away, hesitated and then turned back. "I'm sorry, sir."

The words were of small comfort. Johnson acknowledged them with a resigned nod. "What of other scouts – are they all returned safely?"

"All save Lieutenant Wyatt and his Rangers."

"Wyatt?" Johnson said, more sharply than he had intended.

"Yes, sir."

*God damn*, Johnson thought. He closed his eyes, counted to three, opened them and then nodded again. "Thank you, Thomas. You may carry on."

He watched the captain walk away. In truth, not counting Stryker and his men, the fact that only one scouting party had failed to report back was more than he could have dared hope for. Hearing that it was Wyatt who was still out there, however, did detract from what might have been a greater sense of relief.

Increasing the pace of the march had posed no problem for the troops. It had been done gradually, without histrionics. The civilians, unaware of the order and the reasons behind it, had had no option but to keep up. Thanks to the full moon, the column had been able to remain on the road long after sunset, and an earlier than usual breaking of camp that morning had shortened the travel time to the lake by a significant margin. As a result, the travellers had arrived at the rendezvous just as the early morning mist was rising off the waters of Bulwagga Bay, six hours earlier than had been foreseen.

With embarkation having to be brought forward there was an unavoidable risk of scouts failing to rejoin the column in time and being left behind. At least word of the militia's advance had filtered through to the outriders on the column's flanks; over the course of the evening they had made their way to the rendezvous point, there to await the column's dawn arrival.

But of Stryker's party and the boy there had been no word.

And time had now run out.

The Provincial Marine vessels – the eighteen-gun sloop, *Inflexible*; an armed schooner, the *Maria*; and a flotilla of gunboats and batteaux – and the force of Royal Yorkers and

216

Indians who'd been assigned to secure the site, had been ready and waiting. Under the watchful supervision of the Royal Navy boat crews, the boarding of passengers – military and civilian – had been conducted efficiently and without mishap.

The *Maria*, with its full complement of civilians safely on-board, had already set sail. Running before a brisk south-easterly, she had rounded Orchard Point, the northern tip of the peninsula, and was now making firm headway towards Champlain's deeper waters. In convoy behind her, trailing like ducklings, were the batteaux – troop carriers – flanked by their escort of gunboats.

*Inflexible*, deployed to protect the final stages of the evacuation, remained at anchor, pending Johnson and Scott's transfer, along with the last of the lookouts, while a single shallow-draught gunboat kept station closer to the shore. Despite the serenity of the scene, Johnson knew both crews would be growing restless.

With his back to the water, his shoulders warmed by the sun, he ran his eyes along the shoreline as it extended from the southern end of the bay, where the various sections of the column had been ferried out to the Marine vessels, to the wilder, northern promontories. Several of the more exposed stretches of foreshore were littered with driftwood; entire trees, uprooted and stranded by a succession of winter storms and spring floods, lay in disarray across the sand, some singly, some stacked like lengths of cordage, their bleached trunks as smooth as bone in the morning light.

Movement to the north caught his eye and hope soared momentarily, only to plummet when he saw it was an osprey perched atop a dead stump, flexing its wings in preparation for the morning's fishing expedition.

Scott returned, his features drawn with concern. "We can't wait any longer, sir. We must leave now. Clinton's arrival could be imminent."

Johnson watched the piquets making their way to the boats. Bringing up the rear were the scouts, Boone and Cavett. They touched their caps in salute as they loped past.

"Sir," Scott urged.

217

With a last despairing glance towards the trees, Johnson muttered, "Very well, Thomas. I hear you."

He turned and was taken aback to find the scouts standing behind him.

"Beggin' your pardon, Colonel," Boone said, tugging at his beard with a forefinger and thumb that were speckled with powder burns.

"What can I do for you, gentlemen?"

Boone traded glances with his fellow scout then said, "We know about the missing boy, Colonel, and that you're not going to wait on Corporal Stryker."

Johnson frowned. "I've delayed our departure for as long as possible, Mr Boone."

"Understood, Colonel. Only, Nate and me figured that, if you gave the word, we'd hang back and wait for them, maybe with that gunboat there." He jutted his chin in the direction of the water. "Stryker's a good man. We reckon he can't be that far behind us."

"Neither can the militia," said Johnson. "You were the one who gave the warning that they were gaining on us. As I recall, you also informed us of their strength. Governor Clinton's force is vastly superior to our own. With the exception of the Hooper boy, we got what we came for – and without a single man down, so far. A confrontation now would be entirely wasteful."

"Wasn't aiming for a confrontation, Colonel. We'd just like to give Stryker a chance."

"Lieutenant Wyatt, too, if he and his men are close," Cavett added. "We know they're out there. And you said it yourself, Colonel: it's a long walk home."

"Indeed I did," Johnson acknowledged, then shook his head. "But I regret, gentlemen, that I must decline your offer. Corporal Stryker and Lieutenant Wyatt are both men of initiative and excellent soldiers. They're aware that they will have to make their own way home if they fail to make the rendezvous. I made sure every man was apprised of that before we left St Johns," Johnson added, in a gentle rebuke.

Boone looked as if he was about to demur, but then, thinking better of it, he gave a subdued nod. "Yes, sir. Very good, Colonel. We didn't want to go without askin'."

"There is no harm in asking, Mr Boone. You have shown commendable spirit in doing so. It also says a great deal about your loyalty to your comrades, and I thank you for that."

Boone touched his cap. "Colonel." He turned to his companion. "Let's go, Nate."

There was neither disappointment nor resentment in either man's expression, merely stoic acceptance of a decision made by a superior officer.

Johnson and Scott acknowledged the salute and watched as the two scouts waded out to the waiting gunboat. Then, with a final glance along the shore, the two officers set off for the jolly boat.

It was a short row out to the ship. As *Inflexible*'s crew sprang to their stations, Johnson commandeered a spyglass from the ship's commander and led the way aft. Placing the instrument to his eye, he studied the shoreline once more.

"Any sign of them?" Scott asked after several long seconds had elapsed.

Collapsing the glass, Johnson sighed wearily. "No."

"It doesn't mean they haven't found the boy," Scott pointed out. "Or that they've run into trouble. Both Stryker and Wyatt think they have until midday to get here. We shouldn't assume the worst because they haven't made the boats. And as you reminded Boone and Cavett, they know to continue on foot. It's a fair distance, but not that difficult a journey for men of their experience, especially at this time of year."

Johnson's gaze drifted towards the gunboat. It had yet to get underway.

Behind them the crew were scurrying about the deck as an officer yelled commands: "Top men aloft! Stand by all lines!"

Further south over the stern, Johnson could see the twin peaks of Bulwagga Mountain rising over the surrounding forest.

There was a clatter of blocks behind him as the ropes were hauled in tight. Canvas flapped loudly as the sails tumbled from the yards.

Steadying himself against the rail as the deck shifted, he turned back to his second-in-command as the *Inflexible*'s bow began to come round. As he did so, he caught sight of the gunboat and frowned. Her sail still hadn't been raised.

*Inflexible*'s captain called out to his steersman. "Easy on the helm, Mr Swanson. A point to starboard, if you please!"

Scott followed Johnson's gaze. "She in difficulties, do you think?"

Sluggishly, her sails filling, *Inflexible* began to gather momentum.

As Scott and Johnson looked on, a slim figure at the stern of the gunboat stood and raised his arm.

Johnson extended the spyglass and held it to his eye. "It's Boone."

"Why's he holding his gun above his head?"

"He appears to be signalling."

"Signalling?" Scott ducked as a yard let out an ominous groan above him.

"I'll be damned," Johnson muttered.

"What is it?" Scott asked. "Are they in trouble?"

"Only when I get them home. The damned fools."

Scott frowned as Johnson passed him the glass. Fumbling the telescope to his eye, he focused it on the gunboat, the prow of which was still facing the shore. There didn't appear to be a lot of movement from the men on board.

"I see Boone," Scott said, "and his damned rifle. What's that he's doing with his other hand?"

"Talking."

"Talking? To whom? I don't understand." Perplexed, Scott lowered the glass.

"That's because you've never hunted with the Iroquois. Indian hunting parties travel through the forest in silence when they're after game. They use signals to communicate – hand-talking, they call it. Our Mr Boone is using the sign language of the Mohawk hunters to send us – or rather me – a signal."

Scott blinked, rammed the glass to his eye and watched as the scout continued to open and close his left hand in a sequence of curt gestures. "What's he saying?"

"That we are not to wait. He will follow in due course."

220

"He'll what?" Shocked, Scott nearly dropped the glass.

"It would seem that Boone and Cavett have just added the unlawful seizure of one of His Majesty's gunboats to their expanding list of misdemeanours."

Dumbstruck, Scott stared at his colonel, wondering why he wasn't seeing a more spectacular display of outrage. Then the penny dropped. "Bloody hell! The stupid, stupid buggers! Do you think they're acting alone, or are the boat crew in on this?"

Johnson smiled grimly. "Oh, I'd say most certainly that the crew are part of it. Seeing as Mr Boone's gun doesn't appear to be pointed at anyone."

"Is he mad? Disobeying an officer's a hanging offence."

"Yes, it is," agreed Johnson. "Though, strictly speaking, I don't recall giving either of them a direct order. I believe I merely declined their offer of assistance."

Scott opened his mouth and then closed it again quickly. It was only after a further period of contemplative silence that he finally found his voice. He cleared his throat, leaned in and asked, "Should we alert the ship's captain?"

"Oh, I rather think Lieutenant Schank has enough on his hands at the moment, don't you? A vessel like this, his duties must be immeasurable. Not unlike mine," Johnson added ruminatively, staring back at the gunboat as *Inflexible* pursued her steady course towards the open mouth of the bay. Banging a fist on the rail, he straightened. "By God, Thomas, they may be insubordinate devils, but you couldn't wish for finer men, could you?"

Scott looked at him. "If you mean am I glad they're on our side, then the answer's yes."

The gap between *Inflexible* and the gunboat continued to widen. When it was no longer possible to discern individual faces, Scott handed back the glass. "If Boone and his crew of miscreants do manage to extract Stryker and Wyatt's men, will they be able to cope without *Inflexible* as their guardian?"

"I see no reason why not. It's on the water that they'll be at their safest. Those boats have a fair turn of speed when needed.

The Yankees'll never catch them. The buggers have damn all left that floats."

Three months after the Americans declared independence, a British flotilla led by *Inflexible* had decimated the American fleet at Valcour Island. The British Navy in the guise of the Provincial Marine had ruled the waters of Champlain ever since. That superiority had granted the invasion force unrestricted access into enemy territory.

"So, what happens now?" Scott said.

Collecting himself, Johnson turned. "I suggest we make our way below and see if Lieutenant Schank's cook can't provide us with breakfast and a pot of his strongest coffee."

Wyatt could make out the lake through the trees. Sunlight was creating bright shimmering patterns on the water. Nevertheless, he halted. Something wasn't right. Even if the boats were shielded from his view by the lie of the land, this close to the embarkation point he should have been able to detect a sense of activity.

But there was nothing.

Priming their weapons, the Rangers advanced cautiously.

Fifty paces further on, about to emerge from the trees on to the foreshore, they paused at the sound of a soft *tchuk tchuk* to their right. When the blackbird's call was repeated, Wyatt breathed a sigh of relief. As his fellow Rangers lowered their weapons, a swarthy, bearded figure stepped nonchalantly into view before them.

"Jethro," Wyatt said calmly.

Boone acknowledged the greeting with a nod. "Lieutenant."

"You had us worried. Nate with you?"

"Aye, he's around."

Wyatt indicated the gunboat which was now visible and riding the gentle swell some ten yards offshore. "Not sure she'll carry seven hundred."

"Leavin' was brought forward. Rest of 'em've gone."

"Evidently." Wyatt looked off towards the neck of the bay but there were no other vessels in sight. A pale smudge low down on the horizon to the north could have been a disappearing square of topsail, he supposed, but it was too far away to make out specific details. It could just as easily have been a patch of scrubby headland caught by the sun.

Boone spat tobacco on to the ground. "Colonel had no choice – militia was closing in. Order went out to pick up the pace. Column got here at sun-up. Civilians went first. They're long gone."

"From where?"

Boone frowned.

"The militia – which direction were they coming from?"

"Ticonderoga." The scout pointed at a fold in the hills at the southern end of the bay. "Clinton's leading them."

"Is he? When did you discover that?"

"Yesterday. Late mornin' or thereabouts."

*Before the second runner set off*, Wyatt thought. *So they were already coming at us from two directions.*

"We're the last, then?"

"That we are, 'ceptin' Stryker."

"Stryker's not coming," Wyatt said grimly.

"You've seen him?" Boone asked, surprised.

"What was left of him. He's dead. They all are. We came on them late yesterday. Oneida scouting party caught up with them." Wyatt frowned. "Reverend De Witt was with them."

"Oneida?" Boone sucked in his cheeks, considering the implications. "God damn." The scout stared at the ground and then looked up, his head canted. "De Witt, too, you say? Any sign of the boy?"

"Boy?" Wyatt said.

"The Hooper lad. That's why they were out. Boy ran off and the colonel sent Stryker to look for him. De Witt went with them – volunteered."

"Ah, hell," Billy Drew said.

"There was no boy," a confused Donaldson said.

"Could be the Oneida took him," Boone muttered, as if talking to himself. "Though that ain't likely, if'n they were scouts."

Wyatt shook his head. His mind was racing. "They didn't."

Boone squinted at him. "You sound mighty sure of that."

"Scouts're dead, too. We caught up with them. Save for one. We think he took off, heading for Ticonderoga, probably to meet up with Clinton's militia, pass the word the column was near."

"Didn't Tewanias say there were six riders?" Jem Beddowes interjected.

"The boy *was* on his horse," Boone responded speculatively. "Word is, he went looking for his dog."

Wyatt cast his mind back to what Tewanias had told them. *"One rode through before."*

Suddenly, everything seemed to fall into place. The sixth rider had to have been the boy. Somehow, the Oneida had passed him by but had then chanced upon the search party and laid their ambush.

Which could mean . . .

Boone cleared his throat, interrupting Wyatt's train of thought. "Boat's waitin', Lieutenant. Crew'll want to get underway. Didn't have no trouble persuadin' 'em to wait for a while, but we've overstayed our welcome and then some. We should leave. Colonel's a forgivin' man, but even he has his limitations." Boone looked over his shoulder and made a beckoning gesture. "We'd best get Nate back here."

"The boy's still out there," Wyatt said heavily.

"Boat ain't going to wait."

"Jethro's right, Lieutenant," Donaldson cut in. "Even if Tewanias got to the first runner, there's militia coming up from the south and Clinton's closing in from the east. They're practically on our doorstep. And even if we did go back in there, where would we start looking? Grieves me to say it, but the lad's gone."

Wyatt shook his head. "I made a promise. I said I'd keep him safe."

"And you did. You got him to the Hall and you persuaded the preacher to take him on. It's not your fault the lad ran off. You can't blame yourself for that. You want to blame anyone, blame the preacher."

"Preacher's dead."

224

"And we stand a good chance of ending up the same way if Clinton arrives while we're standin' arguing about it."

An awkward silence fell.

Beddowes, cradling his rifle, looked at Wyatt and said, "We going home or heading out, Lieutenant? It's your choice."

*We*, Wyatt thought. Beddowes had used the word *we* not *you*. He knew then that they would follow him. All he had to do was give the order. Torn between the promise he'd given and his duty to see his men home safely, he hesitated.

Then he heard Boone murmur, "Might not come to that, Lieutenant. Take a look."

The Rangers turned as one. Cavett was on his way back from the far end of the bay at a brisk trot, but it was not the sight of his fellow scout that had attracted Boone's sharp eye.

It was the dog.

Wyatt felt a twist in his gut.

As the men looked on, the animal turned abruptly and retraced its path into the trees. A second later it bounded out again, only to pause and look back. The first to emerge was the boy, leading the horse by its halter. The next figure to appear, to Wyatt's utter amazement, was Tewanias.

"I see it," Donaldson said, his face forming into a wide grin, his soft brogue coming to the fore. "But I don't bluidy believe it."

Wyatt managed to find his voice. "Time to move, Jethro."

While Boone gestured to the boat crew, Wyatt looked off beyond Tewanias and the boy to where the smaller figure of Nate Cavett was jogging towards them.

No, Wyatt realized with a jolt. Not jogging. The scout was running, running hard.

The report split the air with the force of a thunderclap. The explosion that followed as the ball smashed into the gunboat, laying waste her bow-chaser, igniting her powder keg and sending wood and metal splinters through the bodies of the navy crewmen as if they were made of butter, rolled around the bay, scattering wildfowl in all directions.

As the screaming began, the Rangers broke apart, searching

for cover. A patch of grey-white smoke roiling at the edge of the trees beyond Cavett's shoulder showed where the shot had originated.

"Militia!" Beddowes yelled, the warning superfluous.

The gun crew was already ramming a fresh round into the gun's barrel. It was a small-calibre fieldpiece, a three-pounder Grasshopper, Wyatt guessed; British-built, designed to accompany Light Infantry and probably captured when the Americans took Ticonderoga. Capable of being drawn by a single horse or broken down and loaded on pack animals, they were easily manoeuvrable over hard terrain and thus ideal for transporting along heavily forested trails.

A volley of lighter reports rang out. Cavett stumbled and threw his arms up, thrust forward by a projectile striking his back. He did not rise. Less than two hundred yards beyond Cavett's body, men were coming out of the woods; some in uniform, others in civilian dress. Among the leading rank were several brown-skinned figures in breech-clouts: Oneida warriors, from their feathered scalp locks.

The cannon roared again, spitting smoke. Wyatt ducked. This time, the ball landed twenty yards short. Scattering sand and stone, it bounced several times before finally rolling to an undignified halt at the end of a long furrow, one hundred yards past its intended target.

The gunboat was listing heavily with half its crew writhing bloodily in the scuppers. Wyatt saw that some wounded survivors were dragging themselves over the side and into the shallows while others, miraculously unscathed by the detonation, were trying to swim away. It had been a devastatingly accurate shot, and judging by the trajectory of the second ball, possibly a lucky one.

He looked to his men. The Rangers had found shelter behind a couple of beached tree trunks whose entwined limbs formed a natural barricade. Weapons primed, they had not opened fire. The range was too great. It would have been a waste of ammunition.

Tewanias and the boy had been less than a hundred paces

away when they'd left the woods. Now they too were running, trying to make up the ground, the dog leading the way. Somehow, the boy had retained hold of his horse, which, thrown into panic by the cannonfire, was whinnying in terror. As Wyatt looked on, the animal gave a desperate lunge and broke from the boy's grip, galloping off along the shore.

There was another boom. The top of the gunboat's mast and yard crumpled like matchwood. The gunner's aim was improving.

Wyatt slipped Tewanias's musket off his shoulder. As the Mohawk and the boy ran in behind the primitive defensive wall, Wyatt tossed Tewanias his weapon, only noticing at the last minute that the Mohawk already had a long gun strapped across his back: a carbine. As Tewanias took the catch, Wyatt saw the wound in the Indian's side.

"Get behind us, Matthew!" Wyatt urged. "Keep your head down!"

The enemy troops were still beyond rifle range but advancing quickly, using the width of the shoreline, knowing that with the gunboat's bow-chaser out of action they had little to fear from the handful of men opposing them.

A roar came from the direction of the boat. Wyatt's first thought was that another powder keg had gone up, but then he saw an eruption of smoke by the starboard gunwale. Somehow, one of the crew had managed to aim and fire the stern-mounted swivel-gun.

A close-quarter weapon devised to repel boarders, when loaded with grapeshot the swivel-gun was a man-killer. Even when fired from a distance it was capable of inflicting appalling damage.

The front line of attackers folded as the spread of musket balls ripped into them, the air misting with blood. Then the Grasshopper fired a fourth time and the gunboat was struck again. Strakes of decking flicked through the air, spearing into both the dead and the living with the force of crossbow bolts. Wyatt and his men ducked. As the smoke from the swivel-gun cleared, Wyatt saw that the muzzle was pointing impotently towards the water. The body of the crewman who'd fired it was draped, bleeding and lifeless, across the upended barrel. The vessel's mast and spar were now lying in a confused mess across the thwarts.

Wyatt looked for the militia cannon. The gun crew was holding off, possibly for fear of hitting its own men. Boone, crouched down next to him, squinted round the end of the trunks. "Bastards."

Wyatt glanced again towards the ruined gunboat. The men who'd gone overboard were clawing their way on to the stony beach. He turned back. The boy was crouched down next to Tewanias and had his arms clamped around the dog's neck. Having lost one animal to flight, he wasn't going to lose another.

It was Wyatt's turn to peer round the barricade. A few more yards and the militia would be within range of the Rangers' long guns. It struck him that he could no longer see the Indians. He looked towards the wood. Indians did not employ European tactics when they went into battle. They didn't advance in serried ranks; they used whatever natural cover was available. It was what made them such valuable allies and fighters. The Oneida, Wyatt knew, would be advancing through the trees; before long the Rangers would be outflanked.

In his mind's eye he pictured the aftermath of the attack on Stryker's men. De Witt had taken his own life rather than face the brutality of the knife. Wyatt knew that if the Oneida arrived first, there would be no restraining them. Tewanias, he saw, was also looking towards the forest, sensing what was to come.

"Make a run for it?" Jem Beddowes suggested.

*Back into the woods?* Wyatt thought. *Where the Oneida could be waiting in force?*

If it was just the Rangers and Boone, it would have been a strategy worth considering, but they had a twelve-year-old boy to consider. Oneida warriors weren't known for their discrimination and tender feelings. Keeping low, he crawled to the Mohawk's side and eyed the wound. "How bad?"

The look Tewanias gave him verged on the contemptuous. "I am not dead yet."

Wyatt smiled and then his expression hardened. He gripped the Mohawk's arm. "I want you to take the boy."

The Mohawk chief said nothing, but Wyatt could see the significance of his request taking shape behind the dark eyes.

"We'll hold them off, give you time to get away." Wyatt removed his hand and turned. "You gave us quite a scare, lad. You hurt?"

The boy shook his head.

"Good. You're to go with Tewanias. He'll look after you."

"They're coming, Lieutenant!" Donaldson announced.

Wyatt turned to Tewanias. "I need you to do this. We'll follow if we can, but you keep him safe. Promise me?"

Tewanias continued to hold Wyatt's gaze. A second passed, then two. Finally, he nodded.

The boy stared at Wyatt. "Aren't you coming?"

Wyatt smiled. "We'll be along, lad. Right now, our job is to slow the buggers down. You do as Tewanias says. You and Tam, you stay with him, no matter what. He says run, you run. He says hide, you hide. Understand?"

"Yes, sir."

"Good lad."

"Best make it quick," Donaldson warned, cocking his rifle.

"Two hundred and seventy yards, Lieutenant," Boone said. The scout spat out the remains of his tobacco plug, raised himself up, rested the length of his rifle on the top trunk and tucked the weapon into his shoulder. "Fish in a Goddamned barrel."

The Mohawk slipped the Oneida's carbine from his shoulder and handed it to Wyatt, keeping possession of his own gun. The message was obvious: *You'll need all the help you can get.*

"All right, boys." Wyatt said, placing the carbine to one side in readiness. "Pick your targets." To Tewanias, he said, "Run when I say. They'll be in range for us, but you'll be out of range for them."

"Unless the buggers have got rifles as well," Billy Drew muttered.

"Not helpful, Billy," Donaldson said sternly.

The Rangers, as skirmishers, all carried rifles which, although they took longer to load, were more accurate than muskets; useful for shooting at specific targets from a distance, namely enemy officers. Regular troops were issued with muskets, including those

229

on the Continental side, but militia used their own weapons, which because they were used for hunting, tended to have grooved bores.

"Time to find out," Wyatt said. He flicked a glance at Tewanias who, along with the boy, was crouched low, ready to move. "Set?"

The Mohawk reached out, laid his hand on the Ranger's shoulder. "O:nen ki' wahi', Wy-att."

Wyatt smiled ruefully. Words seemed inadequate.

As Tewanias took the boy's arm, Wyatt turned back and raised his weapon. "Aim for the uniforms – they're more likely to be the officers. Pick your targets. Take your first shots from me."

Steadying his breathing, Wyatt signalled that he was ready and the four Rangers and the scout rose as one. Sighting on a blue uniform, Wyatt exhaled slowly, paused, and fired.

The cue taken, four rifles cracked alongside him. As the smoke dissipated, five distant figures were left sprawling.

"Now," Wyatt said.

But Tewanias had anticipated the order and even before the reports had died away, he and the boy and the dog were moving.

When he'd led Jonah out from the trees and seen the boat and the figures of Wyatt and his men, the boy's heart had lifted in the belief that he had at last reached safety and that rescue was to hand. But that feeling had been dashed by the boom of the cannon and the arrival of the enemy soldiers. Now, as he ran from the threat of the smoke and the guns, his mind was in turmoil. He had no idea where he was running to. The only comforting thought was that Tewanias was with him. So long as that held true, he would be safe.

As he followed the Mohawk chief across the curve of foreshore towards the furthest trees, he wondered how long it would be before he saw Wyatt again. When he looked back at the puffs of smoke and heard the rifle shots, a small voice inside his head told him it might not be for some time.

Perhaps never.

After the first volley, Wyatt gave the instruction to fire at will.

Jem Beddowes, having already reloaded, rose to one knee and fired again. "Six down."

"Soon get through the rest of 'em," Boone said, ducking back. His grin was cut short as he bit the end from a fresh cartridge and sprinkled the priming powder into the pan.

Another rifle cracked.

"Seven," Donaldson said.

Billy Drew and Wyatt fired together.

"Shot," Billy Drew said, as two hundred paces in front of them two more uniforms went down.

Wyatt did not respond. Dropping back, he began to reload, his actions calm and precise.

A cry came from the woods to his right; the Oneida, drawing closer.

Wyatt knew it wouldn't be long before they were overwhelmed. The Rangers' rate of fire was such that for every twelve seconds it took to reload, the enemy advanced another fifty yards. Even with five of them firing as fast as they were able, there weren't that many seconds left. Not that many yards either. And by now they were well within range of the enemy's muskets.

Another rifle spoke.

"Ten," Jem Beddowes muttered.

Wyatt glanced over his shoulder. Tewanias and the boy had disappeared. At once it felt as if a great weight had been lifted from him. He twisted and peered towards the advancing militia. "Looks like we might just have time for one more round, lads."

"*Then* can we run?" Donaldson asked.

"Then we run," Wyatt agreed, flinching as a musket ball struck the trunk an inch from his shoulder. More shots began to ring out, thick and fast.

Boone fired then. As he squatted back down there came a muffled grunt and Billy Drew was propelled backwards, his shirt darkened by a large crimson stain. The rifle fell from his hand.

"Billy!" Donaldson spun round.

"Keep firing!" Wyatt yelled.

And then a familiar boom sounded and the Rangers ducked as the shot whirred overhead and landed thirty yards behind them. The ground mushroomed upwards. Debris rained down.

Wyatt spat out an expletive. The gun crew had re-entered the fray, no doubt out of frustration at seeing its men being cut down. The shot, Wyatt realized, had been aimed high deliberately, as a means of calculating the correct elevation; so the next one . . .

Another boom, another whimper of a projectile in flight and, even as Wyatt screamed a warning, the ball found its mark. In an instant, the world was filled with earth and rocks, pebbles and sand, flying splinters, confusion and blood. In the midst of it all, Wyatt felt himself picked up. For one glorious moment it was as if he had grown wings and taken flight. And then came the shock of falling, of hitting the ground and tumbling for what seemed like an eternity before finally coming to rest he knew not where.

As the darkness closed in around him, however, there was no pain. There was only a feeling of peace and immense pride in the courage of the men who had fought by his side during the final stand. Thanks to their actions, Tewanias and the boy had been able to make their getaway.

And a promise made to a dying man had been a promise kept.

# 9

Hawkwood woke to the sound of voices and shadows moving in the darkness of the cabin. A lantern flickered.

Caution made him turn his head slowly. His mind had been swimming with violent dreams. When he felt the cold, hard press of a gun muzzle against his left cheek, he froze.

"On your feet, Mr Smith. Easy does it."

Stagg's voice.

As the end of the barrel moved away, Hawkwood felt for the musket and then withdrew his hand. Given the confined space of the cot, by the time he'd extricated the bloody thing, he'd either have taken his eye out or else received a pistol ball through his brain. And that was without knowing why he was being summoned. Better to wait and see and then make a judgement. Drawing his coat about him, he gathered himself, sat up and swung his boots to the floor.

Lawrence was seated at the table, a subdued expression on his unshaven face. He had a gun to his head, too; held by Stagg. He raised his hands and showed his palms in a gesture of apology.

"Couldn't warn you, sorry. Six of them, one of me."

"And I had the gun," Hawkwood said.

Lawrence smiled ruefully. "And you had the gun."

233

Hawkwood's eyes swept the cabin. Stagg wasn't alone. Three of his crew were with him. Two held pistols; the third one carried a small hand-axe. Presumably, the other two were up on deck; helmsman and lookout.

Hawkwood stared hard at the axe.

"Sit." Stagg pointed with his free hand to the table bench.

Hawkwood did as he was told, making sure, as he sat down, that his legs were on the outside of the bench. The fact that there was no need to brace himself against the angle of the boat told him that *Snake* was either hove to, or as was more likely, turned into the wind, her sails slackened.

"What the hell is this, Stagg?"

"Cyrus, get the musket," Stagg ordered.

Without speaking, the crewman who'd stuck his gun in Hawkwood's face retrieved the weapon from beneath the blanket and passed it to his captain. Stagg transferred the pistol to his belt and hefted the long gun in his hand. He held the stock up to the lantern and squinted as he ran a broad thumb around the lock plate.

"Interestin'. It's got the Harpers Ferry mark." He looked at Lawrence. "Belonged to your father, Mr Jones, yes?"

"Indeed it did," Lawrence said.

"Military-issue, too, I see," Stagg continued in a conversational tone. "Your father a *military* man, then?"

Lawrence lifted his chin. "He was. Served with distinction."

"Did he now?" Stagg said, tilting his head to one side. "That's strange. Y'see they only started making these around ten years ago. Before that they all came from the Springfield armoury. Call me suspicious, but you ain't in the first flush, Mr Jones, so your father would have to be gettin' on a tad, or else he's passed over. Either way, I'm thinkin' it's unlikely he'd ever have fired this beauty in anger."

*Hell and damnation*, Hawkwood thought. *Betrayed by a bloody musket?* He took a deep breath, suspecting there was little to gain by feigning outrage. "What's your point, Stagg?"

"I'm gettin' to that." Stagg laid the musket down at the end of the table and wagged an admonishing forefinger. "Y'know, from the moment we met I kept askin' myself who the two of you might be. Not Smith and Jones, that's for sure."

"That didn't seem to matter a whole hell of a lot when you took our sixty dollars," Hawkwood said.

"Aye, well, that was then. This is now."

"And you've had time to mull things over," Hawkwood said drily.

Stagg snapped his fingers. "Exactly. Mostly, though, I've been thinkin' about that toast you made. To private enterprise."

"What about it?"

Stagg tugged an earlobe. "Got to thinkin' it weren't a bad rule. Figured I should embark on a little private enterprise of my own."

"Glad I was able to help," Hawkwood said. "But I thought that's what you were already engaged in."

"Don't mean I can't take advantage of fresh opportunities when they come along, now, does it?" Stagg countered, unfazed by Hawkwood's sarcasm. His brow puckered. "What's that word they use? Diversify? Well, that's what I'm doin'. I'm diversifyin'." His teeth waxed yellow in the lantern glow.

Hawkwood wondered what time it was. Pale light was filtering through the hatchway. Not quite dawn, he guessed.

Lawrence had relieved him shortly after midnight, in continuance of their arrangement that one of them should be awake at all times. It wasn't surprising that the crew had caught on to their precautions, but Hawkwood hadn't bargained on Stagg using the strategy against them, waiting until they had only Lawrence to deal with before springing their trap.

It was a tactic with which Hawkwood should have been familiar. He'd used it himself, in his duties as a Runner. If you wanted to pick up a suspect for questioning or arrest, you did it before first light, while they were slumbering. That way, you caught them off-guard before they were dressed for flight. Hawkwood was fully dressed but he was on a boat with no route of escape, and he'd been caught napping, literally. But as Lawrence had pointed out, one man against six wasn't the best of odds. It could just as easily have been him on deck and Lawrence in the cot.

Stagg began to pace the cabin. It was a short distance between turns and Hawkwood guessed the man was doing it to intimidate them. He and Lawrence were seated, while Stagg was showing that he was the one with the freedom to move about. Though, given his bulk, he looked more like a bear trapped in a small cage.

As Hawkwood assessed his and Lawrence's options, Stagg paused. "Thing is, I couldn't help but ask myself why you were so set on securing such a swift passage to the border. It weren't the names. Might as well have been Washington and Madison, for all I care. But I did wonder. Not about *who* you were but *what* you were. And d'you know what my first thought was? Them's military."

He looked towards Lawrence, his lips parted. The major said nothing.

"No, it's true. I said to myself, 'Remus, now there's two men who've marched a mile or three in their time.' And that got me thinkin'. If you *were* military, whose military might you be? If you were ours, there'd be no need for you to be sneakin' passage aboard the *Snake*, would there? Hell, Burlington's not more than a skip and a jump away. You could've taken a coach there and hopped aboard a transport. Question was: why didn't you? And then it came to me. It was on account of you ain't on our side." Stagg's smile broadened. "You're on theirs. Which makes you Limeys. And seein' as you ain't in uniform, *that* makes you Limey spies!"

"The hell you say!" Lawrence snapped. "We're no such thing!"

Stagg held up a hand in a gesture of appeasement. "Well, I figured *that* out for myself, didn't I? But it's what I thought *at the time*."

Lawrence stared at him. "So what do you think we are *now*?"

Stagg retrieved the pistol from his belt. "Oh, I don't *think*. I *know*." With his left hand he reached inside his coat. "Known all along, on account of information received."

"Christ's sake, Stagg," Hawkwood said. "Cut to the bloody chase. Even patient men can die of boredom."

The crinkles around Stagg's eyes disappeared as he laid the folded square of paper he'd taken from his pocket on the table by Hawkwood's elbow. Then, standing back, he waited.

Hawkwood unfolded the paper.

Both likenesses looked as though they'd been undertaken in a hurry, which, Hawkwood supposed, they probably had. As a result, they were not of a high quality, accuracy having been sacrificed in the interests of speed and urgent dispatch. Though anyone with the illustrations to hand and with Hawkwood and Lawrence seated in front of them would probably have no difficulty adding two and two and coming up with maybe three out of four. In other words, close enough for a positive identification.

It was the written physical descriptions that left less room for doubt. Everything was there, from their respective heights, hair and eye colouring to their builds and complexions. In Hawkwood's case, prominence had also been given to the faint powder-burn on his right cheek and the two scars above his left one. He had Sergeant Dunbar to thank for that, he guessed.

Highlighted in bold lettering above each of the drawings was the proclamation: $100 REWARD! Below it, in equally bold font, were the words: WANTED FOR MURDER. There then followed a brief but florid description of the brutal acts that had been committed during the escape of an English officer and his accomplice from the Greenbush military encampment. The reward was offered for the capture and apprehension of each man.

"Got that off the guard on the inbound coach from Albany not more'n an hour after we first spoke," Stagg said. "He was handin' 'em out. What's it say there? Two troopers dead, a slew more injured and a stable block burnt to the ground? Sounds like it was quite a night."

"You think this is *us*?"

"Oh, please . . ." Stagg said.

"And if I told you it wasn't?" Hawkwood said.

"That case," Stagg said drily, "I'd say you were probably talkin' to the newly crowned King of Persia."

Hawkwood tossed the handbill aside. Stagg might have been many things but he wasn't an idiot. "So what are you after, more money?"

"Hell, yes," Stagg said. "That's the general idea."

"How much?" Lawrence asked.

"Two hundred dollars is a tidy sum."

Lawrence sucked in his cheeks.

"Can't disagree with you there," Hawkwood said. "Shame we don't have it."

"Weren't askin' you for it," Stagg said dismissively. "Just pointing out it's a tidy sum. And I already got *that*."

"By that, you mean us," Hawkwood said.

"There you go," Stagg said amiably. He stabbed a finger at the handbill. "Got me a promissory note right there. All I need now is the balance."

Hawkwood wondered what Stagg would do if he jammed the handbill into his mouth and started chewing furiously.

"Balance?" Lawrence frowned. "What does that mean?"

"Means whatever you and Mister Smith are carryin'."

"We're not carrying anything!" Lawrence protested. "Damn it, we've paid you all we had!"

"Yeah, right, and as I told you I'm—"

"The King of Persia," Hawkwood said, thinking furiously. "Yes, we got that."

Stagg didn't seem too bothered by the notion that his crew was now privy to his previous financial arrangement. Either the skipper had informed his men of the transaction in the spirit of generosity or else he knew the infraction would be overlooked in favour of higher rewards to come, which only served to further illustrate the *Snake*'s chain of command.

"You expect me to believe the two of you are tapped out?" Stagg shook his head. "Don't reckon that's likely. You wouldn't leave yourselves short. Too risky. Nah, you're carryin'. Sure as God made little green apples, you're carryin'. Only question is, how much?"

As money-making schemes went, Hawkwood had to admit Stagg's master plan had its merits. First pick his and Lawrence's pockets, then hand them over to the authorities for the bounty. Two bites of the same cherry. Stagg and his crew would probably make more from this run than they had from their last half-dozen combined.

"Why wait until now?" Hawkwood asked. "If you'd already worked out who we were, you could have turned us in back at Whitehall."

Stagg pulled a face. "Aye, I could've, but that'd be too close to home. The local militia and I ain't always seen eye to eye in the past. Last thing I want is them stickin' their noses where they ain't wanted. I've got more'n forty tubs of prime potash takin' up space in the hold and a buyer lined up. Much better if we hand you over to the regulars. They'll be less inclined to go rootin' around down below. We'll get paid a sight quicker that way, too. The militia ain't exactly well organized. Most of 'em couldn't find their own socks to shit in them. Chances are they'd want to steal all the glory, too. Don't see why we shouldn't come out as heroes. It'll stand us in good stead with them that matter. Give us a reputation as upstandin' citizens. Might even result in the authorities turning a blind eye to some of our more – how shall I put it? – minor infringements. Won't do us any harm, leastways, you can be certain of that."

"Sounds as if you've thought it all through," Hawkwood said.

"Caught *you* with your breeches down," Stagg quipped.

"Can't argue with that," Hawkwood agreed. "Especially as you're the one holding the gun."

"I knew you'd see it my way." Stagg chuckled at his own wit and then straightened. "Right then, time to tally up. Funny, I was about to say 'Mr Smith', but maybe I should be callin' you Hooper? That's the name they've given you on the poster there." Stagg turned towards Lawrence. "Which'd make you Major Lawrence, yes?"

"No flies on you, Stagg, are there?" Hawkwood said. "But what if we don't want to give you our money?"

Stagg looked at him and then shook his head. "You ain't that stupid. You know you ain't got a choice. Hand bill don't say anything about you being dead or alive. That means they don't care. So either we shoot you where you sit, take your money anyway and wrap you up ready for collection, or you hand it over voluntarily and we deliver you to the military in one piece. That way, at least you'll get to live – until they hang you, that is. An' it means I don't have to put up with you bleedin' out all over my deck. Save a deal of moppin' up. The lads don't like moppin' up. Do you, boys?"

"You call that an option?"

Stagg showed his teeth. "You know what they say: where there's breath there's hope."

"We'll see you well rewarded if you get us to the border," Lawrence said.

"Figured you might say that," Stagg responded, awarding himself a knowing smile. "If'n I were in your shoes, I'd try the same thing. But all things considered, I reckon we'll pass. Not that I don't trust you, of course, as officers and gentlemen – even if you are wanted for killin' two of New York's finest. But we've just rounded Caution Point; Plattsburg's no more'n twelve miles off our port bow. Come late morning, you'll be the army's problem an' we'll be bound for St Johns. That way, everyone's happy."

"Except us," Hawkwood pointed out.

Stagg shrugged. "True, but I don't plan on losin' any sleep over *that*."

"Enough of the talking, Remus. Let's see what they've got."

Lawrence fixed the speaker with a steady gaze, though when he spoke it was with cold menace. "If I were you, my friend, I'd be careful what you wish for."

Before the crewman could formulate a reply, Stagg raised his pistol and aimed it at Hawkwood. "Talkin's over. You first. What'll it be?"

Hawkwood stared about the cabin and took a deep, calming breath. Then, reaching inside his coat, he said resignedly, "Doesn't look as though we've much choice, does it?"

"There you go," Stagg said, a grin forming. "You know it makes sen—"

The word died in Stagg's throat as in one fluid move Hawkwood drew out the pistol he'd cocked when rising from his cot, and shot Stagg through the right eye.

The sound of the gun was incredibly loud. Stagg's head snapped back. Blood and brains splattered the bulkhead behind him. The pistol he'd been holding clattered to the deck.

Lawrence was already rising, going for the man at his shoulder. Hawkwood jerked aside as the second armed crewman threw up his pistol only to discover as he tried to fire off a shot that he'd failed to cock it.

*Amateur*, Hawkwood thought as he came off the bench and swept his spent pistol towards the smuggler's gun hand. The barrel slammed into the wrist as the other pistol discharged. The blow was enough to distract the smuggler's aim. The ball grazed Hawkwood's shoulder and struck the lantern, snuffing out the candle and plunging the cabin into darkness.

Attempting to adjust his eyes to the sudden gloom, Hawkwood launched a foot strike at the crewman's groin. He felt his boot connect and as the man collapsed, he transferred the pistol to his left hand and turned to face the last crew member who was plunging towards him, arm drawn back.

Hawkwood used the pistol to parry the downward blow. Sparks flashed as the hatchet blade caught the side of the flint and drove down against the pistol's lock plate, knocking the weapon from Hawkwood's hand. Before the axe could rise again, Hawkwood drew the knife from his right boot and drove it into the attacker's thigh. A scream pierced the cabin as the blade sank in and Hawkwood felt the warm rush of blood across his wrist and forearm. Releasing the knife hilt, he scrambled to where he thought Stagg's pistol had fallen. But as he turned he sensed the hatchet cleaving towards him for a second time.

The axeman, grievously wounded and losing blood, was already off balance. Hampered by his injury, he missed his target. The blade shaved Hawkwood's arm by a hair's width and thudded into the table. Hawkwood kicked out again, felt the hard edge of his heel connect with something pliant and was rewarded with another ghastly shriek.

As the axeman fell away, a cry of alarm rang out from the pair who'd remained on deck. A clatter of boots sounded as, alerted by the commotion below, one of the two men left his mate on the tiller and raced towards the open hatchway.

A scraping sound came from just above Hawkwood's head. Fearing it was the axe on its way down again, he lifted his arm in a futile attempt to ward off the blow and felt something solid strike his shoulder. For one awful moment he thought it was the blade, but then he realized it was the discarded musket sliding from the tabletop. Pulling the weapon towards him, he pawed back the hammer. A crouching shape loomed into view: the smuggler whose pistol shot had broken the lantern. Hawkwood rammed the musket into the crewman's chest and pulled the trigger.

A flash and another loud report and the man was punched backwards, limbs flopping.

Several violent thuds and a stream of muttered invective came from the other side of the cabin.

"Major!" Hawkwood called, as a fresh shadow arrived in the well beneath the hatch: the topside man coming to his captain's aid.

"Here!"

"Stairs!" Hawkwood yelled.

There was a sharp crack and a pistol ball thudded into the bulkhead at the base of the ladder. Splinters flew. The crewman swore, ducked out of sight and retreated back on deck.

Hawkwood, his eyes now adjusted to the gloom, rose cautiously to his feet, musket in hand.

The cabin lay in chaos. Stagg's body was wedged between the floor and the bulkhead, his once-broad bulk diminished and made insignificant by death. The axeman showed no signs of life. The stiletto had punctured his artery and the deck beneath him was slick with blood. Lawrence's victim was sprawled in the corner of the cabin, his side-turned face a bloody ruin after repeated blows from the pistol butt gripped in Lawrence's right hand. The fourth body was huddled at the foot of the companionway, having been flung there by the force of Hawkwood's musket shot.

The air that had once reeked of tar and sweat was now heavy with the scent of black powder, blood and death.

Hawkwood turned to Lawrence. "You hurt?"

"Nothing a stiff drink wouldn't fix." Lawrence's chest heaved as he regained his breath and stared about him. His clothing was dishevelled and there was a graze across his forehead. The pistol hung down by his side. "Christ, we were lucky. What a bloody mess."

Luck might have had something to do with it, Hawkwood thought, but mostly their survival had been down to his and Lawrence's military experience and their willingness to seize the initiative when it was presented to them. Stagg's crew might have had the weapons and the muscle, but they lacked the brains to make full use of them when under threat.

Setting the musket to one side, Hawkwood resumed his search for Stagg's pistol. He found it on the floor by the table leg. After checking the flint, spring and contents of the pan, he ratcheted the hammer back to half-cock. "There are two left."

"Means we've levelled the odds," Lawrence muttered. He looked towards the companionway. "I doubt either of them'll be too eager to play the hero."

"Maybe not, but the fact remains, they have the advantage. They're up top and we're trapped below. There's only one way out and that's through the hatch."

"We can try bargaining. With Stagg and the rest of their crew down, they're more likely to see reason."

Hawkwood bent, withdrew the stiletto and wiped it unceremoniously on the dead man's shirt. "Or we attack," he said quietly. "Take the fight to them while their wits are still addled. If we wait, all they have to do is keep us pinned down here until we dock. We need to seize this vessel, and the sooner we do that the better."

While Hawkwood returned the knife to his boot, Lawrence considered the notion. "With one loaded pistol between the two of us?" he asked dubiously.

"They don't know that. We cut one of them down and that puts us in the majority."

"Well, I can't fault your logic, but there's one other small snag; can you sail this boat?"

"Don't have to sail her. There's a rowboat."

"Jesus," Lawrence said, sounding mortified. "It's a bloody long row. To anywhere."

"Better than the alternative: ending up in the stockade with nooses around our necks."

"Point taken," Lawrence conceded. "So, what's it to be? Slow and cautious, or do we go out in a blaze of glory?"

Hawkwood drew back the hammer of Stagg's pistol.

"Last one up the stairs is first at the oars."

"Easy for you to say – you're the only one with a full load. All I've got is a bloody club." Brandishing the empty pistol, Lawrence clicked his tongue and then grinned. "So, after you."

Hawkwood was half a step from the ladder when the scrape of a boot at the top of the companionway made them both pause.

"Remus?" a rough voice called tentatively. "You down there?"

*Not any more*, Hawkwood thought. Despite the accepted view that those commanding the high ground inevitably had the advantage, he was confident that the crewman would hold his fire for half a second for fear of shooting his captain.

It helped also that Hawkwood and Lawrence were partly in shadow at the bottom of the companionway, whereas the crewman, in his anxiety to establish who had survived the fight, had allowed himself to be silhouetted against the open hatch.

Half a second was all it took.

Hawkwood's shot struck home before his target could correct his mistake. Clutching his pistol, the crewman fell back with a cry. By the time he'd released his last breath, Hawkwood and Lawrence were on deck, Hawkwood swapping the dead man's pistol for his own on the way.

"Don't!" Lawrence aimed his empty gun at the helmsman's chest. "Whatever you were thinking of doing – don't. It would be most unwise."

The helmsman's face dropped. Fear moved across his features as his hands hovered on the tiller bar.

"Seeing as there's only one of you," Hawkwood said.

"If you don't believe us," Lawrence said, "ask yourself how come we're the only ones on deck holding guns."

"If you've a weapon to hand, tell us," Hawkwood said. "Now."

There was a pause as the helmsman considered his options. Then: "Knife. Back of my belt."

"Toss it over the side," Hawkwood instructed. "You even think of throwing it anywhere else and Mr Jones here will put a ball through your brain. What's your name?"

"Walter . . . Walter Maddox."

A faint splash sounded beyond the boat's hull as the knife hit the water.

"All right, Walter," Lawrence said as Hawkwood moved to the rail. "Both hands on the tiller, there's a good lad. And make sure you keep them there."

The angle and lack of movement of the boat should have been an indication, Hawkwood supposed, but in the mayhem that had followed his awakening it hadn't occurred to him that the *Snake*'s progress might have slowed due to weather conditions rather than as a result of Stagg's orders.

The muted light that had he'd seen filtering down the stairwell was not the pale glow of dawn. No sun could penetrate the bank of fog that surrounded them. Visibility was restricted to half a cable's length on all sides. From the slight curve in the mainsail above him, Hawkwood could see that a small breeze was trying its level best to push them along, but it was a futile effort. They were barely moving.

He turned. "What's our position, Walter?"

"He's talking to you," Lawrence said.

The helmsman dragged his eyes from the bloody corpse at the top of the ladder to the binnacle compass in front of him. He nodded nervously towards an unseen point off the starboard bow. "Remus reckoned we were comin' up on the Two Sisters."

Hawkwood had no idea what the Two Sisters were. Presumably a pair of rocks or islands, not that it mattered. It wasn't as though they'd be landing on either of them. He moved to the compass and saw that they were on a north-easterly heading.

"How well do you know these waters?" he demanded.

Unsure as to what was expected of him, the crewman replied, "Well enough."

"Good. You've just saved yourself a swim."

The crewman glanced at the rail and then back. "You ain't goin' to kill me?" he asked, his voice breaking with relief.

Hawkwood shrugged. "Haven't decided yet. The day is young. Put it this way: you getting us to the border won't do your cause any harm. Do we understand each other?"

The helmsman nodded though there was doubt in his expression.

"Good. Maintain your course."

"And that?" Lawrence indicated the body.

"We'll put it over the side."

"The others, too?"

"Soon as we can bring them up."

"You and me?" Lawrence asked.

Hawkwood shook his head. "Me and Walter. You can take the helm."

Lawrence looked sceptical.

"Just try not to hit anything or run aground," Hawkwood said with a grin. He turned to crook a finger, only to discover that the helmsman's attention was fixed on the area of fog lying off the *Snake*'s starboard transom.

Hawkwood followed the man's gaze. At first, there was nothing and then his ears caught it; a pounding sound, vaguely muffled.

*Thunder?* There had been no suggestion of a storm brewing, and there was nothing in the benign motion of the wash beneath *Snake*'s keel to indicate anything amiss. Other than an inability to see more than a few yards in any direction, the weather conditions seemed unremarkable.

He listened carefully. The thumping noise was growing louder. Although distorted by the fog, it was maddeningly persistent. It was only as he listened for a further second or two, trying to identify which direction it was coming from, that he realized it was too rhythmic to be thunder. And the tone kept alternating, like waves dashing against a rocky shoreline, one after the other, in quick succession.

Hawkwood's blood suddenly ran cold. His mind flashed back to the cross-Channel voyage he'd taken aboard the Royal Navy cutter *Griffin,* when, engulfed by mountainous seas during an appallingly violent storm, both the cutter and his mission had come close to foundering on the Pas de Calais coast.

"What the hell *is* that?" Lawrence whispered.

Hawkwood was too intent on trying to pierce the curtain of fog to reply. There was something profoundly unsettling about not being able to see what lay beyond their bow. And with each second the sound – whatever it was – was getting louder.

The helmsman gasped.

Hawkwood turned to see a dark and monstrous outline materializing at the edge of his vision. And then, just as quickly, it was gone, back into the murk, leaving him with no clear idea of what it was he'd glimpsed. His first thought was that it had been part of a rockface, like the one they'd passed the previous evening. Stagg had referred to the feature as the Palisades, an apt name for the huge granite wall that had risen sheer out of the water to a height of some seventy or eighty feet on the New York side of the lake.

Was that what he'd glimpsed? To add to his confusion, in the brief moment before the shape had melted back into the shadows, Hawkwood could have sworn that high above it he'd seen sparks and an ember-like glow, as if someone was stoking a fire, which made no sense at all.

He was on the point of bellowing uselessly at the helmsman to get them the hell out of there when abruptly the noise changed. Hawkwood knew then that he was not listening to a natural sound, but something else, something man-made, something mechanical.

Something familiar.

And as the realization hit him, the helmsman screamed.

The steamboat was not travelling at maximum speed, but given the *Snake*'s sluggish rate of progress it seemed to erupt from the fog bank with the force of a battering ram, smoke belching, paddles churning furiously. Bright tongues of orange flame shot from the vessel's stack, creating demonic flashes within the swirling vortex of smoke and fog.

As Hawkwood thrust the pistol into his belt and leapt to add his weight to the helm, Lawrence shouted a warning, only to have his words eclipsed by an ear-splitting howl as steam was blasted through the steamboat's hooter vent. Vomiting fire and ash, the vessel bore down upon the *Snake* with the fury of a nightmare come to life, disproving the myth that fire-breathing dragons were only the stuff of fairytales.

The smaller boat stood no chance. Her matte-black hull, dun-coloured sail and lack of running lights meant that she'd been invisible to the steamboat crew until the moment the fog had parted, thus rendering it impossible for evasive action to be taken, by either craft.

The steamboat struck the sloop on her starboard quarter, some ten feet forward of her mainmast.

A thousand tormented souls could not have produced a more terrible sound than that made by the sailboat's timbers as they took the full brunt of the charge. The grinding and splintering almost drowned out the hiss and rumble of the steamboat's engine as her bow surged through what remained of the sloop's exposed foredeck and jib.

As the shock ran through the hull, Hawkwood, flung aside, made a grab for the tiller. By some miracle he managed to hang on. The crewman was less fortunate. With a despairing wail, he was gone, pitched backwards over the starboard gunwale. Limbs thrashing, his mouth opened in one last frenzied plea for help as his struggling body sank beneath the surface.

Arms clamped around the tiller bar, Hawkwood saw that Lawrence had also managed to remain upright and was trying to clamber his way aft. But then, as he watched helplessly, the deck shifted again and as the mast, shorn of its braces, toppled across the thwarts in a confusion of broken spars and torn canvas, the major's legs gave way and he disappeared from view.

The *Snake*'s stern rose sharply. Boots braced against the binnacle, and with the water rushing towards him along the already half-submerged scuppers, Hawkwood knew his only chance lay in abandoning ship. He closed his eyes.

*Christ, not again.*

He'd been in similar straits back on the *Griffin*. Convinced she'd been on the point of capsizing, he'd consigned himself to the mercy of the Channel, only to discover later that the cutter had in fact survived the storm. The thought of making the same mistake filled him with dread even though it didn't take a master mariner to see that the *Snake*, unlike the *Griffin*, was beyond salvage.

He let go of the tiller and clambered to the rail.

*Coat!* he thought suddenly. Realizing that the added weight would surely drag him down, he scrabbled at the buttons. As he did so, a loud groan came from deep within the sloop's stricken hull and the deck rose sharply. The *Snake* was turning turtle. Forget the damned coat. No time left.

As he launched himself over the side, he heard a fresh thudding sound. He didn't have to look to know where the sound was coming from. But as he hit the water and as the shock and the cold drove the air from his lungs, he looked anyway.

The steamboat's paddle blades were creating such a froth it was like staring into a boiling cauldron. A dark object appeared within the turbulence and Hawkwood realized it was a body. Whether it was Maddox or another of Stagg's crew, or even Lawrence, he couldn't tell. Within seconds it was drawn down beneath the revolving blades.

In desperation, he kicked out but his legs felt as heavy as lead. The coat and the water in his boots were pulling him down. He tried moving his arms, but that proved just as difficult. His limbs were refusing to obey the signals sent by his brain. With the cold sapping his strength at such an extraordinary rate, swimming any distance was out of the question. Energy was leaching from his body with each expelled breath. And the paddlewheel was getting closer. Its pull was sucking him towards the maelstrom.

Then his head went under.

Water surged into his mouth and nostrils. He clawed for the surface. This time, his arms were able to obey the command and his head broke through. Coughing out water, he gulped in air.

And something hit him on the shoulder.

One of the paddle blades was his first thought. Terror took over. Without any rational thought of how ineffective such a gesture would be, he tried to bat it away.

And a voice that seemed to come from nowhere yelled, "WHORE!"

He felt another thump, harder, this time against his arm, and the cry came again, clearer this time and much closer.

"OAR!"

A dark shadow materialized above him. He flinched.

"Christ's sake's, man! Grab the bloody OAR!"

*Lawrence?* He thought weakly. *How?*

Something struck the water in front of him. He lunged towards it, found it was the oar's shaft and fumbled his way along its length. The oar was reeled in and the back of his collar was gripped.

"Reach up, God damn it! Here!"

Retching, Hawkwood felt his right wrist grabbed. Letting go of the oar, he reached up with his left hand for the dinghy's gunwale.

"Hold on!"

With a supreme effort he managed to hoist both elbows over the side of the boat. Then, with Lawrence braced against the side and holding on to his sodden coat, he was able to haul himself unceremoniously out of the water. As he lay fighting for breath at the bottom of the dinghy, he felt a comforting hand on his shoulder and heard Lawrence say, "I think the bastard's stopping."

Shivering violently, Hawkwood raised himself up. There was no sign of the *Snake*. The steamboat's aft section filled his field of vision. Sparks were still shooting from her thin smokestack, but Hawkwood saw that she was indeed reducing speed. Her paddles were slowing. Then the beat of her engine changed and he knew she was going into reverse.

Lawrence muttered something. Not catching the words, Hawkwood looked up to find that Lawrence was staring at the name painted across the steamboat's stern.

*Vermont.*

"I'll be damned," Lawrence swore hoarsely. "Whatever the hell that beast is, it looks as if we've caught the bloody ferry after all."

# 10

"Special couriers, you say?"

"Bearing dispatches for General Dearborn. Yes, sir."

Hawkwood tipped the rest of the brandy into his coffee and gripped the mug tightly, grateful for the warmth spreading slowly through his palms and fingertips. He took a swig and wondered how long it would be before he stopped shivering and was able to feel his toes again. A while, probably, though he knew that the tremor in his hands and the throbbing in his head came not only from his submersion in the lake's cold waters and the effects of the brandy but also from the engine vibrations pulsing through the deck beneath his feet, and the turning of the paddlewheels on the other side of the bulkheads.

They were seated in the steamboat's stern cabin, dressed in borrowed jackets and trousers, courtesy of the crew's slop chest. Their own clothes had been taken away to be dried off in the fire room, wherever and whatever the hell that was. The steamboat's captain had assured them that they would be returned in a wearable condition probably within the hour or shortly there-after, which seemed to Hawkwood to be more than a tad optimistic.

The captain's name was Winans. Smartly dressed in a dark blue pea-coat, he was a sturdily built man with close-cropped grey hair, matching beard, a solemn expression and the practice of clasping his hands behind his back as if he was striding across

253

the quarterdeck of a frigate rather than the aft compartment of a smoke-belching paddle boat.

His brisk, economic manner suggested he was not a man who suffered fools gladly. Indeed, this trait had betrayed itself soon after he'd provided his uninvited passengers with their dry wardrobe, at which point he'd demanded to know who they were and what the devil did they think they were doing sailing a vessel without lights?

Hawkwood's response did not seem to mollify him in the least, for he continued glowering at them, leaning across his chart table in an adversarial pose.

"And you were aboard the sloop, why?" he demanded.

To buy himself time, Hawkwood raised the mug to his lips and took another slow drink, exaggerating the shakiness in his grip.

"There's not a lot to tell, sir. Captain Douglas and I were on our way from Albany. We heard the Caldwell road was flooded and decided it would be best if we continued the rest of the way by boat. We got as far as Whitehall but found we'd missed the schooner. Unfortunately, we ran into a little trouble with our choice of an alternative vessel."

Captain Winans' chin lifted. "Go on."

"Damned crew turned out to be Federalist sympathizers, didn't they?"

"On a contraband run," Lawrence cut in. "Bound for St Johns. They thought they could make a bit extra by handing us over to the British."

"Smugglers?"

"That'd be one word for them," Lawrence grated. "Traitorous scum, more like."

Hawkwood smiled ruefully. "We weren't in uniform. I imagine someone spotted the regimental branding on our mounts and took a guess that we might not be what we seemed. It was our own damned fault – we should have been more attentive. Being so close to journey's end made us careless."

"They attacked just before you struck us," Lawrence continued. "Captain Matthews and I managed to subdue a couple of them, but it wouldn't have been long before we were overwhelmed. Might seem an odd thing to say, sir, given what's taken place, but it was a damned good job you happened along when you did." Lawrence hesitated and then enquired speculatively. "You haven't picked any of them up, I take it?"

The reply was curt. "We have not. As far as we've determined, you and Captain Matthews are the only survivors." Winans looked to his first officer for confirmation. "Mr Renner?"

Renner, a dark-haired young man with a round, mobile face and the air of someone trying to appear more mature than his years stood by the door. He straightened. "That's the size of it, sir. Some scraps of wreckage, but no bodies. Fog didn't help us, mind," he added pointedly.

At the mention of bodies, the captain's jaw flexed. Hawkwood guessed that Winans was contemplating the entry this would necessitate in the steamboat's log. Presumably such collisions could have a detrimental effect on one's career prospects.

"You ask me," Lawrence muttered darkly, "drowning was too good for the bastards."

Captain Winans stared hard at Lawrence, his eyes scrutinizing the graze on the major's forehead. He frowned. Then, shoving the charts aside, he drew a notepad towards him and picked up his pen. "I shall require details. The name of the vessel was . . .?"

"The *Snake*," Hawkwood said, "out of Whitehall. The master's name was Stagg."

It was almost comical the way the captain's pen paused in mid-air. A tiny bead of ink dropped from the nib to the notepad beneath, splattering minute black speckles across the open page.

"*Remus* Stagg?" Captain Winans said, glancing towards his first officer, who was staring at Hawkwood, slack-jawed, as though he couldn't quite believe what he'd heard either.

"You knew him?" Hawkwood said. Thinking, *Christ, that's all we bloody need!*

Captain Winans' mouth took on a downward curve as he dabbed the inkstains with the corner of his sleeve. "I think it would be fair to say that we are not . . . *un*familiar with his activities."

"He's a black-hearted rogue, is what he is!" Renner interjected sharply, earning an admonishing glance from his captain.

"*Was*," Lawrence corrected. "Now, he's fish bait."

A pregnant silence followed. Hawkwood watched as an approving smile broke across First Officer Renner's face.

In contrast, as befitting his rank, Captain Winans' expression remained tactfully neutral. After several seconds thought, he cleared his throat. "The crew; how many were there?"

"Six," Hawkwood said. "Including Stagg. If you require names, I can provide a couple. Walter Maddox and one that Stagg called Cyrus. I couldn't tell you any of the others."

*Not that I give a damn.*

Lawrence gave an apologetic shrug. "Can't help you either, Captain. I'm sorry."

Winans absorbed the information in silence and wrote down the names. "I see," he said pensively. "Well, I dare say their families will come forward when the vessel's loss becomes known." He looked at Hawkwood. "And the dispatches you were carrying? What of those?"

Hawkwood shook his head. "As far as we know, they're at the bottom of the lake. We did try to retrieve the pouch, but it all happened so damned quickly. There wasn't time to gather anything. All we have are the clothes we were standing in."

Which wasn't strictly true, for they also had the last of the guineas; half of which Hawkwood had transferred from his jacket to the hollowed heel of his boot. The rest were inside Lawrence's belt.

The captain favoured Hawkwood with an unexpectedly wry smile. "It's fortunate you weren't in your nightshirts then. Though I dare say your quartermaster will be able to replace some of the items you lost."

"I expect so," Hawkwood said. "There was nothing of sentimental value."

*Unless, of course, you counted Lawrence's father's mythical bloody musket.*

Captain Winans continued to stare hard at Hawkwood and

for several seconds his gaze did not falter. Finally, putting down his pen, he placed his palms on the chart table and pushed back his chair. "In that case, I believe our business here is done. I have all the relevant information. Unless either of you has anything pertinent to add . . .?"

"No, sir," Hawkwood said, putting down his drink and rising to his feet. Lawrence did the same.

Winans stood. "Very well. I shall leave you in Mr Renner's capable hands while I attend to my report. *Vermont* has undergone some refurbishment since the . . . ah . . . military requisitioned her services and our passenger facilities are not what they were. Nevertheless, I think you'll find them agreeable enough, at least for the duration of your passage."

Winans looked towards the stern window. "I see the fog's almost lifted. We've an hour yet before we reach Plattsburg. I suggest you make yourselves comfortable until then."

Stepping out from behind his chart table, Captain Winans drew himself up. "I'm sorry we had to meet under such unfortunate circumstances."

"Unfortunate for Stagg maybe," Lawrence said with a smile as he shook Winans' proffered hand. "Not for us. We can't thank you enough, sir. It would have been a damned tiring row had you not stopped to pick us up."

Hawkwood kept his face straight. "I'll be submitting my own report, of course, Captain. General Dearborn will want a full account of the incident. I can't say that I'm looking forward to explaining how Captain Douglas and I allowed ourselves to be hoodwinked by scoundrels, but you may rest assured the general will be fully informed of the role you and your crew played in delivering us from Remus Stagg's clutches."

For a moment Winans appeared disconcerted by this. Then a new light glimmered in his eyes. At first Hawkwood thought it was gratitude he was seeing, but then he realized it was more than that. There was relief there, too.

It confirmed his suspicions; for all his air of authority, Captain Winans had been wary lest he and his crew be held responsible for the collision. Had they been so inclined, the men he knew as Douglas and Matthews could have made his life very difficult by levelling accusations of reckless seamanship or, worse, gross negligence on his part. Those fears had dissipated now that he had discovered the identities of the men who had perished and the nature of their business.

Hawkwood's false admission that he and Lawrence feared they may have been negligent in letting themselves to be taken by Stagg had helped their cause. By massaging the facts and by promising to portray the captain as their saviour, Hawkwood had convinced Winans that the three of them were now allies by virtue of a shared sense of culpability. It meant Hawkwood and Lawrence wouldn't have to look over their shoulders for the duration of the voyage to Plattsburg.

The Northern Army's winter quarters and home to several thousand American troops.

And the very last place on earth they wanted to be.

Watching the gang of stokers feed the supply of pine logs into the furnace's open maw, it occurred to Hawkwood that if anyone was of a mind to wonder what the pits of hell might be like they'd be well advised to pay a visit to a steamboat's fire room.

Never had a place been so aptly named. The heat was ferocious, and the heightened activity and noise made it impossible to follow Renner's attempts to explain the vessel's inner workings, as much of his commentary was drowned out by the pounding of the machinery. The odd words that Hawkwood did manage to pick up between the hissing and the clanking and the roaring of the flames might as well have been in Mandarin for all the sense they made. So, while Renner waxed lyrical about reciprocating engines, steam generators, crank shafts and gauges, Hawkwood and Lawrence exchanged the slop chest's seconds for their own attire – retrieved from one of the boiler rails – and did their best to appear impressed whenever Renner looked to them for a reaction.

They returned to the deck with their ears ringing. The drop in temperature that greeted them was a welcome relief, but it didn't take long for the rawness of the day to make its presence felt. Not that the cold deterred Renner from his determination to extol the rest of the steamboat's virtues.

Forced to pit his voice against the noise from the starboard paddlewheel revolving loudly only a few feet away, his face lit up. "Quite a sight, yes? She'll do five knots fully stoked!"

"Five? Really?" Lawrence arched his eyebrows in dutiful amazement. "Why, that's close to—"

"Six miles an hour!" Renner finished effusively, unconcerned by the spray from the blades misting the air where they stood.

"Well, by God!" Lawrence shook his head as though thoroughly awed by the revelation. "Six!" He blinked water out of his eye and caught Hawkwood's gaze. "Would you credit that?"

"Rain or shine," Renner added, his face and jacket growing damper by the minute. "Makes no difference."

"I can see why she was requisitioned," Hawkwood said. "She must beat anything the British have."

"Oh, they've nothing to touch her. Nothing," Renner responded, guiding them towards the stern, away from the pounding paddles and the relentless deluge. "She'll do Whitehall to St Johns and back in two days. Takes the schooner at least a week, sometimes two."

"I saw the *Paragon* in Albany," Hawkwood said, bracing himself against the trembling of the deck.

"Did you indeed? She's new – launched last year. Twice our tonnage; a little faster, too, I believe." A small smile dimpled the first officer's face. "Fulton always was a braggart. He has a rather annoying tendency to argue that bigger is better." Renner tapped the steamboat's rail affectionately. "That's not necessarily the case."

Hawkwood sensed that a question was expected. It seemed churlish to disappoint.

"Fulton didn't build this boat?"

"He did not. She's the captain's own, born and bred."

"Captain *Winans*?"

"Yes, sir. He and his brother. They started out as ship's carpenters. They worked for Fulton when he built the *Clermont*. Served their apprenticeship, you might say. From that, they were able to set up their own yard." Renner waved a hand towards the Vermont side of the lake. "She was launched at Burlington, back in '09. That's when they set up the Whitehall to St Johns ferry route, to link the gap between the Montreal to St Johns stage and the Whitehall to Troy run. That was before the war, of course; before she was commandeered. In those days, all we carried were civilians and the odd item of freight. Now it's corporals and commissary and whatever else the army wants us to deliver."

As he spoke, Renner jerked his chin towards the steamboat's bow.

Hawkwood looked. It had been dark and foggy when he and Lawrence had been helped aboard, cold and dripping and thankful to be alive. Neither of them had been in a fit state to take an inventory of the tarpaulin-covered objects taking up most of the deck space forward of the steamboat's smokestack and boiler well. Now, with the view transformed by daylight, some of the *Vermont*'s cargo was revealed.

To a civilian, the items would have been of no interest. Hawkwood's familiarity with army ordnance, however, gave him a different perspective. His experienced eye could detect the shape of artillery pieces even when they were broken into components and partially covered over. As far as he could tell from the barrel sizes, they weren't large calibre. Six-pounders, at a guess; each one maybe two thousand pounds dead weight. The rest of the goods stacked closely either side of them could have consisted of anything from rifles to roundshot or even a regimental goat, it was impossible to tell. But the guns stood out.

"Seems a bit late in the season to be transporting field guns," Hawkwood ventured. "I'd have thought everything would have been secured in winter quarters by now."

"You'd know more about that than me, Captain." As he spoke, Renner looked off towards the surrounding forestland. "All I can tell you is it's a good job we've a plentiful supply of fuel on the doorstep, the number of trips we've been making back and forth. If I didn't know any better, I'd have said . . ."

Renner paused abruptly. As Hawkwood and Lawrence waited

expectantly he offered an embarrassed smile. "My apologies. Far be it from me to question the general's strategy. I mean no offence."

"None taken, Mr Renner," Hawkwood countered quickly. "On the contrary, we're most interested in your take on things. Captain Douglas and I have been up on the Niagara these past few months. We've not been privy to all that's happened on the Champlain front. I dare say you've learned by now that generals don't always confide in the lower ranks, so if you've some scuttlebutt you'd like to share, feel free. It might give us an indication of what we can expect when we report to our regiment."

Renner's smile remained. Reassured, his eyes showed a degree more humour than had been there before, though when he finally spoke there remained a note of caution in his voice.

"I was about to say that, given the level of preparations, it seems reasonable to suppose there's something brewing."

"Such as?" Lawrence frowned and drew closer.

"That, I wouldn't know, but as Captain Matthews said, it's late in the year to be moving this much artillery, and yet the army's had us ferrying men and supplies from Burlington at such a rate . . ." Once more, Renner's voice trailed off.

"Yes?" Hawkwood prompted.

Renner made another apologetic face. "At such a rate one would think the army is afraid it's running out of time."

"That'll be due to the weather, surely," Lawrence observed.

"Aye, probably," Renner agreed, but there was uncertainty in his voice. "*Vermont*'s faster than the schooner and she's not hampered by rain or lack of wind. For every return trip the schooner makes, *Vermont* will make three, which would indicate they want the equipment transported as quickly as possible, before the lake's iced in."

"What sort of equipment?" Hawkwood asked.

"That's what I was getting at," Renner said. "It's not just been basic supplies. We've been transporting a lot of armaments, like those field guns." Renner jerked his head at the deck cargo. "Small arms, too, along with powder and shot, of course, and tents. And then there were the troop carriers. I—"

261

"Troop carriers?" Hawkwood said.

Lawrence's head came up. Even though they were out of the paddlewheel's range, his shoulders and coat collar shone with water droplets.

Renner turned. "Batteaux. Well over a hundred of them; it took several convoys. They were quite a sight, I can tell you; strung out in lines on the lake."

Hawkwood didn't have to look at Lawrence to know what he was thinking. It was a certainty that the boats Renner was talking about were the batteaux constructed during the military's takeover of the Whitehall shipyard.

"We were shuttling troops before then, though," Renner said. "If you include the sick and wounded, we must have transferred more than a couple of thousand, all told."

"To Plattsburg," Hawkwood said.

"And some to Cumberland Head. All save the terminally sick. Those we delivered to Crab Island."

"What's at Crab Island?"

"A hospital. It's new. Parts of it are still under construction. Built especially for the war, they say."

"There's not one at Burlington?" Lawrence asked.

"There is, but the good citizens of Burlington didn't want the soldiers filling up their hospital beds." There was an abrasive edge to Renner's voice.

"Why not?"

"They were too sick."

"*Too* sick?" Lawrence echoed warily. "What was wrong with them?"

"Dysentery, typhus, smallpox, pneumonia – take your pick. The pneumonia's proved particularly virulent. It's spread beyond the barracks. I understand there have been more than fifty civilian deaths so far."

Lawrence grimaced. "In that case, you can't blame the towns-folk. But moving men when they're in that condition – that's not good."

"It was General Dearborn's orders, on the advice of Surgeon-Major Lovell."

"That's madness," Hawkwood said. "What if some of the men you took to Plattsburg were sick without anyone knowing? They'd spread the diseases even further."

"That's why the Plattsburg townsfolk haven't welcomed them with open arms either. The army's been forced to set up camp a couple of miles out of town, only there aren't the facilities to house them, which is why they needed the tents, as temporary accommodation until proper huts are built."

"Hell, tents won't see them through the winter. If that's all they've got, a lot more are going to fall ill and a lot more are going to die. They should have left them to see the winter out where they were, then transfer them come the thaw."

"Bloody generals," Lawrence muttered. He threw Hawkwood a knowing look and shook his head vexedly. "Was it ever thus?"

"I heard that Fulton was making a military version of *his* steamship," Hawkwood said after a pause.

Renner looked grateful for the change of subject. "I heard the same rumour, but I doubt there's anything in it. It's too impractical, even for Fulton."

"How so? From what you've told us it would be most useful, given the speed and the fact it's less dependent on the weather."

"It would indeed be useful," Renner agreed. "And you wouldn't have to rely on the wind to bring your guns to bear. But tell me, if *you* were in command of a British frigate and you wanted to put *Vermont* out of action, what would you order your gunners to aim at? Her smokestack? Her masts and rigging? What?"

Hawkwood thought about it. "Neither. I'd aim for one of those." He jerked a thumb towards the paddlewheel, flinging up water behind Renner's shoulder.

"Precisely. They're a big enough target. One well-aimed shot and she'd be dead in the water. Oh, we've masts, a spread of canvas and two steering positions, but without those paddles she'd be a sitting duck and about as much use as a floating bathtub."

Renner stared off thoughtfully towards the New York shore. When he turned back, his expression was lighter than it had been. "I dare say you'll be glad to be back on dry land after your adventures."

"Damned glad," Lawrence responded with a smile. "All this water; it's been the cause of far too much excitement for my liking."

"Then fear not, Captain. It won't be long." Renner pushed himself away from the rail. "Now, if you will excuse me, I'll take my leave. There are duties to which I must attend. Please feel free to explore should the mood take you. Mind where you step, though. I dread to think what the captain would say if one of you went overboard and we had to stop and pick you up again! We're behind schedule as it is and Captain Winans hates to be late. You have been warned!" Renner added with a smile before bidding them farewell and heading off along the deck.

Hawkwood and Lawrence watched him go.

"Plattsburg," Lawrence muttered, leaning back against the rail. "That's damned inconvenient. I had thought our luck was holding." He turned, his face serious. "You think our captain suspects anything?"

Hawkwood straightened. "Hard to say. He strikes me as a man who keeps his cards close to his chest."

Lawrence grunted. "Probably as well we didn't deviate too far from the truth, then. So long as we remember what names we're travelling under. I'd only just got used to Smith and Jones, damn it. Thank God none of Stagg's crew survived. That could have proved awkward."

"True. And the fact that our enemy turned out to be the captain's enemy did us no harm."

"We can but hope," Lawrence agreed. "All things considered, things could be worse. We could be stranded on the Caldwell road, up to our arses in mud."

"I suppose we could try and seize the boat," Hawkwood mused. "Sail her to Canada. Cross the lines that way."

"We tried that once, remember?" Lawrence allowed a small smile to form. "Look where it got us."

"And this time there are no oars, as far as I can tell."

"Indeed." Lawrence grinned. "So, any ideas on where we go

from here?" The major cursed as a burst of spray, carried on the breeze, lanced across their exposed faces.

"Only one," Hawkwood said. "Off this bloody deck. Young Renner might think this is the future of maritime conveyance but if we stay out here any longer we're going to need *another* change of clothes, the amount of water those damned wheels are kicking up. I don't know about you, but I function better in the dry. Let's take our captain's advice and make ourselves comfortable below."

"You'll get no argument from me," Lawrence responded. "After you."

"Not this time," Hawkwood said. "*This* time you go first."

They turned for the companionway, only to find their route blocked.

"Back so soon, Mr Renner?" Lawrence quipped.

The first officer touched his forehead in salute. "Captain Winans conveys his compliments, gentlemen, but he wishes to speak with you."

"Does he?" Lawrence smiled. "Did he say what it's concerning?"

Renner looked apologetic. "Sorry, sir, can't help you there. I'm afraid steamboat captains are often cut from the same cloth as generals. They tend not to confide in the lower ranks."

Lawrence chuckled and clapped Renner on the shoulder. "The lad's a quick learner. Very well, Mr Renner, on the basis that it's got to be a damned sight drier down there than it is up here, we're with you!"

As they went down the ladder and made their way aft, Hawkwood was again struck by how much headroom there was below deck compared to other more conventional craft. Aboard *Vermont* there was no need to adopt a Simian crouch, an occupational hazard common to every sailing vessel Hawkwood had ever been on. Here, you could walk upright without ducking to avoid overhead beams. And with the interior bulkheads painted a uniform white, the steamboat seemed unnaturally roomy compared to a ship of the line, despite its modest dimensions.

As for the cacophony of creaks and groans and the calling of hands to their stations – sounds common to all vessels under sail

– they were non-existent. Instead, there was only the all-pervasive rumble of the paddlewheels pushing her through the water, a constant reminder that *Vermont*'s progress was due to artificial contrivance rather than nature's whim.

The smells were markedly different, too. This vessel was free of the rank odours associated with mildewed timbers or the press of humanity in a confined space. Instead, the over-riding aromas were of grease and burning pinewood.

Arriving outside the captain's cabin, Renner knocked and waited for a reply.

"Enter!"

Renner opened the door and led them in before moving aside. Captain Winans was standing by his chart table, hands clasped behind his back. He gave a taciturn nod.

"Thank you, Mr Renner. You may carry on."

"Aye, sir."

Renner left, closing the door behind him.

As traps went, Hawkwood had to admit that Winans had laid his rather well. Though, if the cabin door had opened outwards instead of inwards it might not have worked. As the door swung back it acted as a screen, masking the uniformed figure who was standing silently behind it. It was only as Renner pulled the door shut that Hawkwood caught the human form at the edge of his eye and turned. As Winans brought the pistol out from behind his back, the blue-coated figure limped into full view.

Eyes dark with fury, his own pistol pointing at Hawkwood's head, Major Harlan Quade spoke in a voice strumming with rage.

"You black-hearted son of a bitch! I've a mind to shoot you where you stand, so help me!"

Hawkwood doubted whether Renner had been party to his captain's intentions. The first officer's delivery of the summons appeared to have been without guile, suggesting he'd not been taken fully into his captain's confidence. It had been a sound move. Had Renner been in on the plan, his demeanour would probably have been a lot more guarded and that might have alerted Hawkwood and Lawrence that all was not as it should be.

"Hello, Major." Hawkwood smiled wearily, though his mind was racing. "How's the leg? Lost the cane, I see. That's good."

A small vein pulsed at the side of Quade's throat like a worm trying to burrow out through his skin. Wrong-footed by Hawkwood's apparent lack of consternation, and perhaps disappointed that he'd not been presented with an excuse to shoot, his gaze moved from Hawkwood to Lawrence and then back again. "You bastard! You Goddamned Limey bastard!" His finger whitened on the trigger.

"Major!" Winans warned sharply.

For a moment Hawkwood had been convinced that Quade's anger would get the better of him, but thanks to Winans' intervention the major stood down. Letting his breath out slowly, Hawkwood looked for the nearest escape route. From what he could see, there didn't appear to be one.

Lawrence, who'd been staring at the American in shock and bewilderment, turned and enquired cautiously, "Friend of yours?"

"Old acquaintance," Hawkwood corrected. "Allow me to present Major Harlan Quade, Thirteenth Regiment of Infantry."

"Ah, yes." Collecting himself, Lawrence brought his heels together and rewarded Quade with a formal nod. "Your servant, Major."

Still simmering, Quade's eyes narrowed as if he was unable to decide whether Lawrence was mocking him or being genuinely courteous.

Captain Winans broke the tension. "It would appear introductions are unnecessary. I suggest you both take a seat."

Hawkwood and Lawrence remained standing. Hawkwood knew Lawrence was waiting for him to make the first move. All he had to do was say the word.

But then Winans laid down his pistol within close reach and said, "As you wish, though if you *are* contemplating something rash, I would advise you to reconsider. I doubt you'll want to risk exiting by the stern windows, and there are armed men posting themselves outside the door even as I speak."

From the passageway there came the sound of boots hitting the deck.

Hawkwood caught Lawrence's eye and gave a small shake of his head.

*Not yet. The chance may come later.*

They took the proffered seats. It was all they could do. The brandy and coffee mugs had been removed, Hawkwood noticed. No home comforts this time around.

Captain Winans picked up a sheet of paper from the table. His eyes hardened.

"You can put that away," Hawkwood said. "We know what it says."

Winans looked down at the wanted poster and then at Hawkwood. "You're not denying you *are* the men described here, Hooper and . . . Lawrence?"

"I don't think there'd be much point. Do you?" Hawkwood said evenly.

Winans' eyebrows lifted. Despite Quade's presence, he'd clearly been expecting a denial. He consulted the poster again. "And these charges?"

"Greatly exaggerated."

"Two men dead?" Quade spat out the words. "Four wounded? You call that *exaggerated*?"

"No, Major. I'd call it casualties of war."

Quade went rigid, as if he couldn't believe what Hawkwood had just said. The pistol rose.

Hawkwood tensed, knowing that if he did try to fling himself aside, Quade would undoubtedly shoot, and at that range he'd have to be the worst shot in the world not to hit his target.

But once again Quade held fire. Instead, he fixed Hawkwood with a cold and calculating glare.

"I doubt the tribunal will see it that way."

"Tribunal?" Lawrence's chin came up. "What tribunal?"

Thinking Lawrence was about to lunge from his chair, Quade took a strategic step backwards. A humourless smile touched his lips. "My country, Major; my rules." He turned to Hawkwood.

"As for you, *sir*, as I'm sure you're aware, the penalty for spying is death by hanging."

"What?" Lawrence gasped. "You're mad! He's no spy!"

*We already had this conversation with Stagg*, Hawkwood thought.

"Then where's his uniform?" Quade responded archly.

"It's at the bottom of the damned lake, of course! The same place as mine!"

Quade shook his head. "I'm afraid that defence won't wash, Major. While *your* bona fides as an officer and a prisoner of war are a matter of record it's clear to me *this* man is of a different hue. I believe him to be an agent, in the pay of the British Government through its representatives in Montreal, sent here to observe the disposition of American troops and to report their strengths and movements to his superiors. Tell me, Hooper, were those two men in the alley in your pay? Was that how you engineered our meeting, so that you could gain my confidence and milk me for information?'

"And I broke one of their arms to make it look real? Sorry, Major, nothing so devious. I was simply a concerned citizen who happened to be passing by."

"You expect me to believe that?"

"That's up to you. It was obviously a mistake. I should have left you there. It would have saved us all a deal of bother."

Quade dismissed Hawkwood's retort with another icy glare and turned to Lawrence. "As for his connection to you, Major; that raises a number of issues. His infiltration of the Greenbush camp, for example, suggests prior knowledge of its layout, no doubt supplied to him by Federalist sympathizers. And we know fine well what *their* agenda is," Quade finished smugly.

"Agenda? What the hell are you talking about?"

"Don't play the innocent. It's common knowledge the war's created divisions along our northern borders. Divisions the British are only too eager to exploit. Who's to say our Captain Hooper – if Hooper is even his real name – wasn't sent here to liaise with Federalist cadres in order to plot further dissent, perhaps to try and persuade the New England states to abandon the Republic and align themselves with the Canadas?"

Lawrence gaped. "Good God! You *are* out of your bloody mind!"

Ignoring Lawrence's outburst, Quade swung back to Hawkwood. "You may think you played me for a fool, sir, but I *will* see you subjected to military justice and hanged, by Christ! You'll not find it so funny when they slip the noose around your neck!"

"You're probably right about that," Hawkwood said. "Though I should warn you that's the second time in a day I've been threatened with the gallows, and the last person who made the threat didn't fare too well. I'm not here to spy. I never was. All I'm trying to do is get home."

"Slaughtering anyone who stands in your way."

"No one slaughtered anyone, Major," Hawkwood said wearily. "It was self-defence."

Even as he uttered the words, Hawkwood knew how pathetic they sounded. Had he been in either Quade's or Winan's shoes, he'd have been looking down at himself with the same withering expression on his face.

He wondered how, of all the boats he could have taken, Quade had ended up on this one.

His medical furlough at an end, the major would have reported to Greenbush for his orders. He'd been due to proceed to Plattsburg to join Dearborn's Northern army, Hawkwood remembered, which should have put him on the Fort Edward road. But as Hawkwood and Lawrence had found out, that was impassable due to storm damage.

That would have left a stage ride either to Whitehall and the schooner's erratic schedule or a longer overland journey to Burlington from where, thanks to military requisitioning, the steamboat followed a more regular timetable. Of the two, the Burlington route would have been the more sensible option.

Thus, presumably, while Hawkwood and Lawrence had been voyaging their way down the lake aboard the *Snake*, a seething Major Quade had been rattling his way north. Arriving at

270

Burlington, he'd secured passage on the most convenient military transport to Plattsburg which, as bad luck would have it, had been the recently commandeered *Vermont*.

It had probably been that simple, Hawkwood reasoned; nothing more than an ill-fated twist of circumstance. A bloody coincidence, in other words, which, ironically, was how he and Major Quade had crossed paths in the first place.

Bugger it.

Hawkwood saw it then, as Quade's jaw pulsed. There was something else gnawing away at the American, beyond the anger brought on by all the baiting. Reading Quade's face, he realized what it was.

Harlan Quade's ire hadn't been sparked by the killing of two soldiers. It was the personal humiliation he'd suffered as a consequence of having recognized the face on the wanted posters as the man who'd identified himself as Captain Hooper. Once the posters were distributed, Quade knew that there was a very real possibility that someone who had seen them drinking together in the Eagle Tavern would come forward. He'd had no choice but to go before his commanding officer and confess, for the consequences if it was left to someone else to reveal the association would be far worse.

That must have been an interesting conversation, Hawkwood mused. Who wouldn't have wanted to be a fly on the wall when Quade had unburdened his soul? And once the word was out, the major's mortification would have been complete.

All things considered, it was a miracle the man had held on to his commission. Had a similar lapse of judgement happened to a British officer, he'd have been reduced in rank – unless he had influential friends, of course. From his previous conversation with Quade, Hawkwood guessed the major didn't have too many of those, an indication that his propensity for castigating senior officers for their failings had won him few allies. The fact he was still a major was probably due to the paucity of regulars with combat experience. In other words, the Americans needed every available officer they could lay their hands on, regardless of whatever serious infraction he might have committed.

In Quade's eyes, Hawkwood was now the enemy incarnate. Thanks to their brief liaison, the major's credibility had suffered a mauling from which he was unlikely to recover any time soon. As a result, he was determined to see to it that Hawkwood paid the ultimate price, even if it meant elbowing the hangman aside and tying the noose himself. Quade's war had become a personal vendetta.

Hawkwood wondered when Winans had been made aware that the two men he'd plucked from the dinghy were not who they purported to be. It had to have been after he and Lawrence had left the cabin and accompanied Renner to the fire room. Presumably, that's when Quade had come crawling out of the woodwork, clutching his wanted poster. But what had alerted Quade to their presence?

From what Hawkwood could remember of their arrival on the boat, the only witnesses had been the half-dozen crew members who'd been on watch. And therein lay the possible answer.

While for those on board the *Snake* the impact had seemed like the end of the world, for *Vermont*'s passengers, billeted below deck, the sloop's sinking could well have passed almost without notice due to the steamboat's greater size and method of propulsion and speed. Put bluntly, so quickly had the traumatic event occurred that the shock and sound of the collision had been obscured by the noise and vibrations created by the *Vermont*'s engine and massive paddle blades.

By the time the more observant passengers had questioned why the vessel appeared to have stopped, Hawkwood and Lawrence had been lifted from the water and bundled below. It was only as dawn reasserted itself, when people had begun to stir, that word of the collision had surfaced. Quade must have learned of it when he left his cabin – a privilege of rank – and overheard crew members talking.

"You're wondering how I knew it was you?" Quade said, as if reading Hawkwood's mind. "Captain Winans apprised me of the events surrounding the collision. I was most intrigued to learn that the men we'd taken aboard were army couriers delivering dispatches to General Dearborn. As the names Matthews and Douglas were unfamiliar to me, naturally I enquired as to their descriptions."

"Naturally," Hawkwood said.

Quade's lips formed a bloodless gash. "You can imagine my surprise."

Hawkwood wondered if it was his imagination or whether he really could detect the faint whiff of alcohol on Quade's breath. He'd picked it up just after he'd sat down, when Quade had leaned in close. It would help to explain why the major might have missed all the excitement. Maybe he'd been at the rye the night before and had been sleeping it off. As if anger and humiliation weren't enough; throw in inebriation and you had a recipe for aggression right there.

"Small world," Hawkwood murmured.

Quade smiled again.

"Ain't it just?"

# 11

Based on what they could see from *Vermont*'s rail – a collection of unprepossessing dwellings fanning out from the steamboat landing – Plattsburg had little to recommend it. Indeed, it was hardly worth coming on deck for, save of course, that Hawkwood and Lawrence had no choice in the matter.

In the absence of a purpose-built brig, Quade had confined them to a windowless storage locker for the remainder of their passage, with two armed troopers posted outside the door in case they'd harboured delusions of escape. The fire room lay on the other side of the bulkhead and the heat and noise generated by the furnace had been unrelenting. The sound of the steamboat's paddles being thrown into reverse – the signal that they were finally about to dock – couldn't have come soon enough.

Which was more than could be said for the manacles that had been secured about their wrists by the escort tasked to deliver them topside, where a gloating Quade had been waiting to greet them.

He indicated the restraints. "I had one of the boat's mechanics fashion them as a precautionary measure. Not too uncomfortable, I trust?"

"I've known worse," Hawkwood said.

The smirk vanished, to be replaced by a frown. Lawrence stifled a grin and, manacles clinking, blew into his cupped hands.

Hawkwood looked over to where the last pieces of cargo

were being unloaded. A wooden hoist had been rigged to offload the cannon and other heavy goods from the boat, while troops had formed a human chain to pass the lighter items down the gangplank and on to the mule-drawn wagons waiting in line on the quayside. He wondered if the soldiers were a permanent on-board fixture or if, like Quade, they'd been on their way to a new posting. Either way, their presence had proved annoyingly inconvenient.

When the last item of cargo had been transferred, the major gave the order for Hawkwood and Lawrence to be taken ashore. Guarded fore and aft, they were led towards the gangplank. About to descend, Hawkwood paused and looked aft to where Captain Winans and First Officer Renner were standing side by side.

Hawkwood inclined his head in a silent acknowledgement, though he couldn't have said what made him do it. At first, neither man reacted. Then, just as Hawkwood turned away, the captain nodded back while next to him Renner smiled ruefully before dropping his eyes towards the deck.

"You do realize," Lawrence whispered from behind, "that fraternizing with the enemy's a capital offence."

Hawkwood spoke over his shoulder. "For them or me?"

"Them," Lawrence responded with a grin. "*Your* name's already on Quade's list."

"I haven't forgotten," Hawkwood said. "But he should have been more careful."

Lawrence frowned. "How so?"

Hawkwood looked to where Quade was brushing a speck of dirt from his sleeve, and smiled ominously.

"Bastard should've carved it in stone."

They were marched away from the quay.

At least two of the wagons had space enough in the back to have accommodated both prisoners and escort, but Hawkwood suspected that making them walk allowed Quade to feed his vanity, basking in his own glory as he rode on the wagon behind. Having suffered the slings and arrows, the major wanted everyone to see that he was the one who'd made the capture. That way, his name and credibility would be restored. Delivering the fugitives in person was to be the cherry on the cake. His loyalty proven, promotion could only be a recommendation away. No wonder he was smiling.

Hawkwood, meanwhile, was studying the road.

The thick coating of mud indicated that it had rained recently but the surface had frozen hard in the interim and the slush trapped between the ridges and in the deeper wagon ruts and around the roots of the trees and in the lee of the buildings where the sun had failed to reach suggested that a fair amount of snow had fallen, too.

Above them the sky was bleached of colour and denser clouds were moving determinedly across from the north. Winter had sent out feelers and a warning that heavier snow could only be a day or two away. When it arrived, hell would surely follow.

Dropping his gaze, Hawkwood looked beyond the lead wagon. They were coming up to the river.

The Saranac did not flow directly into the main body of Lake Champlain but into a small bay on the lake's northern rim. The road traced the bay's western edge. At the point where it turned inland, away from the river mouth, the view opened up, revealing an uninterrupted panorama all the way around the bay to where a protective, low lying, forested promontory formed its eastern shore.

Hawkwood felt his elbow nudged.

"Looks like young Renner's suspicions were correct," Lawrence murmured.

Taking in the scene on the far side of the river mouth and along the adjacent bay shore, Hawkwood was thinking exactly the same thing.

Batteaux – a veritable fleet of them, too many to count at first glance – were drawn up along the shoreline. The smallest were perhaps thirty feet in length while others were almost twice that and much wider in the beam. A number of the larger ones had been layered with planking and lashed together to form pontoon jetties, to which the smaller ones had been secured. Stores had been piled upon them, ready to be loaded.

Some vessels had been hauled on to the beach and over-turned, exposing their flat underbellies, sharp ends and shallow draught. It was a shape that had changed little over the years. It hadn't needed to. Constructed chiefly from pine – though sometimes oak was used for the bottoms and uprights – batteaux had been carrying men and cargo in the Canadas and the northern states for the past two centuries.

Men – soldiers, Hawkwood assumed – were at work on the up-turned hulls. The air resonated with the sound of saws and mallets and with the heady scent of pine. The latter emanated both from the boats' timbers and the sap in the oakum that was used to caulk the seams. The scene was one of intense activity.

His thoughts were interrupted by a strong and sudden shove between his shoulder blades.

"Move!"

Hawkwood kept his temper in check. There was no point in retaliating. Disarming the trooper would have been easy, even manacled as he was. Trouble was, there were four troopers guarding them, all armed with muskets. No one could out-run a musket ball. Besides, where would they run *to*?

A wooden bridge appeared before them. The timbers grumbled loudly beneath the vehicles' weight. Hawkwood gazed down at the swift-flowing water below. No reprieve there. The stream was too shallow to provide refuge. Besides, he'd already suffered one ducking. What was the point of another?

The settlement was changing as they moved inland. More buildings were coming into view. A few whose façades hinted at some kind of public service seemed quite new, suggesting there was more prosperity here than had first met the eye; prob-ably a benefit of the pre-war, cross-border trade with Canada. The rest were the usual mix of houses, taverns, churches, stores and livery stables.

In the spring and summer, with the trees in full bloom, Hawkwood thought the place would probably have looked pleasant and welcoming. But not today, not with the winter skies and the bitter wind blowing off the bay. Though he had to concede that the gloom he attributed to the settlement could have been due to his and Lawrence's collective mood. It wasn't easy maintaining a cheerful disposition with the threat of a hangman's noose looming over you.

It struck him as curious that their arrival had not drawn more attention. A few people had turned their heads to observe the procession from the harbour, but if they noticed the two civilians in greatcoats flanked by soldiers, they gave no sign. From the general air of indifference, it seemed Plattsburg's residents had grown used to the movement of troops and equipment. A string of loaded wagons and a handful of marching men weren't anything new.

Which had to be especially galling for Quade, Hawkwood reflected, given his obvious desire to be the centre of attention. Serve the crowing bugger right. What had he expected, a carpet of palm fronds?

The lead wagon came to a halt and one of the escorts turned. "We're here, Major."

"Here" was a large red-brick building that didn't so much imply civic responsibility as shout it from its gabled rooftop, though notwithstanding the substantial frontage with its white-shuttered windows, clock tower and portico entrance, the words PLATTSBURG COURTHOUSE engraved into its Roman-style lintel did rather give the game away.

As the wagons moved off, a wooden sign to the right of the door caught Hawkwood's eye. Carved into it, with considerably less precision than the words above the lintel, was the designation: HEADQUARTERS, UNITED STATES ARMY, NORTHEN DEPT.

Lawrence, following Hawkwood's gaze, noted the misspelling and rolled his eyes. "Christ," he whispered. "No wonder they're bloody losing."

Hawkwood did not reply. As he surveyed the building, a vision of Remus Stagg's grinning visage came suddenly to mind as did a well-known phrase: revenge is sweet.

If the bastard *was* looking down on them – or, as was more likely, looking up – there was no doubt Stagg would be laughing his bloody head off.

\*　\*　\*

"Can't say as I'm taken with the view," Lawrence said ruminatively. "You'd think they'd have provided us with a decent room. I've a good mind to complain."

"We could always ask to be moved," Hawkwood said.

Lawrence sniffed. "I doubt it'd be much of an improvement. There'd still be bloody bars in the way." Turning away from the cell window, he shoved his hands down into his coat pockets. "Mind you, it's a damn sight better than some barracks I've been in."

*That was probably true,* Hawkwood thought. The cell measured ten paces by ten paces; encasing two hard wooden cots and a bucket in the corner. A thin mattress on each bed and an equally thin blanket to go with it. Not that dissimilar to his last gaol: L'Abbaye, the military prison on the Place Sainte-Marguerite in Paris. The only difference being that this place didn't smell as bad and the guards spoke English.

Hawkwood was surprised they'd been housed together. Maybe there was a shortage of cells. The noises that permeated the building did seem to indicate an unusual number of occupants, given what he'd seen of the place. In fact, the sounds that were audible were interesting in themselves, because prisons in his experience were quiet places, the inmates usually having been cowed into silence either by the confining grimness of their surroundings or by the men placed in charge of them. Any human utterances tended to be the vocalization of despair or as a result of mistreatment, whether it be punishment for rule-breaking to bloody disputes between individuals over some personal infringement.

The rarest human sound in a prison was laughter, but Hawkwood's ears had picked up the echoes of laughter on several occasions. It seemed an odd juxtaposition, though not one worth dwelling upon.

Lawrence lowered himself on to his cot, gazed about him, and sighed despondently. "Well at least we tried."

Hawkwood, stretched out, laced his hands behind his head. "We're not dead yet, Major."

"You have a plan?"

"No."

"Damn." Lawrence smiled. "You do know how to dash a fellow's hopes."

"But I have been thinking," Hawkwood said.

"About what?"

"Those batteaux."

Lawrence regarded him quietly for a second. "Aye, I've been thinking about them, too. If I were a betting man, I'd say young Renner hit the nail on the head when he said there was something brewing."

"They weren't off-loading the boats, they were loading them."

"Indeed. But for what?"

"There's only one thing it could be."

Lawrence looked sceptical.

"It would explain the number of craft, the ordnance, the stores, and the troops – everything," Hawkwood said.

"They could just be preparing the boats for winter."

"You don't believe that any more than I do."

Lawrence made a face. "No, you're right. It did look as though they were getting them ready for use. From what we saw, I'd say they're close to whatever it is they're planning. But an *invasion?*"

"It's not that far to the border. And they have the steamboat to assist them. You heard Renner say how fast the *Vermont* can travel. They wouldn't even have to row the damned boats. They could use the steamboat to tow them. After all, that's how they got them here. They'd reach Canada in no time."

"It'd be madness," Lawrence said, then added doubtfully, "wouldn't it? You said yourself, it's too late in the year."

"Maybe not, provided the snow holds off. Even if it doesn't, they might think it was worth the gamble. With the right troops, they could establish a bridgehead. Then, come the thaw . . ." Hawkwood left the possibility hanging.

Lawrence looked pensive. "I'm not yet familiar with the location of all our garrisons. Where's the nearest one? Does your map tell you?"

"It didn't survive my swim in the lake. I could be wrong, but from memory, there's a military fort on the Île aux Noix, up on the Richelieu River. No idea of its size; it could house a brigade or three men and a dog for all I know."

It was probably just as well, Hawkwood thought, that the map was lost. Had it been found when they'd been ordered to turn out their pockets upon delivery to the gaol, Quade would have seized on it as further proof that he was an enemy spy. Why else would he be in possession of a map illustrating the battle fronts? The fact that it had clearly been torn from a well-respected newspaper available to any Tom, Dick or Harry would not have appeased the major one jot. Quade would simply have applied his own interpretation to the "evidence", insisting that Hooper was using the map to direct him to American positions so that he could conduct his own reconnaissance. In the face of that sort of manic fervour, you just couldn't win.

"So what do we do now? What *can* we do?"

"From in here? Not a damned thing."

Hawkwood fell silent.

"There's that look again," Lawrence said. "What's on your mind?"

"I was thinking about our tribunal."

"Ah. What about it?"

"If Quade was serious and there is one and they insist on doing it by the book, they'll have to call witnesses. Except there aren't any. Not here, anyway. They're all back in Greenbush."

Lawrence's head came up. "You mean they'll have to summon them here, or . . ."

"Take us back to Albany. Either way, it may give us some time."

Lawrence looked sceptical. "From what we saw, I'd say they're pretty advanced with their plans. Even if we *were* granted more time, we could be too late. And I repeat my question; what could we do, anyway?"

"Damned if I know. It would depend on the situation."

"You realize they could just take us out and shoot us," Lawrence said morosely. "It'd save 'em the cost of a rope. And I've a feeling Quade would enjoy seeing us strung up."

Hawkwood smiled. "I told you: we're not dead, yet."

His cellmate did not look like a man convinced. But then, slowly, his lips formed a broad, beaming smile. "Y'know, Captain, you're right. We're not bloody dead, are we? By God, we're not!" His eyes landed on Hawkwood's right boot. "It's also just occurred to me that I didn't see them confiscate that blade you keep hidden."

Hawkwood turned his head. "Funny you should say that."

Lawrence brightened. "Ha! I'll be damned. So, we've one weapon to hand, at least."

"We do."

"At least if it gets rough we can take some of the buggers with us."

"Absolutely."

Lawrence chuckled. "Good man. Onwards and upwards, then. Or as the Bard might have put it: Once more unto the breach, dear friend!"

"Always," Hawkwood said.

Not long after noon, they heard the heavy tramp of boots in the corridor.

Lawrence looked up. "Something tells me that's for us." He sat and swung his feet to the floor. "Then again, best to be prepared. It might be a rescue."

*If it's Jago standing there*, Hawkwood thought, *then there really is a God.*

The footsteps stopped. A key scraped in the lock and the door swung open. There was no Jago; only a brace of unsmiling, armed troopers who appeared on the threshold. Two more waited behind. The escort was back.

"On your feet."

They stood and at a signal from the guard they held out their arms. The manacles were refastened.

"Where are we going?" Hawkwood asked.

"You're being transferred."

"To Albany?"

"You'll find out. Fall in. Try anything, we shoot you dead."

Word of their crimes had obviously spread. As a result of their arrival at the courthouse, no doubt, which had attracted noticeably more interest than their march from the ferry landing, most significantly among the small knot of military personnel gathered inside the court's main entrance.

Though there had been a moment when Quade must have wished their appearance had been rather less conspicuous.

As he'd made the way across the lobby towards the sergeant-clerk on duty, footsteps echoing, Quade had ignored the stares of curiosity. That, of course, had piqued the onlookers' curiosity even more, as he'd known it would. The clerk's head, however, had remained obstinately bowed. Only when Quade announced himself had the sergeant deigned to look up; clearly unimpressed, he informed the major that he was in the wrong building – prisoner processing was next door.

A tense stand-off had followed during which Quade tried to stare the sergeant down, demanding that General Dearborn be informed that Major Harlan Quade of the 13th Infantry was reporting for special duties as ordered and that he'd come bearing gifts. The major had then handed the sergeant the 'wanted' notice, with an instruction to deliver it to the general.

The sergeant – whose eyes had widened briefly as they took in the escort and prisoners – had taken the proffered notice. But instead of scurrying off, he had told Quade that the general was indisposed. And no, Colonel Pike wasn't available either. He was supervising the construction work down at the river encampment.

To his credit, Quade had recognized that another outburst would get him nowhere. Instead he placed his hand on his sword hilt in a significant manner. That had been enough to stir the sergeant to state hurriedly that Colonel Simonds, 6th Infantry, might, after all, be available and would the major care to wait?

The sergeant had disappeared at a trot, returning with the news that Colonel Simonds would indeed grant an audience. However the colonel had given strict orders that both prisoners and their escort must remain behind, detained under lock and key at the colonel's pleasure.

That had been the last time Hawkwood and Lawrence had seen the major. No doubt he was busy promoting himself as man of the hour, acquainting anyone who would listen with a list of Hawkwood and Lawrence's offences and an account of how he'd brought the two dangerous fugitives to justice.

*At least this time we don't have to walk*, thought Hawkwood as they emerged from the gaol's side entrance to find a canvas-covered wagon waiting.

"You'd think the bugger would have come to wave us off," Lawrence murmured as he and Hawkwood were ordered to climb aboard. The escort followed.

As the wagon pulled away, Hawkwood looked back.

*Another time, Quade*, he thought.

"Well, they're not taking us back to the ferry," Lawrence observed quietly.

They'd only been on the road a matter of minutes, but the unfamiliarity of the streets told Hawkwood the major was right. They were not retracing their route. Instead, they were veering west, away from the lake.

The houses began to thin out. A narrow bridge appeared, signalling another river crossing. Still the Saranac, though they were obviously further upstream. Across the bridge, open country beckoned; scattered farmhouses, meadows, empty ploughed fields, bordered by a thick band of trees into which the road disappeared.

"Where the devil *are* they taking us?" Lawrence muttered. "Can't say as I like the look of this."

*You realize they could just take us out and shoot us.*

A statement spoken partly in jest. Now, though, as they entered the woods, the words didn't seem quite so amusing. Hawkwood studied the guards' faces for a clue. There was nothing in the troopers' expressions to suggest that their charges were under any immediate threat, but that didn't render the situation less worrying. Hawkwood thought about the knife in his boot. Hard to draw it and fight with manacled hands. Not impossible, though, if push came to shove.

By Hawkwood's reckoning they had travelled about three miles from the town when Lawrence sniffed suddenly and frowned.

"You smell that?"

"Hard not to," Hawkwood agreed.

Twisting in their seats, they looked over the wagon driver's shoulder.

A gap appeared in the trees ahead. As the wagon emerged from the woods, Lawrence let out a gasp.

Hawkwood had lost count of the number of bivouacs he'd had to endure during his two decades of soldiering. Irrespective of the country or the terrain, they all had one thing in common: the stench, of unwashed bodies, cooking-fire smoke and shit. Mostly shit, because there were never enough latrines. The rag-bag collection of tents and crude shelters that was spread out before them was no exception.

Just as well it was winter, Hawkwood thought. Had it been the height of summer, God knows what the stench would have been like.

"Dear God," Lawrence muttered in awe. "What an utter bloody shambles."

It was an acute observation. With drifts of woodsmoke rising from the sea of tents and makeshift accommodations, the scene looked more like a squalid gypsy encampment than a military one. This was no Greenbush.

The camp must have covered tens of acres, most of them hacked out of the forest to judge from the huge number of tree stumps that had been left to poke up between the tents and the campfires and the various roosts that the troops had built for themselves from whatever materials there had been to hand, from cut-down spruce branches to uprooted bushes and strips of birch bark.

To make matters worse, the site wasn't even flat. The bulk of the accommodations ranged across the side of a steep hill. Thick stands of pine occupied the high ground while the lower reaches ended in bluffs at the foot of which could be seen the river, flowing between gaps in the trees. Despite there being two prime

286

ingredients – timber and water – within easy reach, it wasn't the first place Hawkwood would have chosen to set up a camp.

And it was still expanding. At the edges of the wood, trees were being felled and branches lopped and stripped to provide material for small wooden cabins, two rows of which had already been raised along the crest of the hill.

It was hard to estimate the number of souls in situ, despite the amount of canvas on view, as there seemed just as many men making use of bivouacs as there were in tents, while some of the shelters at the bottom of the hill looked to be made from little more than pitched blankets. There had to be a couple of thousand troops at least.

Hawkwood recalled the conversation they'd had with Renner. Transfixed by the scene before them, it wasn't hard to see why the people of Plattsburg – who probably numbered less than a thousand – didn't want their town to be overrun by this many military personnel, especially if there was sickness in the ranks.

"If they don't get the rest of those cabins up soon," Lawrence observed quietly, "there's a lot of poor buggers who won't see Christmas."

Hawkwood wondered about camp discipline, for he could see that not everyone was engaged in the building work. Pockets of cold and hungry-looking men were huddled around the fires. From the air of despondency that hung over the place, and from the looks on faces, a high percentage of the occupants appeared to have already given up the fight.

The wagon cranked its way up the slope, heading towards an area of levelled ground upon which several tents had been pitched in the lee of two large, sentry-guarded huts and a quartet of spindly wooden poles from which fluttered a limp Stars and Stripes and a trio of equally despondent regimental pennants.

The wagon halted. A uniformed officer stepped forward.

Quade.

"Seems I spoke too soon," Lawrence muttered as he and Hawkwood obeyed the order to climb down.

Beckoning the escort, Quade led the way to one of the huts. Officers' accommodation, Hawkwood guessed. It didn't matter if you were building a garrison or a temporary camp, officers' quarters always took priority.

"Wait here."

Ignoring the sentries' lacklustre salutes, Quade entered the hut and disappeared. Two seconds later, he was back.

"Bring them."

Inside the hut, four men were gathered around a table strewn with documents. They looked up as Quade re-entered.

"The prisoners, Colonel," Quade announced.

Two of the men at the table were in uniform. As the escorts took up position behind Hawkwood and Lawrence, guarding the door, one of the uniformed men stepped forward.

Young, early to mid-thirties, Hawkwood decided, for there was no grey in his hair, which was full and wavy save for some thinning around the temples, giving him a high forehead and lending an elongated look to his features. Lantern light played across pale skin, a pair of dark eyes, a sharp nose and slightly prominent lips which, had they belonged to a woman, might have been described as petulant.

He stared at the prisoners. After what seemed like a full ten seconds of silent appraisal, he announced, in a hard and clipped tone, "My name is Zebulon Pike. I hear you killed two of my men."

*Hell and shit*, Hawkwood thought.

"You have anything to say?" Pike asked.

Another extended period of silence ensued.

"It would seem not," Lawrence said.

Hawkwood saw the second uniformed officer's eyes narrow.

A nerve flickered along Pike's left temple. "You're Lawrence," he said slowly.

"I am he."

Pike nodded thoughtfully. His head swivelled. "Which makes you Hooper."

Hawkwood did not reply. What was the man expecting him to do – fall to his knees and beg forgiveness? That wasn't going to happen. Hell would freeze over first.

He looked past Pike's shoulder at the rough log walls seamed with mud and at the earthen floor. There was nothing remotely comfortable about the cabin's interior. A part-drawn curtain separated the main floor space from a sleeping area to the rear in which the corner of a metal bedstead and a large wooden chest could just be seen. Other than that, few concessions had been made with regards to either privacy or the rank of the occupant. A cast-iron stove stood against one wall, while the rest of the furniture, like the hut itself, was sparse and functional, consisting of a table, four plain chairs and a small campaign desk. Various uniform items and a sword hung from a row of hooks on the wall beside the door.

Hawkwood switched his gaze to the three men standing by the table. The second uniformed officer was a far more imposing figure than Pike – tall, well over six feet in height, with a stout, well-proportioned build and an upright posture which, even if he had not been in uniform, would nevertheless have marked him out as a military man. The dark hair, swept back from a stern face gave a hard, gritty edge to his features. He, too, wore the uniform of a colonel.

Of the remaining pair, one was a white man; the other was an Indian. Both were clad in loose-fitting, knee-length blue calico smocks and brown leggings. The white man also wore an open-fronted buckskin coat; the Indian had a russet-coloured cloak folded over his right shoulder. While they were dressed in a similar fashion, the main difference between them lay in their colouring and their facial hair. The white man's hair was straggly and flecked with silver, accentuating his grizzled features. His chin was hidden behind a short beard. The Indian's head was shaved, save for a thick tuft of hair atop his skull from which hung a single grey feather. A silver ring decorated his left nostril and matched the rings in each ear and the circular gorget around his neck. Most noticeable were his facial tattoos which took the form of two patterned lines. They ran, like rows of stitching, from his left brow to the base of his right jaw. One skirted the inside of his right eye, the other the outside, giving the unsettling impression that the flesh of his face had been separated into three parts and sewn back together by an unsteady hand.

Hawkwood's eyes flicked to the Indian's medallion. It was

embossed with a design, hard to see in the lantern light, but with enough definition to make it recognizable as the crude outline of a bear.

His scrutiny of the room's occupants complete, Hawkwood returned his gaze to Pike.

The colonel was a lot younger than Quade's remarks back in Albany had implied, which only made it all the more strange that he would want to re-introduce pole-arms to frontline combat. He must have been in his cradle during the Revolution. Had he *any* first-hand experience of war?

"What can we do for you, Colonel?"

Pike blinked. Another moment of hesitation passed, at which point understanding seemed to dawn. "Ah, yes, I see. Major Quade did warn me of your propensity for impertinence."

"It's a curse," Lawrence said drily. "But then the major does tend to have that effect."

"Best be quick, Colonel," Hawkwood said. "There's none of us getting any younger."

Pike's chin rose. His expression hovered between confusion at being addressed so dismissively and doubt over how to frame a commanding reply.

Finding his voice, he said, "You were brought here because I wanted to meet you face to face; to see for myself what sort of men you were."

A thin sheen of sweat shone along the colonel's hairline. Hawkwood hadn't noticed it at first and wondered why that should be. The stove's door was propped open to allow heat from the burning logs to circulate, but it wasn't oppressively warm in the hut, or at least it didn't seem so to him.

"You flatter, us, Colonel."

"Then you misread my intention. It means only that I can have you shot with a clear conscience."

"Shot?" Lawrence said. "What the devil happened to the tribunal?"

Removing a handkerchief from his jacket, Pike dabbed his lips, swallowing with distaste as he did so. "There will be no tribunal."

"Colonel Simonds ordered us detained," Hawkwood said, wondering if it was his imagination or whether there was a wheeziness in Pike's voice that hadn't been there a moment ago.

"Colonel Simonds does not command here. *I* do."

Hawkwood saw the eyes of the other colonel flicker.

Lawrence turned to Quade. "You bastard."

Quade smirked.

An expression that said it all.

Perhaps it had been the sergeant's attitude at the courthouse or the lack of adulation he'd received, but something had persuaded Quade that his best chance of seeing Hawkwood punished was to take the initiative himself. Perhaps it had been Colonel Simonds who'd pointed out that if military justice was to be dispensed in strict accordance with Army regulations, then Quade might have to wait to see it enacted. And it was liable to be a very long wait, given that a tribunal would be a long way down the army's list of priorities, below sorting out accommodation for the troops and several rungs below the plan for an invasion – if that's what the activities along the lakeshore were in aid of.

Angry and frustrated at having been, as he saw it, let down by yet another senior officer's incompetence, Quade had decided to take his grievance directly to the man he should have gone to in the first place: Colonel Zebulon Pike. In Albany, Quade had been less than complimentary about Pike and his notion of how to re-equip frontline troops. Since then, it appeared the major had undergone a change of heart; a pragmatic reversal based on Quade's realization that, if he was to see retribution visited upon Hawkwood, he would need a powerful ally. And who better than Colonel Zebulon Pike, commanding officer of the troopers Hawkwood had killed in Greenbush? No one could accuse Quade of not seizing his chance. By presenting Hawkwood and Lawrence to the colonel-in-charge, Quade would see his own worth increase and both he and Pike would have their revenge.

And justice, true military justice, as viewed by Major Harlan Quade, would be served. Quickly and comprehensively.

Moreover, when the rank and file learned that their officers had exacted swift and fulsome revenge for the killing of their comrades, their allegiance to Quade and Pike would be that much stronger. If asked, they would follow those officers to hell and back.

"Major Quade believes you're a spy as well as a murderer," Pike said, bunching the handkerchief in his fist. There were minute beads of perspiration lining up across the top of his upper lip, Hawkwood noticed. The man was looking decidedly less well as the conversation progressed.

"The major has a vivid imagination," Hawkwood said. "Not that it matters, seeing as you're going to shoot us anyway. But I've had better things to do, frankly. Hell, until Quade dragged us here, I didn't think you had anything worth spying on."

Hawkwood saw the two white men at the table tense. Pike's chin came up again. "Explain yourself!"

"This place," Hawkwood said. "This camp, the condition of your men. They're in no fit state to fight a war. I doubt they were up to the job even when Madison threw down the damned gauntlet back in June." He flicked a glance towards Quade. "Your regular troops have had no fighting experience. Neither have most of your officers, save for people like the major here. Those who did fight in your revolution are likely too damned old to be efficient. General Dearborn, for example. That's why you call him 'Granny', yes?"

Hawkwood had picked that up from the newspapers. It was debatable whether it was a term of affection or ridicule. He saw Quade flinch.

"And your men are housed in this hellhole while the militia have buggered off home for Christmas. It's no wonder you suffered bloody noses at Detroit and Queenston. If Quebec could see this place, they'd be wondering what all the fuss was about. You Americans are no threat. I wasn't sure about that until the major shipped us here. Now I've seen it with my own eyes, I know it for a fact."

"You know nothing!" Quade cut in. "Soon, you'll see—"

"Major!" Pike said sharply, before running the handkerchief across his lips.

"If you're thinking about the boats," Hawkwood said, "we saw those too. Mind you, that many, they'd be hard to miss." He smiled at Quade. "Cat's out of the bag, Major. You should have brought us the long way round."

"You've got yourself quite an armada, Colonel," Lawrence said. "We're impressed. We heard about the batteaux back in Whitehall. Didn't put two and two together until we came here, though."

"I'm still not convinced," Hawkwood said. "Can't see the snow holding off for much longer. Winters here can be a bitch. So, if you're going, you'll need to move soon. Meanwhile, your men are dropping like flies. It doesn't look promising."

Then Pike coughed.

It wasn't a small cough, the sort to subdue a tickle at the back of the throat. Neither was it a polite cough that a person might use to draw attention to what was about to be said. No, this was a sudden, deep, wet, throat-clearing cough that started down in the lungs and exploded in a crescendo of hacking and hawking that sounded as though Pike's internal organs were being torn loose and would soon be expelled across the insides of the hut.

Hawkwood and Lawrence took a step back and watched as Pike launched into a series of cacophonous eruptions which, one after another, expectorated large gobbets of yellow-green phlegm into the handkerchief he was pressing desperately to his mouth. The spasms continued for several seconds until, finally, eyes watering and clutching his belly, Pike managed to haul himself to a nearby chair where he collapsed in a heap, chest heaving as he fought for breath.

The officer at the table was already moving to Pike's side, concern flooding his face. Pointing to Hawkwood and Lawrence, he rapped out an order to Quade. "Major, get them out of here! You!" he snapped to one of the escorts. "Fetch Surgeon Gilliland – now!"

As the escort made a rapid exit, the officer turned to the white man behind him. "Wine, Amos! Quickly!"

Hastily, the civilian poured wine into a glass from a decanter on the table. He handed it to the officer, who, holding the glass to Pike's lips, watched anxiously as the colonel gulped the liquid down. "Easy, Zeb, easy. The doctor's on his way."

Looking up, he cursed. "God damn it, Quade! I told you to get those bastards out of here! Secure them in one of the huts. We'll deal with them later."

Quade stared down at Pike and then jerked his head at the remainder of the escort. "Out."

"*Wait!*"

The croak had come from Pike. His fellow colonel opened his mouth to object but Pike brushed him away. Pain creased his face. Quade had turned, but it was Hawkwood that Pike addressed, through gritted teeth.

"Consider this a delay, Hooper. It sure as hell ain't a reprieve. I *will* see you shot. I'll give the order to the damned firing party myself."

"I'll bear that in mind, Colonel," Hawkwood said as a shove from behind thrust him towards the door.

They had only just made it outside when a fresh bout of coughing began.

"All this way," Lawrence said, "when they could have left us in the damned gaol. At least there were beds." He shook his head and smiled grimly. "We do end up in the most forlorn bloody places, don't we?"

They were in one of the recently erected huts. Spacious, it wasn't. Neither was it furnished. Four log walls, and a shingle roof. Shavings littered the floor and the walls were only half-caulked. There was no window either. From that omission Hawkwood suspected the hut was probably intended as enlisted men's accommodation rather than an officer's. At the moment, though, with no fireplace, as far as protection against the weather was concerned, it wasn't much more than a wind-break secured with a clasp and padlock.

Lawrence cocked an eyebrow. "You reckon Simonds knows we've been brought here?"

His voice was couched low. The padlock wasn't the only device keeping them in the hut. Quade had stationed two armed men outside the door. If there was any justice, they'd be slowly freezing to death.

Hawkwood blew into his cupped hands. "My bones tell me it's all Quade's doing."

"Sly bugger. He gave the order and rode on ahead. Got his two penn'orth in first. Probably knew Simonds would have other things on his mind. Equipping all those batteaux, for example." Lawrence smiled ruefully. "I believe we hit a nerve in there, don't you? Good God, if looks could kill." Peering about him, he let out a grunt. "Y'know, I used to think it was only the poor who didn't have a pot to piss in. Seems it applies to prisoners, too. I doubt we treat captured Americans so harshly."

Lawrence stared down at his manacled wrists. "Bastards aren't taking any chances. It doesn't bode well, does it?"

Lawrence's features lay in shadow. With the onset of twilight, the only light that penetrated the windowless hut came through gaps in the walls. And as their cell grew darker it had become colder, too. But at least they had their great-coats. Some of the soldiers they'd seen on their way through the camp didn't even possess that luxury. Hawkwood wondered how many men had perished from sickness and exposure since the camp had been set up. Now he and Lawrence had usurped someone's valuable living space, and all because Quade had a temper.

Lawrence joined Hawkwood on the floor, pulling his coat beneath and around him as best he could. "I hope whatever Pike's suffering from isn't catching. The bugger looked as if he was on his last legs."

"He's in good company," Hawkwood said, thinking again of the men festering in the encampment below them.

"Makes me wonder if they're going to have enough men to man those boats," Lawrence said, his voice a murmur. "From what I saw coming up the hill, there's not many that looked in fighting shape."

"That's why they stuck them out here."

Lawrence frowned. "Well, yes. Renner told us the locals didn't want them spreading disease."

"That's not what I meant."

"Then, what?"

"It's not just a question of the townsfolk not wanting them. The reason the sick men have been moved here is because the army doesn't want them contaminating troops who are fit."

"You mean the able men are housed elsewhere?"

"It's a thought."

Lawrence pursed his lips. "It'd make sense. Closer to town, possibly?"

"Renner said they've been ferrying troops to Cumberland Head. That's the opposite side of the bay. Maybe there's another encampment there. Though some might be more conveniently located. There's a good chance they're being housed in the gaol."

"Because?"

"I heard laughter – and there's not many find those places amusing. It's no palace, but I think there are men in there who are relieved to be living within brick walls rather than canvas ones. It'd be cramped, so there wouldn't be vast numbers – a couple of hundred, perhaps, kept relatively warm and fed and grateful for it because they know the alternative is a transfer to this place if they do fall ill." Hawkwood shrugged. "They may have set up tents within the walls that we didn't see."

"So young Pike drew the short straw stuck out here."

"And paid the price," Hawkwood said. "Looked like he's sick as a dog, too."

"I doubt he'll stay here," Lawrence said, "if he's as ill as he looks. Him being a colonel, they'll probably move him into town, commandeer someone's house. Losing foot-sloggers is hard enough, but senior officers are in serious short supply." He scratched his unshaven chin. "Those two not in uniform were an intriguing mix; the Indian, especially. Fearsome-looking fellow, despite the jewellery."

"Oneida," Hawkwood said, without thinking. "Bear clan."

Lawrence tilted his head. "And how in God's name would *you* know *that*?"

"Another long story," Hawkwood said, after a pause.

Lawrence leaned back against the wall and regarded Hawkwood with wry amusement. "Now, why did I know that's what you were going to say?"

Lawrence waited expectantly but when Hawkwood stayed silent he ran a hand across his own stubbled jaw. "Before I crossed the border, I was told the Yankees employ their own force of native intelligence gatherers. They call it their Observer Corps; Indians commanded by white officers. I'm wondering if that's what those two were." Adding in a subdued tone, "I'm told they're exceedingly cruel to their captives. That they torture the living and mutilate the dead."

Hawkwood drew his legs up and rested his hands on his knees. "It's nothing new. The Spanish irregulars castrate French prisoners. It's a way of spreading fear among their enemies."

"It's barbaric," Lawrence said, with a shudder.

"It's war," Hawkwood said.

Lawrence looked at him.

"It's why we put up with it; why we want them on our side. It's why people like you, me and Grant are sent in behind enemy lines on recruiting expeditions. In Spain it was the *guerrilleros*. Over here it's the Iroquois. We'd be foolish *not* to use them."

Lawrence's right eyebrow rose in query. "No matter what atrocities they might commit?"

"Better to have them inside the tent pissing out than outside the tent pissing in."

Lawrence thought about that. Falling silent, he rested his head back against the wall. When he glanced to his side, he saw that Hawkwood's eyes had closed. Staring at the hard, scarred face, Lawrence smiled to himself. Finding sleep was like exploiting the presence of food and water. You took advantage of it whenever you could because you never knew when the chance to rest would come again. And at least they had shelter, unlike many of the poor devils outside. It was cold but both of them had known worse, having survived winters in the Spanish mountains when four wooden walls would have been considered a luxury.

Thinking about what he knew of Hawkwood's past history, Lawrence pondered upon the chain of circumstances that had thrown them together. It was truly remarkable that their paths should have crossed again, and in America, of all places; the pair of them strangers in a strange land. And yet a question nagged. Hawkwood, after only one brief sighting and without any verbal reference, had known both the tribe and the clan of that nameless Indian warrior. How was that possible? There had to be a logical explanation. But what that might be, Lawrence had no idea.

Taking a leaf out of Hawkwood's book, he closed his eyes. Conserve energy when you can, that was the soldier's creed. It was only as his eyelids drooped that he realized just how weary he was. Despite the cold, sleep came quickly.

It was still dark when he opened his eyes. He didn't know what time it was. He was about to consult his watch when he looked to his side and saw that Hawkwood's head was turned and that his eyes were also open. The glow of a lantern wavered through the gap in the logs. Footsteps sounded. Then came the grate of the padlock being released.

They climbed to their feet as the door swung open.

"Hot food and a warming pan would be nice," Lawrence murmured.

It wasn't to be.

A gruff voice ordered them outside.

They emerged to discover four troopers armed with muskets. A horse-drawn wagon waited behind them.

Hawkwood studied the troopers. They were dressed against the cold in long grey coats, black shako caps and scarves. There was nothing odd about that, save for the scarf wrapped around each man's face so that only his eyes and the bridge of his nose was visible, thus rendering him effectively anonymous. That was why the order to leave the hut had sounded so gruff, Hawkwood realized; because it had been muffled.

*What? They think we wouldn't know they're the same quartet who transported us here?*

And then it dawned on him that the troopers' faces were concealed not because he and Lawrence might recognize them, but to hide them from anyone else who happened to observe their departure. At the back of his brain, a warning bell began to ring.

One of the troopers – Hawkwood assumed it was the one who'd given the order – jerked a thumb towards the wagon.

"Where to now?" Hawkwood asked.

There was no reply.

A lantern hung from a strut behind the driver's seat. It provided little illumination, though in its vapid glow Hawkwood saw that the back of the wagon held two upright, bucket-sized wooden casks.

The first pair of troopers boarded the vehicle. Only when Hawkwood and Lawrence were seated did the second pair climb up after them. At which point, the first pair split up, one into the driver's seat, the other to the front of the wagon, where he angled himself so that he faced backwards. As the second pair settled themselves down in the rear, the driver clicked his tongue and with a flick of the reins the wagon moved off.

Hawkwood looked out over the encampment. There was a moon but it wasn't shedding much light and it was hard to make out details. Shrouded figures moved among the tents and bivouacs. Other blanketed forms lay huddled around the edges of the cooking fires. No laughter here. Instead, the night was broken by harsher sounds: the whimpering of the sick and the suffering. Hawkwood shivered as a chorus of coughs and groans, carried upon the breeze, broke out across the hillside, contaminating the night.

"Dear God," Lawrence whispered, his expression mirroring his horror.

Their path, Hawkwood saw, was heading downhill, away from the main encampment, towards the woods.

"You know when I said the last time that I didn't like the

look of where they were taking us?" Lawrence murmured, following Hawkwood's gaze. "Well, now, I *really* don't like where we're going."

The trees drew them in. Noises from the camp began to fade. There were no animal sounds, no night screeches, no rustling in the undergrowth. There was just the creaking of the wagon boards and the splintering of pine cones beneath the wheels as they trundled across the forest floor. Their escorts had yet to utter a single word.

Hawkwood's eyes flickered towards the casks. One of them appeared to be leaking. The liquid seeping from the crack in the staves looked like watery gruel. There was no smell coming off them, or at least none that he could detect. Surreptitiously, he allowed his gaze to linger on the leaking cask's lid. It looked secure enough, though what might have been a trickle of the same soupy liquid had formed a thin rime around the lip. It was hard to see clearly in the darkness.

As if from a great distance, he heard Stagg's voice in his ear.

*I've got more'n forty tubs of prime potash takin' up space in the hold . . .*

As the words came back to him, he realized what he was most probably looking at and a knot formed in his stomach.

The wagon's right front wheel hit a tree root and the vehicle bounced. A fresh line of seepage appeared around the rim of the cask lid. Hawkwood saw that they were nearing the edge of the wood.

*Another part of the camp?* he wondered. They hadn't travelled that far, perhaps half a mile.

"Smells like a bloody latrine," Lawrence muttered under his breath, as the trees thinned out and the clearing opened up before them, and at once his face crumpled.

With the forest casting black shadows across the open space, Hawkwood's first impression was that he was looking at a clutch of wooden fence posts that had been left in the ground to rot. It was only as the wagon drew closer to the hummock in which they were planted that he realized these weren't fence posts at all, they were shovel handles. And the hummock wasn't a natural hummock, either. It was a mound of excavated soil.

And as Lawrence uttered a despairing, "Sweet Jesus!" the stench rose to meet them. Fighting back the bile surging into his own throat, Hawkwood saw the edge of the pit.

# 12

The wagon rolled a few yards further before jolting to a halt.

*One chance*, Hawkwood thought. *That's all we're going to get.*

The driver applied the brake and his companions rose to their feet. The two troopers at the rear of the wagon hefted their muskets in one hand and jumped down. Turning, they prepared to supervise their prisoners' descent.

Hawkwood slammed the flat of his boot against the leaking cask, aiming it towards the nearest trooper. At the same time, he pulled his wrists apart, drawing the stiletto from his left sleeve with his right hand as he did so, praying that Lawrence would be as quick to react as he had been aboard the *Snake*.

He'd transferred the knife from boot to sleeve when he'd squatted down in the hut, thinking there might be a chance to exact damage before the end came, but it was only as he'd pushed himself to his feet that his fingers had hooked themselves around the half-bent nail that had been lying in the dirt beneath his right buttock. With his movements hidden by his coat sleeves and with the noise of his endeavours masked by the rumble of the wagon, he'd used the nail to unpick the lock securing the manacle to his right wrist.

Jago, he thought as he felt the band separate, would have been proud of him.

There had been no time to release the left manacle, so as he withdrew the knife – and as Lawrence launched himself at the driver – he used his left hand to curl the chain and the full weight of the empty shackle against the temple of the trooper standing behind him, the impact making itself felt the length of his arm. As the trooper rocked back, Hawkwood pivoted.

The cask, meanwhile, had found its target. It had caught the first trooper in the upper chest, knocking aside his musket and discharging a wave of milky-grey fluid up and across the only exposed part of him: his eyes. Dropping his musket and clasping his hands to his face, the trooper began to shriek.

Recovering from the shock, the remaining escort threw up his musket as Hawkwood followed Lawrence over the side of the wagon. As he dropped, he heard the crack of the gun – loud and sharp in the night air – and then he hit the earth and rolled. Winded but unhurt, he came up with the knife in his hand.

The trooper who'd fired, knowing there was no time to reload, scrambled for his companion's weapon. As Hawkwood charged round the back of the wagon, the trooper raised the gun, his finger curling around the trigger.

Hawkwood grasped the musket barrel just as the trooper fired. Turning his eyes from the flash, he felt the recoil in his left arm as he pushed the muzzle aside and brought the stiletto round in a stabbing arc. The rapier-thin blade pierced the trooper's scarf and entered his neck just below his jaw bone.

Hawkwood stepped away as the trooper fell, clutching his throat. The scarf slipped, revealing eyes widening with incomprehension and pain.

The trooper who'd received the contents of the cask was still screaming. His fingers were clawing at his face. The scarf had been ripped away and it looked as if he was trying to tear his skin off. The cask lay open next to him. Liquid was draining out of it.

Ignoring him, Hawkwood turned in time to see that the trooper he'd struck with the manacle had regained his feet. Upon seeing Hawkwood, he levelled his gun.

A figure rose up behind him.

Lawrence, his savage expression accentuated by the lantern

light, drove the musket butt against the base of the trooper's skull. The trooper fell forward on to his knees and then face down on to the wagon's deck.

Breathing hard, Lawrence stared down at the comatose form. "Goddamned bastard." He looked at Hawkwood and said wearily, "This is getting to be a habit, my friend."

Hawkwood wiped the stiletto blade on his sleeve and slid the weapon inside his boot. The trooper doused with the contents of the cask had curled into a foetal ball. His hands were clamped to his face. He had stopped screaming. The sounds bubbling from between his fingers were no longer human.

Taking care to avoid the spillage, Hawkwood moved to the trooper he'd knifed. It was the same one who'd given the order to board the wagon. The trooper's mouth had frozen into a rictal grin. Blood from the fatal throat wound had pooled on to the ground.

Hawkwood went through the trooper's pockets. He didn't know if the key to the manacles would be there, but it was a place to start. If the search proved fruitless, he would have to search the rest of them. Failing that, it was back to the nail, assuming he could find it in the dark. It had been dropped during the fight. He cursed his clumsiness. He should have been more circumspect, but then there had been other things to worry about.

His fingers touched metal. Surely, they couldn't be that lucky?

He pulled out the key. Maybe manacles were at such a premium that they couldn't afford to discard any of them. It took only seconds to attend to the remaining locks. Lawrence massaged his freed wrists, wincing as he did so.

"You're hurt?" Hawkwood said.

"Just a bit bruised. All this brawling's a reminder that I'm not getting any younger." He stared down without sympathy at the trooper who'd been hit with the barrel and grimaced. "How did you know the casks contained lye?"

"I didn't. It was a guess. I saw one of them was leaking and I remembered Stagg telling us he was carrying potash. They make lye by soaking wood ash in water. The trench back there, stinking like a latrine? That's the way it smells when they use lye to render down dead bodies."

Lawrence stared at Hawkwood with the same expression of horror he'd shown earlier. "I'm not going to enquire how you know that."

He gazed bleakly towards the pit and then at the shovels which, isolated on the mound of soil, looked uncannily like a row of truncated burial crosses.

A movement on the wagon caused them both to turn quickly. The trooper Lawrence had toppled with the musket was coming round. His scarf no longer covered his face and he'd lost his cap.

Between them, they dragged him from the wagon and on to the ground. Using a set of manacles, they secured the trooper's arms behind his back and propped him against a rear wheel. Withdrawing the knife from his boot, Hawkwood squatted down and pressed the point against the trooper's already bruised and bloodied cheek. "Who ordered this? Was it Quade?"

The trooper's gaze fastened upon the bodies of his companions before moving to the face of the man holding the knife to his skin. There was no mercy in his captors' eyes, the trooper saw. Fear flooded through him. As the knife blade moved down towards his jaw, he tried to jerk away, only to crack his head against the wheel rim. Moaning, he nodded.

"*And* to keep quiet about it?"

Another nod, more fearful than the first.

Which confirmed why they had worn caps and the wraparound scarves, Hawkwood thought.

"What's your regiment?"

The trooper found his voice, though the reply came out as a whisper. "F-Fifteenth Infantry."

"Pike's boys," Lawrence grunted.

"Quade told you we'd killed your comrades back in Greenbush, yes?" Hawkwood said. "Told you it was a chance to get even?"

Hawkwood moved the knife down to the trooper's throat and applied pressure to the blade, piercing the skin. Blood welled beneath the stiletto's point. "Y-yes."

"Got them to do his dirty work," Lawrence said coldly. "Scheming bugger."

In the moonlight, the trooper's face reflected a sickly pallor. In contrast, his jowls hadn't been near a razor for several days. The smell coming from him suggested he hadn't washed for a while, either, though the odour rising from the nearby pit could have had something to do with that.

Hawkwood sat back on his haunches before leaning in again. "The boats; how long before they depart?"

The trooper looked confused at the change of subject. "Boats? I don't—"

Hawkwood pressed in with the knife. "Last chance."

Opening his mouth as if he were about to reply, the trooper paused. A new expression stole across his face. Suddenly, before Hawkwood and Lawrence's startled gaze, his eyes rolled back into his skull and a dribble of saliva emerged out from the corner of his mouth and trickled down his chin. His head lifted momentarily and then, like a puppet whose strings had been cut, he lolled forward; as his jaw fell open, his body gave a small shudder, sagged, and then went still.

"Good God!" Lawrence exclaimed, stepping back quickly.

Hawkwood withdrew the knife and searched for the trooper's pulse with his fingertips. "He's gone."

He stared at the trooper's face for several seconds and then rose to his feet.

"I've seen this before," Lawrence murmured, gazing down at the dead man. "In Spain. A young subaltern got kicked by a cavalry horse. Went down as if pole-axed. Took several minutes to come around. Swore he was fine, finished his duties and then dropped dead an hour later. Surgeon said the blow had caused some sort of blockage in the brain that took a while to reveal itself. Looks like hitting this one with the musket did more damage than we thought." Lawrence gnawed the inside of his lip. "Just when the conversation was getting interesting, too, damn it."

"What about the driver?" Hawkwood asked.

Lawrence shook his head. "Neck's broken."

Hawkwood was about to ask Lawrence if the break was due to the fall or judicious use of the manacles but decided there wasn't much point. It wasn't as if it would make any difference to their current situation.

"Best we were on our way, before they discover we've gone. The shots will have carried."

Lawrence looked back towards the woods and the track that had brought them to the clearing. "I doubt that way's feasible. Any suggestions?"

"Continue north, same as before."

"Steal a boat?"

"Not likely. I've had enough of bloody boats."

"I'm glad you said that." Lawrence eyed the wagon. "Horses?"

"They're not saddled. Besides, in these woods they'd be more trouble than they're worth. We'll be quicker on foot."

Lawrence nodded. "Very well. Though I suggest we see what these fellows are carrying. With luck they'll have powder and shot, in which case we can make use of the weapons."

They checked the bodies by lantern light. Hawkwood searched the pockets of the trooper struck by the lye barrel, ensuring none of the caustic liquid touched his skin. The trooper neither stirred nor made a sound, though the almost imperceptible rise and fall of his chest indicated that he was breathing. The pain which had caused him to lose consciousness must have been beyond terrible. Lye devoured flesh like molten fire. The trooper's natural reflex would have been to clamp his eyes shut, but Hawkwood knew that wouldn't have made any difference. He stared down at the state of the trooper's hands and face. Even when he moved the light away, the darkness couldn't conceal the horrific damage done to the man's exposed skin and what remained of his eyes bore no relation to what had been there before. Some things, Hawkwood thought, were worse than death.

Further examination of the troopers' pouches produced lock covers and cartridges. When he rifled the driver's corpse, Lawrence discovered a small tin containing flint and steel and a wad of char cloth, which he pocketed, along with two pemmican strips another of the troopers had been storing inside his jacket.

After helping themselves to a pouch, a scarf and a canteen each, they were ready to depart. The lantern would have been useful for travelling at night, but they knew it would only draw attention to their presence, so they doused it. Then, taking their bearings and leaving the bodies where they lay, they headed into the woods.

They heard the river a while before it came into view and used the sound as a guide. Reaching the water took some time, however, and no small amount of effort for the descent through the trees in darkness was steep and made slippery and hazardous by the rains.

When they finally found themselves on the bank, Lawrence stared out across the swift-moving torrent. "Here we go again."

It wasn't that far to the other side – sixty or seventy yards at the most – but they knew that trying to traverse even a relatively short distance presented a huge risk. In daylight it would be hard enough. At night, doubly so. Added to which, it wasn't only the speed of the river that was worrying, it was the depth of it. Wavelets breaking energetically over the rocks in the middle of the current suggested that although it might not be that deep, the flow was impressive. Even if they did make it across, it was inevitable they'd end up wet and, as a result, a lot colder.

Several dots of fire light were visible through the trees to their right; reminders that the encampment was only a short distance away. How far exactly, it was hard to tell. In their present situation, the glow from just one fire would be enough to pose a threat.

Hawkwood cast his eyes back to the far shore. He judged it to be formidably steep on that side, too, though it could have been the trees casting unhelpful shadows. They came down very close to the water's edge. He looked to his left. The river didn't seem so broad in that direction. It was also further away from the camp. He tapped Lawrence's shoulder and they set off along the bank. The rush and tumble of the water was loud in their ears and passage proved harder than it looked. There wasn't much shoreline and their progress was hampered by rocks and tree roots.

They had covered some fifty paces when Hawkwood spotted what looked like a suitable crossing point. Several low-lying islets protruded from the middle of the river bed. Composed of pebbles and clumps of weedy vegetation, the largest wasn't more than a yard or so in width, but its effect was to divide the river into two narrower and, hopefully, fordable streams.

Hawkwood slid the musket from his shoulder and removed the strap. Then he took off his coat, boots and socks. Convincing himself that it wouldn't be for long, he wrapped the coat around his footwear and used the strap to secure the bundle across his shoulder. He checked to see that Lawrence had followed suit, then using the musket as a steadier, he steeled himself and waded out into the water. The temperature of the stream almost made him gasp out loud, as did the strength of the current. The algae-covered rocks were very slippery underfoot. Those that weren't felt as sharp as knives. Even with the musket as a support and planting his weight firmly, it was all he could do to remain upright. But if his years in the army had taught him one thing, it was the value of dry boots; they'd be worth their weight in gold when he got to the other side. *If* he got to the other side. He paused momentarily as Lawrence stepped after him. Then, tentatively, leaning into the flow, they inched their way out into the river.

It took three or four cautious steps before they got used to the awkward contours of the river bed and the power of the water. Even so, progress was agonizingly slow and it seemed as though an age passed before they eventually reached the safety of the nearest islet, by which time they were soaked to their thighs and Hawkwood could hardly feel his toes for the cold. But the tactic had worked. They were well over halfway to their objective.

"Jesus," Lawrence gasped. "We should have brought the bloody horses and let *their* arses get wet."

Cheered by the realization that they were almost there,

with less than twenty paces separating them from their goal, Hawkwood shouldered his pack once more, swore under his breath then set off. And wondered immediately how it was possible that one side of a river could be colder than the other.

He knew it was his imagination but it did feel as though his feet were turning into blocks of ice. It would have been easy to return to the isle and persuade himself that it would do them good to rest a few moments before completing the remainder of the crossing, but with the bank now so tantalizingly close he knew they had to keep going. And so, pushing all thoughts of rest to the back of his mind, he allowed his concentration to focus wholly on where to place his feet.

So he had no idea that Lawrence was in trouble until he heard him cry out.

Hawkwood was less than a dozen paces from safety when he heard the commotion behind. Even with the river creating noise all around them, the splash and grunt were loud enough to alert him that Lawrence had stumbled. He turned quickly, almost losing his own balance in the process, to find Lawrence on his knees, half in and half out of the water, his face a pale oval, his coat bundle about to slide off his shoulder and the second musket nowhere to be seen.

Without thinking, using his own musket as a prop, Hawkwood made a grab for Lawrence's arm, and failed completely. It was a reach too far. As the current took hold, Lawrence's feet lost their purchase again and he began to slide.

No time for hesitation. Crouching as best he could to counteract the tug of the water, Hawkwood grasped his own musket by the barrel and swung the butt towards his struggling companion.

It worked, though more by luck than judgement. As the musket sheered towards him, Lawrence managed to seize the neck of the stock with his left hand.

Fearful that Lawrence would not be able to maintain his grip, Hawkwood crabbed his way down the length of the gun and grabbed Lawrence's wrist. Only then did he realize that Lawrence was still holding his musket in his other hand. It was the one thing anchoring him to the river bed. With the water surging around them, they clung together until Lawrence, using his gun as a fulcrum, managed to push himself to his feet. Then, slowly, arms linked, they fumbled their way across the remaining few yards of river and up on to the bank.

Lawrence, breathing hard from the effort, stammered his thanks.

"Only returning the favour, Major," Hawkwood said as they dropped their bundles and weapons on to the ground.

Tension lined Lawrence's face but he smiled weakly. "What was that about a boat?"

He put a hand to his left side. Then, realizing that Hawkwood had seen the action, he tried to hide it by straightening.

And failed.

"God damn it," Hawkwood said. "You *are* hurt!"

"It's nothing," Lawrence said quickly, though the way his lips compressed told otherwise.

"You're a damned poor liar, Douglas," Hawkwood said. "Show me."

Lawrence sighed, but made no effort – or did not have the strength – to resist as Hawkwood stepped forward. Up close, Hawkwood saw the rent in Lawrence's jacket and, when he lifted the garment away, a corresponding one in the sodden shirt beneath. Apprehensively, he peeled the material back. It wasn't that easy to see, but his heart sank at the sight of the dark discolouration surrounding the puckered entry wound in Lawrence's abdomen, just above his left hip.

"Christ, you've been shot!"

"I know," Lawrence said, teeth chattering.

Hawkwood swore again. Before Lawrence could argue, he probed Lawrence's lower back, breathing a sigh of relief when his fingers found the exit wound. Lawrence jerked at the touch. Hawkwood took his hand away and tried to recall the sequence of events.

Only two muskets had been fired during the skirmish. Determining the source of the shot, therefore, wasn't difficult.

It had to have come, Hawkwood realized, from the weapon he'd deflected.

"Well?" Lawrence said. "Will I live?"

"It didn't hit bone, far as I can tell; just flesh and muscle. It went through, too, which is the good news, but there could be matter in the wound. Is there much pain? And don't bloody lie."

"Not much at the moment. I was lying earlier, but right now I'm half numb from that bath I've just taken. I can walk, if that's what you're asking."

Looking across the river towards the camp, he shivered again. "We can't stay here. Quade will be wondering if his execution squad completed their task. They don't report back to him, he's going to come looking." He smiled wryly. "We should have buried them all in the bloody pit. That would have kept the bastard guessing."

"Wagon and horses, too?"

Lawrence reached for his coat, grimacing as he leaned down. "I'd have got you to do the heavy lifting."

Hawkwood unpacked his bundle and put on his socks. He watched anxiously as Lawrence unrolled his coat and stepped into his boots. They had survived the ordeal because, remarkably, the coat had escaped total submersion. It had also been wrapped tightly. As a result it was only slightly damp on the inside and therefore wearable. The same could not be said for Lawrence's jacket and beeches, which had taken the brunt of the ducking. They were wet through.

"Wait," Hawkwood said, as Lawrence went to fasten the coat. "Give me your scarf. Open your shirt."

Lawrence did as instructed. Hawkwood took his own dry scarf and rolled the ends to create two pads which he pressed firmly on to the entry and exit wounds. Instructing Lawrence to hold them in place, he tied the second scarf around Lawrence's waist to keep the makeshift wadding secure. "It's a good job the water was so damned cold. It'll help staunch the blood flow, at least for a while. We'd best find somewhere to set a fire and dry off. I can take another look at it then. I reckon we've got a bit of time; they won't come after us before daybreak."

313

"You're positive they'll come?" Lawrence asked, fastening his coat and re-attaching the strap to his musket.

"We've just bested another four of their men. It's the second time we've made Quade look bad. He'll be spitting blood." Hawkwood hoisted his gun over his shoulder. "Plus we know about their invasion plan. They won't want us reaching the lines with that information."

"Even though we don't know *when* they're planning to launch?" Lawrence said.

"That won't hold them back. If they can stop us, they will."

"They might bring the date forward, knowing that we know."

"They might. Either way, we'd best get going. Can't stand here nattering all bloody day. Quicker we move, the quicker we'll warm up."

"Why, Captain Hawkwood," Lawrence grinned, shouldering his musket, "I never took *you* for an optimist. Who'd've thought?"

A mile north of the river they came upon a cabin. Lying in a hollow and half-hidden by thick vegetation, at some time in its life a falling tree had demolished part of a side wall and a corner of the roof. The old stone chimney had survived intact and it had been its squared outline set against the natural tangle of the surrounding woods that had caught Hawkwood's eye. Wary of disturbing any forest predator that might have chosen the ruin as its den – though any animal would have heard them coming a long way off – they approached with caution before finally ducking through the open doorway.

"Home's home, be it never so homely," Lawrence quoted softly as they surveyed the Stygian interior.

Ignoring the smell of mould and abandonment, and anxious to warm themselves, it did not take long to get a fire going in the old hearth. Despite the damp and the fetid odours, there was no shortage of fuel. Pieces of broken furniture littered the dirt floor: an up-ended table, a worm-eaten dresser splattered with droppings and splinters of wood that might have come from the back and sides of a rocking chair. The fire glow revealed decaying roof beams festooned in cobwebs, along with corners and ledges ankle-deep in twigs and leaves and dried animal scat.

Also strewn among the debris were the remains of smaller household articles: some holed and rusted pots, a wooden pail and shards of crockery that had looked like slivers of bone in the gloom. Several large metal hooks were embedded in the chimney breast, from which cooking pots had once hung. They made use of these to suspend their wet clothes above the flames to dry, though not before Hawkwood had made a careful study of the rents in Lawrence's jacket and shirt.

Teasing the torn edges of the material around the entry hole in each garment back into their original position with his fore-finger and thumb, Hawkwood examined how closely the edges fitted together. It was a crude way of judging if any material had been shorn off by the musket ball and forced into the wound. Thankfully, from what he could see, the volume of the material looked to be intact. It wasn't a fool-proof method of detecting the possibility of foreign intrusion, but it was the only measure they had to go by, under the circumstances.

Inspecting the wound again, Hawkwood was relieved to discover that there didn't appear to have been significant blood loss since the makeshift bandage was applied. The main concern now was the risk of infection. Having seen the state of the troopers and the encampment, there was no telling what manner of dirt had become engrained within the fibres of their clothing.

Both men understood the consequences of allowing wounds to go untreated. For now, though, they had no option but to deal with the injury as best they could with the materials available, which were precious few. The priority must be to keep the wound as clean and as dry as possible.

A further search of the cabin brought to light a treasure trove in the shape of a dented tin mug. Using water from one of the canteens to swill it out, Hawkwood refilled it and placed it at the side of the fire. When the contents began to bubble, he removed it from the ashes, waited a few minutes, then, taking a strip from Lawrence's already torn shirt and dipping it into the water, he ignored his patient's muttered expletives and swabbed the wound as best he could, before reapplying the pads and the make-do bandage.

Lawrence dug out the strips of pemmican he'd found and passed one to Hawkwood. Clad in their greatcoats and huddled over the fire, they chewed on them while they checked the arms and ammunition. The cartridges had been well packed in the troopers' pouches and had retained their integrity. The muskets they dried and cleaned as best they could after their immersion in the river. As they worked, they felt the warmth returning to their bones.

When the time came for them to depart, they did so with some reluctance, torn between the desire to linger in front of the fire and the knowledge that to stay would invite the risk of capture.

The good news was that both sets of breeches were dry, as was Lawrence's shirt. His jacket still held some residual dampness, but it was wearable, if slightly scorched in places.

Extinguishing the fire, they made their exit. Outside, the night seemed twice as cold as it had before they had taken shelter, giving them one more pressing reason to keep moving.

As they left, Hawkwood took one last glance over his shoulder. A year or two and the ruin would be impossible to spot, even in the light of day. Perhaps that was how it should be. It was from the surrounding timber that the materials to make the cabin had been hewed, so it seemed only fitting that the forest should reclaim what had been taken now that the occupants had departed.

It turned out that the occupants had not travelled far. In a patch of moonlight less than thirty paces from the ruin, dwarfed by the trees looming above them, stood two simple wooden crosses. Canted and choked by weeds, they too would soon disappear, absorbed by the woodland as if they had never existed.

A memory of two other small wooden crosses, erected in the shadow of a spreading oak tree, flashed into Hawkwood's mind. Were *they* still standing, he wondered, or had the forest moved in to claim them, too? It was too dark to see if these forgotten markers carried inscriptions. Had the people who'd dwelled here been buried in haste as well? Had there been anyone to speak over *them*? Though, in the grand scheme of things, what difference did it make? It wasn't how you died that mattered; it was how you lived. And in the end didn't Nature always have the last word, anyway?

"Matthew?" Lawrence enquired softly.

Hawkwood, half lost in thought, turned.

"Are you all right?"

As his mind returned to the present, Hawkwood nodded. "I'm fine."

Lawrence peered at him, unconvinced.

At that moment, Hawkwood felt something cold alight upon his cheek. He glanced up. The air was filled with tiny white flakes. They were floating down through the trees in eerie, spectral silence. He felt the caress again, first upon his brow and then his eyelid. He blinked it away.

The snow had come.


"Christ in Heaven! Four men dead! And that's not counting Greenbush! Who the hell are these bastards? They're going through our boys like a two-man army!"

Colonel Cromwell Pearce was fuming.

While Major Quade was thinking feverishly.

The sick in the camp were dying at an increasing rate. Because of that, it had become impractical to conduct individual interments. It was customary, therefore, to bury collectively at first light the bodies of those men who'd died during the night, while the poor souls who'd expired during the day were laid to rest a couple of hours after dusk. It had also become the practice to store the bodies in one of the huts until the allotted times and from there to transport them in numbers to the burial ground in the backs of wagons.

Formal funeral services had also been suspended. In light of the steadily rising death toll, it had been decided that there was no longer a need for the men to gather to pay their respects en masse at every burial. The mood in the camp was grim enough without twice-daily funerals serving as reminders of the rapidly

317

deteriorating conditions. For the sake of morale, the onerous duty of disposing of the dead was carried out with as little ceremony as possible. After the chaplain had performed a brief eulogy as the bodies were taken from the morgue hut and laid in the wagons, the burial detail would proceed unaccompanied into the woods to take care of the rest.

It had been the morning detail that discovered the troopers' corpses out by the burial pit, whereupon the alarm had been raised.

And Quade had received his summons.

For when a corporal who'd risen to take a piss in the early hours reported seeing some winter-clad soldiers and a wagon parked outside the hut that housed the two British prisoners – who were then checked upon and found to be missing – the troopers' deaths took on a whole new meaning, as did the two faint musket shots a number of the camps' inhabitants later remembered hearing, though they hadn't taken any notice of them at the time.

Quade had been ordered to report first to the tent adjacent to the medical hut where the bodies had been delivered. He did so in a state of stunned disbelief. It shouldn't have been the troopers lying there. It shouldn't have been anyone. His orders to the escort had been very specific. Wait until everyone in the camp was likely to be asleep. Remove the prisoners from their hut. Take them into the forest and kill them. Dispose of the remains. In other words, make them disappear. Four against two. How hard could it be?

The answer lay stretched out before him. All four, Surgeon Gilliland explained, had died from different causes. The first from a knife wound to the carotid. The second from a broken neck. The third, who at first didn't appear to have a mark on him other than an injury to his cheekbone, upon further examination had suffered a contusion at the base of the skull; he had died of a haemorrhage inside the brain. As for the fourth man . . .

The gorge had risen in Quade's throat when he'd seen the extent of the trooper's disfigurement: a face so badly burned it looked as though each eyeball had been gouged out with a pair of fire tongs.

Surgeon Gilliland identified the damage as having been caused by a solution of lye, thrown, splashed or poured over the trooper's face, a diagnosis confirmed by the burial detail's observations at the killing site. Death had been caused by a swelling of the nasal passages due to ingestion of the same liquid, which had cut off the trooper's air supply. Death, Gilliland had confirmed, would have been a merciful release.

Quade's mind was in turmoil. How in God's name had it come to this? How had two men, both of whom were fettered, managed to gain the upper hand over four armed soldiers and wreak such catastrophic damage? Thus preoccupied, he presented himself before the colonel to confirm the troopers' identities; they were indeed the men he had charged with delivering the prisoners from Plattsburg gaol to the encampment and, subsequently, with guarding the prisoners' hut.

At which point Colonel Pearce had let his feelings be known, forcefully.

Quade was reporting to Colonel Pearce because Colonel Pike was no longer in the camp. Upon the orders of Surgeon Gilliland, who'd diagnosed severe pneumonia, he'd been moved to a more comfortable billet in Plattsburg. Now under the care of a local doctor, he would be bled copiously and dosed with opium, antimony and digitalis until his illness subsided. Colonel Pearce, 16th Infantry, was Pike's deputy. It was to him that command of the encampment had been transferred.

"Well, Major?" Pearce demanded. "Any Goddamned thoughts?"

Assuming a mystified expression, Quade shook his head. "I'm sorry, Colonel. I'm at a loss. Clearly, they were operating under some misguided initiative of their own."

"Initiative?" Pearce growled.

Quade had prepared himself for a possible cross-examination, though not for the purpose of speculating on how four men had ended up dead. He'd assumed the alarm would be raised when the prisoners were reported missing and that he would be summoned on account of his previous contact with them; not because of this. This was the last thing he'd anticipated.

But while he'd been shaken by the troopers' deaths and repelled by their injuries, he was also aware that, crucially, there was no one else left who knew that the men had been acting under his orders. So, while defeat appeared to have been snatched from the jaws of victory, Quade was at least secure in the knowledge that his role in the night's events would never be known. Still, it wouldn't hurt to distance himself further. It wasn't as if the dead could retaliate, was it?

"The men *were* Fifteenth Infantry, sir. Colonel Pike's regiment – same as the men killed at Greenbush. Perhaps, with the colonel indisposed, they weren't prepared to wait for justice to be served upon the prisoners and decided to dispense their own brand of vengeance. Loyalty to the regiment's a powerful incentive among the rank and file, Colonel. It's what binds them."

Quade was rather pleased with that last statement. There was, in fact, an element of truth in it. When he'd suborned the troopers into his scheme, he'd done so using Colonel Pike's name. They had been led to believe that, prior to his confinement, the colonel had ordered the death of the British spies who had slain two members of the 15th Infantry. The troopers, aggrieved by the Greenbush slayings and intent on retribution, had not questioned the order. So far as they were concerned, it had come down from their colonel. Therefore they were not being asked to commit murder but to deliver justice.

Quade pressed on. "Or it could be, sir, that they were averse to the prisoners being housed in one of the huts while brave American soldiers were out in the cold with only a blanket to keep them warm." Adding, with a helpless shrug, "Who knows what was going through their minds? I fear that's something we may never fathom."

"Meanwhile," Pearce snarled, "we've two armed British spies running loose around the countryside! God damn their eyes!"

It was hard to tell from the colonel's menacing glare whether the curse was aimed at the insubordinate dead troopers or the two men who were now on the run. Best to remain silent, Quade thought.

Never having dealt with Pearce, he found it difficult to read the man. He knew that the colonel was about his own age, though they were from different backgrounds. A widower, Quade had heard, and a descendant of Scots-Irish immigrants, Pearce had been a soldier for almost twenty years, serving mostly with volunteer units, rising eventually to the rank of Major General, 3rd Division of Militia. It had been President Madison who, a month after the outbreak of hostilities, had called upon his services and appointed him colonel of the 16th Regiment.

Quade was reflecting on what that said about the quality of regular senior staff officers when the door opened, allowing a cold blast of air to enter. A sentry poked his head in.

"Captain Walker's here, Colonel."

"What?" Pearce barked, annoyed at the draught and the interruption. "Ah, yes, very well. Send him in."

The sentry stood back as two figures entered the hut, one dressed in a buckskin coat and wide-brimmed hat, the other wearing a dark cloak.

"Amos," Pearce said. He inclined his head towards the captain's companion. "Cornelius."

The Oneida warrior bowed his head briefly in return.

"You heard?" Pearce said to Walker.

Throwing Quade a glance of acknowledgement, the bearded man removed his hat. "I did."

Pearce clicked his tongue. "Damnedest thing. The major and I have been discussing the matter. Question is, can we catch the bastards?"

Walker pursed his lips. "Any idea how long they've been gone?"

Pearce gnawed the inside of his lip. "We've a witness: Corporal Travis. He was out taking a piss some time after midnight. Dark, of course, but he could see the wagon up by the hut. In the early hours, other men reported hearing shots in the distance. Only when the alarm was raised did they put two and two together. Our best estimate is three, maybe four hours ago."

"We're assuming they'll be heading north?" Walker asked.

"Correct."

"How well do they know the country?"

Pearce looked at Quade.

"I'm not sure," Quade said.

Walker moved briskly to the table, the Indian at his shoulder. Pearce and Quade followed. Among the papers were several maps. Walker selected one and spread it out. Quade, looking over his shoulder, recognized the outline of Champlain and the north-western part of the state, most of which was blank space. There were shaded areas running north to south to indicate mountainous terrain, while several spidery lines radiating outwards from the west shore of the lake were clearly rivers and tributaries. Dark bean-shaped blobs stuck to the ends of the rivers were, presumably, less significant bodies of water; they could have been small lakes or large ponds for all the information the map provided. None were named. Very few towns featured on the map. Plattsburg was annotated, as was Willsborough to the south and Chazy and Champlain to the north. A solid, inked line struck out north-west from Plattsburg to a dot on the map, marked Chataugay, which looked to be in the middle of nowhere. There, the line forked. One fork continued west, terminating at a spot marked Bombay. The other veered south-west through dots marked Malone and Hopkinton before disappearing off the edge of the map. No other settlements were shown.

"Military road," Pearce said in answer to Quade's frown. "Built along old Indian trails. Not as substantial as it looks. Not much more than a bridleway in parts. Right, Amos?"

The bearded man nodded absently and tapped the map just above the dot marked Champlain, where another roughly drawn line ran from a point at the top end of Lake Champlain west to the St Lawrence River. Tracing it with his fingertip, he said, "The border. Runs all the way to St Regis. Ain't no fences, though. Settlements neither. North or south of the line, all you're looking at is wilderness. That's hard country, nothing but backwoods and rivers. Not even people. Hard going for those that know it. Damned sight harder for them that don't."

"You're saying we *can* catch them?" Quade said.

Walker continued to look at the map. "I'm saying maybe."

"The weather might help," Quade ventured. "If the snow persists. It should slow them down."

"Might do," Walker agreed, nodding thoughtfully. "We know *anything* about them?"

Pearce looked at Quade. "Major? You came up from Greenbush. What can you tell us?"

"So far as Lawrence is concerned, nothing."

"And Hooper?"

Quade hesitated, then said, "In my opinion, he's the dangerous one."

"Because?" Walker said.

"It was Hooper who engineered Lawrence's escape. He assaulted an officer in order to obtain a uniform which enabled him to infiltrate the Greenbush cantonment. He tricked his way into the guardhouse to secure Lawrence's release. The reports from the men on duty there indicate he killed two soldiers and injured at least two more. That was after setting the stables alight to create a diversion."

Walker's eyebrows lifted.

"He purports to have returned recently from the continent – France," Quade added, and then wondered why he'd felt the need to say that.

"France?" Pearce queried.

"Part of the story he concocted in order to pass himself off as an American officer. Said he'd been there on behalf of the president." Quade snorted derisively.

"Did he indeed?" Pearce said, interested, in spite of himself. "Doing what?"

"'Unspecified duties' was how he termed it. Said he'd been assigned to Dearborn's command in order to pass on his knowledge of British military tactics. Not that it matters, since he's patently not who he claims to be."

"Perhaps," Pearce murmured.

"Sir?" Quade said.

"It's been my experience that even the most pernicious deception often contains an element of truth."

Quade frowned. "I don't follow, Colonel."

"Perhaps he really was there. Maybe not France, but on the continent, as you put it. His conduct thus far indicates a strong familiarity with military matters. He's certainly a soldier, and a well-trained one at that. About our age, would you say, Major? Give or take a few years. Given that Britain's been at war with the French pretty much these past twenty years, he's had plenty of opportunity to hone his craft. If he wasn't in France, my guess would be the Peninsula. Either way, it would confirm your point about him being dangerous. Hell, the trail of bodies he's left behind tells us that much.

"So, in answer to your question, Amos, I think it's safe to assume that, while they might not be familiar with the country, they'll be used to campaigning, which makes them used to hardship. We send anyone after them, they'll have to be good."

Walker's eyes flicked to the Indian and then back to Pearce. "They are, Colonel. Don't you worry about that."

Pearce eyed Cornelius and the tattoos across his face. "You'll send some of your observers?"

"It's our best chance. They can travel a damned sight faster than white troops." Walker squinted at Pearce. "My question, Colonel, is when they do catch up with them, you want them dead or brought back?"

*When, not if,* Quade noted.

Pearce, who'd been looking at the map, straightened. "Dead would be acceptable. Proof of death would be required."

A look passed between the two men. Walker turned to his companion but did not speak. The Oneida, his face like stone, returned his gaze.

*He wants their scalps,* Quade realized; the image this conjured up, usually unpalatable, took on a more pleasing dimension. To Walker, he said, "Won't the weather hamper your men, Captain?"

"Not by much." Walker grinned. "Always a track to follow, if you know what to look for."

"And if they manage to cross the border? Will your men continue the pursuit?"

Walker waved a dismissive hand at the map. "What border? Oneida don't recognize borders, Major. Their ancestors have hunted this land for a thousand years. Hell, longer than that. Didn't need no maps then; don't follow them now. A line on a piece of paper don't mean shit to them. So, don't you worry none about borders – they won't."

"It's not their reaching the border that bothers me," Pearce snapped. "It's two spies passing on word about our flotilla."

Walker nodded thoughtfully. "You're right. Getting to the border ain't the same as reaching the lines. They'd have a ways to go before they do that. Not far, but it'll give us more time to catch them."

Pearce looked pensive.

"They'll be trying for Île aux Noix?" Quade said.

The island lay in the middle of the Richelieu River, which flowed out of Champlain and ran due north all the way to its confluence with the St Lawrence, some forty miles above Montreal. Like so many strategic fortifications in the region, it had changed hands over the years. The French had built the ramparts, the British had captured them and the Americans had taken them during the Revolution, losing them a year later following their retreat from Quebec, at which point they had returned to British hands. Since then, the original fortifications had been extended and a shipyard added and it had become the Crown's main frontier post in the region.

Pearce and Walker exchanged glances. It was Walker who spoke. "That's the nearest garrison of any size. But it ain't the closest outpost."

Turning to the map, the captain pointed to a spot in the hinterland west of the Richelieu and north of the borderline, where there was a small drawn symbol half the size of the captain's fingernail and shaped like a squat, square-sided mushroom. "That is."

At the end of the captain's gnarled fingertip was a dot marked Lacolle.

"Goddamn it to hell," Pearce said.

\* \* \*

The snow had fallen steadily for more than two hours before it began to ease. By the time dawn finally arrived the land was covered in a crisp white blanket while every leaf on every tree was decorated with a coating of hoar frost. Finding a path across the icy ground, through hollows and along ridges and over half-frozen streams where one slip could easily lead to a turned ankle or worse, had become a test of endurance. As a result, what had begun as a purposeful hike soon slowed to a weary trudge.

There had been no signs of human habitation since the cabin but plenty of evidence in the snow telling them they were not alone. Animal tracks abounded. Deer and hare slots, mostly, though on one occasion they had come across a set that was recognizably feline in nature. A lynx, Hawkwood deduced from the size of the pug marks, hoping he wasn't mistaken and that it wasn't one of the bigger mountain cats out on the prowl.

He tried not to think about the signs they were leaving in their own wake. Maintaining caution, they had avoided open ground as much as possible, sticking close to the treeline where the cover was better and where the surface was less prone to indentation, using established deer trails whenever they could.

Every so often, they paused and took stock. As yet, there was nothing to suggest that the Americans had taken up the chase, but Hawkwood was not about to let that lull him into a false sense of security. Had the roles been reversed, the fact that his quarry had established a lead would not have deterred him from pursuing them.

He and Jago had once chased a smuggler halfway across the English Channel, at considerable risk to themselves; there had been no question of allowing the bastard to escape, not with the blood of two British naval officers and several French prisoners of war on his hands. Memories of his own recent escape from Paris also came to mind; he'd been followed every step of the way by a policeman named Vidocq because Hawkwood had killed one of his officers.

Between them, he and Lawrence had taken the lives of at least six American troopers. No commander could afford to let that go unpunished, else he would lose the respect of his men. The Americans might be some way behind, but they were coming. The only hope was to reach the British lines before their pursuers caught up. And before the snow began to fall in earnest. Which was not going to be easy, with Lawrence's strength flagging.

Though he was trying hard not to show it, the wound was clearly causing Lawrence considerable discomfort. Constant movement over rough terrain had started it bleeding again. But there was no prospect of rest and recuperation. If the weather stayed as it was, it could take two days to reach their goal, and any deterioration would lengthen the journey considerably. They could not afford to drag it out longer by halting for frequent rest breaks. Telling themselves that the quicker they reached the lines, the sooner a doctor could take a look at Lawrence's wound, they pressed on, not even stopping to eat.

Chewing strips of pemmican as they walked had helped keep the hunger pangs at bay, but their dwindling supplies wouldn't sustain them for the rest of the journey. Hawkwood was keeping a watchful eye out for game. There wasn't time to rig traps and catch prey, but they had weapons and ammunition, making it possible to hunt for food. They also had the tools to light a fire. Water wasn't a problem, either, not with so much snow about. And there were plenty of streams and they had canteens. The main concern was finding shelter.

Their chances of finding another ruined cabin were so remote as to be nonexistent. They needed to find something though; the prospect of spending a night in the open did not make the heart sing. Hawkwood hoped some refuge would present itself soon, because from the sky's sullen tint, the earlier snowfall had only been a foretaste of what was to come.

By late morning the sun had yet to show itself. While the frost had eventually disappeared, the woods remained snow-bound and eerily gloomy, wrapped in an expectant hush, as if the day was holding its breath. Occasionally a bird's twitter would interrupt the silence, but for the most part the only sound, apart from their breathing, was the soft crunching of snow beneath their boots.

The deer trail gradually petered out. Snow-capped rocks and boulders began to break up the surface ahead of them. Piled atop and against one another as if by some giant hand, they reminded Hawkwood of the ruined fortifications they'd sailed past on their voyage up the lake. He thought longingly of his stinking cubbyhole on the *Snake*; that had been the last time he'd had anything approaching a decent night's sleep.

For Lawrence wasn't the only one who was feeling the pain of the march. Hawkwood, too, was tiring. Just the effort of lifting one foot in front of the other had begun to tell. And if *he* was fighting to stay awake, then Lawrence had to be suffering tenfold with that wound in his side. To reassure himself that all was well, he looked back over his shoulder to find that Lawrence had come to a halt several paces away, his face as white as the snow. He was breathing hard and clutching his side. Hawkwood stepped forward quickly, just in time to catch him as he swayed and almost fell.

Lawrence swore, straightened, and then offered an apologetic smile. "Not as hale as I thought I was, damn it."

"We'll stop a while. Rest our legs."

Lawrence did not demur. As Hawkwood reached beneath his arm to help him to a nearby boulder, Lawrence let go a rueful sigh. "I'm not sure that'll make much difference."

Hawkwood wasn't listening.

One hundred paces away, within the trees, he'd seen movement.

"What?" Lawrence asked, suddenly alert.

It had been no more than a hint; a shapeless form, half-hidden, that had been there one second and gone the next.

"Matthew?" Lawrence said cautiously.

"I thought I saw something . . ." Hawkwood let go of Lawrence's arm and slid the musket from his shoulder.

Lawrence squinted back the way they had come. With no sunlight filtering light down through the canopy, the woods were draped in shadow, differing shades of grey against the lighter-coloured snow. Even with so many trees devoid of foliage, trying to penetrate the forest's interior was well-nigh impossible. It might as well have been twilight rather than close to midday.

They waited and watched. All was silent. No birdsong, Hawkwood noticed.

Lawrence fingered his musket apprehensively. "I don't see anything."

Hawkwood didn't either. Seconds slid by. The tension began to ease. Fatigue, he suspected, was making him see things that weren't there. Fear of pursuit, too. That was all it could be.

And then . . .

If a whisper could take form, that's what Hawkwood saw, as whatever it was passed ghost-like through a gap in the trees, dark against the snow but with insufficient texture for identification to be made.

"I see it!" Lawrence hissed. He eased back the hammer on his musket. Hawkwood did the same.

They counted off the seconds. One . . . two . . .

There was a sudden blur of motion. Hawkwood's heart leapt into his mouth as an antlered buck burst from the woods less than seventy paces away and bounded into an area of deeper brush, where it was immediately erased from view.

They stared after it.

"Sweet lord!" Lawrence breathed. He lowered his gun and shook his head in weary amusement at having been alarmed by nothing more threatening than a nervous whitetail.

They kept their eyes on the spot where the animal had vanished. It did not reappear.

"Would have looked nice in a pot," Lawrence murmured wistfully.

Hawkwood used the heel of his hand to release the lock on his musket, conscious of just how hard his heart was hammering. A bloody deer. That's all it had been.

But spooked by *something*, he thought uneasily.

A call rang out from the woods close by and to their right.

*Blue jay*, thought Hawkwood. There was no time for a warning. He spun, heeling the musket hammer to full cock.

Lawrence swore as a brown-clad figure burst from the forest on their left. Hawkwood fired. The figure was thrown back with a cry, a war club pitching from his hand. Another musket banged. Hawkwood felt a tug on his sleeve as the ball sliced through his coat, then Lawrence pushed him towards the shelter of the boulders.

It occurred to him that the first warrior might have sprung the attack in order to draw fire, because once a musket was discharged, it took too long to reload in close-quarter combat. He was about to warn Lawrence to save his shot when a second warrior sprinted from cover. With no time to aim, Lawrence turned and brought his musket up quickly. Instinctively bringing the gun against his belly to brace it, he pulled the trigger and the long gun spoke. The recoil slammed against Lawrence's wound. He staggered and started to go down, his face twisting in agony and remorse at seeing his shot go wide.

The attacker celebrated Lawrence's miss with a high-pitched bark. Tomahawk in hand, he sprinted forward. Hawkwood felt his innards contract as three more painted warriors ran from the trees. Two were armed with a short-barrelled carbine each; the third carried a sword and club.

Hawkwood pivoted towards the struggling Lawrence. "Up, dammit!"

Lawrence, teeth gritted, clambered to his feet just in time.

The lead warrior had covered the ground incredibly fast, heels kicking up the snow. Hawkwood had a split-second's glimpse of a red-and-black painted face and bared teeth above a faded grey shirt and buckskin leggings, then the hatchet blade was whipping towards him.

Sweeping the musket across his body, he felt the impact as the tomahawk's shaft struck the gun barrel. Parrying the blade aside, he drove the musket butt into the warrior's throat. There was a crunch as the cartilage gave way, then his attacker hit the snow. By this time Hawkwood had already dropped the gun, scooped up the tomahawk and turned to face the next threat.

Hunting in packs, predators cut out the weakest animal from the herd, run it to ground and then move in for the kill. The

Oneida were applying the same tactic. Either they had detected from Lawrence's spoor that he was injured or they'd been watching from the trees for some time, waiting until he showed signs of fading before launching their attack. Two of the remaining three Indians were running towards him. The third had Hawkwood in his sights.

The hatchet was a weapon for which he'd found little use in either his army days or in his career as a Runner. Some skills, however, were never forgotten. They simply remained dormant until called upon.

The first warrior was less than five strides from Lawrence when Hawkwood let fly. The Oneida crashed to the ground with the tomahawk blade embedded in the back of his skull.

Which left Hawkwood without a weapon, save for the stiletto in his boot. It wasn't enough. He reached for it anyway.

The carbine's report sounded incredibly loud. Hawkwood felt a sharp, searing blaze of pain across his forehead. As he went down, he caught a brief sight of Lawrence jabbing his musket at one of the remaining attackers, while at the edge of his vision he saw the fifth warrior – presumably the one who'd shot him – draw a knife from the beaded sash at his waist.

Hawkwood tried to rise. Through the blood that was seeping into his eyes he saw Lawrence stumble. As his adversary let out a triumphant bray and raised the war club above his head to deliver the coup de grâce, Hawkwood heard another, closer, crow of victory and looked up. The shooter stood above him.

With great deliberation the Oneida laid his gun to one side, drew his knife and placed a knee on Hawkwood's chest. Taking hold of a clump of Hawkwood's hair with his free hand, he pulled it tight. Pain shot through Hawkwood's skull. Half-blinded, he pawed weakly for the top of his boot, knowing the stiletto was out of reach. The Oneida bent and pressed the point of his knife against Hawkwood's scalp and grinned.

From behind them came a piercing scream, followed by a swift pattering sound.

*Lawrence!* Hawkwood thought despairingly.

And then the grinning face above him shuddered under the impact of a war club, crushing the side of the skull. So fast and so vicious was the strike that Hawkwood's attacker made no sound. There was only a sickening crunch followed by a loose thump as his body sagged sideways on to the snow.

And then a deafening silence.

Hawkwood looked up, taking in the bloodied war club and the hand that held it. A dark form, dressed in a buckskin coat and broadcloth leggings floated into view. Behind it, other similarly clothed figures were moving among the bodies. Hawkwood recoiled as a hand reached towards him. A fresh bolt of pain ripped through his head as he tried again to reach his knife.

Then a voice spoke. It seemed to come from a long way off. "She:kon, Kahrhakon:ha. Skennenko:wa ken?"

*Kahrhakon:ha.*

A name from the past. *Hawk.*

Hawkwood blinked away blood and tried to focus. His skull felt as if it was on fire. A face materialized above him, unpainted. Strong, stern, almost haughty features, not young, set below a shaven scalp surmounted by a topknot decorated with two white feathers.

Weakly, Hawkwood looked to the side and saw that the Indian who'd been about to dash Lawrence's brain to a pulp was sprawled on the ground, a dark stain spreading across the snow beneath him. Lawrence had collapsed against a boulder, musket in hand. He was staring at the body before him and at the three Indian warriors who were examining the scattered corpses. He turned towards Hawkwood, a look of total bafflement on his face.

Hawkwood squinted upwards. The figure hadn't moved. As he made to wipe the blood from his eyes so he could see, the action sent another white-hot bolt of lightning through his skull and the figure began to dissolve. Then a hand took his.

Feeling the strength in the grip, Hawkwood focused again and stared at the tall warrior and the war club he was holding, dripping with the Oneida's blood. A knot formed in his throat.

It couldn't be, he thought. Tears pricked his eyes and then his vision blurred again.

In the same language as before, the voice commanded: "Lie still little brother."

And darkness descended.

# 13

Crouched on Hawkwood's chest and no more than a foot from his nose, the mouse stared back at him through bright, black eyes. As rodents went, this one wasn't that big; five inches of sleek furry body, complemented at the sharp end by a large head and impressively pointed snout and at the blunt end by three inches of shortened tail. It looked more curious than alarmed, until Hawkwood raised his head, at which point, with a nervous twitch of its whiskers and a quick flick of its tail, it was gone.

Hawkwood closed his eyes and sank back down. It took a couple of seconds for the realization to sink in that, when he'd lifted his head, it hadn't hurt; well, not much. Which made a change. He tried again. Willing himself to sit up, he got as far as resting his weight on his elbows – a small victory in itself and more than enough to be going on with.

No mouse this time. And no real pain either, not unless you counted the dull ache hovering at the back of his eyeballs as he waited for his vision to adjust to his surroundings. Even then, the darker recesses remained obscured by the smoke curling up from the cooking fires.

He touched a hand to his head and ran his fingers tentatively over what felt like some sort of sticky paste. The smell gave an indication of the ingredients: softened pine resin mixed with deer tallow and beeswax. The traditional remedy for cuts and wounds.

Above him he could see the slatted underside of a storage platform and the furs and blankets that lined the sleeping compartment's walls. Protruding over the edge of the platform he could just make out the corner of a woven reed mat and the bottom curve of an iron cooking pot. Other objects were strung from the posts that supported the partitions at each end of the compartment and which, in turn, formed part of the longhouse's timber frame: wood-splint baskets, an infant's carry-cradle, mixed articles of clothing – including his coat – a pair of snow shoes, a carry pouch and assorted clubs, bows, knives and a quiver of arrows. Above the central aisle the joists were festooned with provisions: strips of dried meat competed for hanging space with smoked fish, corn husks, slices of dried pumpkin, herb garlands and several bleached animal skulls.

His ears picked out the low murmur of voices, but when he turned his head the only person he could see was a slight, round-shouldered, grey-haired figure kneeling with its back to him, tending the fire adjacent to his own sleeping ledge. He transferred his gaze to the opposite partition – a twin of the one in which he lay – and to the supine form half-hidden beneath a layer of beaver pelts. Relief rose within him when he saw the steady rise and fall of Lawrence's chest beneath the coverings. Immediately, his mind flashed back to the fight with the Oneida and the aftermath. Then his head began to throb once more. Sensing the onset of confusion, he lowered himself down.

A hand on his shoulder returned him to the present. He started and found himself gazing up into the wrinkled features of an elderly, grey-haired woman who was holding a small wooden bowl towards him. The figure from the hearth; he assumed she'd been instructed to wait until he or Lawrence showed signs of life before administering her potions.

"Onighira," she commanded, pressing the steaming bowl gently to his lips. Her eyes, he saw, were grey and cloudy, the inevitable result of a life spent in smoke-filled interiors.

Hawkwood raised himself up and took a cautious sip. It was some sort of herbal brew. Beech-bark tea, most likely, and slightly bitter to the tongue. But there was comfort in the warmth as it coursed through his insides.

Three gulps later, the old woman withdrew the bowl and retired silently to the fire. Setting the vessel down, she padded off into another darkened area of the longhouse, her footsteps making no sound on the hard-packed earthen floor.

With the taste of the tea lingering spikily at the back of his throat, Hawkwood pushed the blankets and furs aside and swung his feet to the ground. He was relieved to discover that the earth did not rise up to meet him, though it did tilt slightly. Encouraged, he stood up. Only then did the world start to spin. He sat down quickly and waited, eyes closed once more, for the motion to stop.

He had no sense of time, so it could have been either seconds or several minutes later when he sensed that someone else had arrived and was watching over him. Presumably the old woman, discovering that one of her patients was awake, had gone to report the fact.

"Mat-huwa, skennenko:wa ken?"

He knew then that it wasn't a dream.

Shadows, cast by the firelight, played across the cloaked warrior's face, accentuating the patrician features and the deeper lines that had been added since Hawkwood had last gazed upon it. The dark eyes, however, were as keen as he remembered.

"You look well, rake'niha," Hawkwood said, his throat constricting. "The years have been kind." He rose to his feet. This time, the world stayed where it was.

"Your words flatter me, Mat-huwa," Tewanias said as he clasped Hawkwood's hands in his own. "But my heart is glad to see you."

There was more grey in the hair than Hawkwood remembered, but as they embraced he detected a firmness in the Mohawk chief's frame that would have been envied by men half his age. Remarkable for someone who'd survived more than sixty winters.

They separated in silence, but did not release their hold, each gripping each other's forearms as if reluctant to break the spell.

337

Before either of them could speak, a second cloaked figure appeared at Tewanias's right shoulder: the warrior whose timely intervention had saved Hawkwood and Lawrence's scalps.

"Cageaga," Hawkwood said.

The tall warrior gazed back at him, his face angled laconically. "So, you *do* remember."

Without warning, and before Hawkwood could react, the Mohawk tapped a finger against the side of Hawkwood's head. Pain flared momentarily.

"It's good to know you still have the skull of an elk, little brother. I am also pleased to see that you have not forgotten *every*thing you were taught."

He presumed Cageaga was referring to his throwing skills. Back-handed compliments had always been the taciturn warrior's preferred form of encouragement.

"I had a very good teacher," Hawkwood said.

It occurred to Hawkwood that he was conversing in a tongue he'd not used for more than half his lifetime. And yet, retrieved from the same store of memory that by some miracle had granted him the skill to launch the tomahawk with such devastating force and accuracy, it seemed to come as naturally as breathing.

The Mohawk warrior considered the response, before nodding thoughtfully. "Ea, that is true."

With Tewanias and Cageaga at his shoulder, Hawkwood crossed the aisle to Lawrence's side. The major's coat had also been removed. His complexion had regained some of its colour. His breathing was strong and even. Gently, Hawkwood lifted away the covers and raised Lawrence's shirt. Had they been in a British Army medical tent, a regimental surgeon might well have recoiled at the sight of the poultices affixed to Lawrence's skin. Composed from what appeared to be mashed vegetable root, moss and frog spit, they looked to be the last thing anyone would choose to draw infection from a gunshot wound. In the absence of a sawbones, however, they were the best treatment Lawrence was going to get and Hawkwood was prepared to place his trust in them. He replaced the covers and turned away. "He's a brave man."

"He will be cared for," Tewanias said. "Do not worry." He took Hawkwood's arm. "Let us sit."

They retired to the fireside. Seated on a mat, Hawkwood drew his legs up beneath him and held his hands out to the flames. His mind was in a whirl. When he looked up he found Tewanias was regarding him gravely.

"I did not think our paths would cross again, Mat-huwa."

"Nor I," Hawkwood said. "And yet you show no surprise. Why is that?"

Tewanias's gaze dropped. He stared silently into the fire for several seconds before answering: "Your return was foretold."

Despite the fire's warmth, Hawkwood felt a chill run across his back and shoulders. "By whom?"

"One who is no longer with us."

Hawkwood waited.

"Ayonhwathah," Tewanias said.

Hawkwood searched his memory. A grainy image began to form. "I remember. He told us stories around the fires at night. I called him Tota."

*Grandfather.*

Tewanias's face softened. "As did we all."

"My heart is made heavy by his passing. When did this occur?"

"It has been four days since his spirit crossed over to the sky world," Tewanias said solemnly.

The day we left Whitehall, Hawkwood calculated.

He thought about the wake that would have been held for the old man and the rites that would have followed, the days during which the mourners would have lain face-down upon their sleeping mats, enveloped in their robes, without fires to warm them, eating their food cold and leaving the longhouse only at night and as secretly as possible.

He held his hands out to the flames, grateful for their warmth. Had they arrived prior to Ayonhwathah's crossing, he knew the longhouse's interior would have been as dark as night and as cold as the snow-bound woods that surrounded it.

It was on the tip of his tongue to enquire how the old man had known of his imminent return, but he knew there would be no rational answer. In matters of prophecy, one did not question the how or the wherefore, any more than one queried the existence of Ha-Wen-Neyu, the Creator of all things, when the evidence was everywhere around you. One had only to gaze upon a snow-capped mountain or a crystal-clear lake or watch an eagle soar to know the works and wisdom of the Great Spirit, whose voice could be heard in the wind and whose breath gave life to all the world.

Hawkwood posed the next question carefully. "Did Ayonhwathah give purpose to my being here?"

Tewanias shook his head. "He did not. He spoke only of when, not why."

"*When?*" Hawkwood said.

"Ea, he said that on the seventh day, following the birth of djutu'weha' – the moon of great cold – Kahrhakon:ha would return, to warm himself at the fires of the Kanien'kehá:ka."

Hawkwood digested that. "How did you know where I – we – would be?"

"We did not know."

"But you *were* looking for me?"

"We were searching, but not for you alone."

"I do not understand. Then how did you find us?"

The two warriors exchanged looks. It was Tewanias who answered.

"We know soldiers of the Yan-kees have been gathering at Senhahlone – what the whites call Platts-burg – and that they have been joined by our enemy, the Oneniote'á:ka. Their runners have been seen to the north and east. They have been drawing ever closer. Fearing attack, we sent scouts into the forest to watch the trails and to give warning. When Cageaga found the Oneniote'á:ka's spoor, he thought they were searching for us, not you.

"We knew no matter what path *you* were on, it would bring you here. We did not think it would happen the way it did, that our enemy would bring you to us. Cageaga tells me you fought well."

"I am flattered by Cageaga's words. All Kanien'kehá:ka know him to be a great warrior."

340

"The scars on your face tell me there have been other battles," Tewanias observed softly.

*Too many*, Hawkwood thought, but he smiled and said, "A few."

Tewanias gazed at him perceptively. "You have the look of a soldier, Mat-huwa. One who serves in the army of the Great King, perhaps?"

"Yes," Hawkwood looked towards the sleeping Lawrence. "We both do."

It was easier to reply in the affirmative rather than to try to describe his true profession, which would have no useful meaning to either of the men seated opposite him. In any case, his past life seemed to have developed the alarming knack of intruding upon his current vocation, so his answer wasn't that far from the truth.

"You are here to make war on the Yan-kees?" Cageaga enquired.

"That was not my intention."

Cageaga frowned. "I do not understand."

Hawkwood thought for a few moments and then said, "I was sent by King George's war chief to the land of les français to spy upon the enemy of the Great King. I was discovered and forced to flee. I hoped to find a ship to carry me back to England, but I was delivered here, to America – Anówarakowa Kawennote – instead. Now I am trying to get to Canada. From there I will find a ship to carry me back across the great water."

"And your friend?" Tewanias asked. "He was sent to make war on les français too?"

"No. He *was* sent to America to make war against the Yankees. We were both captured and held prisoner in Senhahlone. We escaped and Yankee soldiers were killed. Now they hunt us. There is a price on our heads."

"*That* is why the Stone People wanted your scalps?" Cageaga asked. "To sell to the Yan-kees for bounty?"

"Yes."

It was safe to assume the Oneida had indeed been in the service of the Americans. Hawkwood recalled his visit to Colonel

341

Pike's hut, and the civilian who'd been lurking in the background with his Oneida companion. Their presence and the subsequent attack confirmed Lawrence's testimony that the Americans employed native irregulars to carry out special tasks, including, it appeared, the chasing down of fugitives. Given the skills required to pick up a trail and follow it across inhospitable ground and through even more inhospitable weather, it made sense. Hawkwood thought of the signs he and Lawrence had left behind; not so obvious to white men, but as good as a map to the Oneida.

Had Quade dispatched them? With the colonel indisposed, it was possible Quade had given the order, just as he had given the order to the burial detail. Had it not been for Cageaga's intervention, the corpses lying in the snow would have been his and Lawrence's. Hopefully, the Oneida having failed in their mission, they would be safe now.

Or would they? Hawkwood turned to Tewanias. "Why do you fear an attack?"

There was a long silence. Tewanias drew his cloak closer about him. Smoke from the fire drifted in front of his face. "The Yan-kees say this is their land. We say it is not. They will send their soldiers to take it from us."

"They will try," Cageaga murmured ominously, "and they will fail."

Hawkwood waited.

"Much has changed since you left us, Mat-huwa," Tewanias said. Small amber reflections of light glowed in the corners of the Mohawk chief's dark eyes.

"Tell me."

Tewanias turned his head away from the flames so that one side of his face was pooled in shadow.

"When you first came to us, I told you of the history of our people and how it was the Peacemaker's vision of the tribes coming together as one under the Tree of Great Peace that gave breath to the Rotinonshón:ni."

"I remember," Hawkwood said.

"And how the sachems of the Six Nations would meet in

342

friendship around the great fire at Onondaga?"

Hawkwood nodded.

Tewanias paused, gathering his thoughts. "During those times it was said that the land ruled by the Rotinonshón:ni was greater in measure than all the sky; from the banks of the Oiqué – what the whites called the Hud-son . . ."

". . . to the river the People of the Cave Country call the Tanasi," Hawkwood finished. "I have not forgotten."

"And we told you how the whites came," Cageaga muttered, his voice dripping with scorn, "with their guns and their one true God."

"That, too," Hawkwood said, wondering where the conversation was leading.

"And we thought that was good," Cageaga growled. "The whites offered us trade: guns for furs. With guns, the Rotinonshón:ni could defeat their enemies, the Wendat and the Abenaki, so we welcomed these new friends. We let them build their houses and their farms. But with the passing of each winter more whites came, spreading their shadow across the land. The Rotinonshón:ni became fearful; some left their homeland and went west, to Ohíyo. Others went north, to Canada. The rest stayed. But soon, they learned that the whites had brought other things besides their one true God and their guns."

Hawkwood waited.

"They brought sickness," Cageaga hissed, "and they brought war. And we have been paying with our lives and our lands ever since."

"First, it was the English fighting les français," Tewanias said, drawing his cloak about him. "The Rotinonshón:ni were divided. Those Kanien'kehá:ka who had travelled north chose to fight on the side of les français. Those who remained fought for the Great King. Kanien'kehá:ka fought against Kanien'kehá:ka. But when the soldiers of the Great King defeated les français, a treaty was signed so that all men – the Rotinonshón:ni and the whites – could live in peace and the lands of the Rotinonshón:ni would remain free for all time."

"And like fools we believed them," Cageaga snorted. "For too long we have let ourselves be tricked by the white man's promises."

In a more moderate tone, Tewanias continued, "And war came again. This time it was the Yan-kees who fought the soldiers of the Great King. The people of the Rotinonshón:ni were made to choose sides. Many villages were burned. Many warriors crossed over to the sky world. The great council fire at Onondaga was allowed to die, never to be lit again. And when the war was over, a new treaty was agreed. This time, when the whites made their mark upon the paper, to share out the lands won and lost, the Rotinonshón:ni were ignored."

"Did *we* not count?" Cageaga broke in, his mouth twisting with anger and disgust. "Were *we* not owed respect?"

"The Kanien'kehá:ka who fought for the English were afraid the Yan-kees would punish them," Tewanias said. "Knowing this, the English offered them shelter in Canada. Many departed to join their brothers in Kahnawá:ke and Ahkwesáhsne. Others moved across Kaniatarowanénhne to new villages, to Ohswé:ken on the far side of Erie and to Kenhtè:ke."

Kaniatarowanénhne, Hawkwood knew, was the St Lawrence River. "But not all?"

"No. Even though they had defeated the English, the Yan-kees promised that the lands of the Rotinonshón:ni would remain free to any who wanted to stay. We took them at their word and some of us stayed.

"In the beginning, the Yan-kees' word was true, but as time passed they broke their promise. They allowed more of their people to enter the lands of the Rotinonshón:ni. Their farms became villages and their villages became towns. The whites thought if there were more whites than Rotinonshón:ni, the Rotinonshón:ni would forget their old ways and live as the whites lived and we would let them take the rest of our lands."

"And they were right," Cageaga growled. "The Stone People and the People of the Marsh and the Great Mountain all took money from the Yan-kees in exchange for land, while their warriors adopted the white men's ways, turning to drink and wickedness. They had no right to sell land they did not own!

344

The Great Spirit did not *sell* the land to the Rotinonshón:ni! He *gave* it to the Nations for safekeeping. In return, the land gives us shelter, the food in our bellies, the clothes upon our backs. When we of the Kanien'kehá:ka look upon the mountains and the forests, we see the power of the Great Spirit. But when the white man looks upon the land he sees only profit. Now the whites are too great in number and we are too few. Though we have tried to protect the land from them, we have failed."

"Before you came to us the first time, Mat-huwa," Tewanias said, "our prophets warned us that we would have to leave the home of our ancestors and find another place far from the reach of the Yan-kees. So we left our village for a new home, in Atirú:taks, the hunting grounds of the Kanien'kehá:ka, where we knew the whites would be afraid to enter, where you lived with us. We were happy there, but when the war between the whites ended, when we learned that our leaders had sold the last of the Kanien'kehá:ka land to the Yan-kees, we knew the Nations were broken beyond mending."

"That was when the Yan-kees told all Kanien'kehá:ka that those who did not want to join our brothers in Canada could remain, but it had to be in a place of the Yan-kees' choosing. I have seen such places," Cageaga said bitterly, his face twisting. "The whites call them . . ." he paused, trying to fold his tongue around the word he was searching for ". . . reservations. I did not know that word, but I saw what it means. The Kanien'kehá:ka cannot live in such places. So we came here, to the last strong-hold of our people. If the Yan-kees want to take this land, they will have to fight us for it. We will defend it against them and they will know our anger."

*Here.* Hawkwood realized he had no idea where "here" was.

"The Kanien'kehá:ka know it as Kanièn:keh," Tewanias said, reading his confusion. "After the homeland of our fathers."

Land of the Flint. Hawkwood understood then.

"This village is named Gaanundata."

Flattened Mountain. As he pondered upon the significance of that name, Hawkwood's wound began to throb again. It felt as if a small mallet was beating time against the inside of his skull. The smoke wasn't helping, either. It was catching at the back of his throat, though it could also have been the after-effects of the bark tea. He heard a low grunt from behind him. Tewanias and Cageaga looked towards the sound. Hawkwood turned.

Lawrence was on his feet.

Hawkwood rose quickly. "How are you feeling?"

The major gazed about him, frowning at the strange artefacts strung around the walls, wrinkling his nose at the combination of smells contained within the longhouse's dim-lit interior. "What is this place? Where are we?"

"Safe," Hawkwood said.

Lawrence considered that. "How did we get here?"

"By a miracle," Hawkwood said, as he wasn't sure in his own mind about the exact sequence of events that had taken place following the bloody run-in with the Oneida.

He had thought that Lawrence might have remained conscious throughout and been in a position to fill the gaps for him, but it sounded as though the major must have succumbed to the pain of his own wound. Presumably Cageaga and his warriors had fashioned travois stretchers out of coats or blankets, and transported the two of them through the snow to this safe haven. Action that had undoubtedly saved their lives, for without it, Hawkwood knew, neither of them would have survived a night in the open.

Lawrence put a hand to his side and let go another half-stifled grunt. Lifting his shirt, he stared dolefully at the unsightly wad of vegetable matter clinging to his flesh. Touching the mess he raised his fingertips to his nose and sniffed. "What in the name of . . .?"

"Don't worry," Hawkwood said. "It won't kill you. You're in good hands."

Lawrence grimaced. "I'll take your word for it." He indicated the bloody graze and the salve on Hawkwood's scalp. "And you?"

"I'll live."

A faint smile played across Lawrence's lips which slid away as

346

his focus shifted past Hawkwood's shoulder to the two warriors watching them silently from the fire. His eyes narrowed.

"Who are they?"

"Kanien'kehá:ka," Hawkwood said. "Mohawk."

"Mohawk?" Lawrence switched his gaze back to Hawkwood. His expression changed. He frowned. "I heard you talking. You were speaking their language."

Hawkwood wondered if he was imagining the suspicious tone in Lawrence's voice. "It's been a while. I'm a little rusty."

Lawrence stared at him. "I don't understand."

"You remember that long story I mentioned?"

"How could I forget?"

"Same story, different chapter." Hawkwood smiled.

Lawrence's eyes continued to rake Hawkwood's face. Then his chin came up. "Dammit, I knew you were holding something back! I had a feeling you knew more about this country than you could've picked up from a stolen map. Am I right?" Giving Hawkwood no opportunity to respond, Lawrence went on: "That Indian back at the encampment – I had my doubts then. You knew his tribe *and* his clan. And now we have these fellows, with whom you've been conversing like a native. What the devil—"

Suddenly Lawrence broke off. He seemed to sag, as if retracting into himself. Finally, he let go a sigh. "Forgive me. The last thing I want is for there to be distrust between us. If it hadn't been for you, I'd be rotting in a prison cell, or worse. I can only assume you've had your own reasons for keeping things to yourself. But look at it from my point of view. If nothing else, being kept in the dark's bloody annoying! You have to give me something, even if it's to prevent me from going mad!" He threw Hawkwood a beseeching look.

Placing a hand on Lawrence's shoulder, Hawkwood said, "My apologies, Douglas. You're right, you deserve an explanation. And you'll have it – in the morning. Will you settle for that?"

"I don't suppose I've any bloody choice, have I? Very well, morning it is. But by God I *will* hold you to it, see if I don't!"

347

He jutted his chin towards the two figures waiting behind Hawkwood's shoulder. "Are you going to introduce me? I take it these fellows do have names I can pronounce?"

"That they do," Hawkwood said, relieved to be back on firmer ground.

"Excellent! In that case, I'm most anxious to make their acquaintance."

Hawkwood led Lawrence to the fire.

"Major, meet Broken Twig, war chief of the Turtle Clan and Dogs Round the Fire, war chief of the Wolf Clan. Though you might find it easier if you address them as Tewanias and Cageaga. It was Cageaga who came to our aid."

Turning to the two warriors, Hawkwood said, "Ontiaten:ro' ne ki – Roren." *This is my friend – Lawrence.*

Lawrence held out his hand. "I thank you both, gentlemen. Chief Tewanias, Chief Cageaga, it's an honour to meet you. We are for ever in your debt." He looked at Hawkwood. "Er, how do you say—"

"Niá:wen," Hawkwood said, pre-empting him.

"Niá:wen," Lawrence said, bowing formally. He glanced sideways. "Though it don't do justice after what they've done for us. Do they speak English?"

"When it suits them," Hawkwood said, earning himself a reproving look from Tewanias.

Both warriors took Lawrence's proffered hand, but their faces remained impassive.

"Roren," Tewanias said.

"Roren?" Lawrence looked to Hawkwood again.

"It's how they say Lawrence."

"Is it indeed? Well, I've been called worse. What do they call you?"

"We're on first-name terms. It should be Watio, but I've managed to get them as far as Mat-huwa."

Tewanias, with great formality, showed Lawrence to a space by the fire, poured some bark tea from the pot resting on the hearthstones into a wooden bowl and held it out.

Lawrence eased himself down carefully, accepted the bowl

with both hands and took a cautious sip. Running his tongue along his lips, his brow furrowed. "Interesting."

"Three sips are considered polite," Hawkwood said.

Lawrence took three swallows under watchful eyes. Placing the bowl down, he picked a tiny piece of bark from between his teeth. "It has medicinal properties, I take it?"

"Only if you've run out of leeches," Hawkwood said. He thought he saw the corner of Cageaga's mouth twitch, but decided it must have been a trick of the firelight.

Tewanias spoke. "Roren, satonhkária'ks ken?"

"I'm sorry, I don't—" Lawrence began.

"He asks if you're hungry." To Tewanias, Hawkwood said, "Tiohrhen:sa sata:ti." *Speak in English*.

"My God, when *was* our last meal?" Lawrence shook his head. "Damned if I can recall. I could eat a bloody horse." His eyes shot to his hosts and a mortified look crossed his face. "Er, I didn't mean—"

Hawkwood smiled. "It's all right, Major. I doubt that's on the menu."

Tewanias beckoned. A figure appeared. It was the old woman from before. Tewanias spoke to her softly. As she left, Tewanias turned back.

There was an awkward pause, as though each was waiting for one of the others to speak, a silence broken eventually by Lawrence, who enquired of Hawkwood, "How much have you told them?"

"Some of it. They know we've been trying to get to the border and why the Oneida wanted us dead."

"The invasion?"

"Not that part, not yet."

The old woman reappeared with a young girl by her side, slender and pretty, her eyes cast shyly down. Both carried wooden bowls and spoons, which they handed out wordlessly before slipping away as silently as they had arrived.

"Tesatská:hon, Roren." Tewanias indicated the bowl in Lawrence's hand and switched to English: "Eat. It is deer. The Kanien'kehá:ka do not eat horse."

349

Lawrence reddened.

"Unless all the deer have been eaten," Cageaga murmured under his breath.

But by then, neither Lawrence nor Hawkwood were listening.

Venison, horse or squirrel, Hawkwood wouldn't have cared. He'd eaten all three at one time or another during his military service, as had Lawrence. Soldiers on the march weren't particular when it came to foraging. If it could be skinned, spitted or stuffed in a pot, they'd eat it.

What mattered was that it was food and it was hot and quite possibly the best meal Hawkwood had eaten since stepping off *Larkspur*'s gang plank. The fact that it helped disguise the lingering taste of the tea didn't hurt, either, while the rounded cornbread rolls served with each bowl proved a useful tool for mopping up the last drops of juice from the meat.

"By God, if I only had my pipe to hand, I'd die a happy man," Lawrence said, as he set down his empty bowl. "My compliments, Chief Tewanias. That was as fine a stew as I've tasted."

Hawkwood was about to tell Lawrence that he could dispense with Tewanias's title when, to his amazement, Tewanias, after rummaging inside the pouch he carried beneath his cloak, produced two small clay pipes, each around six inches in length. With great solemnity he placed one of them in Lawrence's palm.

Lawrence stared at the object in astonishment. "I'll be damned!" He beamed as Tewanias handed over his tobacco pouch. "Sir, you are a gentleman after my own heart!"

Cageaga took out his own pipe and helped himself to a fill of tobacco. Lighting up, he passed the pipe to Hawkwood. Hawkwood had never taken to the habit, but accepted the pipe as it would have been discourteous to decline. Steeling himself, he took a puff, circulated the smoke inside his mouth for what he considered an appropriate amount of time, and exhaled, trying not to let his eyes water, then returned the pipe to Cageaga.

As he watched the other three puffing contentedly, he found it hard not to compare the unlikely scene before him with a tableau from any of the London clubs lining Pall Mall, where pillars of the aristocracy would round off their dinners in a fug of tobacco smoke, a glass of port within convenient reach. The only constituents missing here, he decided, were the port, the armchairs and evening wear. Though he knew that while Lawrence was enjoying his pipe as a complement to the stew, Tewanias and Cageaga were engaged in a much older ritual. Tobacco was considered to be a gift from the Creator. The exhaled smoke carried one's thoughts and prayers to heaven. More significantly, no man was without his pipe when important matters were to be discussed.

Timing was everything.

"We must talk." For Lawrence's benefit, Hawkwood spoke in English. He addressed Tewanias. "The Yankees are not seeking to attack the Kanien'kehá:ka."

Tewanias's head came up. He wafted tobacco smoke away from his face. "You know this, how?"

"We were there. We have heard their words. We have seen their guns. They are gathering to attack the English, across the border in Canada. That is why they are at Senhahlone. That is why the Oneida were chasing us – not just because we killed the Yankee soldiers, but to stop us reaching the border. Now, Lawrence and I must warn the soldiers of the Great King that the Yankees are sending troops to attack them. We need your help."

"Our help?" Cageaga said, taking his pipe from his mouth. "Is this what Ayonhwathah foretold? That you would return to ask our help to warn the English? This seems a very strange reason. I do not think that is why you are here."

"I do not think that either," Hawkwood said. "I think I am here to warn the Kanien'kehá:ka, too."

It was Tewanias's turn to frown. "You said the Yan-kees were not seeking to attack us."

"I believe that to be true. But if the Yankees do cross the border and the English are defeated, then all Kanien'kehá:ka are in danger."

"How are *we* in danger?" Cageaga demanded. "It is not *our* war."

"Not yet. But it will become your war. The same way white men's wars that have gone before became your wars."

"That is—" Cageaga began.

Tewanias held up a hand. "Let him speak."

Hawkwood considered his words carefully. "It is the intention of the Yankees to drive the English out of Canada and from Anówarakowa Kawennote. If they succeed, all the villages of the Kanien'kehá:ka will disappear for ever, like the ashes from the great council fire. It will be as the last time when the Yankees defeated the soldiers of the Great King. A treaty will be signed and the Nations will be forgotten. The Yankees will say that land granted by the English is theirs by right of conquest. The Yankees' government will make the Kanien'kehá:ka leave their villages and they will sell the land. They will tell the Kanien'kehá:ka that they must live where the Yankees decide."

"In . . . reservations," Cageaga said dully, his pipe forgotten.

"Ea, in reservations," Hawkwood confirmed.

"You believe this to be true?" Tewanias asked.

"I do."

"The Kanien'kehá:ka could fight," Cageaga said.

"On their own, they would lose. The Yankees are greater in number than the Kanien'kehá:ka. You could not hold out against them. You know that."

"Perhaps the Yan-kees will sign their own treaty with the Kanien'kehá:ka?"

Hawkwood could tell that the question was posed more in hope than expectation. "They did not honour the last treaty, why should they honour the next one?" he pointed out.

Cageaga fell silent.

Tewanias took a draw on his pipe. "If you warn the English, can they defeat the Yan-kees?"

"Yes," Hawkwood said. "The soldiers of the Great King have known many wars; more than the soldiers of the Yankees. They are better fighters. They will win."

Tewanias sat back. Lowering his pipe, he regarded Hawkwood for a long time. Finally, he spoke. "I will have my warriors show you the path."

"Niá:wen," Hawkwood said, before reverting to English once more. "Do you know *where* the English soldiers are gathered? The nearest English garrison?"

The expression on Tewanias's face made it plain that he'd expected Hawkwood to have that information. There were two, he told them. One large and one small.

"Where?" Hawkwood pressed.

The main garrison was located on the Île aux Noix.

Hawkwood and Lawrence exchanged glances.

"And the other?" Hawkwood asked.

"It is only a . . ." Tewanias searched for the word. He shook his head, looked to Cageaga for help and, when none was forthcoming, said helplessly and with some frustration, ". . . maison en bois?"

*A wooden house?* Hawkwood thought. Lawrence appeared equally mystified. Then a thought struck.

"A blockhouse?" Hawkwood ventured.

Tewanias thought about it. "Ea! Blockhouse. Yes!"

"Where?" Hawkwood asked.

"There is a small village, lived in by whites. It has no name in the Kanien'kehá:ka tongue."

"What do the whites call it?"

"Lacolle," Tewanias said.

# 14

Of the two locations, Lacolle was the closest. It lay, Tewanias informed them, on the bank of a tributary of the Richelieu River, a little over two leagues to the south-west of Île aux Noix. Hawkwood hadn't heard "league" used as a measure of distance for some time. Two leagues was, as near as he could recall, about seven miles.

How many troops were billeted at Lacolle, Tewanias didn't know. It didn't matter; the number was immaterial. There were British soldiers manning the blockhouse and there had to be communication between the village and the main garrison. If they could make it to the former, they could then get word to the latter.

"So when do we leave?" Lawrence asked.

"You need rest," Tewanias said, nodding towards Lawrence's wounded side.

"Dawn it is, then," Hawkwood said.

When he opened his eyes, it took a second or two to orient himself. Then he inhaled and it all came flooding back. There were certain odours that were an inevitable consequence of a significant number of people taking up occupancy in an enclosed space: stale air, woodsmoke, rendered animal fats, dirt and dogs and the sweet-sour miasma that arose whenever humans exercised their full range of bodily eructations. The longhouse reeked.

Neither was it silent. Someone broke wind with gusto and it was as if a signal had been passed. In no time, the walls were vibrating before an onslaught of snores, grunts, groans, coughs, belches, snuffles and farts. Morning had definitely arrived.

He had slept well, though and for that he was grateful. No headache, either.

Through the smoke opening in the roof he could just make out a patch of grey sky. Below the opening, the fire was smouldering. Blanket-covered humps littered the floor where those most vulnerable to the cold, the children and the elderly, had spent the night on mats close to the hearth.

Sensing movement to his left, Hawkwood turned and found he was not alone. A whiff of sweat and bear grease rose towards him; not too unpleasant when compared to the smell of the longhouse taken as a whole, but on the gamey side, nonetheless, especially when you weren't used to it. As the sleeper's arm moved, Hawkwood saw it was Cageaga, looking just as disgruntled with his eyes closed as he did when he was awake.

The desire to empty his bladder was suddenly overwhelming. It was warm beneath the furs but he knew he'd have to go sooner or later and, as he was awake, it was probably best to get it over with. Dropping his feet to the ground, he fumbled into his boots, reached for his coat, and picked his way carefully around the slumbering bodies towards the entrance.

The drop in temperature hit him as soon as he stepped outside. Snow had settled deeply throughout the village. The outer defences had provided some protection but with their dark, bark-constructed walls, the three longhouses nestling inside the log palisade looked like burnt loaves topped with white icing.

He wasn't the only one up and about. Several hunched figures were picking their way to or from the latrine pits. Heads down, tucked into their blankets and furs, no one appeared to notice that he was not one of their own, or if they did, they had more pressing matters on their mind. He wondered if there would be any familiar faces among them.

"Damned tea," Lawrence said from behind, cutting into his

thoughts. "Goes right through you. Where's a fellow go when he needs to piss?"

Hawkwood turned. "How are you feeling?"

"I'm getting there," Lawrence said, his breath fogging. "I saw you get up. Thought it best to follow. Didn't want to go blundering about with my breeches unbuttoned."

"This way," Hawkwood told him.

Business over, they re-emerged into the open and fastened their coats. It was a relief to be breathing clean air after the heavy smell of the longhouse and the latrine. Hawkwood was in no rush to go back inside.

"I was told the Iroquois lived in log cabins like the whites," Lawrence said, looking around him. "Not like this."

Following Lawrence's gaze, Hawkwood saw how the village must look to an outsider.

"Most do, probably, but traditional Iroquois houses were always built like this. It made it easier to abandon them when the tribe moved."

"Moved?"

"Every twenty or thirty years, when the land stopped producing crops, the tribe would gather up their belongings and look for a new spot where the soil was fertile and the hunting good. Then they'd start all over again with what tools and materials were to hand. The forest would grow back over the old village and in time you'd never know they'd been there."

"Carrying their homes on their backs."

"Something like that."

"Does this mean Tewanias and his people don't expect to be here for long?"

It was a good question.

"I think they know they can't hide for ever. Progress will come, whether they like it or not and they'll have to make a decision. Stay or leave."

"If they leave, where will they go?"

"Canada. There won't be any other option."

"And if the Americans are victorious?" Lawrence said. "What happens if they take Canada?"

"It's up to us to make sure that doesn't happen."

Despite the assurance he'd given to Tewanias, Hawkwood wondered whether that might be easier said than done.

"You're worried for them, aren't you?" Lawrence regarded him closely.

Hawkwood nodded. "You may think me unpatriotic or a bloody fool, but it strikes me Tewanias's people have more right to this land than either King George or Congress. They've fought for it, tended it, built their villages, raised their families and yet it's been stolen from them. What you see is all they have left – and if the Americans have their way, they're not even going to have this. They've become exiles, Major; exiles in their own damned country."

For a long moment, Lawrence was silent. Then he said quietly, "I saw the way you and Tewanias talk to one another. This is not the first time you and he have met, is it?"

"No."

Lawrence absorbed that, then said, "There was a word you used when you were speaking with him, when you asked for his help. Rag . . . rargay . . . something?"

"Rake'niha," Hawkwood said. "It means 'my father'."

As the ramifications of that statement sank in, Lawrence let out a gasp.

"It's time we talked," Hawkwood said.

"You lived with them for *how* long?"

"Eight years, nearly."

Lawrence stared back at him. "I don't know what to say."

"Not what you were expecting?" Hawkwood said.

Lawrence shook his head. "How could it be? I'll be damned! It's not often I'm at a loss, but this time . . . you actually lived as one of them!" Lawrence's brow furrowed. "But why didn't Tewanias deliver you safe home?"

"He did. He took me to *his* home."

Lawrence spread his hands. "I meant to Canada, an English home."

"He was honouring the promise Gil Wyatt made to Will

Archer: that he'd keep me safe. Wyatt placed me in Tewanias's care. Tewanias saw it as his obligation to a friend. Besides, what *English* home would that have been? The Archers weren't my blood relatives, but after my father, they were the only family I'd known. There *was* no one else. If I had been taken north, I'd have been placed in an orphanage or a workhouse and left there. Tewanias decided the best thing for me was to remain with him, and that's what happened. I was adopted into his clan."

"There was no animosity towards you, being white?"

"Adoption's common practice among the Iroquois. Or it used to be. The Nations have always known that, if they're to survive, the population has to be maintained. War, tribal disputes, disease, old age, they all have an effect. They'd adopt to replenish the blood, taking in prisoners captured in battle or refugees seeking sanctuary from other tribes. They don't discriminate. Black, white, Indian – makes no difference."

"But what about . . ." Lawrence began helplessly, as if searching for something to ask, yet not knowing where to begin: ". . . schooling?"

"I'd been to school. The Archers saw to that. Their farm was only an hour's ride from town. There was a schoolhouse at the back of the church. I could read and write. I knew my numbers. The Archers had books. Will took me hunting, taught me to shoot. At that age, I didn't need much else. It was Tewanias who gave me my first French words. He'd learnt the language from Huron captives taken during the war against the Frogs. I seemed to have the knack."

"You never wanted to return to your own world?"

"My *own* world? The Archers were dead. I had nothing to go back to. In any case, where would I go? Not the farm. Too many bad memories. Besides, it would have been confiscated by then, or burnt down. No, I was safer with the clan."

Lawrence smiled.

"What?" Hawkwood asked him.

"You keep saying 'clan'. I'm half Scots, remember? I know all about clans. My mother was a Macintyre."

"There you go, then. It's not that different. The Scots have the Macintyres, McPhersons and the rest . . ." Hawkwood smiled ". . . and the Iroquois have the wolf, turtle, bear—"

"Hawk?" Lawrence said.

"There *are* hawk clans, among the Seneca, Onondaga and Cayuga. Not the Mohawk. They only have the three."

"Despite the name?"

"Mine or theirs?"

Lawrence smiled.

"The name has nothing to do with the bird. Mohawk's not even a Mohawk word. It's what the whites call them. Kanien'kehá:ka is how they refer to themselves. It means 'People of the Place of the Flint'. Supposedly, it refers to the tribe's ancient sites along the Mohawk River. The place was a good source of the stuff. They used it to make arrowheads and tools."

"So why Mohawk? Because of the river?"

"The river took its name from the tribe, and it's only the whites that call it that. Mohawk's a much older word. It's from the Abenaki. They're ancient enemies of the Kanien'kehá:ka. It's what *they* called them."

"Does it have a meaning?"

"It does," Hawkwood said.

Intrigued by the change of tone, Lawrence frowned. "What is it?"

"Man-eater."

Lawrence paled.

"Don't worry. I'm pretty sure it *was* venison in the stew. And no, Douglas; I've not tasted human flesh. If they did consume their enemies, it was long before the Nations came together and the Rotinonshón:ni was formed."

"They still scalp their enemies, though."

"Yes, they do."

There was an awkward pause.

"If you're afraid of the answer, Major, don't ask the question. Best let it lie."

"You're right. My apologies. Even if I thought I should ask,

I'm not sure I really want to know. Was that when you learned to fight?"

Hawkwood nodded. "The Iroquois teach their sons how to hunt and how to use weapons, how to stalk, track, ambush and survive in the wilderness. Most boys have been on their first hunt by the time they're ten. I was considered a late starter, though I did know how to shoot.

"Even their games are a form of training. There's one they play, with sticks and a ball. They set up a gate at opposite ends of the field; it could be a tree stump, a couple of poles set in the ground, anything. The object is to drive the ball through your opponents' gate only using the sticks. There's no limit to the number of players or the size of the field. In the old days, there'd be hundreds of players and the goals could be a couple of miles apart. Some games went on for days."

"Like a battle," Lawrence said.

"Exactly. And there's no quarter given. Players often end up with split skulls or broken arms and legs. A few even die. It's called *Tewaarathon* – the Little Brother of War. Gives the young bloods a chance to test their mettle. Swinging a stick in a mêlée's good training for swinging a club or a tomahawk."

"Is that how *you* learned?"

"Yes. Cageaga was the one who taught me. Showed me how to throw a tomahawk, too. I've seen him hit a corn husk at sixty feet."

Lawrence smiled. "Well, from what I've seen, it's stood you in damned good stead. But how did you get from there to taking the King's shilling?"

The question was met with silence. Sensing a mood change, Lawrence frowned and looked up, to discover that their walk had taken them out of the village and beyond the palisade. Fifty yards of open ground separated them from the edge of the forest. They weren't alone. A couple of the village dogs had latched on to them and were loping back and forth across the snow, tongues lolling.

"There was a girl," Hawkwood said.

"Ah." Lawrence allowed himself a knowing smile. "There usually is."

Then he saw the look on Hawkwood's face and the smile slid away.

Hawkwood stared off towards the woods. "Her name was Ehrita."

Lawrence waited. Instinct told him the best thing was to remain silent.

Hawkwood turned. "It means 'Moon' in Kanien'kehá:ka. She was Cageaga's sister. He'd taken me under his wing. At that time, she was as thin as a stick, annoying, always getting in the way. As we grew older, I started to realize she wasn't as annoying as I'd first thought."

"How old were you?"

"Sixteen, seventeen, maybe. Old enough to have noticed how she was changing. How we all were. It's strange, looking back. I could throw an axe, shoot a bow, hunt, skin and gut a deer, and yet women were a mystery. Still are, if I'm honest." The mention of her name had conjured her image in his mind's eye: "She had the longest hair, right down to her waist. I can see it now. Hair so black it seemed to turn blue when the light hit it, dark as ravens' feathers. I thought she was the most beautiful creature I'd ever seen."

"You were . . . sweethearts?" Lawrence said, and immediately looked embarrassed at having used the word.

"Not in the way that you mean. That's not how the Iroquois are brought up. Marriages tend to occur late and by arrangement between the clan elders. It was tradition for a young warrior to be paired with an older woman – a widow, often as not – the idea being to give them a companion more experienced in the affairs of life.

"I wasn't born into the tribe so I didn't know any better. As we got older, we knew something was happening between us, though we didn't know what to do about it. Cageaga saw it. He could read the signs."

"He disapproved?"

"Far from it. He could see I cared for her and that she felt the same. I'm not sure he understood it any more than we did. But I remember he took me aside one day and warned

362

me that if I was to ever make her unhappy or cause her pain, he'd kill me."

Lawrence smiled. "I rather think all older brothers say that."

"True, but the difference with Cageaga was that *he* meant it."

"He'd have killed you?"

"In a heartbeat. Then he'd have gutted me like a rabbit and left my innards out for the crows."

"You said he was your friend."

"He was, but he'd have done it, just the same."

Pondering this, Lawrence was struck with a sense of foreboding. "Something happened?"

"Yes."

"To the girl?"

"Yes."

"By your hand?"

"Not mine, no."

*Let him tell it*, Lawrence thought.

Hawkwood took a breath. "The men were on a hunting trip. We were gone two days. While we were away, strangers came and abducted three of the women. Ehrita was one of them. It was a while before anyone knew they were gone, before the alarm could be raised."

Lawrence didn't dare speak.

"We weren't sure who'd taken them. At first, we thought it might have been an Oneida raiding party. Their lands were to the south and every so often they'd travel into the mountains to hunt and there'd be the odd skirmish. You asked about animosity? Between Oneida and Mohawk, it's never gone away."

"*Were* they Oneida?"

"No." Hawkwood turned. "Your mother was Scottish. She ever tell you about the reivers?"

Lawrence's head came up. "That she did. They were raiders who plied their trade in the borderlands. Stealing livestock, mostly, but anything that could be transported was fair game. You're saying *that's* who took the women?"

"Not reivers, but a similar breed. Freebooters – soldiers without an army, looters and thieves. The sort of scum who find

it easier to steal from others than earn an honest crust."
Hawkwood's eyes turned dark. "There were six of them. Made
them easy to track."

"You caught up with them?"

"It took us a day and a half, but yes. With four of them, at
any rate. They'd made camp and were . . . availing themselves
of the women."

Lawrence didn't have to ask what that meant. The expression
on Hawkwood's face was description enough.

"You killed them?"

"Not immediately, no."

Lawrence's mouth went dry.

"We questioned them first . . ."

Lawrence stared at him.

". . . then gave them to the women."

Lawrence didn't dare blink.

"Then we killed them. I'd never heard men beg before. And
I do mean beg, literally."

"But you got the girl – Ehrita – back?"

"No. The last two had taken her with them. We split our
force. One half returned to the village with the women we did
rescue. The rest of us, including Cageaga, continued the chase.
We caught the fifth one the next day."

Lawrence remained silent, sensing there was worse to come.

Hawkwood shook his head. "He didn't have her, either.
We put him to the knife. It didn't take long. He got quite talkative
towards the end; told us the sixth man had taken her to be
sold."

"Sold?" Lawrence echoed.

"To a ferryman who ran a trading post up on what the
Mohawk called the river of black water. Name of Harker; I
remember that. It was carved into the wood above his door."
Hawkwood closed his eyes. Took a breath, opened them again.
"Because I was white, it was decided that I should go on alone
to reconnoitre, while the others stayed hidden."

He broke off and stared down at the ground. Then, raising
his head, he continued: "There was a dog, scratching at an

outhouse door behind the store. I found her inside. There were bruises across her face and a rusty saw blade on the floor beside her. She'd used it to open her wrists. She'd let herself bleed to death rather than suffer more violation."

Lawrence saw that Hawkwood's fists were clenched. "Oh, my dear fellow . . ."

"They were in the cabin, sharing a bottle; the sixth man and the trader, laughing over something. They didn't see me at first; didn't put up much of a fight, either, when I confronted them. The drink saw to that. They tried to get away but they weren't quick enough. They died screaming. I wanted them to feel what she must have felt. I thought no more about taking their lives than I did slaughtering pigs for offal."

Lawrence's face had turned white.

"My mistake was not knowing there was a woodsmen's camp close by. They heard the screams and came running; got there as I was coming out. I had the knife in my hand and my clothes were covered in blood. It didn't take them long to discover what I'd done. Then one of them found the outhouse. You can guess the rest."

"They thought it was you who'd killed her?"

"Three dead and a wild man holding a bloodstained blade – what would you have thought?"

"What happened?"

"They held a vote: deliver me to the authorities or save themselves a two-day journey and carry out the sentence themselves. They decided on the latter."

"Sentence?" Lawrence said cautiously.

"They hang murderers, Major."

Lawrence sucked in his breath.

"There was a barn next to the outhouse with one of those beams above the door for hoisting up grain and flour. Someone found a rope. It didn't take long. They were quite cheerful when they pulled me up."

He closed his eyes, heard again the coarse laughter ringing in his ears as the rope had slipped, causing his body to swing and his heels to rake against the side of the barn.

When he opened his eyes he realized his hand was touching his throat and Lawrence was gazing at him in horror.

"They say I stopped breathing, that I died. Perhaps that's true. What I do know is when they saw the men haul me up, Cageaga and the others came to my rescue. They attacked the hanging party, killed two, drove the rest back into the woods. They cut me down, torched the post, took Ehrita's body and carried us both to the ferry boat. They used it to escape downriver."

"Good God," Lawrence breathed.

"When the mourning period was over, I told Tewanias that it would probably be best if I left the village. The witnesses at the trading post would have alerted the authorities. I didn't want to bring the risk of reprisal down upon the tribe. There was a possibility that we could be tracked and the village discovered; if it was found to be harbouring killers of white men, it would go badly.

"Tewanias gave me his blessing and I left. I think he knew, even then, that change was coming, to the tribe *and* the Nations, and it was the right time for me to return to my own world. Not that I had any notion of what I was going to do. For a while I drifted, town to town, never staying long. Eventually I made my way to Boston, took a labouring job, kept my head down."

"You thought they might be after you?" Lawrence said, doubt entering his voice.

"It sounds stupid, but yes. In the end I thought I would be safer at sea."

"Sea?" Lawrence's eyebrows rose in further astonishment.

"I'd heard there was a merchantman looking for crew. I signed on as a deck hand. The only decent thing about my time aboard was the first officer. He was from Amiens. In between watches and heaving my guts over the side, I was able to improve my French."

"How long did you serve?"

"Until our first port of call: Cork."

"Ireland! You, too!"

"If that month taught me anything, other than conjugation, it was that I'd never earn a living before the mast. I couldn't wait to disembark. A week later I took that shilling you mentioned.

I thought the army would be the place to hide, to start anew. It also seemed the right thing to do, maybe a way of saying thank you to Gil Wyatt and his men for what they did for me."

"You never saw them again?"

"No. Tewanias told me they all died in the attack on the beach."

Lawrence's face softened. "You joined the army to honour them."

"Enlisted in the Fifty-first Regiment of Foot. They were in Ireland on garrison duty.

"John Moore's regiment?"

"He was a major then. I served with him in Corsica until he left. I met up with him again at Shorncliffe when I was put forward for training with the Rifles. I had keen eyesight and I was a good shot. Skills that served me well."

"And you've been putting them to excellent use ever since," Lawrence said. "But Hawkwood? How did you come by *that* name?"

"The clan's name for me was Kahrhakon:ha. It means Hawk. I don't remember why I added the 'wood', but Hawkwood seemed to fit. I kept Matthew because it made life easier – I knew I was less likely to be caught unawares. Same reason we posed as Matthews and Douglas."

"You could have told me," Lawrence said, after a lengthy pause, with more than a note of reproof in his voice. "Why didn't you?"

Hawkwood watched the dogs cavort. The larger one had shaggy brown hair and floppy black ears and when it stopped to scratch its belly its face adopted a lop-sided grin that sent a faint shiver through his heart.

"It was a long time ago; another life. I couldn't decide whether I wanted to remember it or put it all behind me."

Lawrence thrust his hands into his coat pockets. "I can understand that, but you can't run from the past, Matthew. No one can. There's many who've tried. They've all failed." He tilted his head and looked Hawkwood directly in the eye. "Were you ashamed of *yours*?"

Hawkwood considered that.

*Not all of it.*

Uncertain what to make of his silence, Lawrence continued: "I hope that wasn't the case, because I've never known a man with less reason to be ashamed of who he is and what he stands for. I'll say it now, Captain: it's been a privilege knowing you and that's God's honest truth. Don't look at me like that. I ain't one to gush, but it had to be said. Ah, now I've embarrassed you. My apologies."

Lawrence smiled ruefully at Hawkwood's lack of response. "While we were locked in that prison hut, I made a comment that implied all Indians were only one step away from being Barbarians. I was wrong. If that's what made you think you couldn't confide in me, I apologize." He pointed towards the longhouse. "Those two chiefs of yours, Tewanias and Cageaga, have more nobility in them than the feckless arse-lickers who make up the bulk of His Majesty's officer corps; only reason most of *them* ever got a commission is because Daddy bought it for them."

"The noble savage?" Hawkwood said.

"You've read Dryden?"

"I have. There's no need to look *so* surprised, Major."

Lawrence smiled. "'When wild in the woods, the noble savage ran . . .' Quite a line, ain't it? Y'know where he took it from?"

Hawkwood shook his head.

"'Tis said he stole the phrase from a Frog explorer called Lescarbot. Lescarbot went on expeditions to Canada. Maybe he was referring to the Iroquois when he penned it."

"I'll ask Tewanias if he knew him," Hawkwood said drily.

"Doubtful. He'd have to be two hundred years old."

"Perhaps not, then," Hawkwood said.

He turned towards the woods. Beyond the dogs, which were dashing around like demented wolves, nothing stirred. There was a strange, almost ethereal, beauty in the way the trees, weighted with snow, stood so silently. It could have been a scene from a child's fairy tale about an enchanted forest that on the outside looked peaceful and serene, while deep within its heart there lurked dark and terrible dangers.

A spindly wooden structure at the edge of the trees caught Hawkwood's eye. At first he thought it was a drying frame, but he knew the villagers would not have erected such a thing outside the palisade. Then he realized what it was. He did not look to see if Lawrence was behind him as he set off towards it.

A raised outline in the snow beneath the bark platform showed where the funeral fire had been lit.

"What is it?" Lawrence asked, looking up.

"A burial scaffold."

"They leave the bodies out in the open?"

"For a period; it's to shorten their path to the sky world, and to make sure they're dead."

Lawrence looked at him.

"To be on the safe side," Hawkwood said.

"Then what?" Lawrence enquired, not without some trepidation.

"They either wait until the body rots and bury the bones, or else they bury the body after the fire's allowed to die down." Hawkwood pointed to the snow-covered hearth stones. "Or they store them in their lodges."

"Dead bodies?"

"Yes."

Lawrence thought about that. "And when they move the village?"

"They collect the bones from each clan and bury them in a common grave." Hawkwood smiled. "Would you like to change your opinion about them not being Barbarians?"

Lawrence smiled back at him. "No. I meant what I said. Is this where Ayon—" Lawrence's brow creased. "I'm sorry, I don't recall his name – was laid?"

"Ayonhwathah? Probably."

Lawrence fell silent. Hawkwood knew the major was wondering how many corpses there might be stored beneath the longhouse's roof and how near he'd been to them.

"Do you ever think of her: Ehrita?"

The question caught Hawkwood off-guard. He turned away. "Not often."

*But when I do, it cuts like a knife.*

Another excited bark sounded. The dogs had latched on to a scent and were off, heads down, following a trail of sunken paw prints that disappeared into the trees.

Letting them go, Hawkwood and Lawrence retraced their steps. Entering the palisade, they found Tewanias waiting for them. Cageaga stood at his shoulder. With them were three armed warriors, dressed in furs and leggings and with snow shoes upon their feet.

"The scouts have brought news," Tewanias said. "The Yan-kees are marching."

"Damn it," Lawrence muttered. "I was hoping we'd have more time."

They were seated around the fire. The scouts were wolfing down a breakfast of reheated stew and bark tea. From the speed they were eating and from the appreciative sounds they were making, Hawkwood guessed they hadn't eaten a hot meal for a while. All three were lean and muscular. They must have covered a lot of ground in the night and yet, beyond their obvious hunger, not one of them looked wearied by their trek.

They had greeted Hawkwood and Lawrence's presence with silent nods, though Hawkwood thought he saw a flicker of recognition flash across their faces when introductions had been made and his own name given. He wondered how much Tewanias had told them. As they ate, they kept stealing glances towards him.

"What road do the Yankees take?" Hawkwood asked.

"They march north."

"Not west, towards Gaanundata?"

Tewanias acknowledged the implication. "No. There is a road, begun many years ago by the soldiers of the Great King, which goes from Senhahlone to Canada."

"The same road that goes to Lacolle?" Hawkwood said.

"Ea," Tewanias said.

"How many soldiers?"

"The scouts say more than four hundred."

"Not a large force for an invasion." Lawrence frowned.

"Big enough to take a blockhouse, though," Hawkwood pointed out, "and gain a toehold. They manage that and Dearborn can follow with the rest of the army at his leisure. They're probably mobilizing the main force now." He turned to Tewanias. "What about artillery? Were there guns? Cannon?"

Tewanias consulted his men. "They say no."

"Well, that's something at least," Lawrence said.

"Guns wouldn't be that easy to move, given the roads. They'd need horses and they're in short supply. It takes six to draw a six-pounder and four to pull a caisson. Plus you'd have to feed and water them."

"Which would slow them down." Lawrence continued to look pensive. "How many men does it take to man a blockhouse in the back of beyond?"

"Not nearly enough."

To Tewanias, Hawkwood said, "Lacolle is close to the Richelieu, yes?"

"Ea."

"So if they capture the blockhouse, they'll control the river. If they control the river, there's nothing to stop them barging the rest of the troops up from Plattsburg, along with their artillery. That'll give them their bridgehead. It's only seven miles from Lacolle to Île aux Noix. Bring up enough men and they can cut off the garrison. Seize the island and they have themselves a naval base inside Canada. Then, come the thaw, it's downriver to Montreal and Quebec. Once they have Quebec, they have the continent."

"All for want of a nail," Lawrence murmured. "Assuming they *are* heading for Lacolle, you think we can warn the defenders in time?"

"Maybe." Hawkwood turned to Tewanias. "Tell me about the road."

Like most wilderness roads, it had begun life as an Indian trail before being adopted by the British as a means of transporting men and equipment during the war against the French. Following the Revolution, it fallen into disuse for a while. As settlements were hacked out of the wilderness it had enjoyed a gradual resurgence, though it had never been considered a major turnpike. That had changed with the resumption of hostilities between Britain and America, when it had again found favour as a conduit along which the American army could move troops and equipment to protect its northern border.

Travelling north from Plattsburg to the border, the road passed through two settlements, both straddling rivers: Chazy and Champlain. The latter was situated three miles from the border and roughly eight from Lacolle.

"What are you thinking?" Lawrence asked.

"That we find a place to intercept, assess the column's intention and its weakness, then carry the information to Lacolle as fast as we can."

Taking the knife from his boot, Hawkwood looked to Tewanias for confirmation and used the point of the blade to scrape a crooked line in the dirt. "Plattsburg, Chazy, Champlain, Lacolle, yes?"

Tewanias inclined his head.

"The border's here." Hawkwood drew a horizontal line severing the road north of Champlain. "Where are *we*?"

Tewanias pointed with his finger to a spot due west of Chazy.

"How many leagues from Plattsburg to Champlain?" Hawkwood asked.

Tewanias's eyes narrowed. "Seven."

"And Gaanundata to Champlain?"

"Four."

Hawkwood leaned back and tapped the knifepoint on the dirt.

"I see what you're getting at," Lawrence said. "We cut across, get to the road before them. You think it's possible?"

"Maybe."

Lawrence stiffened. "Damn it. There's that bloody look again. You've thought of something else, haven't you?"

"Maybe while we're at it we can slow them down a bit."

"Oh, yes? And how do you propose we do that?"

"Same way we dealt with the Frogs in Spain."

"Remind me."

"With a little help from our friends."

Lawrence stared at him, then his eyes widened.

Hawkwood grinned.

"Well, you said you were here to recruit the natives. Now's your chance."

The mood in the longhouse was sombre.

The dozen or so warriors gathered around the fire listened in silence as Tewanias explained why they had been summoned to council. Seated on Tewanias's right, Hawkwood watched the firelight play across their faces. Most of the men were Tewanias and Cageaga's age, though a couple were slightly younger. Elders and chieftains from the three clans – Turtle, Wolf and Bear – their expressions ranged from stern to quizzical.

When first assembled, there had been little emotion on display, but then Tewanias had called Hawkwood and Lawrence forward. As Hawkwood entered the circle, Tewanias had referred to him as Kahrhakon:ha. That had drawn an instant reaction. Heads had lifted and eyes had narrowed as he and Lawrence resumed their places. Hawkwood had been careful to maintain a neutral expression throughout.

When Tewanias had finished speaking, it took only a second or two for the significance of the argument placed before the council to sink in.

A sedate-looking elder, introduced as Sonachshowa, cleared his throat. "To consider taking up arms against the Yan-kees is a most serious matter. You tell us their soldiers do not march on us. If that is true, we have no need to raise our weapons against them."

"They do not march upon us today," Tewanias said, holding the older man's gaze. "But they will come. Sooner or later, they will come."

"It has been many winters since the Kanien'kehá:ka took to the war trail," another gaunt-featured warrior pointed out.

"That is why our young men grow soft," a third warrior growled, a comment that was met with a chorus of low grunts, though whether in approval or opposition, it wasn't easy to tell. "They would rather hunt than make war."

"And what is wrong with that?" another warrior asked. "If it stops us going hungry."

The third warrior showed his teeth. "It is the destiny of boys to become warriors. How can they prove themselves men unless they have known war? Peace will be the ruin of our nation. If young warriors are not given opportunity to test themselves in combat, they will lose their manhood and turn into women."

"If we strike against the Yan-kees now," another warrior put in, "perhaps they will think twice about coming."

This statement was also met by muttering – though this time slightly more in agreement, Hawkwood thought – as well as a couple of thin smiles.

"But if we extend the hand of friendship to the Yan-kees, will they not leave us in peace?" Sonachshowa enquired.

"That is what the Jesus Delawares said," Cageaga cut in sharply. "And look what happened to them. The Yan-kees destroyed their village and killed their women and children."

"Many years have passed since then," the sedate elder said.

"That does not mean we should forget," Cageaga said. "The Yan-kees are not to be trusted. Remember Tippecanoe."

Hawkwood listened to the exchanges and held up his hand. "Have I permission to address the council?"

The murmurs subsided. Hawkwood glanced at Tewanias. Tewanias nodded.

"Some of you may know my name," Hawkwood began. "I am Kahrhakon:ha, adopted son of Tewanias. As my father has told you, my friend and I are soldiers for the Great King beyond the Water and we are being hunted by the Yankees. We were making our path to Canada when we were attacked by scouts of the Oneniotèá:ka. Had it not been for my brother Cageaga, our scalps would, even now, be hanging from the lodge walls of the Yankees' general."

He had their attention.

"What Tewanias says is true; the Yankees *will* come."

"Even if we do not take up our weapons against them?" the sedate elder repeated.

"It will make no difference," Hawkwood said.

374

"What if we were to side with the Yan-kees? What then?" someone asked.

The question was met with several sharp intakes of breath.

Tewanias shifted uneasily on his haunches. "We would be shamed for ever in the eyes of our brothers in Canada."

Hawkwood shook his head. "From what my father has told me and from what I know, whether you fight for the Yankees or the Great King will make no difference. The Yankees will take your land whether they win or lose. If they defeat the English, they will take not only Kanièn:keh but also the land of the Kanien'kehá:ka in Canada. If the English win, they will not take Anówarakowa Kawennote back from the Yankees. That means the Yankees will still be free to take Kanièn:keh and they will send you to live on reservations."

At the mention of the word, heads lifted. Hawkwood saw foreheads crease and eyes darken.

"The old ways will be lost for ever," Cageaga said. "Not only will they take our land, they will make us pray to the white man's god."

"The English will not take your land. They will grant you land, as they did before," Hawkwood said. "In Canada. Do not doubt my words. If the English win, you will have homes. If the Yankees win, you will not. But in exchange, the English want your help."

Several of the elders turned to each other and spoke in hushed asides.

"The man who sits at my side is an officer in the army of the Great King," Hawkwood said. "He has told me that Kanien'kehá:ka warriors from Ohswé:ken and Kenhtè:ke and the other villages in Canada are, even now, fighting at the side of English soldiers. With their help, great victories have already been won on the Ne-ah-ga and at Mackinac.

"Nor are the Kanien'kehá:ka in Canada the only nation to take up arms against the Yankees. In the west, Tecumseh of the Shawnee also fights for the English king. If the men of Kanièn:keh join the English they will fight alongside their brothers from Ahkwesáhsne. Like some of you, the Ahkwesáhsne did not want to fight. But two months ago they were attacked by the Yankees who stole many gifts given to the Ahkwesáhsne by the English. They threatened to burn the village and they built a blockhouse – *une maison en bois* – so that they could control the Ahkwesáhsne. Is that what *you* want? The Ahkwesáhsne asked for help. English soldiers went to their aid. They forced the Yankees to surrender so that the Ahkwesáhsne could be free to choose their friends."

"Perhaps the Ahkwesáhsne fought with the English out of fear," a long-haired warrior suggested.

"It was only because the Ahkwesáhsne land lies on both sides of the great water that the English helped," put in the elder sitting next to him. "If the Yan-kees take the river, the English will not be able to keep their army fed. They were thinking of themselves."

Cageaga raised his hand. "All here know the Yan-kees fear the Kanien'kehá:ka. If the western tribes and our brothers in Canada have taken up arms, how can we stand by and do nothing? We must consider what our brothers and Tecumseh of the Shawnee would think if those gathered at this council chose not to fight the enemy of our race. I do not want to be thought a coward by the Shawnee."

Before anyone could react to that, Cageaga went on: "Do not forget that the Stone People march with the Yan-kees. It was the Oneniote'á:ka the Yan-kees sent after our brother." He indicated Hawkwood. "There are those here who have suffered under their knives. By joining with the English, we can avenge those who have died and bring honour to their memory."

Hawkwood could see minds at work. Avenging the murders of friends and loved ones was difficult in peacetime, but in times of war it was considered a legitimate enterprise.

"But we are too few in number," another elder interjected. "The Yan-kees are many. We are surrounded."

"You would not be facing the Yankees on your own," Hawkwood said.

Lawrence leaned in close to Hawkwood's side. "Would it be all right for me to speak to them, if you translate my words?"

"Speak slowly and I'll try." To the gathering, Hawkwood said,

"My friend, Lawrence – Roren – wishes to address the council. He speaks for the Great King beyond the Water."

A few of the elders swapped glances but no voices were raised in objection.

"You have the floor, Major," Hawkwood said.

Lawrence eased his crossed legs into a more comfortable position and looked around at the warriors gathered before him. He took a calming breath.

"The Great King knows well that the Mohawk are fearless warriors who have fought bravely on the side of the English soldiers against the French and the Americans." He paused, allowing Hawkwood to relay the message. "That was many years ago. Once again the Great King is asking for help from his Mohawk brothers, against an old enemy who now seeks to drive both the English *and* the Mohawk from their homes. The Great King believes that if our peoples fight together, as one army, we will defeat the Americans. In exchange for your help, the Great King will see you rewarded with food and clothing, as well as blankets, hunting supplies and tools—"

"And guns?" The query came from a hard-faced warrior with a silver nose ring and a shell gorget around his neck.

"Yes, and guns, too. The army will also pay wages to any warrior who fights for the Great King. War chieftains will be given the rank of captain and receive officers' stipend."

"The English have smooth mouths," Cageaga cut in. "We have heard white men's promises before." Speaking in Mohawk, he glanced towards Hawkwood. "Why should we trust the English any more than we trust the Yan-kees? Did they not betray us when they placed their mark upon the last treaty?"

Hawkwood did not react, knowing that in posing the question, Cageaga, despite his clear allegiance to Hawkwood and by association Lawrence, was playing devil's advocate, and in the process cementing his reputation as a sceptic, in case Hawkwood's request for help was rejected. It was a shrewd move.

Hawkwood translated Cageaga's words into English.

Lawrence continued. "I know that many times the whites have promised much and delivered little. The Great King knows this and he is deeply sorry. When that treaty was signed between the English and the Americans, the Great King made his mark in good faith, believing the Americans would honour *their* mark. It was the Americans who broke the treaty. My friend Matthew has spoken of how the Americans will take all Mohawk land for themselves. The Great King has agreed, by signed treaty, that all land he grants to the Mohawk nation will remain Mohawk, for all time. This *I* promise."

Hawkwood looked around the faces of the men present. "My friend, Roren, does not lie. I say this not as a soldier of the Great King but as Kahrhakon:ha, adopted son of Tewanias, war captain of the Kanien'kehá:ka. I swear on this, the totem of my father."

Hawkwood pulled aside his collar, his fingers brushing the ring of bruising round his neck.

The amulet had yellowed with age and had been worn even smoother by years of constant handling. Hawkwood saw the expression on Tewanias's face as he held it in front of his throat. It was a look that he would never forget.

Concealed beneath his shirt, the bone carving had rarely seen the light of day. When it had, those that commented upon it or queried its provenance had soon learned to curb their curiosity. Soldiers of all ranks carried a talisman; a medallion or a coin, even a musket ball that had been dug out of a wound and placed in a pocket. The turtle amulet had become as much a part of him as the scars on his body and the stiletto concealed in his boot. Whether, like the knife, it had protected him over the years, he did not know and would never know, but many a time on the eve of battle he had found himself manipulating it between his fingers in the same way a God-fearing private might touch a crucifix or a priest his rosary.

He tucked the amulet away.

Emboldened by the reaction to Hawkwood's intervention, Lawrence said, "And if other tribes see that the Mohawk have joined with the English, they too will fight against the Americans, which will also assist the Mohawk. When the English win, all, including the Mohawk, will celebrate a great victory."

"Never forget," Cageaga said, "it was the Yan-kees who took our land. It was the Yan-kees who were responsible for the breaking of the Rotinonshón:ni. For those reasons and because the English gave sanctuary to our brothers, we must answer the call of the Great King. There are some here who would want us to lie still and hold down our heads, but I am Cageaga of the Kanien'kehá:ka. I will paint my face and be a man and fight the Yan-kees as long as I live!"

Cageaga's eyes blazed as he placed the flat of his hand on his chest. The gesture, by common consent, brought the respective arguments to a close. As discussion broke out around them, Tewanias turned and said quietly to Hawkwood. "Go now. Prepare for your journey. The council will make its decision."

"What do you think?" Lawrence asked as he slipped his shoulder through the musket strap. "Will they help us?"

"Hard to tell. The war captains and the peace chiefs will have their say. It may be put to the families and the clan mothers."

"The clan mothers? The *women* have that much influence?"

"It's the women who rule the clans. They help elect the chiefs. When a man marries, he joins his wife's clan, not the other way round. The tribe couldn't function without them."

"I'm learning something new about these people every minute," Lawrence said.

Hawkwood smiled. "There's another thing that might surprise you?"

"What's that?"

"If it wasn't for the Iroquois, the Rifles might never have seen the light of day."

Lawrence looked at Hawkwood askance.

"It's true. Sixty years ago, we were out here fighting the French. Some Iroquois fought on *their* side. That's where the name comes from, by the way: Irinakhoiw – it's Huron for 'black snake'. Only the Frogs couldn't pronounce it correctly. They knew the Indians' value, though: these were warriors who were at home in the forest, they could travel light and they could live off the land. They were a bloody sight better shots than the regular troops, too. The French used them to harass the enemy flanks and pick out and kill the officers. Sound familiar? It's one of the reasons our light companies were formed. John Moore and our other commanders realized the benefit of irregulars who could move fast and fend for themselves, without supervision.

"Over the years, skills were honed, uniforms changed colour, muskets were replaced. The Rifles were the end result. They fight in small groups, hitting the enemy hard and moving on before it can retaliate. They spread panic. It's what the Indians do and they're experts at it." Hawkwood smiled then. "And you know the best thing about using them?"

Lawrence shook his head. "What's that?"

"They don't need training."

It was more than an hour before Tewanias reappeared, Cageaga at his shoulder. They approached, their faces grave.

"This doesn't look good," Lawrence murmured softly.

Cageaga was the first to speak. "The council has spoken."

Hawkwood waited. In truth, he'd been expecting the deliberations to go on for a lot longer. The early verdict did not bode well. He prepared for the worst.

"We are with you," Tewanias said.

# 15

The troops left Plattsburg well before first light, without fuss or ceremony. From the town, the column skirted the curve of Cumberland Bay, crossed over Dead Creek bridge and turned north on to the Chazy road.

Harlan Quade, riding just behind the van, hunkered into his coat, massaged his right thigh and wished he was somewhere warmer; Tripoli, for instance. Though he recalled that during the march across the desert to Derna, the heat and the flies had been ferocious, while the nights had been as cold as the proverbial witch's tits. Here, at least, there wasn't that much disparity between day and night-time temperatures. There weren't any flies either. Perhaps he should be thankful for what he had. He was in his own country, after all; for the time being, anyway.

And at least there was a road. They didn't have to forge a path out of the wilderness, which, only a few years ago would have been a requirement. In this country, where even a cart track was considered a godsend, good roads had become lifelines, especially in times of war.

As darkness gave way to dawn, the mood of the troops lifted and by sun-up the sound of their progress had become a determined tramp. The men's breath clouded the air as they marched while around them frost clung to the trees like droplets of white lace.

The order to advance had come from Colonel Pearce, retaining command due to Colonel Pike's continued confinement. The objective: to capture and hold the blockhouse at Lacolle and create the first stepping stone on the road to Montreal, Quebec and the subsequent expulsion of the British from the Canadas, at which point the Revolution would have reached its natural conclusion.

The colonel was not expecting serious opposition. It had been reported that Lacolle was staffed by only a token force – forty or so militia and a couple of dozen native irregulars. Four regular companies would be more than enough to secure the ground; regulars, because the militia had been deemed unreliable after the fiasco at Queenston when they had refused to cross the river. Though the point was moot since the latter were all back in their homes and bedding down for the winter anyway.

There had been a worry that sickness spread by patients brought to Plattsburg from Burlington would reduce the number of troops available for the mission, but by segregating the fitter men, Pearce and Pike had ensured that there were more than sufficient numbers to staff the final assault of the year before the northern roads became impassable. At the moment, the snow was an inconvenience rather than a barrier and the lure of establishing a bridgehead while the British posts at both Lacolle and Île aux Noix were so conveniently under-manned was too attractive to ignore.

Île aux Noix, being the larger of the two outposts, housed more troops than Lacolle. It boasted a detachment of Royal Artillery equipped with three-pounder guns and companies of the 100th Regiment of Foot. On paper, at least, it appeared that the American force was outnumbered. Colonels Pearce and Pike, however, were counting on the element of surprise to swing the odds in their favour.

News that a relatively small column of US infantry was on the march was unlikely to set pulses racing on the other side of the border, unlike, say, the forward advancement of several thousand men and an entire artillery battery – though they were ready to follow, by both barge and road, as soon as the first position was secured. The fact that the men were travelling light, without tents or equipage, would lead an observer to assume that the manoeuvre was no more than a transfer of personnel, which happened all the time, particularly with America anxious to reinforce its defences against the threat of a possible British invasion.

The Provincial Marine did have at its beck and call an armed schooner and three gunboats, but they'd already been laid up for the winter. Pearce and Pike knew, therefore, that if their troops could secure the river and bring up reinforcements at speed, they could isolate the garrison – including the Marine – by cutting off the isle's main supply routes. The British commander would have little choice but to capitulate, as Hull had done in Detroit.

The one fly in the ointment had been the escape of the two British spies. The fact that the Oneida had yet to return bearing their scalps was not necessarily an indication that their quarry had evaded capture. But despite his faith in Amos Walker's irregulars, Colonel Pearce was not prepared to stake everything on their success. To guard against the eventuality that Hawkwood and Lawrence had managed to deliver word of the invasion, he had decided to bring forward the attack so that, even if forewarned, the British would not have time to mount a viable defence.

That was the plan. And Major Harlan Quade was determined to see it through, even though his thoughts were for the most part engaged elsewhere, wondering how it must feel to be a fugitive, knowing there was an Oneida hunting party on your tail. It was enough to give a person sleepless nights. A picture formed in his mind: two corpses, lying stripped and mutilated in the snow.

Warmed by the image, he smiled broadly.

Cageaga and Tewanias set the pace. Hawkwood, Lawrence and the nine chosen warriors followed in single file behind.

Thirteen was a pitifully small number when ranged against upwards of four hundred, as Lawrence had pointed out, adding, "Let's hope it ain't a portent."

383

The village was too small to provide more, Hawkwood had told him. And Tewanias had to leave men behind to protect the families. "Besides," he'd added, "we don't need that many. We only need enough."

"To do what?" Lawrence had asked.

"Scare the bastards shitless."

For reasons he couldn't quite understand, that statement had sent of a shiver of apprehension down Lawrence's spine. The feeling was not dispelled when he'd seen the warriors who would be accompanying them.

Dressed for winter in buckskin coats, leggings and calf-length moccasins, with long guns strung across their backs, they might have passed for a hunting party about to set off after game had it not been for the accoutrements and additional weaponry they were carrying: swords, war clubs, knives and tomahawks. At Hawkwood's request, a couple of the men also carried bows. Not all wore scalp locks. A few of the younger-looking ones had full heads of tied-back hair. Even with their features unpainted they looked fit and formidable.

Tewanias introduced them by name and clan affiliation, each man responding with a saturnine nod. Hawkwood heard the names Effa, Opio, Alak and Deskaheh and hoped he'd remember the others when the time came.

As they'd made their way from longhouse to palisade, the women and children and the men who were staying to guard the village gathered to watch them depart.

Whereas new recruits setting out from an English hamlet might be expected to march off to the sound of fife and drum, the departure from Gaanundata was accompanied by a subdued, almost mystical, silence. No one waved. No one called a farewell. Taking the path to war was not a joyous occasion but one which demanded great solemnity, born of the understanding that some of those who were leaving might not return. As they headed for the woods, Lawrence took the opportunity to glance over his shoulder. No one had remained at the entrance to see them leave. The villagers had already returned to their fires.

For the first mile, the path led downhill. Descending the slope, Hawkwood looked back. It was not difficult to see how Gaanundata had got its name, nor why it had remained hidden. Protected on three sides by densely wooded, near-vertical slopes and on the other by a deep river gulley, access to the site was via a narrow deer track that snaked its way up through the forest from the gulley floor. Had they been seeking the place on their own, it was doubtful they'd have found it, even with directions. Not until the top of the bluff was reached, where the trees thinned out, did the palisade come into view. In the light of day, a person could easily pass within one hundred paces of the wall and not know it was there. In a gathering gloom, with snow falling thickly, it would have been next to invisible.

Walking in line, the ground crunching crisply beneath his feet and with musket to hand, it occurred to Hawkwood that it had been a good few years since his last forced march, leading a band of guerrilleros in pursuit of a French reconnaissance patrol. It had been a hard slog, alternating between trotting and walking, over difficult terrain, some of it mountainous, most of it forested. Not that much different to the country they were traversing now, except here there was snow instead of scree.

The snow shoes made the going easier, though there was defin-itely a knack to wearing them. Only the toe end of the foot was attached to the shoe. The trick, as Hawkwood remembered and as Lawrence soon learnt, was to keep the heel elevated and the feet well-spaced and not to lift the foot too high off the ground. In order to don the shoes, they had dispensed with their boots, which would have placed strain on the rawhide webbing. Instead, both were wearing knee-length moccasins.

Though the shoes were not built for speed, once they'd grown used to the odd, sliding gait that was required they were able to maintain a decent stride. The moccasins helped, for they provided both comfort and suppleness; especially useful when wading a stream or river, for their flexibility offered a much better grip than boots would have done.

Mindful of Tewanias's fears that Oneida scouting parties were increasing their range, there was little talking. It was as if each man was held in thrall by the stillness surrounding them; stillness that only ever seemed to occur in thick, winter-bound forests. Occasionally, a bird would sing out or a tree branch would snap under the weight of snow. When that happened, they would halt and stand in silence for a minute or so before moving on, but there was never a sight or a sound to suggest the enemy was close.

At one point, Lawrence broke the spell.

"Y'know this could be a wild-goose chase. Just because a column's on the march don't mean it has Lacolle in its sights. We're going to look like damned fools if all they do is stay this side of the border or turn left at Chazy."

Hawkwood spoke over his shoulder. "I'd rather look a fool for crying wolf than not cry at all and discover we were right in our suspicions. At least this way we can make our own reconnoitre. In any case, our troops have to be warned about the bigger invasion threat."

"Think we can beat the buggers to the mark?"

"Hard to say. They've had a head start, but if we keep to the pace, we may have a chance. That many on the move, they'll have to call a rest at some point, which might work in our favour. If they're riding, the officers' horses'll need watering. The troops too."

"To keep 'em regular, you mean?" Lawrence grinned.

It was an old joke. People tended not to drink enough water in cold weather, a failing which often led to constipation – a curse of winter campaigning. It made Hawkwood wonder about the state of the troops at the river encampment. Though from the smell that had hit them on the approach, constipation would seem to have been the least of the camp's problems.

"The Iroquois might be able to run thirty miles and fight a battle at the end of it," Hawkwood added, "but I can't see a Yankee column doing that. They'll want to pitch camp and gather themselves before the assault, if there's to be one, which will give us more time to catch up."

"I'm wondering what in God's name possessed 'em to march in December in the first place," Lawrence muttered. "I said before; this is no time to launch an offensive."

"That's probably the reason," Hawkwood said. "They know our troops won't be expecting an attack. Plus they'll be wondering about you and me and how close we are to the lines and whether we've managed to pass a warning. They'll want to strike before reinforcements can be called up."

Lawrence shook his head. "If it was your decision, would you attack now?"

"You're asking me? I'm the one who's considering going up against four hundred troopers with a handful of Indians and two white men trying to walk in snow shoes. What the hell do I know? Some would call us mad."

"Fair point," Lawrence conceded. "Still . . ."

"If I was to wager on why the Yankees are marching, I'd put my money on dented pride."

Lawrence blinked. "Come again?"

"They've had a bad start to the war. Mackinac, Detroit, Queenston – all defeats. The buggers are smarting. They need a win, something to stir the blood and raise the spirits."

"And for that they're going to attack a blockhouse?"

"Which guards an important river. Giant oaks from little acorns, remember? They're looking beyond Lacolle. They've Quebec in their sights. Seizing control of the Richelieu would be a nice way to see in the new year. There's many who'd see it as an early Christmas present."

"I'd rather have a cask of Madeira," Lawrence quipped.

Hawkwood didn't respond. He looked up. A gap had appeared unexpectedly in the clouds, revealing a widening patch of pale blue. It was the first clear sky they'd seen in days.

The sun shines on the righteous, Hawkwood thought.

Or it was supposed to.

Arriving at Chazy, the column halted. Quade gave the men permission to smoke and brew coffee. Those wishing to attend to more basic needs headed into the surrounding forest. An

387

hour later, bellies replenished, bladders emptied and bowels voided, coffee dregs were poured on to the fires and the column moved off.

It was early evening when the woods finally gave way before them and the lights of Champlain village twinkled into view. A collective sigh of relief ran through the ranks.

Being close to the border, the village's inhabitants had become used to the comings and goings of the military, but the place was small and they were not disposed to giving the troops free run. Quade took the column across the river and on to a site a mile to the north-east to set up camp. In the absence of tents, spruce branches were cut to make temporary bivouacs beneath the trees. Fires were lit.

Quade met with his officers.

"Less than two miles to the province, gentlemen. We've made excellent time."

He looked around the semicircle of uniforms: a captain and two lieutenants from each company.

"We may be on our own ground but I do not want the men complacent. Set piquets. Two-hour watches. Make sure the fires stay lit. They will keep the cold at bay."

Quade drew out a pocket watch and consulted the dial. "Silent réveillé at five-thirty. Inform your sergeants that I want all troops to check their weapons upon muster. Random inspections to be carried out. Anyone whose musket is not serviceable or who has damp powder is to be put on a charge. Punishment will be severe. Remind them they are regulars and not the Goddamned militia. Carry on."

Watching the officers disperse, Quade helped himself to a mug of coffee. Adding some whiskey from a silver flask, he took a sip and rolled the drink around his tongue.

In the aftermath of the Greenbush incident, he was all too aware that the upcoming assault was likely to be his last chance to redeem himself. Both the Greenbush commandant and, latterly, Colonel Pearce had made it plain that the only reason Quade had retained his authority was because of the shortage of combat-experienced officers. One more wrong move and his name would

388

be added to the list of officers who'd vanished into obscurity. Quade was determined that was never going to happen.

Lacolle would be his reprieve.

By Hawkwood's reckoning, they'd been on the move for more than eight hours when, in the gathering dusk, Tewanias and Cageaga halted.

"We are being followed," Cageaga said softly, speaking in Mohawk.

There was no alarm in his voice, which struck Hawkwood as odd.

"Oneida?" asked Lawrence, when the announcement was translated for his benefit. Looking anxiously through the trees, he slipped the musket off his shoulder. "You think they've found us?"

"I don't think so," said Hawkwood, frowning as he watched Tewanias. The war captain was staring back the way they had come with what appeared to be weary resignation.

"You might as well join us, boy," Cageaga called softly. "I can smell you. You are also making more noise than a herd of elk."

For a while there was no sound and nothing moved, and then there came the pad of footsteps across snow and a wiry figure detached itself from the shadows beneath the trees and came forward slowly. Several of the warriors grunted in surprise as the figure's face caught the light.

Cageaga hissed through his teeth.

"Well, well," Lawrence murmured. "And whom do we have here?"

The newcomer, Hawkwood saw, was younger than the rest of Tewanias's men, probably by four or five years. His hair was long and black and thick and fell over the collar of his hide coat. A carbine, war club and a provisions pouch were slung over his shoulder. A knife hung from a sheath at his waist.

"Who is he? What are they saying?" Lawrence asked Hawkwood as Cageaga, his face taut with anger, began to berate the newcomer in a tone that would have done justice to the Inquisition.

"His name's Kodjeote. He's Cageaga's nephew. He says he's come to fight."

"You mean we have another young buck out to prove himself. Seen a fair few of those in our time, haven't we?"

"He's reminding Cageaga that he's eighteen and that Cageaga was younger than that when he got his first tattoo."

"His first what?" Lawrence said, thinking he'd misheard.

"It's how warriors keep a tally of the men they've killed. Cageaga's are on his thigh."

Lawrence's gaze dropped to Cageaga's buckskin leggings and then rose again as the young warrior began to remonstrate with his uncle.

"He's saying if it wasn't for him, they would never have known of Kahrhakon:ha's return."

"Kahrhak— That's you," Lawrence said, when he saw the boy's eyes flicker towards Hawkwood.

"Kodjeote's also telling them that he's a man not a boy and that he's one of the best hunters in his clan. He says now that he's proved that, he deserves the right to prove himself a warrior."

"Christ, lad," Lawrence said softly. "Be careful what you wish for."

"Cageaga's pointing out that deer do not shoot back. Kodjeote's saying his brother is here, so why shouldn't he be allowed to come with us?"

"His brother?" Lawrence looked towards the other warriors, who were following the exchange with rapt attention. A couple of faces showed curiosity, others impatience, while one or two wore the expression older boys the world over assumed when a younger boy asked to join their game. Turning back to Hawkwood as the heated discussion continued, Lawrence hissed, "Now what?" as Tewanias stepped forward to stand at Cageaga's shoulder.

Hawkwood listened. "Tewanias is telling Kodjeote that his task was to stay and help protect the village. By disobeying his elders, he's placed the village at risk. Kodjeote says that if they send him back, he'll follow us anyway."

Lawrence's eyebrows rose. "I'll wager that's not gone down well."

Hawkwood saw Cageaga's face darken again. "You might say that."

"Gives us an extra man, though," Lawrence offered quietly.

Hawkwood did not respond.

"You're not going to intervene?"

Hawkwood shook his head. "This is between them."

"Well, from the look on Tewanias's face," Lawrence murmured, "I'd say we're about to get a decision."

They watched as Tewanias took Cageaga aside and placed a hand on his shoulder. The other warriors maintained their silence, their faces inscrutable in the fading light. The young warrior's eyes remained fixed on a point between the two captains. When, after several minutes the men broke apart, his head lifted defiantly. Cageaga's expression, Hawkwood saw, looked as if it was set in stone. It was Tewanias who delivered the verdict.

"Tewanias has told him that he can come, but he is to obey orders without question and he is to stay close to his brother. They'll deal with him when they return home."

"So it's fourteen now," Lawrence said, adding sotto voce. "Things are looking up."

As Kodjeote joined the others Hawkwood saw one of them reach out and tug the younger man's hair. As Kodjeote turned, his tormentor favoured him with a grin and nudged him with an elbow. The brother, Hawkwood guessed. It was the warrior who'd been introduced to him as Deskaheh.

"We're wanted," Lawrence said.

Hawkwood followed his gaze to Tewanias, who was standing next to a glowering Cageaga and beckoning for them to approach. The two war captains led them through a thin stand of trees to where a river lay across their path.

They had forded at least half a dozen water courses during their journey, all without mishap and with only one detour

– around a small area of swampland three miles to the south. Thankfully, from what Hawkwood could see of it, this river didn't appear to be much of an obstacle either. But it wasn't the river that had drawn Tewanias's attention.

The Mohawk chieftain pointed across the water to the woods on the opposite shore.

"Canada," he said softly.

In that instant the weariness slid from Hawkwood's bones. He heard Lawrence gasp and felt a touch on his shoulder. He turned. Lawrence grinned and held out his hand.

Hawkwood grasped it firmly.

*All we have to do now*, Hawkwood thought, as they removed their snow shoes, *is find the enemy*.

It was still dark when, ten minutes after the first soldier had been awakened by kicks to the soles of his boots, the last of the troops cast off their frost-stiffened blankets and emerged from their bivouacs. To everyone's relief, no snow had fallen during the night. Instead, they found the countryside shrouded in fog.

Wood was added to the campfire embers and as coffee pots were replenished and ablutions performed the officers looked to their horses while the troops, under the watchful eyes of the corporals and the sergeants, attended to their weapons.

At the appointed hour, with the fog thickening, Quade gave the order to move out.

"Maybe we were wrong," Lawrence suggested.

"Maybe," Hawkwood said.

Hawkwood surveyed the road, which wasn't that impressive, considering it was supposed to be the main highway linking Quebec Province to the United States. No more than a track through a wood, it certainly didn't match the Dover post road or the road he'd travelled on from Boston to Albany. But then, given the time of year, traffic was bound to be light; so light in fact, as to be non-existent, to judge by the lack of imprints. There were a few animal tracks, but no vehicle marks and certainly nothing to suggest that upwards of four hundred men had passed by recently.

Hawkwood wasn't sure whether to be pleased or disappointed.

After fording the river, he'd persuaded Tewanias and Cageaga to continue the trek eastwards. Travelling at night through a winter landscape, most of which was primeval forest, was not generally advisable, but while the moon was bright enough to see by, it had made sense to go as far as they were able. They'd managed another two miles before eventually calling a halt.

Confident they were safe from human threat, they'd constructed lean-tos out of branches, with a snow wall in front to shield and reflect the heat from the fires. After setting watches, the night had passed without event. Breakfast had consisted of pemmican washed down with water from their canteens. Moving off before the sun rose, another hour's hike had seen them to the road.

"So?" Lawrence said. "Cut our losses, head for Lacolle?"

Hawkwood was about to reply in the affirmative when an owl hooted in the woods to their right. No one moved. Poised at Hawkwood's shoulder, Tewanias said softly, "Someone comes."

Hawkwood did not query the warning. He trusted Tewanias's instincts implicitly, knowing the owl call had been voiced by one of the Mohawks who, with others, had been deployed to watch the road, both north and south of their position.

As he shifted his grip on his musket, a stocky, buckskin-coated warrior, war bow in hand – Hawkwood remembered his name as Chohajo – materialized at Tewanias's side and spoke rapidly into the Mohawk chief's ear. Tewanias nodded, then informed Hawkwood: "Two riders."

"How far?"

"Close."

"Friend or foe?" Lawrence murmured.

"Let's find out," Hawkwood said. Turning, he issued swift instructions to Tewanias. "And await my signal, rake'niha. There must be no noise."

Hawkwood saw Cageaga's mouth split into a vulpine smile.

"With me, Douglas," Hawkwood said.

They stepped out on to the road.

It was a short while before the riders came into view for they were not travelling fast but at walking pace, employing caution. With the snow muffling the sound of their horses' hooves and the fog distorting their shapes, they looked more like ghostly apparitions than flesh-and-blood mortals and it took another second or two before Hawkwood was able to pick out details.

Both riders were wrapped against the cold in long coats, scarves and caps. The peaked, drum-shaped headgear left little doubt that the riders were military. The way they were advancing made Hawkwood suspect that in the semi-darkness and the fog, his and Lawrence's presence had yet to register.

Slipping the musket strap on to his left shoulder Hawkwood dropped his right hand down by his side so that it was concealed by his coat. Lawrence held his gun cradled across his chest.

The riders advanced another few yards before it dawned on them that they did not have the road to themselves. They pulled up quickly.

"Gentlemen." Lawrence stepped out and smiled up at their startled expressions. "You'll oblige me by dismounting."

Hawkwood watched the indecision creep over their faces. It took a moment for the lead rider to find his voice.

"By whose authority?"

"That would be mine," Lawrence said. "On account of I'm the one with the gun."

Neither horseman responded. After exchanging glances with his companion, the lead rider dropped his right hand down by his side.

Damn it! Hawkwood thought, half a second before the rider drew the pistol from his saddle holster.

Lawrence brought his musket up.

"No!" Hawkwood said sharply.

The tomahawk that Hawkwood had been holding concealed behind his coat flew from his hand in a blur. As the rider fell back with the blade buried in his right shoulder, Hawkwood lunged towards the horse's halter, grabbing it as the second rider, stunned by the attack, hauled on his reins and wheeled his horse about, Lawrence snapped his musket to his shoulder once more.

"No, Douglas!" Hawkwood warned again, as horse and rider careered off in the direction from which they'd come.

"Shit!" Lawrence cursed. He threw Hawkwood a look of exasperation.

"Wait," Hawkwood said.

Lawrence turned just in time to see several shadows detach themselves from the forest and converge upon the fleeing horse and rider. It was the fact that they did so in utter silence that made Lawrence's pulse skip a beat.

The horseman's indecision was his downfall. Alarmed by this fresh threat, he tried to pull his horse around. This time, the snow got the better of him. As if sensing panic from the man on its back, the horse shied and then reared, throwing its rider to the ground. Relieved of the weight, hooves scrabbling, the animal managed to regain its balance but, instead of bolting, it remained rooted to the spot, haunches quivering. Within seconds, one of the warriors had taken hold of its halter, while his companions moved swiftly toward the horseman who lay sprawled, face down, in the snow.

"Sorry, Douglas," Hawkwood said. "I didn't want the sound of the shot carrying."

Lawrence shook his head. "No apology necessary."

Hawkwood handed Lawrence the reins of the horse he was holding and moved to its rider, who'd landed face up. His eyes were open but from their glassy stare it was clear he was dead. His head, Hawkwood saw, as he tugged the hatchet free, lay at an unnatural angle, indicating he'd died from a broken neck and not the wound to the shoulder. Death had come quickly so there was little blood. The rider's shako lay a few feet away. There were no insignia on his coat, but a red collar and blue uniform jacket showed beneath it.

Lawrence looked down at the corpse. "Well, they're Yankees all right. Outriders for the column?"

"That'd be my guess."

Spying the dead man's pistol, Hawkwood picked it up, brushed off the snow and handed it to Lawrence, who checked the powder before sliding it into its holster.

"Question is, how far out in front are they?" Lawrence muttered.

"Don't know." Hawkwood peered along the road. At that distance the fog was too thick to penetrate. "But I know a man who does."

They made their way to where the second rider had been hauled to his feet. He, too, had lost his cap. His hair was wet and dishevelled. He looked, Hawkwood thought, both dazed and terrified by the sight of the bloodstained tomahawk.

"Name and rank?" Hawkwood snapped.

"H-Henry Nevens, Lieutenant." Adding quickly, "Sixth Regiment of Infantry."

"You're scouts for the column, yes?"

The lieutenant's gaze remained fixed on the hatchet.

"Didn't catch that," Hawkwood said, inclining his head as though deaf.

The lieutenant swallowed. "Y-yes."

"How far behind is it?"

Hope flared in the man's eyes at the thought of his compatriots appearing out of the mist to save him, but it was a vision dashed as Hawkwood laid the flat of the tomahawk blade against the lieutenant's pale cheek. "Don't lie. I'll know if you lie and I'll let my friends ask the questions. You understand me?"

A sound, halfway between a gasp and a croak, emerged from the lieutenant's throat. "Not far . . . a mile . . . I'm not sure."

"How many men?"

"Four companies."

"Who leads them?"

"The lieutenant blinked. It was not a question he'd expected. "Major Quade."

"Well, well," Lawrence murmured.

"Their objective is Lacolle, correct?" Hawkwood said.

The lieutenant hesitated then nodded.

"Is the main army still at Plattsburg?"

The lieutenant hesitated again.

"Come on, lad," Lawrence said. "You done well so far. Don't ruin it."

"C – Colonel Pearce leads them to Champlain."

"To await news of victory before advancing at the double, no doubt," Lawrence said. He looked at Hawkwood. "Well?"

Hawkwood led Lawrence to one side. "Take the horse, Douglas. Ride to Lacolle. Warn them."

Lawrence frowned. "There are two horses."

Hawkwood turned. "Rake'niha, I need a man to guide Major Lawrence the rest of the way."

Tewanias called to the warrior who was holding Lieutenant Nevens' horse.

"I take it this means you're going to try and keep the buggers occupied?" Lawrence said.

"If we can. With luck, it'll give you time to alert Lacolle so they can send for help."

Lawrence bit his lip.

Hawkwood smiled. "It has to be you, Douglas. You're the better rider."

Lawrence looked towards Tewanias and his warriors. "And you're the one who speaks the lingo."

Tewanias approached. At his side, Lawrence's appointed guide.

"Oneas ronwa:iats," Tewanias said to Lawrence before correcting himself with a smile. "His name is Oneas. He has some English."

As his name was spoken, the Mohawk swung himself effort-lessly into the saddle.

"Always useful," Lawrence said. He looked across to where the lieutenant was being held and his face froze.

"You should leave now, Douglas," Hawkwood said.

Lawrence hesitated, made as if to speak, and fell silent. Then he tucked in his scarf and mounted the horse.

Tewanias raised his hand and spoke in English. "Goodbye, Roren. We will meet again."

"I hope so, sir," Lawrence said. "It's been an honour." He turned back to Hawkwood. His mouth was set grim.

"O:nen ki' wahi', Major." Hawkwood held out his hand. "Safe journey."

Lawrence paused, then grasping the hand, he said, "You, too, Captain. I'll see you in Lacolle, God willing." Releasing his grip, and as if discomforted by the prospect of parting, he turned his horse and rode to where his guide was waiting.

God, Hawkwood mused as he watched them disappear into the darkness, would have little to do with it. The devil, on the other hand . . .

He looked for Tewanias.

"We should hurry. The Americans must not know we've been here. Take the body into the woods. Cover all traces of blood."

"It will be done. And the one who lives?"

Hawkwood did not reply.

"If we let him go, he will warn the Yan-kees," Tewanias said.

"I know."

Tewanias held his gaze.

"I know," Hawkwood said again.

Tewanias turned and spoke to his men. Hawkwood looked towards the captured lieutenant and took a deep breath.

Watching Hawkwood approach, Nevens straightened. From his expression it was not hard to read his mind. Seeing his companion cut down so brutally, not by an Indian but by a white man, had, no doubt, been as shocking as the deed itself. The threat to hand him to the Indians for questioning had probably awakened countless childhood memories and tales of bloodthirsty natives. The sight of Lawrence and Oneas departing had only added to his fear. It was obvious his mind was racing, trying to come up with a way to save himself.

It was a futile exercise.

Hawkwood was almost level with them when Cageaga stepped behind the lieutenant. In a move so fast that it had barely time to register in Hawkwood's brain, he drove the head of his war club against the base of the lieutenant's skull. Nevens collapsed without a sound.

Squatting down next to the body, Cageaga drew his knife.

"Yahtea!" Tewanias's command cut through the air.

Cageaga paused. He looked up, staring first at Hawkwood and then at a point over Hawkwood's shoulder. Hawkwood turned. Tewanias did not speak either but remained where he was. His eyes were on Hawkwood. They moved to Cageaga. He shook his head. "Yahtea," he said again.

No.

Showing no emotion, Cageaga returned the knife to its sheath and stood up. Tewanias looked back at Hawkwood, held his gaze for another second and then turned away.

Hawkwood crossed to the body. He did not look for signs of life for he knew there would be none. The blow, delivered by an adept, had been meant to kill. He presumed Tewanias had sent Cageaga a signal while his back had been turned. It had been a deliberate act, designed to deny Hawkwood the task of having to carry out the sentence himself.

At least, Hawkwood assumed that had been the reason; that Tewanias had directed Cageaga to deliver the blow because he'd thought Hawkwood might balk at killing a man in cold blood. Hawkwood wondered about that and then realized there might have been another reason. Tewanias hadn't acted to spare Hawkwood from killing Nevens but to save him from having to make the decision whether to do so or not.

They carried the bodies off the road and into the forest and concealed them beneath spruce branches and snow. The few drops of blood that had been spilled were easily dealt with.

Tewanias then recalled the lookouts, who reported that the column was still nowhere in sight.

Which gave them time, Hawkwood hoped, to look for a killing ground.

Goddamned weather, Quade thought, though he knew, despite the damp and the poor visibility that the fog couldn't have come at a more opportune time for it gave his attacking force a distinct advantage. In parts, it was almost impossible to see further than a hundred yards in any direction. If conditions persisted, they'd be on top of the British positions before the Limeys even knew they were there.

By Quade's estimation, they had crossed the border a little over a mile back, though the measurement was somewhat nebulous due to the fog and because every mile of forest looked like every other mile of forest. Moreover there had been no actual physical barrier to deter the column's advance; indeed, had it not been for the crude marker half-buried at the side of the track, on the northern face of which was chipped a very rough letter Q and on the opposite the letters NY, it would have been hard to tell where one country ended and the other began.

From the maps he'd studied, Quade knew there was a creek up ahead. Not that wide, he'd been advised, or deep, but the banks were steep enough to have required the construction of a simple log bridge to facilitate the movement of wheeled traffic.

When the end of the bridge came into view, Quade found himself buoyed by an unexpected yet undeniable frisson of pleasure. The real border may already have been crossed, but there had been little sense of occasion. It was only now, as he approached the crude-cut, snow-covered timbers, that the true meaning of what he was about to achieve struck home. Caesar may have had the Rubicon and Washington the Delaware, but to Major Harlan Quade, the crossing of this narrow, insignificant creek felt just as symbolic.

It also occurred to him, then, that he should have made his way to the front of the line to lead the troops over himself, but by the time the bridge appeared through the fog, the van was already halfway across. Annoyed with himself for having missed an opportunity, Quade had little option but to follow on behind.

The van had reached the far bank and Quade was only a yard or two away from guiding his horse on to the span when the first call came from the woods on the other side: three screeches in swift succession, answered a moment later by a similar squawk from within the trees on the opposite side of the road.

Crows, Quade thought. He hated the damned birds. They reminded him of churchyards and tombstones.

The next sound was more animal than birdlike: a shrill bark that set the nerve ends jangling. It sounded like a dog fox staking claim to its territory. The fog added to the unearthly quality of the moment. So much so that Quade felt a cold shiver dart along the back of his neck.

Though that was as nothing compared to the way his heart leapt into his mouth when, upon hearing a sudden shout, he saw, through a break in the fog, several dark shapes explode from the trees and fall upon the vanguard troops, howling and hacking like beings possessed.

A low grunt came from Quade's left. He turned quickly, in time to see Captain Carradine, 6th Infantry, who'd been riding alongside him, slump sideways and then topple from his saddle. Quade gaped at the feathered shaft sticking out of the captain's chest.

Meanwhile, across the bridge, savagery ensued. The sergeant was the first to go down, his throat slashed and pumping blood. A second trooper managed to draw back the hammer on his musket only to die from a crushing blow to the skull before he could pull the trigger. Two of his companions suffered a similar fate. A corporal, more alert than the rest, managed to bring his gun to bear, only to take a knife cut across the belly, which gutted him like a fish. Dropping his musket, he fell to the snow, hands clasped around his spilling entrails. Another trooper fell with an arrow in his neck.

Gathering his wits, Quade hauled on the reins and yelled at the men marching behind him.

"Form up! Form up!"

A burly sergeant, who'd already sensed the danger, rapped out a command and a phalanx of troopers broke from the main body and ran forward. Further down the line, other NCOs were bellowing at the men to turn and protect the flanks.

Quade stared anxiously across the bridge. Disbelief gripped him. He could make out vague shapes but with the drifting fog it was hard to distinguish friend from foe or how many attackers there were. Behind him, the support troops fingered their weapons nervously as war cries and screams rent the air. A musket spat, but it was impossible to see who'd fired the shot, or if the ball had found its mark.

Quade drew his sword. "With me!"

He kicked his horse forward. He was three-quarters of the way across the bridge with the troops on his heels when he saw the shadowy figures darting away from his advance. The attackers, he realized, were breaking off from the fight. Having seen the imminent arrival of a superior force, they were fleeing, back into the forest.

Heathen bastards! Too cowardly to stand and fight!

It was only as he reached the end of the bridge that a more disturbing thought suddenly pierced his subconscious. And as two dishevelled figures appeared out of the murk – a corporal, his arms around a wounded trooper, then others following close behind, some hurrying, some staggering – it hit him.

"No!" he screamed.

The musket volley sent shock waves through the air. The fog was lit by powder flashes. Two men went down. A third trooper spun away with an arrow in his shoulder.

Flinching, Quade felt the wind of a ball as it winnowed past his left ear.

"Back!" he yelled. "Fall back!

The bulk of the troops coming up behind him were quick to obey, though a handful, ignoring the orders and the risk, broke ranks to run forward and help drag their injured comrades to safety. Another volley sounded, this time from the southern side of the bridge. Troops from the column had formed a defensive line along the creek and were returning fire, although there was little to aim at beyond fog, shadows and smoke.

Quade, anxious to present a less conspicuous target, dismounted quickly. As Captain Carradine's riderless horse cantered past him, he spied the corporal from the vanguard and pulled him close. "Report! What did you see?"

Not yet recovered from the shock of the attack and from the effort of helping his wounded comrade to safety, the corporal blinked. "Savages, Major! They came out of nowhere."

"I know that, damn it – I saw them! How many?"

The corporal blanched, his breath clouding. "Can't rightly say, sir. Never got a chance to count. Seven or eight maybe. Not many, but they were on us before we knew they were there. We got off a round or two, but . . ." The corporal shook his head helplessly before casting a terrified eye towards the forest over his shoulder.

Quade looked back across the bridge. The smoke was dissipating fast. The bodies of the dead were coming to light. They were sprawled across the snow like piles of empty sacking, the majority of them on the north side of the creek. A couple lay on the bridge, while both the trooper shot by an arrow and Captain Carradine had ended up face down on the bank. Of the attackers there was no sign. Presumably, they were back in the woods, reloading, and waiting.

But who in God's name were they?

There had been nothing from the scouts to warn that the enemy had been primed. All the signs had indicated that the redcoats were still a-bed. But, then, the attackers hadn't been redcoats, they'd been Indians, which was even more confusing. Where had they come from? Were they scouts for a bigger party, perhaps?

Quade was considering that possibility when a fresh outburst of musketfire came from the other side of the bridge. Ordinarily, given the range, the shots might have gone wide or dropped short, but a couple had found their targets due to the troopers being closely packed together. The reports were followed by a chorus of triumphant yelps, answered immediately by a retaliatory fusillade.

"Hold your fire!" a sergeant roared as he looked for an officer and fresh orders. "Wait till you can see the bastards!"

Fifty yards along the line, a private stared in disbelief at the arrow sprouting from his chest. He fell forward, his weight snapping the shaft in two. Galvanized by the prospect of further arrows raining down, his companions immediately loosed off their muskets.

The shots were met with more derisory whoops.

"I said cease firing, damn it!" The sergeant caught Quade's eye. "Savages are taunting us, sir."

That they were, Quade thought, and wondered how many guns were deployed among the trees. The ambush had been typical of the hit-and-run tactics perfected by irregulars. On this occasion it had also served to lure the column into a counter-attack which had led to the second ambush. It had been a well thought out move. Quade chided himself for not anticipating it. Men had died because he'd been slow on the uptake. It wouldn't happen again.

He looked up. It might have been his imagination but it appeared that the fog was starting to thin. A dull light was permeating through the trees, turning the snow from grey to white. Dawn wasn't that far off. He realized suddenly that there had been no catcalling for a minute or two. He wasn't sure which was the more terrifying; the catcalls themselves or the silence that preceded them.

He ordered a casualty count. Six confirmed dead and eight wounded. There would be more to come, as those numbers were based on the troopers whose fates had been witnessed by their comrades and on the number of walking wounded who'd made it to the safe side of the bridge. Some bodies were still on the north side of the creek, their condition unknown as they were too far out of reach. Quade bit back an expletive and wondered how many of the wounded were able to walk and, more importantly, fight. Wounded men constituted a greater inconvenience to an army than dead ones because they could slow the rate of the march and it took a disproportionate number of personnel to care for them. Dead men didn't need tending. They only needed burying.

Not that the number of casualties had depleted the fighting effectiveness of the column to any great degree. Six dead out of more than four hundred, though worrisome, was not a cata-strophic loss. The effect the deaths would have on the rest of the troops, however, could not be dismissed. Many would have seen the bodies of their comrades scattered across the snow and, human nature being what it was, they would be wondering who might be next. Such fear could prey on the mind, especially when it involved Indians. The word would be spreading. Were more on the way, coming to reinforce the ambushers?

The corporal had spoken of seven or eight warriors. Quade was prepared to gamble that the total number of attackers was indeed small, perhaps a dozen to fifteen guns at the most. Notwithstanding the bridge having the potential to be a killing ground, there was a limit to the firepower such a small number of shooters could discharge successfully against a much larger body of well-armed troops. All he needed to do was get the men across the bridge. Force of numbers would do the rest. But he'd have to move fast.

It was said a bad workman blamed his tools. Hawkwood had enough faith in his own ability as a marksman, however, to know that in all likelihood it had been a fault with the musket that had caused him to miss the shot, though in his own defence Quade had only been in view for a second. Had it been a Baker rifle, the chances were Quade would now be lying in the snow with a bullet through his heart. But that wasn't the case. As a result, by the time Hawkwood had reloaded, he was wondering if he wouldn't have been better off using a damned bow.

That thought notwithstanding, the trap had worked well, thanks to Tewanias who, when Hawkwood had enquired about a possible place of ambush, had known exactly the spot to head for. The forest and the fog had lent the necessary cover and, while it was no Thermopylae, the bridge had provided an ideal choke point.

But although breathing space had been won, the respite was likely to be short-lived. It wouldn't be long before Quade led his men back over the creek and Hawkwood knew that when that time came, his meagre band of warriors would have no option but to give way. Though that didn't necessarily mean they would run.

If his time in Spain with the guerrilleros had taught him anything it was that you didn't have to meet the enemy head-on to be effective. Havoc could be visited upon a foe in many ways, if the right strategy was employed. Hawkwood's strategy was based on the Iroquois understanding of forest warfare and the Americans' fear of native auxiliaries, which was why he'd told Tewanias and Cageaga to use their traditional weapons – tomahawks, clubs and knives – and that no quarter was to be given.

It was also why he'd wanted warriors armed with bows. Swift to deploy – an Iroquois warrior could launch fifteen arrows in the time it took to load a musket – the bow had the advantage of being a silent killer, capable of delivering death without warning. To the Americans, it was a weapon used by savages who lived beyond the borders of civilized men, who fought without honour, who treated their prisoners in ways too awful to mention. A bow, when added to an arsenal, could instil terror. And it had done just that.

Hawkwood had guessed that its use might also lull Quade into believing that his men, greater in number and armed with muskets and cold steel, were the superior force when compared to illiterate aboriginals whose weapons were those derived from wood and sinew.

And so it had proved, but it had been a ruse that could only be used once.

Quade, knowing the element of surprise had now been lost, would be reassessing the situation. He'd be calculating how many were arrayed against him and how best to retaliate. He would also be seething with rage that his plans had been thrown into disarray. Thus caution was liable to be thrown to the winds, giving way to impatience and rash decisions. Or so Hawkwood hoped.

From what he knew of the man, there was no way, having come this far, that Quade would simply scurry back to Plattsburg, tail between his legs. Knowing it was imperative that he got to Lacolle before word of his advance reached the garrison at Île aux Noix, he'd be intent on securing his goal.

So, with the fog starting to disappear, it wouldn't be long before he made his move. For Major Harlan Quade was a man with something to prove, a man whose career depended on the success of this mission. And there was no way he'd allow a paltry wooden bridge and a handful of ignorant savages to stand in his way.

# 16

As he followed Oneas down the snow-covered forest track, Lawrence wondered how and where his guide had learned to ride. There had been no horses in the village and yet, watching how the Mohawk controlled his mount, it had become clear this was one warrior who was at home in the saddle.

It had to be in the blood, he'd decided. Domesticated dogs traced circles when lying down because that was how their wolf ancestors had flattened vegetation to make their beds; the habit was inbred. Perhaps it was the same with the Mohawk. Maybe they were descended from a race of ancient horse lords? Given their range of skills, it would have been interesting to have had warriors of the Kanien'kehá:ka fighting alongside him in Spain. That would have given the French something to think about.

The fog had precluded all thoughts of hard galloping and with no familiar reference points Lawrence was unsure how far they were from their destination. They had to be close. They had passed over a creek a mile or so back; the impact of the horses' hooves on the bridge timbers had sounded like drumbeats as they had cantered across, even with the depth of the snow. A short distance further on, they had come across the first sign of military activity.

Initially, as they approached, it had been hard to make out the exact shape of the structure. Only as they slowed and drew closer and the fog parted before them did Lawrence realize what he was seeing.

Felled tree trunks; angled across the road as if they'd been borne aloft by some cataclysmic event and then deposited from a great height. The result was an abattis; a crude barrier constructed to deny vehicular access to attacking forces, which probably explained the lack of wheel marks earlier on. Any locals would have known about this deterrent and would have found an alternative route. An enemy transporting guns and wagons and other heavy equipment would be halted in its tracks until the barrier had been removed or destroyed. A properly constructed abattis, used in conjunction with a ditch and a gun battery, was a formidable rampart, easily capable of disrupting an advance. This one was a lot simpler, but it was nevertheless a very effective form of defence.

In order to pass they would have to guide the horses along the verge between the logs and the edge of the wood, rather as he and Hawkwood had had to do when negotiating the military road on their way to Whitehall. In doing so, Lawrence could see by the cuts in the timber that the trees had only recently been felled.

Beyond the defence work, the road lay open once more. It occurred to Lawrence that, if Quade was coming, if Hawkwood and Tewanias's warriors failed in their efforts to delay his advance, the log jam certainly would. Not for long, perhaps, but every second counted and the longer it took the column to reach Lacolle, the better. As they urged the horses on, he wondered if any more obstacles lay ahead.

The shot came out of nowhere.

Lawrence ducked as Oneas threw up his arms. At the sound of the second report, his horse let out a whinny and he felt the shudder as the ball thudded home. His mount stumbled then immediately recovered and he thought they were safe – until he leaned forward and the horse's front legs buckled. The next thing he knew, the road was coming up to meet him. Fearful that he might be struck by a flying hoof or crushed by the weight of the animal collapsing on top of him, there was little he could do save pull his feet from the stirrups and try to roll clear.

Any hopes that the snow might cushion his fall were displaced as soon as he hit the ground. There was no give in the surface at all. It was solid earth beneath snow. The musket slung across his shoulder didn't help, and when the stock caught the base of his spine as he landed, the pain of it knocked the breath from his body and brought tears to his eyes. Winded and half-stunned, for one terrible moment he wondered if he'd actually suffered permanent injury. When he found he could feel his arms and legs, relief surged through him.

Wincing as another stab of pain scooted across his lower back, he pushed himself off the snow. Oneas lay forty paces away. Remarkably, his horse had not run off. Instead, it was waiting only a few yards further on, trembling but unharmed. The fact that it had remained in attendance, as it had done when its previous master, Lieutenant Nevens, had taken his tumble, suggested it was army-trained and not intimidated by either gunfire or the loss of its rider.

Lawrence looked for the source of the shots. He ducked back down behind his mount's heaving flank as two figures emerged from the woods on the other side of Oneas' body: a white man and an Indian. The white man was dressed in a fur-lined buckskin coat and wide-brimmed hat. The Indian wore a similar coat but his head was bare, revealing a greying scalp lock. Both carried long guns and both were instantly familiar. It was the pair from Colonel Pike's head-quarters, the Oneida warrior and the individual whom Pike's fellow colonel had addressed as Amos. Lawrence swore softly. It looked as though he'd just found Quade's advance scouts.

A rattling sigh broke from his horse's mouth. The animal shuddered and then grew still. Across the snow, the two shooters advanced cautiously.

And Oneas' right arm moved.

To Lawrence, it looked as if the Mohawk was trying to raise himself. He did not succeed. Moving swiftly and silently, the Oneida warrior ran forward, pulled a knife from his waist, bent down, and drew the blade across Oneas' exposed throat.

As, gingerly, Lawrence eased the musket strap from his shoulder.

411

He fired as the Oneida rose to his feet. The ball struck the Indian in the upper chest and he was thrown backwards. The white man paused in a half crouch, as Lawrence tossed the musket aside and picked up the pistol he'd taken from his saddle holster. "Move an inch and I will shoot you dead."

Lawrence, ignoring the stabbing twinge in his back, wondered if the fall had reopened his other wound. His side felt damp, but that could have been from the snow.

The buckskin-clad man straightened. There was no expression of surprise, though when he looked at the body of his companion and then back at Lawrence and caught sight of Lawrence's moccasins, he frowned. As his gaze shifted to Lawrence's face, his eyes hardened. "You're a hard man to kill, Major."

Lawrence smiled grimly. "Not for want of trying, though, eh?" His pistol aimed at the bearded man's face, he walked forward. "Forgive me, we weren't formally introduced."

"Amos Walker. Captain."

"Your servant, sir," Lawrence said wryly. "Now, I'd be obliged if you'd drop the gun."

Walker looked at the gun in his hand and then up at Lawrence and gave a rueful smile. "It's empty. Didn't get a chance to reload. But then you'd guessed that; right?"

Lawrence wondered if he shouldn't remove the smile by simply shooting the man there and then, but at the back of his mind there hovered the thought that if he could save the shot he should do so. He wasn't sure why.

Walker shrugged and lowered the weapon to the ground. His eyes narrowed as they tracked the woods over Lawrence's shoulder. "Well, I guess this explains why my observers never reported back. No Hooper?"

"No," Lawrence said. "On your knees; hands behind your head."

Walker hesitated then did as he was told. "Ah, well, one dead out of two ain't bad."

Keeping the pistol aimed at the other man's chest, Lawrence hoped desperately that the surviving horse wasn't about to bolt. Its ears had pricked up and it had pawed the ground when he'd taken his shot, but to his relief, it had remained in place, allowing him to grasp the saddle horn with his left hand. Pain flared again and he wondered if he'd be able to lift himself up without falling flat on his back. He saw Walker's shoulders tense and knew the American was probably thinking the same thing.

Using the reins to guide the horse around so that its body was between Walker and himself, Lawrence gritted his teeth, and raised his left foot into the stirrup. Then, resting his right hand, which was still clasping the pistol, on the cantle, he hoisted himself up. His back protested but he could tell the pain was easing.

"Nicely done," Walker observed. "Now are you going to shoot me?"

Lawrence shook his head. "It is tempting. Believe me, it is, but I've seen more than enough killing for one week."

Without waiting for a response, he kneed the horse into motion.

Walker stared after him, then, moving quickly, he scooped up the musket and let out a sharp two-toned whistle.

Lawrence was already accelerating into a canter as the three painted, scalp-locked figures ran from the trees in front of him.

No time to think, only to act. Praying his mount would obey, he spurred the horse forward.

The nearest Oneida scout looked mesmerized by the half-ton of horse flesh bearing down upon him. As he fell beneath the hooves, Lawrence turned the pistol on the second attacker. There was hardly time to aim but he was too close to miss. The gun spoke and the Oneida spun away clutching his groin. The third warrior raised his carbine to his shoulder.

His discharged pistol now transformed into a dead weight, Lawrence employed it in the only way possible. He threw it. He knew there wasn't a chance in hell that it would hit its target from the back of a moving horse, but it was all he had left.

It missed, though not by much; passing close enough for the warrior to flinch and alter his aim for a second. As Lawrence galloped past, the Oneida threw up his carbine once more.

Lawrence heard the crack and felt the burn as the ball

shredded his sleeve and then he was clear and galloping. His heart flew.

As behind him, another report sounded.

It had taken Walker eleven seconds to re-load and his target was at the limit of the weapon's effective range when he fired. Through drifting smoke, he saw Lawrence duck and cursed as the fleeing horse and rider were swallowed up by loitering fog.

Lowering the gun, he moved quickly to the body of the warrior Lawrence had shot. He bent down and laid his hand on his friend's arm. Cornelius was a war captain and had been recruited by the Continental army back in the Revolution. His first scouting mission had been for General Sullivan during the '99 campaign to lay waste the Iroquois homeland.

Walker had been a lieutenant with George Read's 2nd New Hampshires when they'd met, at the battle of Newtown, where Cornelius had saved his life during Joseph Brant's counter-attack on the slopes above the Chemung River. They'd scouted together ever since, leading reconnaissance missions for the rebel army throughout the rest of the war. And now, with a fresh conflict having broken out between old enemies, they had resumed their duties, scouting enemy territory, working in advance of the main force, from Tippecanoe to Gananoque and from Queenston to Quebec.

When Cornelius's eyes blinked open, Walker gasped.

The Oneida chief frowned. Cautiously, he sat up and reached a hand to the back of his head. It came away bloody. He peered at it in mystification, then at Walker. His eyes widened. Grasping the gorget that hung round his neck, he stared at its engraved surface. The dent made by the musket ball was plain to see.

"Son of a bitch," Walker breathed as he realized what must have happened. Lawrence's shot had hit the gorget with sufficient force to knock Cornelius off balance but then, by a miracle, had glanced away. As Cornelius hit the ground, the back of his head had collided with whatever hard object lay covered by the snow beneath him. Walker looked. It was a small flat-topped rock. Droplets of blood patterned the snow that had settled on top of it.

He helped Cornelius to his feet. A red trickle ran from the

Oneida's scalp lock down on to the back of his neck. He ignored it. Both men turned as the surviving warrior who'd run from the trees approached, carbine in hand. He did not ask after Cornelius's health, but muttered under his breath, as though castigating himself for having missed his shot. His eyes moved to the body of the Indian Cornelius had dispatched with his knife, at the ruined throat and at the three decorated braids that sprouted from a four-inch square tuft of hair on the dead warrior's crown. Walker and Cornelius followed his gaze.

"Kanien'kehá:ka," Cornelius murmured softly, his lips curling with contempt.

Walker frowned. What, he wondered, was Lawrence doing in the company of a Mohawk?

As the crackle of musket fire came faintly from the south, all three men turned.

The column was under attack.

Bent low over the horse's neck, Lawrence could feel the blood trickling down his back.

*Walker, you bastard.*

The ball had hit him high on his right side, in the meat of his shoulder. The impact hadn't been that great. No more than if someone had struck him with a clenched fist. At first there had been only a slight numbness, but then, aggravated by the movement of the horse beneath him, the pain had started.

With his guide dead, there was no option but to stick to the road. Where he was in relation to his destination, he had no idea. He'd seen no signposts, though the snow could well have covered them. The woods remained thick and impenetrable on either side. There were no buildings, no farmsteads, just the snow and the forest. And then more forest.

With every movement, a spasm of pain shot through him. Each time, he grunted at the shock of it. His hands braced either side of the horse's withers, he pressed down, forcing his weight into the stirrups. It was all he could do to hang on. Every hoof thud was agony.

The end was not long in coming.

Lawrence knew his strength was failing and that his mount had sensed that all was not well. Cold was creeping into every pore of his body, from his legs to his back and from there to his arms, hands and fingers. It was becoming harder to concentrate. Even the horse's head was cast down, as if it had been made weary by the weight of the injured man on its back. Little by little, Lawrence could feel himself slipping away.

He'd tried compensating by adjusting his grip on the reins but each time he did that the horse had sensed his indecision. As a result, progress had slowed from a canter to a trot and finally to a plodding walk.

They were close to a standstill when he eventually relinquished his hold. He'd tried desperately to loop his arms around the horse's neck in an attempt to hang on, but as the animal turned its head and looked at him with its big brown eyes as if to query what it should do next, his strength finally gave out and he slid sideways out of the saddle and on to the unyielding ground below.

He lay there, unmoving, the snow wet against his cheek, vaguely aware of the horse standing over him, as if it was waiting for him to remount. He tried to push himself up but fell back. It was probably easier, he decided, not to move. It was certainly less painful. Sleep, he thought, would be a blessing. All he had to do was close his eyes and drift away. Why fight it? He felt the horse's warm muzzle on the back of his neck. In the same instant, there was a faint vibration in the ground beneath him.

Through half-closed eyes, Lawrence saw a shadow appear between the horse's legs. There was movement on the road and the sound of hoofbeats. A second shadow appeared behind the first, then another. The horse whickered. A voice called out; an order or an exclamation of warning. He couldn't tell which. The words were indistinct. A shaft of pain lanced down his back. He tried lifting his head, but the effort proved too much.

A pair of boots stepped into view, then a second set – black military-issue – along with the hem of a coat and the tip of a scabbard. Voices sounded, faint, the words no clearer than they had been the first time.

The boot-wearers made their way towards him, scuffing up snow. Someone bent down. Lawrence felt a hand on his shoulder. Pain flared. He tried to speak but all that came out of his mouth was a dry whisper.

Another voice spoke, close enough to him so that this time Lawrence heard every word. Words that pierced him like a knife.

"*Qu'avons-nous ici?*"

"*C'est un cheval Américain!*"

"*Il est blessé! Récupérez le chef de bataillon! Vite!*"

No! Lawrence thought as his exhausted brain absorbed what he was actually hearing. It wasn't possible! It couldn't be, not after all they'd been through. He tried to rise, to struggle, but strong hands held him down. A wave of despair swept over him at the thought that they had battled this far, overcoming obstacle after obstacle, to be so close to freedom.

Only to be taken by the Goddamned French.

Cageaga regarded the black paint smeared across Hawkwood's face and smiled wolfishly. "Like old times, little brother."

Cageaga's features were broken up by three horizontal black bands, across his jawline, nose and the ridge above his eyes. Tewanias's face was divided by two colours: red from chin to cheekbone, black from cheekbone to brow. The other warriors were similarly daubed. The reason for the paint was threefold; as notification that the men were on the war trail, to put fear into the enemy and to break up the shape of the face so that skin tones – most relevant in Hawkwood's case – were not visible against the darkness of the forest.

There were bloodstains on Cageaga's hands and wrists. Cageaga had led the assault on the van. The war club he carried across his shoulder was the same one that had killed Lieutenant Nevens and the Oneida warrior who'd been an inch away from removing Hawkwood's scalp. The club head still bore traces of the Oneida's and the lieutenant's blood, darkly visible beneath the new stains caused by the blood and brain matter that had leaked from the skulls of the dead troopers.

Hawkwood was glad Lawrence had not been there to see

417

Nevens' death or the attack. The major might well have rescinded his new-found admiration for Tewanias and his warriors had he witnessed the savagery that had been employed. Clubs and edged weapons caused hideous damage and Hawkwood had told Cageaga to employ them to good effect; an instruction the Mohawk war captain had obeyed to the letter, even to the taking of scalps, four of which now hung from the warriors' belts. If Quade wanted a war, Hawkwood intended to see to it that the bastard got one.

Cageaga touched Hawkwood's arm. "They come," he whispered softly.

Hawkwood looked behind him. It was unlikely the morning sun would break through to any great effect, but if it did, Hawkwood wanted it at their backs. Even low in the sky, its rays would be diffused and broken by the trees and, when reflected off the snow, would throw multiple shadows which, like the face paint, would help confuse what was surely an already unnerved enemy.

Oneas and Lawrence's departure meant they were now twelve. Engaging the column in a pitched battle, therefore, was out of the question. That would amount to facing Quade on his own terms, an option that was not only impractical but monumentally foolish, not to say suicidal. The column obviously possessed the greater firepower and in a face-to-face confrontation the Mohawk couldn't hope to prevail. But what they lacked in numbers they would make up for with stealth manoeuvrability and surprise.

Under the cover of the fog, Tewanias had recalled all but one of his warriors to the east side of the road and placed them some thirty paces inside the wood and roughly five paces apart. While it gave each man a view of the track, the trees provided cover, like arrow slits in a castle wall. The intention was that by firing and then moving swiftly to a new shooting stand, the troops would be fooled into believing there were more attackers than there actually were. That masquerade wouldn't last long – it couldn't – but until the realization set in, even if it took just minutes, the plan was simple: kill as many of the enemy as possible, starting with the officers and NCOs.

Hawkwood eased back the hammer on his musket. The fog had thinned considerably, revealing a restricted but advantageous view of the road and the bodies of the infantrymen strewn across it. He turned his eyes to where a phalanx of soldiers was setting off across the bridge.

Unless Quade was even more callous than anyone supposed, he would not march his men past the scene of the attack. To do so would mean the column would have to step either around or over the bodies. No commander in his right mind would order his men to do that. The likely scenario was that Quade would halt and deploy troops along the road to protect his flanks, thus allowing the wounded to be assessed and the dead consigned to collection by a burial party, which suited Hawkwood well, for it would present the Kanien'kehá:ka with their second killing field. It would, however, put the ambushers at greater risk, bringing them within closer range of the column's guns.

He kept his eyes on the bridge. The first troops had crossed the creek and were advancing cautiously, but with determination, in two single files, one on either side of the road.

Hawkwood glanced to his side. Cageaga was crouched over to his left, Tewanias to his right. Hawkwood could see a pulse beating along the line of Cageaga's throat. Beyond Tewanias, the rest of the warriors were well concealed within the trees.

Hawkwood looked for Quade. Two mounted officers rode behind the advance party but neither of them was the major. The likelihood was that Quade was holding position on the south side of the creek, awaiting word that the enemy had dispersed.

The forward troops arrived at the first body. At the sight of the bloodied corpse, a corporal stumbled away and vomited into the snow. As the advance party took up outward-facing positions along the edges of the road, fingering their weapons nervously, a squad of troopers moved in to check for signs of life.

Hawkwood, knowing there would be none, sensed movement to his left. Cageaga was regarding him expectantly. Hawkwood shook his head.

Not yet.

On the road, one of the troopers – possibly a surgeon's mate – turned to the mounted officers. The lead officer – a captain, probably, though his rank was not apparent from his coat – nodded brusquely, murmured something, and watched stone-faced as the bodies were lifted and deposited at the side of the track. The second officer glanced about nervously, scanning the wood. For a moment it seemed he was staring directly towards Hawkwood's position. Lowering his face and narrowing his eyes so that the whites were reduced in size, Hawkwood remained still. The officer's gaze moved on.

As soon as the bodies had been removed from the line of march, the lead officer raised his hand to indicate that the column should proceed. The troops fell back into step; even from a distance, they looked relieved to be on the move.

Hawkwood waited until the first section had passed. Only as the mounted pair drew abreast of his position, did he turn to Tewanias. Acknowledging the signal, Tewanias cupped a palm to his lips and with the tip of his tongue pressed against the roof of his mouth, emitted a string of short, staccato bird calls.

The first shot came from within the forest on the west side of the road. Even as the lead officer began to topple, another shot sounded and a second stab of flame and a billow of powder smoke appeared a couple of yards to the right of the first report. The men in the column were already turning towards the threat; a move which left their backs unguarded.

Using the trunk he was crouched behind as a brace, Hawkwood sighted and fired. The shot took the second officer between the shoulder blades, pitching him from the saddle.

And the Mohawks' guns began to speak.

A sergeant and two privates went down beneath the first volley. Hawkwood, already reloading, counted under his breath. "One . . . two . . . three . . ."

He was at four when the second volley crashed out.

Two more troopers went down.

Hawkwood and Tewanias had split the warriors into three groups. By alternating fire, it gave each group the opportunity to move position and reload while the others took their turn to shoot. Allowing time for reloading, three to four shots every five to six seconds were never going to persuade the column to turn tail, but it was one way of maintaining a rate of fire. Not a fast or a heavily concentrated one, admittedly, but the consistency would cause some of the troops to keep their heads down. At best, it was only a delaying tactic, but if it stymied the column's advance even by as little as a yard it would have served its purpose.

Hawkwood had borrowed the decoy trick from the Spanish guerrilleros and had kept one warrior – Effa – with two long guns, the second taken from one of the dead soldiers, concealed on the side of the road opposite his main ambush force. At a given signal – in this instance, Tewanias's bird call – the decoy had opened fire, drawing the enemy's attention, causing them to turn and leave their backs exposed, perfect targets for Hawkwood and the warriors who were lying in wait behind them.

The trap sprung, the first Mohawk shooters had immediately shifted positions, but by this time the troopers, realizing they'd been duped, were returning shots, aiming at the dissipating powder bursts. The forest resounded with the sound of gunfire. Smoke clouds swirled along the edge of the road. Musket balls whined and ricocheted through the trees, thudding into trunks and shredding leaves.

The third group fired. Hawkwood did not look for the outcome but braced himself against a tree, took aim on a trooper and squeezed the trigger. The trooper dropped. Moving quickly to his new stand, Hawkwood withdrew a fresh cartridge from his pocket, bit into it and felt a tug on his arm as a musket ball caught the sleeve of his coat.

Where the hell are you, Quade?

The answer came as the forest to the rear of Hawkwood's position erupted in a crescendo of flame and smoke. Hawkwood pivoted, feeling the pressure of air against his skin as another ball thrummed past his right cheek and thudded into the tree beside him. He saw a warrior – it might have been Niah – jerk and spin away, his black-painted features misting red as a ball exited his skull.

Quade! You clever bastard!

The major, it seemed, had laid a trap of his own.

Sensing that another ambush was a distinct possibility, Quade, using what was left of the fog as cover, must have dispatched men across the creek somewhere downstream; at which point, all they'd had to do was wait until the ambush party gave away its position. It explained the overt nervousness of the two mounted officers, who'd known their assignment had been to draw the enemy's fire.

Hawkwood spat the ball into the barrel of his musket and ducked as a fresh broadside, this time from the road, ripped into the trees around him. A cry came from his left as another of Tewanias's warriors – Alak – fell back, venting blood as a ball tore through his throat. Withering fire was now coming from two sides.

Cursing, Hawkwood tapped the butt of the musket against the ground to seat the ball and was about to swing the weapon up when a hand touched his shoulder. He heard Tewanias's voice in his ear. "Hatskwi! We must move, now!"

Hawkwood took stock. It was hard to see how many uniformed shapes were advancing as the smoke through which they were moving was almost as impenetrable as the fog that had gone before, but it was safe to assume that Quade would have calculated the number of ambushers from the shots fired and deployed his men accordingly; in other words, in a significant number.

Quade's mistake had been in failing to prevent his front rank from firing too soon.

A musket could propel a ball more than two hundred and fifty yards, but its effective range was only eighty or ninety at best. Judging by the location of the smoke, the troopers were beyond that. If they'd had the patience to hold their fire for another thirty paces, their surprise would have been complete. As it was, in their haste to engage, instead of cutting off an escape route, they had, inadvertently, provided one, by virtue of the fact it would take them some time to reload, giving their quarry an extra few seconds.

As Tewanias signalled to his men to pull back, Hawkwood raised his musket again and looked for a final target, to keep the troopers' heads down. Unable to get a clear shot at the soldiers in the wood, he turned back to the road, sighted on a corporal shaking powder into his pan, and fired. As the corporal fell away, his hand clutching his half-primed weapon, Cageaga clicked his tongue in satisfaction and then flinched as a ball smacked into a snow-laden bough inches from his feathered topknot. "Come, Mat-huwa! The smoke will hide us!"

*From your lips to God's ear*, Hawkwood thought.

But either God wasn't listening or He'd turned a deaf ear, because shouts went up the second they broke from cover, drowned instantly by the crash of musketry, much closer than before.

As he watched a warrior whose name he did not know spin away, it struck him that, in the furore, fewer shots had come from the column. With smoke hampering their aim, the troops on the road had been shooting mostly at shadows and while a couple of shots had found their mark – possibly more by accident than design – the majority had struck foliage. As a result they had clearly become worried about shooting their own men by mistake, a fear that was not reciprocated by the troops in the forest, who, from the noise that marked their positions, were spread out in a longer line than their first volley had suggested, and closing fast.

"There, Major! The bastards are running! See?"

Quade, sword in hand, followed his lieutenant's pointing finger. His head was throbbing from the sound of the guns, for the soldiers were firing at will now and the air was heavy with the smell of burnt sulphur and saltpetre, so much so that his eyes had begun to water. His leg was beginning to ache like a bitch as well. But then a gap in the smoke allowed him to catch a glimpse of a shadowy form slipping between the trees ahead of him and his pulse quickened.

Relief surged within him, for there had been a moment, wading across the icy creek, when he'd wondered if his gamble to draw the ambushers into his trap would work. Now, with the enemy in disarray – and secure in the knowledge that they were indeed few in number – he was able to breathe once more. To judge from the exchange of fire between the ambushers and the troops in the column, the strategy had cost him a number of men, but their sacrifice had been for the greater good. With the ambush foiled, the advance could continue unhindered. Lacolle was only a short step away and victory remained within their grasp, though the element of surprise might well have been lost if the sound of the gunfire had reached the ears of the British. Quade tried not to think about that as he addressed the lieutenant at his side.

"Tell the sergeant to keep the men in open order. Extend the line. We must drive them towards the road. We will hem them in there."

"Sir!"

A shot rang out close by. Quade turned to see a trooper bearing corporal's stripes standing a few yards away, pointing his smoking musket at a crumpled form in a buckskin coat lying by his feet. There was a wound in the corpse's belly, which had been leaking blood on to the snow, and a hole in the painted forehead.

Turning, the corporal caught Quade's eye and grinned as he reached into his pack for another cartridge. "Don't look so fierce now, Major, do they?"

Quade stared down at the mess that, only seconds before, had been a man's face. It was unlikely, he thought, that anyone would look fierce with holes in the front and back of his skull, be they white man or Indian. He looked away as someone unleashed a shot at a fleeing shape and saw a scalp-locked figure throw up its arms and pitch forward.

*Like ninepins!* he thought, but turned back when he heard the corporal say, "Ah, Jesus," in a mixture of anguish and disgust.

424

The corporal was nudging something away from the dead warrior's belt with the muzzle of his gun. A bloody strip of skin with hair attached. The hair was sandy-coloured with streaks of grey running through it.

The corporal said bleakly, "I think it's Sergeant Carmody, sir."

Part of him, at any rate, Quade thought.

Carmody had been the sergeant in charge of the van, one of the soldiers who hadn't made it back across the bridge.

"Murdering bastards," the corporal muttered. He turned. "What should we do, Major?"

Quade assumed the corporal was referring to the scalp. It was on the tip of his tongue to reply that there was little they could do as the late Sergeant Carmody had no further need of his hair. Instead, he said, "We exterminate them, Corporal; as many as we can. That's how you deal with vermin."

As he followed Tewanias's weaving figure, Hawkwood counted the number of warriors running with them.

Some of Tewanias's men had managed to lay down covering fire as they'd made their escape, but with the troops closing in behind, not everyone had had time to reload and so their shots had soon petered out, leaving their backs vulnerable to their pursuers. What had begun as an ambush had fast become a desperate rearguard action and Hawkwood didn't have to look back to know that their trail was so obvious that a blind man could follow it.

All told, they appeared to be four men down; a sizeable toll, and not just for their party. Gaanundata was a small village. Even the loss of four fighters would leave a scar; one that would take a long time to heal. Born into a culture where, notwithstanding their expertise, adult males were, by tradition, full-time providers and only part-time warriors, it said a lot for Tewanias's authority that the survivors had decided not to cut their losses and leave Hawkwood to face the column on his own – though they would have been within their rights to do so.

Another flurry of reports sounded and he ducked. Looking

around him, no one appeared to be hit, which made him wonder if the troops had either lost sight of them or were just poor shots. His throat constricted when he saw what appeared to be smoke ahead. His first thought was that somehow the enemy had managed to outflank them. But then he realized, as the ground turned to porridge beneath him, that it wasn't smoke at all but mist congregating over water. And it wasn't Quade's men who'd cut off their escape route; Nature had provided her own inimitable barrier.

Only quick thinking by one of Tewanias's men prevented Hawkwood from being sucked into the bog. He was up to his knees and going down when the nearest warrior to him – Chohajo – thrust out his war bow, allowing Hawkwood to grasp the tip so that he could be pulled to safety. As his feet found firmer ground and he caught his breath, it struck him that Lawrence would have appreciated the irony of the situation after his own experience during their crossing of the Saranac.

All humorous thought quickly evaporated when he saw what lay before them.

With pockets of mist drifting across its surface like steam, it was impossible to tell how far the mire extended or which areas were solid and which were swamp. The fact that the cold had not penetrated the ground to the extent that it had become safe to walk upon was a warning not to be ignored. Had he struggled, he'd likely have sunk in a lot deeper. Attempting to cross such a treacherous area was asking for trouble.

Tewanias grasped Hawkwood's arm. "This way, Mat-huwa!"

We're being herded, Hawkwood realized when he saw the direction in which Tewanias was leading them. He saw then just how well Quade had played the game, forcing them towards the road and the column's waiting guns.

Hawkwood thought about the road. Quade would have been briefed on the terrain before leaving Plattsburg. He'd have known about the swamp as a place to avoid. All he'd needed to do was drive Hawkwood and Tewanias's men towards it, knowing they'd be forced to make a detour, with only two directions available to them: east, which would place them at the mercy of Quade's extended right flank; or west, into the path of the advancing troops. This was the option Tewanias had chosen.

*Because he knows that if we can get to the road first,* Hawkwood thought, *we can make it. Maybe.*

But even as the thought formed he saw Tewanias raise a hand. Every man froze. Hawkwood looked towards the trees ahead and the shadows within them.

*Soldiers from the column. They've got there first, damn it.*

There was a crack and a bright spit of flame. The report was followed by two more, so close together as to sound almost like a single detonation. Hawkwood threw himself behind a stump. From the corner of his eye he saw the warrior called Aqueia sag, a red flower blooming across his chest.

The other Mohawk took cover. Save for Tewanias, who, for perhaps half a second, stood as if nailed in place. For one awful moment, it seemed to Hawkwood that the war captain had been hit. But then, before his astonished gaze, as if launched from a sling shot, Tewanias began to run, not for shelter but towards the shooters.

*God's teeth!* Hawkwood thought wildly, but then he realized that Tewanias had been counting the shots. And as the surviving Mohawk rose as one behind their leader, Hawkwood was up and running, too, musket in one hand, tomahawk in the other.

Wolves were at their most dangerous when cornered. Therefore, despite the troops' exuberance at having located the enemy, there was still an understandable reluctance in attempting to track the Indians in their natural lair – the forest. Their decision to opt for firepower rather than a hand-to-hand confrontation had resulted in a gap opening up between the chasers and those being chased, with a consequent lull in the shooting. The sudden reports, therefore, were as good as a lit beacon.

*Yes!* Quade thought exultantly, when he heard the gunfire. *The column! We have them!*

Hurriedly, the major sheathed his sword. Drawing his pistol, he summoned his men to him and raced towards the sound of the shots.

Hawkwood knew he had only seconds to cover the ground before the shooter he was running at could fire off a second shot. Madness, but he ran anyway.

He was fifteen paces short when the brim of the shooter's hat lifted and his features came into view. It was Pike's scout, Amos. The man who, if Lawrence's observation was correct, had sent the Oneida trackers after them with orders to kill.

He saw the scout mouth the word, "You!" as the long gun's muzzle came swinging round. The bore looked about a mile wide.

Hawkwood hurled the tomahawk, aware as he did so of Tewanias veering to one side and curving his war club towards the Indian to the scout's right. The third shooter – also an Indian – was turning, knife drawn, to face the warriors rushing in behind.

The scout's reactions were commendably fast. As the hatchet left Hawkwood's hand, Walker twisted aside and threw the musket barrel across his body to deflect the spinning blade. The threat countered, he swung the long gun down and pulled back on the trigger.

There was no finesse in Hawkwood's attack, only brute strength and momentum. His rising shoulder hit the musket barrel as Walker fired. The force of the charge swept Walker off his feet and carried both men to the ground, Walker's gun trapped between them. As the scout's head went back, Hawkwood rammed his knee up into Walker's groin. Immediately the scout's grip on his musket loosened, enough for Hawkwood to slam the butt of his own gun down against the bridge of the scout's nose as hard as he could. A second blow was unnecessary but he followed through anyway. Walker died with the look of surprise etched on to his bearded, pulverized face.

Fearful for Tewanias, Hawkwood spun round to find the Mohawk captain standing over his opponent. The facial tattoos

428

and the nose- and ear-rings identified him as the warrior who'd been present in Pike's hut. He was alive and trying to rise, but his eyes were glazed in pain. The bone in his right elbow – struck by Tewanias's war club – jutted from his skin and blood was flowing from the back of his right leg where the tendon had been severed just behind the knee.

Tewanias held his war club loosely in his hand, his chest rising and falling. As Hawkwood rose to his feet, Tewanias hammered the club head against the defeated warrior's temple, killing him instantly. Then, quickly, drawing his knife, he laid the club aside, squatted, and ran the knife blade around the feathered scalp lock. Ripping it free with a howl of triumph, he held it aloft before sheathing the knife, retrieving his club and tucking the bloody trophy into his belt.

Hawkwood turned to where the body of the second Oneida warrior lay face down in the snow. Tewanias's men had claimed their revenge. Clubbed and then hacked into ribbons, the corpse looked like something left on a butcher's block.

Hawkwood picked up his tomahawk and cleaned it of snow. Tewanias caught his eye. Words weren't necessary. They had been lucky; there had only been three shooters. But where were the rest?

And then Cageaga looked behind him and hissed, "They are coming! Run!"

It had taken Quade only a second to realize it wasn't the column. The lack of sustained gunfire had told him that.

So who . . .?

Then he heard the howl.

Quade's hair stood on end. Primal, more animal than human, the sound matched the war whoops heard when the van had come under attack at the bridge. Quade didn't like to think what it might mean.

Moments later, he came upon the bodies.

Staring wordlessly down at Amos Walker's stove-in face – partly in horror, partly in shock – the thought that ran through his mind was that at least the scout's corpse had not been mutilated, unlike the remains of the two Oneida warriors who lay sprawled alongside him. Not that it would have made much difference, given the damage that had been inflicted upon the man's skull. From what Quade could see, there had been no attempt by Walker's attacker to stun or incapacitate. The blow – or blows – had been delivered with but one purpose: to extinguish life.

Another thought then struck him. Why only three bodies? Walker's party had included four Oneida scouts. Where were the other two?

Native irregulars were, in Quade's experience, prone to retreat when they knew the odds were stacked against them. As they would have regarded Walker – or, more likely, Cornelius – as their leader, the others had probably felt disinclined to continue the fight once those two were killed. Had they taken advantage of the surrounding cover and slipped off into the woods? If so, then God rot their cowardly black hearts.

A chorus of fresh gunshots interrupted his thoughts, followed by the lieutenant's excited voice.

"We have them in sight again, Major! You were right! They're making for the road!"

The lieutenant's observation was cut short as more brisk reports echoed through the trees. Quade heard a nearby voice exclaim loudly, "Christ, Jed, you couldn't hit a barn door!"

Quade recognized the corporal with whom he'd exchanged words earlier.

"God damned misfire!" the shooter protested.

"Move aside, then! Let the dog see the rabbit!"

Then Quade heard the corporal say in a puzzled tone, "Damn! I do believe that's a white man . . ."

Quade stared off to where the corporal was squinting down the barrel of his gun. In a slight dip in the terrain he saw several figures running in a crouch across a clearing, their zig-zagging forms dark against the snow. The significance of the corporal's words was immediately apparent, for one of the trailing figures was dressed in what appeared to be an army greatcoat. Taller than his native companions, even from a distance, there was something uncannily familiar about the figure's bearing.

*No!* Quade thought. *Not possible!*

He pivoted, thrusting the pistol back in his belt. Caught by surprise, the corporal could only gape as the major ripped the musket from his hands and swung it to his shoulder.

And fired.

# 17

Hawkwood did not look around, for the shot had sounded no different to any of the others that had bracketed them as they ran, but when he heard the muffled exclamation, he turned quickly.

"I am hit, Mat-huwa," Cageaga gasped. He sounded vaguely surprised as he tipped forward into Hawkwood's arms.

Hawkwood felt liquid warmth against his right palm. He lifted it from Cageaga's back and found the blood. "It's only a scratch."

Cageaga groaned and gave a twisted smile. "You are a poor liar, little brother. You always were."

"And you talk too much, old man. Save your breath."

A shout went up behind them. Hawkwood looked towards the source in time to see a dark-clad figure, long gun in hand.

Quade.

And then the smoke closed around the bastard and he was gone. But there would be others in attendance. Awkwardly, Hawkwood looped his own gun over his back and, taking Cageaga's carbine, he placed an arm around the wounded man's shoulder. "On your feet."

Cageaga groaned and then coughed. Pain contorted his features. A line of pink froth oozed from between his lips and trickled down the corner of his mouth.

"Get up!" Hawkwood said sharply.

Cageaga grimaced and then spat. "I can taste blood. I think my insides are bleeding."

"Hold on to me," Hawkwood said. "We can make it together."

"To where, little brother?"

Hawkwood's stomach contracted. It had been a simple question, yet Cageaga was right. The blood he was coughing up indicated that the ball could well have penetrated a lung, in which case the wound was fatal.

In the Peninsula, there had been times when Hawkwood had left injured men behind, knowing they'd have a better chance of survival if they were taken prisoner and cared for by French surgeons the same way that, by unwritten agreement, French wounded were treated by British field surgeons. In the current theatre, however, no such etiquette would apply. A rabid dog stood a better chance of survival than a captured Mohawk, especially one who'd led a scalping party against American troops. Confirmation of that had been the isolated, single musket shots that had sounded behind them. They meant Quade's men had found wounded warriors and were administering their own version of the last rites.

He looked for the other Mohawk but they were no longer in view. Only the tracks of their moccasins were visible. A ball thudded into an adjacent stump. Another quick glance over his shoulder revealed a glimpse of a blue uniform jinking through a break in the trees, then another, and another, accompanied by a flash of scarlet collar.

Quade?

When he'd glanced back the first time, the major's stance had made it safe to assume that he, Hawkwood, had been in Quade's sights when he'd pulled the trigger and not Cageaga. Which begged the question: how long had he known that Hawkwood was alive and a participant in – if not the instigator of – the ambush at the bridge?

It would explain his relentless pursuit. Any other officer, having seen the enemy routed, would have pressed on with the prime objective, which was not to hunt down ambushers but to capture a blockhouse. But Quade, still smarting from their previous encounters, would know that if the sound of gunfire had carried as far as the British outpost there was a high probability his mission had been severely compromised. Now that he knew Hawkwood was the disruptor of his plan, he'd want to settle the score personally.

Well, the bastard would just have to wait his turn, along with every other mother's son.

"Up, damn it!" Hawkwood urged as he took Cageaga's weight.

Another shout came from behind them. Risking a look over his shoulder, Hawkwood saw a shako-capped form, musket raised.

Oh, Christ, he thought.

And then there was a crack and the soldier fell.

Hawkwood turned to see two figures running forward through a curl of smoke. One was Tewanias, the other was Kodjeote.

"You were told to stay close to your brother!" Cageaga gasped.

"Then you would be dead," Tewanias said, as Kodjeote looped his discharged carbine over his back and hooked an arm under Cageaga's other shoulder. With Tewanias protecting their backs, Hawkwood and the young Mohawk half-carried, half-dragged the wounded warrior into the trees.

Quade, his mind reeling, his shoulder buffeted by the musket's recoil, swore savagely as the four figures disappeared from view.

*Hooper? How in the name of Christ . . .?*

Spinning, he tossed the musket back to its owner, who was staring down at his dead comrade in shock and disbelief. The ball had entered the trooper's right eye before he'd got a chance to fire, leaving a fist-sized hole in the back of his skull and scattering brain matter in a wide arc. A stained and battered shako lay in the snow several feet away.

*Hooper!* Quade thought again as he took a handkerchief from his sleeve and wiped the trooper's blood from his cheek. Bloody Hooper! Even with what had looked like streaks of dirt across his face, Quade had recognized him. What the hell did it take to kill the bastard?

Though it probably explained Walker's death, he reasoned. It had to have been Hooper who'd killed the scout. Had it been one of Hooper's companions, Walker's scalp would have been taken.

"Well, I have him cornered now, by God!" muttered Quade, mentally consulting the map. If his recollection was accurate, the road wasn't that far. The creek couldn't be much more than half a mile back and they were moving in the right direction, so the road had to be just to the left of them. And the enemy's tracks were leading the way.

"Move!" Quade barked. "With me!"

Scooping up the dead trooper's primed musket and with his troops at his shoulder, he set off in energetic pursuit.

Stealth was no longer a factor, for either the hunters or the hunted. While Quade's men might not have been banging drums or blowing horns, their intention was clearly to flush their prey, like boar from a thicket, towards the road and into the path of the advancing column.

A sucking sound came from the back of Cageaga's throat. "If you carry me, you cannot outrun them. You will all die or you will be captured. To become a prisoner of the Yan-kees would be worse than death." Cageaga's fingers found Hawkwood's wrist. "I will be dead before they take me. Your war is yet to be fought. Go now!"

"No," Hawkwood said again.

About to respond, Cageaga coughed. Another droplet of blood broke from between his pressed lips.

Kodjeote and Tewanias looked at Hawkwood in mute appeal. While foliage could provide temporary concealment, it was no protection against musket fire. They had to move, before the jaws of Quade's trap closed upon them.

Or, failing that, find somewhere to make a stand.

But to make a stand, you needed something solid at your back and Hawkwood couldn't see a damned thing that came close to fitting that category.

Except . . .

He stared. There was something there, through the trees. What it was, he couldn't make out exactly, but it had caught his eye in the same way the chimney of the ruin where he and Lawrence had warmed themselves had trapped his attention: by not quite fitting in with its surroundings.

And then an image arose of another time and another place – a small hilltop village in Portugal called Vimeiro and the defences placed across the narrow roads leading to it – and he realized what he might be looking at. Quickly he drew Tewanias's attention. The war captain frowned and then saw what Hawkwood was alluding to. His chin lifted. "Ea!"

In the next instant Tewanias was calling his remaining warriors to him and they were half-running, half-stumbling – not away from the edge of the wood, but towards it.

They were one hundred paces ahead of the column's front markers when they broke from the trees.

Close to, the abattis looked less like a defensive wall and more like a stockade that had collapsed under the weight of snow piled upon it. But right then, Hawkwood would have settled for an upturned rum cask if it helped provide cover.

It took a second for the troops in the column to react, possibly because some in the first rank had thought they might be Quade's men and so had not opened fire immediately. This gave Hawkwood and the Mohawk the few extra yards they needed. It also gave Effa – the decoy – the opportunity he had been waiting for to rejoin his fellow warriors. Bursting from the trees on the other side of the road, he sprinted towards them, carbine in hand.

And as the cry from the soldiers went up, the shooting began.

Effa staggered but recovered and continued, blood running from the wound in his leg, stippling the snow behind him. Hawkwood and Kodjeote, their arms still linked around Cageaga's shoulders were bunched together and so presented the most tempting target. They were ten paces from safety when Hawkwood felt the strike high up on his left arm, propelling him forward so that he almost fell into Cageaga's path. For a moment, Kodjeote had the weight of two wounded men hanging from him, but then as Hawkwood regained his balance, Tewanias grabbed his collar and with musket rounds striking the ground about them, they threw themselves down behind the log pile.

Breathing hard, Hawkwood picked himself up and peered over the top of the nearest trunk. The shooters had paused to reload while the soldiers behind them were moving up quickly to fill the gaps in the line, though none seemed prepared to engage in a full-frontal assault, which gave the Mohawk valuable seconds in which to reload as well.

Pain bloomed through Hawkwood's left bicep and shoulder and he sensed the blood seeping down the inside of his sleeve. When he tried forming a fist, it felt as though someone had just stuck a red-hot poker through his flesh. He examined his coat and saw the blood-soaked gash in the material, indicating the ball had scored rather than penetrated his flesh. There was nothing he could do in the meantime, though, except grit his teeth and bear it; after all, it wasn't as if a field surgeon was going to put in an appearance. Awkwardly, he fumbled in his pouch for a fresh cartridge.

Lawrence should have made it to the British lines by now. But would there be time to marshal a defence? Though it seemed aeons, the initial ambush back at the bridge had been only an hour ago. And since then, what had they achieved? The invading force remained intent on capturing its objective, whereas Hawkwood's war band had lost half its number. Tucking in his neck as musket balls struck the trunks and cut through the air around them, he wondered whether they'd succeeded in putting so much as a dent in the Americans' plan. Had the entire errand been nothing more than a waste of good men?

Their aim had been to distract Quade from his course by nipping at the column's flanks for as long as possible. They had achieved only a modicum of success. Quade had lost officers and NCOs, but the ensuing disruption to the chain of command had not been enough to stem the assault.

Which left Hawkwood one of seven men – three of whom

were nursing wounds – attempting to hold the line against four hundred.

But as redoubts went, this was better than some he'd had to defend. With the swamp only a short throw to their left, the abattis had been well sited. Assuming there was marshland on the opposite side of the road too, they were unlikely to be outflanked. An attack would have to come from the front.

"You are wounded, Mat-huwa!" Tewanias said, alarmed.

"It's only a scratch," Hawkwood heard a voice beside him say. He saw Cageaga smile weakly.

Hawkwood shook powder into his musket's pan. He had four cartridges left. Tewanias and the others were no doubt equally low on ammunition.

*So we'd better make what we have count.*

Though, he knew, even as he made the promise, that the chances of keeping up a sustained rate of fire were non-existent. There would be an opportunity for perhaps one re-load before they were over run because by then their muskets would probably have become fouled with use anyway.

A hand touched his arm. He looked to his side and was astonished to see Cageaga hauling himself up.

"My gun, little brother. I may not be able to run, but I am not yet dead."

Wordlessly, knowing better than to argue, Hawkwood passed him the carbine.

"Good." Cageaga checked the load. Satisfied, he raised the gun – wincing as he did so – on to the top of a log and sighted along the barrel. Accentuated by the black paint, his eyes glittered like coals.

"Now," he murmured, bloody spittle landing across his chin, "let them come."

This time when he heard the reports, Quade knew it had to be the column. Powder bursts, like exploding puffballs, were visible through the trees. Gripping the musket, he plunged towards them.

Not wishing to run into crossfire, Quade emerged on to the

road some yards behind the forward skirmish line. He looked for Captain van Roos, the officer he'd left in charge of the column, but he was nowhere to be seen. Neither were any enemy bodies, Quade noted, with a growing sense of misgiving. He'd hoped for at least one or two. Hooper's among them, preferably, but any of his Indian friends would have sufficed.

He saw van Roos' lieutenant hurrying towards him, a sergeant at his shoulder. The lieutenant's name was Dettweiler. It was evident he was relieved to see Quade, but it was just as apparent that he was the conveyor of bad news. He straightened and touched the peak of his shako in hasty salute, while eyeing the musket in Quade's hand.

"Well?" Quade's eyes went unerringly to the bloodstains down the front of the lieutenant's jacket.

It was as he'd expected. Upon re-crossing the bridge and engaging with the enemy, the column had taken additional losses. Captain van Roos had been among those killed in the first exchange. The dead also included a sergeant and five troopers. Three men, including Lieutenant Smalley from the 6th Regiment, had received wounds. It was the captain's blood on the front of Dettweiler's tunic. The lieutenant had held the captain as he'd died.

"Tell me you at least got *some* of the bastards," Quade snapped.

A nerve twitched along the lieutenant's jaw. An observant man might have interpreted the reflex not as a measure of worry but as the manifestation of contempt towards a senior officer who was prepared to show more interest in the fate of the ambush party than the welfare of his own soldiers. Quade appeared not to notice.

"I regret they struck the road ahead of us, Major. But we do have them pinned down."

*Christ Jesus!* Quade thought. *Must I do everything myself?*
"Where?"

Staring through the smoke to where the lieutenant was pointing, he saw the abattis for what it was and subdued the impulse to scream out loud. There'd been no mention of that in the report on the British defences, which could only mean it had been erected in the last few days by the Crown forces as they'd retreated from the frontline into their winter burrows. Why the hell hadn't Walker and his scouts or the outriders brought word about the wretched thing? Unless Walker had been on his way to report when he'd been killed. And, come to think of it, where *were* the outriders?

Quade swore beneath his breath. He resisted the urge to look at his watch, knowing they should have been entering Lacolle. By now the blockhouse would have been in sight and within his reach, if it hadn't been for that Goddamned Hooper.

He wondered where Lawrence had got to. Had he missed him in the woods? Was he trapped behind the abattis with the others? Well, he could bloody die with them, in that case.

Quade stared again at the barrier. *I can do this*, he thought desperately. *And if I can rid myself of Hooper at the same time, that'll be two birds with one stone. Three, if you include his compatriot.*

He turned to Dettweiler. "How many are there?"

The lieutenant looked beyond Quade's shoulder. "Seven, sir, as far as we can judge. Six hostiles and a white man, though we had to look twice as the fellow appears to be wearing war paint. Sergeant Brody here believes the natives are Mohawk, by their markings. We think three of them may be wounded, including the white fellow."

*It's not all bad news, then*, Quade thought.

No mention of a second white man, though. He wondered if that meant the Oneida had caught Lawrence and killed him. One could but hope. But that led to a more pertinent question: how, in the name of Hades, did Hooper come to be travelling with a band of Mohawk? Yet another enigma to add to what was fast becoming a lengthy list.

"Only seven? Why haven't you attacked?" Quade demanded, eyeing the troops, most of whom were being held in formation, save for the skirmishers who had found cover along the edge of the trees from where they could watch and await further orders and direct fire as necessary.

"We were awaiting your return, sir."

*To lead the charge, you mean*, Quade thought. *Against seven men?*

He searched for signs of guile but Dettweiler's face remained maddeningly neutral, as did the sergeant's.

*I do not have their respect*, Quade realized; the revelation forming a hollow pit in his stomach. He turned towards the abattis. The shooting had died away. The enemy were not engaging either. Saving their shots, Quade deduced. Then another possibility struck him. Maybe they want to parley?

Lieutenant Dettweiler broke into his thoughts. "Your orders, Major?"

Quade turned to the sergeant and passed him the musket. "Find a home for that and tell the skirmishers to prepare."

"Sir?"

"We're going to put the bastards out of their misery. It's what you do with wounded animals. And when that's done, we will resume our mission. We will march to Lacolle with all dispatch and take their Goddamned blockhouse before the morning is out."

The sergeant frowned but responded, "Yes, sir. Very good, sir."

Quade saw what looked suspiciously like an expression of doubt pass over the lieutenant's face. As the sergeant moved out of earshot, he fixed Dettweiler with a cold eye. "Something on your mind, Lieutenant?"

Dettweiler hesitated then drew himself up. "Permission to speak freely, Major?"

Quade nodded curtly. "Out with it."

"It's just that the sounds of our exchanges may have carried. It's possible the British now know we're coming."

"And . . .?" Quade stared at him for several seconds. "Are you implying we should turn back?"

"Sir, I—" the lieutenant's voice faltered.

"Because that's what it sounds like," Quade said, knowing there was never going to come a time when he would admit he'd been having the same thought. Not now that he had Hooper in his sights.

Dettweiler shifted uncomfortably. He knew there was no point in retracting the statement; he'd already committed himself. "I'm sorry, sir," he said stiffly, "but I believe I would be remiss in my duty if I did not remind the major of the losses we've taken during this morning's engagements – at least two dozen men killed or wounded."

Quade raised an eyebrow. "Remiss in your duty? Really? Well, perhaps, Lieutenant, it would be remiss of me not to issue you a reminder of the penalty for questioning the orders of a senior officer."

Dettweiler coloured. "Sir, you misunderstand. I'm not questioning your orders, I am merely—"

"Drawing my attention to the casualty list? Yes, well, I thank you for your insight, Lieutenant. You may consider your duty done. And while I share your concern regarding our dead and wounded, you seem to have overlooked the fact that we are at war. And in war, losses are, sadly, inevitable. We will, therefore, proceed as ordered. We've been entrusted with this mission by Colonel Pike. I do not intend to disappoint him. Do you?"

Dettweiler, stung by Quade's accusation and with his resolve wavering, was given no time to reply.

"I ask you this," continued Quade, "do you suppose Captain van Roos and Captain Carradine would want us to turn back?"

*Quite possibly*, Dettweiler thought. Instead he said carefully, "No, sir."

Quade jabbed a finger. "Indeed. We thrashed the Limeys once and, by God, we can do it again. Only this time, it'll be permanent. This time, we'll sweep them off the whole damned continent! You say there are, what, *seven* hostiles? Damn it, man, we're sixty times their number! I doubt they've more than twenty rounds between them. It'll be like an elephant stepping on an ant. Our armies have suffered enough embarrassment these past few months. It is my intention to redress the balance. You think we can't defeat a handful of savages who blacken their faces and stick feathers in their hair?" Quade glowered at the lieutenant. "Well, do you?"

"No, sir."

"Damned right; 'No, sir'! Then we are in agreement, are we not? This ends here and it ends now."

Conscious of Cageaga's laboured breathing close to his ear, Hawkwood raised his head cautiously. After the initial ferment, the shooting had dwindled away and an expectant and uneasy hush had fallen over the road, as if every man – with the exception of Cageaga – was holding his breath.

He thought about a stretch of barren foreshore and a barricade of uprooted, sun-bleached trees behind which a small band of loyal Rangers had fought to the bitter end. Lawrence had mentioned something about coming full circle in a conversation they'd had on the *Snake*. Maybe it happened to everyone, sooner or later.

He thought, too, about the men around him.

They should not be here. Their village needed them. They should be in their longhouses, gathered around the fires with their families. They should not be preparing to die.

He turned to Tewanias. "Leave me your guns. Make your escape. There's a time to stand and a time to retreat. This is not a good day to die, rake'niha; not for a king you will never meet, who lives across an ocean you will never see."

Tewanias looked back at him. "You think that is why we are here? If that was so, these men would have left the fight when the Yan-kees attacked us in the woods. We are Kanien'kehá:ka. We fight the Yan-kees because they and the Oneniote'á:ka are our enemy, and we stay because of the totem you wear beneath your shirt. It is the same totem handed to me by my father, who received it from his father before him. I have no son of my own. That is why I gave the totem to you. You are Kahrhakon:ha, adopted son of Tewanias, war captain of the Kanien'kehá:ka. We do not fight for the Great King beyond the Water, Mat-huwa. We fight for you."

Hawkwood stared at him, a lump forming in his throat.

"Then can we fight them now," Cageaga urged. "Otherwise, we will be here all day. I do not think I will last that long."

Hawkwood placed his hand lightly on Cageaga's shoulder. "You forget – it is just a scratch."

Cageaga awarded them with a ferine smile.

Hawkwood removed the tomahawk from his belt. "They'll want to finish it quickly. There may only be time for one shot. Tell your men to pick their targets. Aim for the officers and the sergeants. Then be ready to fight."

"Ea," Tewanias said, and relayed the order, sliding the war club from his shoulder. Around him, the remaining warriors began to shed themselves of their clubs and edged weapons, placing them within easy reach.

Hawkwood saw Kodjeote exchange looks with his brother.

Peering over the logs, Hawkwood searched for Quade but couldn't see him. Then his attention was caught by a small knot of men standing off to the side, behind the skirmish line. As he watched, the knot broke apart and Quade was there, pistol in one hand, sword in the other.

Hawkwood raised the musket, ignoring the pull on his wounded arm and sighted on Quade's chest. It was a long shot, literally, but there might not be an opportunity to take another. Taking an even breath and holding it for a count of three, he squeezed the trigger.

At the exact same instant as the road – and Quade with it – disappeared behind a cloud of smoke as the skirmishers opened fire.

In that split second between his shot and the eruption of the smoke, Hawkwood thought he saw Quade stagger, but by then his view was obscured. He swore in frustration.

Then out of the smoke, the bayonet men came running. Hawkwood knew there would be no time to reload; the troops in the forefront of the attack were too close. At least the narrow width of the road meant they were bunched together, so it would be a very poor marksman who wouldn't find a target within the first volley.

The Mohawks' muskets crashed out around him, filling the air with flame and smoke and the stench of rotten eggs. Hawkwood saw a corporal jerk back as if on a string, his face a bloody mask, his scream louder than the sound of the guns. Next to him, a private staggered as a ball took him in the

445

chest. Sinking to his knees, he fell face down, his hands curled around the musket which lay trapped beneath him. Two more troopers in the first rank tumbled like skittles, their blood misting the air.

But as the Mohawk rose to shoot, they, too, became targets. Effa, already nursing the wound in his thigh, shrieked as his jaw was shot away. Chohajo, having loosed off his musket and knowing there was no time for a second shot, turned to his bow. He was able to loose two arrows before a musket ball shattered his left wrist. A second ball struck his left temple. And as he toppled backwards, the Mohawks' guns fell silent.

Cageaga snatched up his tomahawk. Through gritted teeth, he let out a growl. "I am Cageaga of the Kanien'kehá:ka. If I am to die today it will not be as an old man waiting for death. It will be as a warrior, with my blade buried in a Yan-kee heart!" He gripped Hawkwood's arm. "I will wait for you in the sky world, little brother! I will save you a place by the fire."

And before anyone could stop him, he had stumbled from shelter, knife drawn and tomahawk raised, and launched his wounded body at the advancing troops.

Hawkwood heard Tewanias yell, not in warning or out of fear but in anger and support. As the war chief followed Cageaga out from the sanctuary of the log wall, with Kodjeote and Deskaheh at his side, Hawkwood was only half a pace behind, knowing in his heart that they should have stayed put.

But better to go down fighting than die like rats in a trap.

Shouts of alarm rose as the troopers caught sight of the painted figures charging towards them through the smoke.

Even though he was severely weakened, remarkably, Cageaga was able to parry the first bayonet thrust with ease, using the blade of his tomahawk. But as he slashed his knife, severing the trooper's hamstring, a musket ball struck his left hip. A second took him in the shoulder and he fell back, surrounded by a ruck of blue and brown tunics. He was still fighting as the bayonets and musket butts drove him to the ground where, finally, beaten down, he sank beneath the soldiers' boots and the snow around him turned dark with blood.

As Cageaga disappeared from view, Hawkwood scythed his tomahawk blade towards an exposed throat and felt the blade bite. Tugging it free, he saw Tewanias curve his war club against a musket stock. On the other side, Deskaheh and Kodjeote had also hurled themselves into the fray. War clubs rose and swept down. A man shrieked and a musket spat and Kodjeote was flung backwards. Deskaheh screamed with anger as he saw his younger brother shot down.

Sensing a presence behind him, Hawkwood ducked and was halfway through the turn when he felt a stunning blow against his right shoulder. He staggered and saw Deskaheh look towards him and shout something unintelligible. A scream came from nearby, but whether it had been uttered in pain or rage, he couldn't tell. A pistol cracked.

He looked for Tewanias and saw him hammer his war club against a trooper's jaw. Then another blow landed across his back and he felt a sharp burn as a bayonet scored his thigh. He tried again to turn but, weakened, slipped on the trampled snow. He heard his name called and saw it was Tewanias battling towards him, and then he saw a trooper drive a musket butt between the Mohawk chieftain's shoulder blades. As Tewanias fell, the trooper reversed the musket and drove his bayonet into Tewanias's lower back. Hawkwood's cry of despair was cut short as something hit him at the base of his skull and the next thing he knew he was falling.

Still conscious when he hit the ground, his shoulder protested as a gun butt thumped into his side. Through half-closed eyes, he saw a figure pushing through the mêlée, sword in hand.

Quade's face was stained with blood and dirt. There was a rent in his coat and a darkening patch showed where Hawkwood's musket ball had scored across the top of his left arm. The hem of his coat was damp with mud and melted snow. Beneath the blood and the dirt, his expression was venomous. Hawkwood braced himself for the final thrust. Instead, as the sounds of fighting ceased, he heard Quade snarl angrily, "Get him up!"

They hauled him to his knees. A pistol muzzle was placed against the back of his skull. Focusing through a wash of pain, he looked around at the carnage and the gorge rose into his throat. Beyond where Tewanias had fallen, Cageaga's corpse would not have been recognizable had it not been for the broken feathers and the beading on his buckskin coat. The back of his skull and his shoulders were thick with blood and one leg was twisted beneath him. His tomahawk lay within inches of his outstretched hand.

Like rag dolls tossed aside in a fit of childish rage, the bodies of Deskaheh and Kodjeote lay intertwined, beaten and bloody. Around them, a dozen uniformed corpses bore witness to their defiance. Most had been felled by gunshots, but the rest displayed the wounds of close-quarter battle. As he watched, a trooper placed his musket against Deskaheh's skull and pulled the trigger.

"Spare me your revulsion," Quade said, observing Hawkwood's expression, as the echo of the shot died away. "Given what your savages did to their comrades, it's no more than they deserve. At least we're putting them out of their misery. Better a ball to the back of the head than a lingering death."

Hawkwood fought back rage and stayed silent, knowing any response would have been inadequate. There were no sympathizers here. While some of the troopers were sifting among the bodies of their comrades, looking for signs of life, others loitered, fascinated by the white man with the painted face. The hostility in the air could have been cut by a knife.

Quade stared down at him. "Proved quite the savage yourself, haven't you, Hooper? Even got that damned muck on your face. You think that makes you one of them now?" he added sneeringly.

Hawkwood looked back at him. "I was always one of them, Quade."

The sneer was replaced by a frown.

Hawkwood's head had at last begun to clear. "I assume a tribunal is out of the question?"

The frown slid away, to be replaced by a thin smile, devoid of humour. "We've been through that, remember? Though, even if that hadn't been the case, you wouldn't qualify." The corner of Quade's mouth lifted. "Ah, but then you won't be familiar

448

with General Hull's proclamation that no white man found fighting on the side of an Indian is to be taken prisoner?"

There was a coppery taste at the back of Hawkwood's tongue. At some time he must have bitten through it; probably when he'd been struck on the head. He spat out blood. "Last I heard, General Hull was being held in Quebec. I'm not sure his proclamations carry much weight any more."

Quade shook his head. "Ah, but they do, believe me. Not that it matters, anyway. We've already established you're a spy and . . . well, you know the punishment for that."

"Best get on with it, then," said Hawkwood wearily. "There's a blockhouse awaiting your attention. I assume that's still your objective?"

"Nothing to stop us now," Quade said.

Hawkwood looked up at the sky. "You'll have to move quickly. I'd say there's more snow on the way."

Quade peered heavenward.

"Been a hell of a morning, Major," Hawkwood said.

Dropping his gaze, Quade stared at him for perhaps two or three seconds. "And the last one you'll ever see."

Hawkwood dropped his hands to his knees. "Maybe, maybe not; the day's not over."

Before Quade could respond, an officer appeared at his shoulder. "All the hostiles are accounted for, Major." He stared down at Hawkwood as if mesmerized.

"Very good," said Quade. "See to the wounded. Get the men back in line. Prepare to move out. We've wasted enough time."

The officer hesitated and then responded curtly, "Yes, sir." With a lingering look towards Hawkwood, he moved away and began issuing orders.

Quade was silent until the officer was out of earshot. Then he said, "Y'know what pleases me the most? Knowing my face will be the last one you'll ever see. It's why I told my men not to kill you."

Hawkwood let his hand drift to the top of his right moccasin. He could taste blood in his mouth. "I'm flattered."

"Ah, yes," Quade said sarcastically. "And there it is – the attempt at levity. Your friend Lawrence fancied himself as a wit, too, as I recall. I don't see him, by the way. Where is he?"

"Damned if I know. We got separated."

Quade shrugged. "Pity. It would have been nice to have had you both together. No matter, we'll just have to make do. All right, Corporal – when you're ready."

Hawkwood felt the pistol muzzle lift away from his scalp. "No blindfold then?"

This time there was no smile. "I told you; I wanted you to see my face."

"My apologies," Hawkwood said. "I forgot." Glancing to one side, he saw a trooper lean over Tewanias's body and aim his musket downwards. His breath locked as his fingers reached the hilt of the knife in his boot.

"God's sake, Corporal," Quade snapped. "Just do it."

The sound of the shot was louder than expected and Quade's eyes widened in shock.

As the corporal's skull blew apart.

Hawkwood threw himself down as musket rounds tore into Quade's men. The trooper who'd been about to shoot Tewanias in the head was now face down, his brains dribbling into the snow. Hawkwood looked back towards the abattis, to where soldiers in light grey uniforms and black bearskin caps were appearing through the smoke. Muskets boomed again. Pandemonium ensued. More troopers went tumbling.

Hearing a scream of rage, Hawkwood turned in time to see Quade's sword slashing down towards him. He hurled himself to one side. The stiletto was in his hand, but he needed a more substantial weapon. He had no idea where his own tomahawk had fallen, but Cageaga's was there in full view. Transferring the knife to his left hand, he scrambled towards it, his wounded shoulder screaming in protest.

He was halfway to his feet when Quade came in again, blade held high, to deliver a vicious downward stroke that would have cleaved bone had it connected, but by then Hawkwood had the tomahawk in his right hand and was able to parry the strike away. As he rolled, the heavy blade sheared past his injured arm, missing it by a hair's breadth.

Using the tomahawk as a brace, Hawkwood pushed himself up. His head was swimming and the world, which seemed to be enveloped in nothing but smoke and noise, tilted alarmingly.

There was a fresh cut on Quade's scalp, probably a graze from a musket ball, and blood now covered most of his face. He was breathing hard. With a manic cry, he attacked again: a reverse cut to Hawkwood's right side. Hawkwood, managing to recover his balance, sucked in his stomach and slammed the tomahawk against the descending edge. Shock ran through his arm as steel met with steel. Sparks skittered along the colliding blades. From all sides there came shouts and crackles of musketry.

And then Quade's injured right leg suddenly buckled and his boots lost their grip.

It was enough of an opening. Hawkwood's moccasins gave him the traction he needed. Reversing his hold, he rammed the stiletto into Quade's right bicep. Quade shrieked and pulled back, sword dropping. Letting go of the knife, Hawkwood pivoted. Curving the tomahawk round in a full-blooded strike, he drove the blade deep into Quade's neck.

Quade made a sound halfway between a sob and a gurgle. Blood spurted as Hawkwood pulled the hatchet free. Quade's body collapsed on to the snow.

Hawkwood tossed the hatchet aside and sank to his knees as chaos continued to erupt around him. The pain in his shoulder was exquisite. The blue uniforms were pulling back as more grey uniforms appeared, wreathed in smoke from the guns. Other figures were there, too, running among them; scalp-locked warriors, brandishing clubs and guns.

*Tewanias.*

Desperately, Hawkwood crabbed towards him.

Blood oozed out of a rent in the back of Tewanias's coat. He groaned as Hawkwood pushed the trooper's body aside and turned him over. Then his eyelids flickered and he opened his eyes. "Mat-huwa?"

"I am here, rake'niha."

Tewanias grunted and tried to rise. Hawkwood held him down, pressing his hand against the wound.

Tewanias grimaced. Gripping Hawkwood's arm, he pulled himself up. He stared desolately around him, at Cageaga's bloodied, crumpled form and at the bodies of the others. "We are the last?"

Hawkwood nodded. "Ea."

Hurt filled Tewanias's eyes when he saw Deskaheh and his brother. He looked up, past Hawkwood's shoulder.

Hawkwood turned and stared up at the figure standing behind him dressed in an unbuttoned military greatcoat, a rifle-green uniform showing beneath it, a scabbard hanging from his hip.

*What the hell was an officer of the 95th doing here?*

His heart rose. And then he saw the cap and the differences in the tunic and accoutrements suddenly became apparent. This wasn't the 95th.

"Captain Hawkwood?"

The enquiry had been made in a distinctive Gallic accent.

Cradling Tewanias, Hawkwood looked at the grey-uniformed men who were moving among the bodies, checking for life and retrieving weapons. Others – marksmen – were attempting to pick off targets among the American back markers.

"Yes," he responded cautiously.

"Lieutenant-Colonel Charles de Salaberry at your service, Captain."

"Colonel," Hawkwood said.

The officer smiled. "Do not worry, Captain. We are Voltigeurs Canadiens. We're on your side."

Hawkwood let go a breath. He could see the man was intrigued by the paint on his face. The colonel's gaze moved down and he frowned. "You're wounded?"

"I'm all right. My friend is not."

The colonel dropped to his haunches. "I will see he gets attention."

"Major Lawrence?" Hawkwood said.

"Ah, yes." De Salaberry smiled again. "A very brave man."

"You're from Lacolle?"

452

"We are quartered close by. We found him on the road."

"How many are you?" Hawkwood asked.

"Three hundred and forty. We are a combined force, French Canadian mostly; Voltigeurs, Embodied Militia, Voyageurs, plus some Mohawk auxiliaries."

"Mohawk?"

"From Kahnawá:ke."

Hawkwood felt Tewanias stir.

"This is Tewanias, Colonel," Hawkwood said. "He is also Mohawk. He and his men were—"

De Salaberry laid a hand on Hawkwood's arm. "I know who he is. Major Lawrence told us of your plan to delay the column." Staring forlornly at the bodies of the dead warriors, he added softly, "And I see you have paid a heavy price."

Tewanias shifted and emitted a sharp gasp.

"We need a surgeon," Hawkwood said.

Regret showed instantly on de Salaberry's face as he rose to his feet. "I'm afraid our surgeon is not with us. He was called away from the post yesterday. We have his assistant, however – Lieutenant Hersey. He will supervise the transfer to Lacolle."

"You've a wagon?" Hawkwood enquired hopefully.

"No wagon, either, I'm afraid. We will have to improvise. We will construct a litter."

Hawkwood looked past de Salaberry's shoulder.

The colonel saw what had caught Hawkwood's attention. "He insisted on accompanying us. He was most . . . ah, persuasive."

Lawrence was propped between two of de Salaberry's men. It was obvious they were the only things keeping him upright.

"Fortunately," de Salaberry added, "I was able to deter him from leading the charge."

"That would be a first," Hawkwood said, watching the anguish creep across Lawrence's face at the sight of the dead warriors.

"Lieutenant Hersey, our medical assistant," de Salaberry explained, as a green-jacketed officer approached at a run.

As the lieutenant crouched to examine Tewanias's wound, Hawkwood stood up and walked forward.

Close to, Lawrence looked even paler than he had from a distance. "I'm so sorry," he said.

"What the hell for?"

"This." Lawrence gazed despairingly at the carnage around him. "We were too damned late."

"No, Douglas. You weren't. The bastards are broken. They're on the run."

"But Tewanias? His warriors?"

"His men are gone but Tewanias is alive. The medic's attending him now."

Lawrence's face twisted with pain. "Goddamned bastards!"

"You're hurt." Hawkwood went to reach out. "How . . .?"

"I fell off my damned horse."

Hawkwood stared at him.

"On account of I was shot."

"Shot? God's teeth! Not by . . .?" Hawkwood's gaze swung accusingly towards the two Voltigeurs.

"Lord, no! It was that bloody Observer fellow we saw back at Plattsburg. I ran into his scouting party. His name's Walker, by the way, God rot his socks."

"*Was* Walker," Hawkwood said.

"What?"

"Not is," Hawkwood said. "Was."

It took a second for the emphasis to sink in. Lawrence's eyes widened.

"I had a run in with him, too."

"The devil you say! And . . .?"

"He lost."

"Good," Lawrence spat savagely. "Serves the bastard right." His chin lifted. "And our friend, Quade? I don't suppose . . .?"

"He didn't make it, either."

"Then, by God, the drinks are on me."

"And don't think I won't hold you to that," Hawkwood said wearily.

For the first time, Lawrence allowed himself a weak grin. "Well, someone had better hold me, because if they don't, I'm going to fall on my arse. By Christ, Matthew, it's good to see you!"

Drawing himself up, he shrugged off the two Voltigeurs, held out his hand and took an unsteady pace forward.

And promptly collapsed.

As de Salaberry's men bent to help him, Hawkwood spun quickly. "Colonel!"

De Salaberry looked round.

"We're going to need another litter," Hawkwood said.

They transferred Tewanias and Lawrence to Lacolle on litters crafted from cut-down branches. The litter-bearers were Kahnawákeró:non warriors who carried out the task at their own insistence when it was discovered that Tewanias was known to their war captain – though the two men were from different clans. The Mohawk auxiliaries, also with de Salaberry's full agreement, made litters for the bodies of Tewanias's men, so that they, too, could be removed from the place of battle.

Hawkwood, hurt but in no serious need of assistance, commandeered Lawrence's horse.

Arriving at Lacolle, it was not hard to see why the Americans had thought their plan would work. There was nothing to the place. Built on the north bank of a small river, there was no settlement as such, just a stone house, a stable and a sawmill. The blockhouse was the dominant feature. Squat and square and two storeys high, with firing slits cut into the thick log walls. There were unglazed windows with shutters for defence. The first storey overhung the ground floor and there were slits in the overhang floor so the defenders could fire down upon any attackers, not unlike a medieval donjon. Around the blockhouse was a small tented village and several crude huts; accommodation for extra troops and the auxiliaries, de Salaberry explained.

Originally, the post had been built to protect the sawmill as well as a signal beacon, sited to the east where the river flowed into the larger Richelieu River and which, in times of emergency could be used to alert the garrison at Île aux Noix.

*So they wouldn't have needed to ride there for help,* Hawkwood thought. *If there'd been time for someone to get to the beacon, they could have just lit a fire.*

The post housed forty-five militia and twenty-three Mohawk auxiliaries, who might have been able to defend their position against three times their number, but to fend off four hundred attackers for any length of time would have been wishful thinking. What Quade hadn't allowed for had been de Salaberry and his Voltigeurs and the other militia units and auxiliaries who'd been quartered in the nearby woods and on farms a couple of miles further along the Lacolle to Montreal road. The Americans' intelligence had been lacking on every count.

The surgeon's name was Brossard. Having returned to the post from visiting a militia captain with a broken leg, he turned his attention to the now conscious Lawrence in a hastily arranged surgery set up in the blockhouse. It wasn't the worst field hospital Hawkwood had been in, by any stretch.

"God must have been looking down on you, Major," the surgeon declared cheerfully as he examined the wound, grunting as his probing discovered the ball lodged only a centimetre beneath the skin. "I suspect most of its energy was spent on the journey from muzzle to muscle, which suggests either weak powder or else the shooter was at the limit of his range. If so, it was a remarkable shot," he added admiringly, as he extracted the offending projectile with the aid of a small pair of forceps.

He looked equally fascinated when he was directed to the wounds in Lawrence's abdomen, to which wads of congealed root and moss still adhered. To Hawkwood's utter surprise, Brossard murmured in appreciation as he peeled away the poultices.

"These native medicines are a wonder. The Indians have forgotten more about the healing properties of forest plants than we'll ever know. I've adopted a number of their remedies myself and have found them to be most efficacious in the treatment of wounds and maladies."

Humming quietly to himself, Brossard retrieved a clay jar from his supply cabinet and measured out a handful of the earthy-smelling contents. Grinding them into a powder with a pestle and mortar and into a paste with the addition of what looked like melted beeswax, he applied the salve in an even layer to each of Lawrence's wounds, though not before dousing the areas liberally with half the contents of a small whiskey bottle, prompting an impressive stream of obscenities from what, up until then, had been a relatively passive patient.

"My father was a physician, too," Brossard explained, when Lawrence had stopped blaspheming. "He marched with Montcalm and learnt many secrets from Huron medicine men." He added smilingly, "And now, here we are: sons of French soldiers along with Huron and Mohawk who were once sworn enemies, all coming together to serve an English king. Life is strange, is it not?"

Lawrence, he advised, if all went well, would be fit enough to travel in two days.

Tewanias's deeper bayonet wound was of greater concern. Swabbing it as best he could, Surgeon Brossard then took the unusual step of consulting his patient for advice. Tewanias sent word for the Kahnawákeró:non war captain, who in turn summoned his own healer, Brossard being happy to defer to native lore.

Fascinated, Hawkwood watched as, between them, medicine man and surgeon – using ingredients from Brossard's pharmacy mixed with herbs from the healer's pouch – set about concocting their own potions which they then administered both directly to the wound and orally. They would know the benefit, the Kahnawákeró:non healer told them, by the morning of the third day.

Tewanias, while not ready to fight a battle, was on his feet by the evening of the second day, when Colonel de Salaberry came and took Hawkwood aside.

"If the major is fit, you must both depart in the morning. I have dispatches for the military authorities in Montreal. A courier will be leaving here at first light. You can travel with him. From Montreal, Major Lawrence can return to his duties. As for you, Captain, it's late in the season but there should be a schooner available to transport you downriver to Quebec. From there, you will be able to secure passage to England. Do not delay, otherwise there will be no journey home, certainly not for you, not for another four months. The weather will not permit it."

I'll bear that in mind," Hawkwood said, and went to tell Tewanias the news.

"I am deeply sorry, rake'niha," were his first words.

The Mohawk war captain stared into his eyes. "For what?"

"For bringing death to your village."

Tewanias frowned and gathered his blanket around him. "Did you speak false words to the council?"

"I spoke what I believed to be the truth."

"Then you should not feel blame. Cageaga, Effa, Deskaheh, Chohajo and the others were Kanien'kehá:ka, men of free will. The choice to follow you was theirs, as was their choice to leave, which they could have done at any time. They knew the danger."

"Wives are without husbands, rake'niha." Hawkwood thought about Kodjeote and added, "Mothers are without sons."

"Wives and mothers are also Kanien'kehá:ka. They will understand."

"It would have been better if I had not returned."

Tewanias laid a hand upon his arm. "No, Mat-huwa. Do not say that. The Great Spirit guided you here for a purpose. It was in order for us to meet again, so that you could open our eyes to the threat from the Yan-kees and we could make ready for the battle that lies ahead."

"And Cageaga and the others?"

"We will carry them back to Gaanundata and prepare them for their journey into the sky world."

"We?" Hawkwood said.

"Hickonquash, war captain of the Kahnawákeró:non, and some of his warriors will travel with me. A number are blood kin to the people of my village."

"Will you remain in Gaanundata?"

"That, I do not know," Tewanias said heavily.

"The Great King beyond the Water has promised you land in Canada. You will be safe there."

"The council will decide. Hickonquash will speak with them also."

"The Americans will know that you helped us defeat their soldiers."

Tewanias's head lifted. From the way he held himself, Hawkwood knew that while the Mohawk chief looked as though he was on the mend, there was a possibility that the wound would yet prove fatal. The next few days would be critical.

"What is your meaning?"

"The Americans will seek to punish those who fought with the soldiers of the Great King."

"Ea, that may be so, but now the Yan-kees have tasted our wrath and they will know the Kanien'kehá:ka will not be cowed."

"It was always so," Hawkwood agreed. "And I will make it known how warriors of the Kanien'kehá:ka fought and gave their lives so that all the peoples of Canada can remain free."

A shadow moved across the Mohawk war captain's face. "And will you return to Anówarakowa Kawennote – America?"

"I do not think so, rake'niha."

Tewanias gazed at him. "Then let us be grateful for the days we have been given. Let us spend our last evening by the fire and talk of old friends and brave warriors who are no longer with us, and when the morning comes and the fire has turned to ash, let us remember these times and pray to the Great Spirit to guide our footsteps from this place."

"I would like that," Hawkwood said softly.

Snow had fallen during the night, but it had been a light feathering and not enough to deter the colonel from sending out his dispatch riders: one to the garrison on the Île aux Noix, the other to Montreal, via the north road.

"Gentlemen," De Salaberry greeted Hawkwood and Lawrence warmly, "I confess I'm rather sorry to see you go. It's been a while since we had such . . . stimulating company. Major Lawrence, I do not know how long this war will last, but it would not surprise me if our paths were to cross again. When that time comes, I only hope that it is under less . . . shall we say . . . dramatic circumstances."

They were in de Salaberry's quarters, which weren't a whole lot different from Colonel Pike's back in Plattsburg, Hawkwood noted. There were the same Spartan furnishings – bed, dresser, desk, chair and campaign chest – and the same earthen floor. The only difference was the open fire instead of a metal stove.

"So long as your surgeon remembers that whiskey's for sipping and not for slopping, I shall look forward to it, too, Colonel."

De Salaberry grinned. "I will tell him. Though, it might have been worse. He could have used my best cognac."

Lawrence chuckled and then winced.

"Be sure to have your wounds looked at again by the surgeon in Montreal," de Salaberry added chidingly.

"I will, sir. Thank you."

"No, Major. Thank *you*."

De Salaberry turned to Hawkwood. "And I have a message from Surgeon Brossard for you, too, Captain. Get *your* wounds checked, as well. They may not be vexing you at the moment, but we both know what conditions are like on-board ship. The last thing you need is for an infection to take hold while you are at sea. I'd hate to think of them wrapping your remains in a sail and dropping you overboard weighted down with lead shot."

"Can't say as I'd like it, either, Colonel," Hawkwood said.

De Salaberry smiled and held out his hand to each of them in turn. "Good, then I wish you both a safe journey."

The colonel returned to his desk and Hawkwood and Lawrence left the room. They were half a dozen paces away when the door opened suddenly behind them. The colonel stuck his head out and smiled. "Forgive me, gentlemen. I almost forgot . . ."

Both men paused.

The colonel raised a hand. "Joyeux Noël!"

And with that, he turned his back, re-entered the room and closed the door.

Hawkwood and Lawrence looked at each other.

"Well, it can't be worse than my last one," Hawkwood said.

They made their way outside. The dispatch rider bound for Île aux Noix had already departed. The Montreal-bound courier was waiting with the horses.

Turning up his collar and adjusting his borrowed cap, Lawrence mounted carefully. "If I fall off this time, at least I'll have you to catch me." He glanced around him. "I thought Tewanias might be here to say his farewell."

"We've already said our goodbyes," Hawkwood said. \

Lawrence looked at him, unsure.

Hawkwood did not reply. Lifting the reins, he caught the dispatch rider's eye. "After you, Corporal."

With that they set off, walking their horses away from the post. It wasn't until they were clear of the tents and beyond the perimeter that Hawkwood looked back over his shoulder. The place was waking up. Smoke rose from the blockhouse chimney and from the campfires; bodies were gathering around them in preparation for the queue to the cook tent. From one of the huts, a figure emerged, tall and dressed in a dark cloak. For a second it did not move, but then, slowly, a hand was raised.

Hawkwood reined in and lifted his right hand in acknowledgement. He watched as the figure held the pose before it turned and disappeared. Steering his horse around, he found Lawrence had been watching him. Hands resting easily across his pommel, the major waited as Hawkwood drew level.

No words were spoken as they kicked their horses into motion and followed the corporal down the snowy, forest track.

# EPILOGUE

"Quite a sight, ain't it?" Sir George Prevost spoke from behind Hawkwood's right shoulder.

It was hard to argue. Indeed, it would have taken an idiot or a blind man to disagree, for the view from the chateau's window was more than "quite a sight". It was spectacular.

The chateau was the Chateau St Louis, the official residence of the Governor-in-Chief of the Canadas, probably the only title grand enough to match the building's extraordinary location. Built on the rim of a terrifyingly high, near-vertical bluff, the chateau overlooked the confluence of the Charles and St Lawrence rivers. It was, Hawkwood thought as he stared out at the scene spread below him, like standing on the edge of the world.

He wondered how far the view extended. Miles, probably side of miles on a clear day. Today wasn't that clear, though, for the a light sleet was falling. Nothing, however, not the ordinary cold, pewter-coloured sky, could detract from the out over the aspect on the other side of the glass. His gaze crouched at the slanted rooftops of the lower town and the a small sprinkling foot of the bluff, across the mile-wide river.
of lights on the eastern shore. évy; it's where Wolfe

Prevost followed his gaze. "Pointe three months to take pitched camp during the siege. Too him of us. How he managed the city. The Heights are to the s th to get troops and cannon up those damned cliffs beats me. Hell of a thing," Prevost murmured, as if he couldn't quite believe the deed had been considered, never mind accomplished.

Wolfe, Hawkwood knew, was General James Wolfe, who, a little over half a century before, after scaling the aforementioned cliffs, had defeated the French general, Montcalm, on the Plains of Abraham, the plateau that lay just outside the city's walls. The battle had cost both generals their lives, but the Crown's forces had prevailed and the victory had led, ultimately, to Britain gaining control of what had been, up until then, French Canada.

He looked northwards, to the basin, a broad expanse of gun-metal grey water framed by bleak, snow-covered hills and dotted with the sails of vessels battling gamely through rising swells.

"Your ship leaves on the morning tide," Sir George said, reading Hawkwood's mind. "She's the frigate, *Ariadne*. She's carrying dispatches for our masters in London. Fast, I'm told. You'll be home within a month, all being well. I must say you're dashed lucky you arrived here when you did. Another few days and there's a good chance we'd have been iced in, leaving you stuck here until March."

The Governor put his head on one side and said speculatively, "Glad to be going home, I expect, after your adventures. How long will you have been away?"

Hawkwood thought back. "Three months."

*seemed longer.*

no\diers and sailors, eh? You'd think we'd be used to it by

Ha\

*any mo*\od felt like saying, *But I'm not a bloody soldier; not a soldier, a*\en though he knew that wasn't strictly true. Once

Sir George\'s a soldier.

his father's regi\ld know that better than anyone, having joined Rising through th\t, the 60th Foot, as a twelve-year-old ensign. held the posts of lieu\nks, after service in the West Indies, he'd of Dominica before bei\ant-governor of St Lucia and governor Scotia and, eventually, Pre\ppointed lieutenant-governor of Nova

A not-too-tall, not-too-s\dent of Lower Canada.

\ut man, with thick side-burns

framing affable features, Prevost's demeanour reminded Hawkwood more of a yeoman farmer than an army commander and senior diplomat, but his record spoke for itself.

"It'll be Christmas aboard, then," Sir George followed on cheerfully. "Hard tack and holly. Extra rations of grog, though, eh?" He grinned.

*Christmas?*

Hawkwood kept forgetting. Not that it mattered. It was the thought of another bloody sea voyage that occupied his mind, rather than a round of festive sea shanties, if there were such things. He supposed he would find out soon enough. He groaned inwardly.

"You said your goodbyes to Major Lawrence?" Sir George asked.

"I did, sir, yes."

"And how was he?"

"The surgeon said he should make a good recovery."

"Splendid! Though not the most tolerant of patients, I'm told." There was humour in the statement.

"No." Hawkwood smiled at the recollection. Lawrence swearing fit to bust as Surgeon Brossard poured the whiskey.

"Well, I'm glad he's on the mend. We need men of his ilk."

*Ilk?* Hawkwood thought.

The ride from Lacolle had taken the full day, with a change of horses at the halfway mark, a small, unobtrusive inn and livery stable sequestered by the army for just such a purpose. By the time they arrived at Longueil, the dark had fallen. A cold fog covered the St Lawrence but it hadn't prevented them seeing the lights of the city twinkling on the far bank.

The last ferry of the evening had departed so they'd found accommodation in an army guardhouse, a relic from the town fort, which had been deemed unsafe and torn down a couple of years earlier. The guardhouse's state of repair had suggested its own demolition wouldn't be long in following, but for the one night it had provided a warm, dry billet and that was all that was required.

They'd caught the ferry the next morning and the dispatch rider had escorted them to military headquarters, where a clerk in the Adjutant General's office had been sent to secure Hawkwood a berth on a Quebec-bound schooner leaving at midday. Lawrence had accompanied him to the quay.

"Seems odd to be saying farewell," Lawrence said, smiling. "Reminds me of London. We meet, we enjoy a brief period of excitement and then we say our goodbyes."

"I'm not sure I'd call what we've been through a 'brief period of excitement'," Hawkwood said. "But each to his own."

"Hah!" Lawrence let go a laugh. "Well, then, let's say that time spent in your company is never dull."

"Dull would be nice," Hawkwood said, "once in a while."

"Then here's hoping for a very dull voyage home, my dear fellow." Lawrence held out his hand. "O:nen ki' wahi', Captain."

Hawkwood smiled. "You, too, Major."

The two men had shaken hands at the foot of the schooner's gangplank. Lawrence's last words as Hawkwood turned to board were, "I know it's against your better nature, but this time, Captain, do *try* and stay out of trouble."

Sir George turned away from the window. He looked pensive. "Y'know, I can't decide if we were lucky or if the Americans were just incompetent."

Assuming from the lengthy pause that followed that he was expected to supply some pearl of wisdom on the subject, Hawkwood said cautiously, "They were so desperate for a win, I doubt they thought it through."

*Well, Quade didn't, at any rate.*

Sir George looked at him. "You make it sound like a game of cricket. Just as well we bowled the buggers out, eh? Explains why the Yankees never took it up!"

*Dear God*, Hawkwood thought. *Shoot me now.*

The Governor's face turned serious. "If they *had* achieved their objective, it would've been a close-run thing. We're spread too thin. I have less than six thousand regular troops at my disposal – and that's for the whole country. London can't spare us reinforcements. Europe takes precedent."

"What about the militia?"

"On paper, around seventy thousand in Lower Canada. That might sound more than sufficient, but the Yankees have a hundred thousand – and more waiting in the wings. In truth, I doubt either side has any idea how many will rally to the flag."

"So you need all the help you can get?"

"Indeed we do. I am exceeding grateful that, in this particular case, we had the help of your Mohawk friends – and I have affirmed that gratitude in my dispatches to Lord Bathurst."

Hawkwood wasn't sure if he was supposed to say thank you, Lord Bathurst being the Secretary of State for War and the Colonies and therefore a figure of some importance. But he was still a bloody politician and Hawkwood, as a rule, despised politicians – present company currently excepted. So, instead, he said, "Thank God for de Salaberry, too. If it hadn't been for his arrival . . ."

"Indeed," said Sir George. "Good thing I listened to him. It was at his insistence that I agreed to set up the Voltigeurs. They've certainly proved their worth. A hard taskmaster, I'm told, but needs must when the devil drives, eh?"

"Frankly, sir, he could have turned up wearing a cap and bells and I wouldn't have minded. He was there when he was needed. That's what counted."

Sir George laughed. "Cap and bells! Now, there's a sight I'd pay to see! Y'know, he fought a duel once. Cut his rival in half, it's said."

Hawkwood wasn't sure how to respond to that, either, though he recalled there had been a slight but interesting indentation on de Salaberry's forehead which could well have been an old scar from a sabre slash.

"How are *your* wounds, by the way?" Sir George enquired.

"Mending, sir; thank you."

Fortunately, the bayonet graze had been just that; inconvenient but not life-threatening. The wound in his upper arm had needed more attention, a process that had involved several sutures along with the liberal use of Surgeon Brossard's rapidly depleting stock of alcohol and another herb poultice, courtesy of the Kahnawákeró:non medicine man.

Currently, his entire arm and shoulder ached like the devil – the cold didn't help – but Hawkwood knew the Governor was only being polite when he'd asked after his health. It was what politicians and commanding officers did by way of conversation when they couldn't think of anything else to say.

"Capital! And your . . . ah, other companion, Chief . . . Tewanias?" Sir George frowned. "Declined the services of de Salaberry's surgeon, I understand; preferred to be treated by his own people. Is that right?"

*Not exactly*, Hawkwood thought, but it would have been splitting hairs to contradict.

"Can't say as I blame him; some of the army butchers I've come across over the years," Sir George added good-naturedly, moving to the fire and turning his rear to the flames. He fixed Hawkwood with a keen stare. "Will he fight for us?"

"Sir?"

"Chief Tewanias. Will he fight for us?"

Hawkwood considered his reply. "The Lacolle engagement cost him some of his best warriors. His village is not large. It can't afford to lose that many men. He'd prefer it if he didn't have to fight at all."

"I fear that die was cast the moment he agreed to side with you and Major Lawrence," Sir George said grimly.

"He's aware of that," Hawkwood said, more curtly than he had intended.

Sir George appeared not to notice. "He knows there is land for them here in Canada?"

"He does."

Sir George, Hawkwood had discovered, wore three hats. As well as being Governor-General and Commander of the British Forces, he was also Superintendent of Indian Affairs and therefore responsible for overseeing the relations between the British government and the First Nations.

"The Americans are unlikely to accept his village's neutrality now that blood's been spilt," Sir George said, lifting his coat-tails to be closer to the fire's warmth.

"He knows that, too, sir."

"He fought for us before, didn't he?"

Hawkwood knew the information would have been in de Salaberry's dispatch. "It was a long time ago."

"Then let us hope old loyalties die hard," Sir George murmured. "History will remind him that the Americans cannot be trusted. They'll never let him rest. Not now."

*Once a warrior*, Hawkwood thought, *always a warrior.*

"And we would be negligent if we did not try to take advantage of that fact," Sir George said, throwing Hawkwood a meaningful look.

Anger flared briefly in Hawkwood's chest but then subsided as it occurred to him that he was hardly in a position to pass judgement. Sir George's statement and the argument that Lawrence and he had put to the council when they'd asked Tewanias for help were not that far removed from one another.

"Tewanias is his own man, Sir George. It's true he's unlikely to favour the American cause. He'll either fight for the King or he'll not fight at all. But his village has taken a mauling in lives lost. He may well choose the non-combatant option. In any case, the final decision will not be his to make. That will be up to the tribal council."

"Then let us hope the council comes to the right decision."

*For them or you?* Hawkwood wondered.

Sir George looked thoughtful. "A future task for our Major Lawrence, perhaps? I'll have words with Colonel Pearson. He could dispatch the major to make a fresh overture on our behalf."

Hawkwood said nothing, thinking: *That's what got us into this bloody mess in the first place.*

Something must have shown on his face, for Sir George, perhaps in the realization that he'd been discussing military strategy with a man who was no longer a serving officer, then fell silent. Colonel de Salaberry, after two evenings of convivial discussion back at Lacolle, had been made privy to Hawkwood's status and his reason for being in America. It was inconceivable that he would not have revealed something of Hawkwood's background in his report. Not in great detail, perhaps, but he was sure to have informed his superior of Hawkwood's former army service, with the emphasis on the word "former". All this was conjecture, Hawkwood knew, but had he been in St George's boots, he would have exercised a degree of caution, too.

"Anyway, it's something to consider," Sir George said, lowering his coat-tails. "For I suspect we've seen the last of the fighting this year, which'll give the Yankees time to lick their wounds and reflect on their catalogue of defeats. With luck, they'll sue for peace. It would be nice to look forward to spring, knowing we won't have to watch our backs."

Sir George looked towards the window. "I doubt we can say the same for Europe, though, eh? Can't see Bonaparte capitulating any time soon – Frog bastard!" Turning, he smiled. "Forgive me. It's this damned weather; makes a fellow prone to dyspepsia. Now, is there anything you require? You've managed to secure accommodation for this evening, yes?"

"Yes, sir."

In an inn close to the waterfront; the bill settled by army scrip, courtesy of the Adjutant General's office.

"Very good. Then I won't keep you. I suggest you treat yourself to a decent supper as well. It'll give you something to remember when you're tapping the weevils out of your biscuits!" Sir George extended his hand.

"Nothing wrong with weevils, sir," Hawkwood said as they shook. "They help take your mind off the cheese."

Sir George was left chuckling as Hawkwood closed the door behind him.

Passing quickly through the anteroom, he headed for the door. He had to step aside to make way for the entry of another visitor, a tall, elderly man, slightly stooped with a ruddy-complexioned face topped with a thatch of thinning, silvery-white hair.

By the time Prevost's secretary had risen to greet the newcomer, Hawkwood had left the room, unaware of the look he'd attracted

470

as the white-haired man paused and gazed after him, forehead creasing.

In answer to the knock, Sir George rose from his desk. The door opened and the secretary showed his visitor in.

Sir George greeted the white-haired man warmly. "Delighted to see you, my dear fellow! Please, do take a seat. May I offer you a brandy?"

There was the merest pause, as though his visitor's mind had been preoccupied, but then his invitation was accepted with a nod. "Thank you. Most kind."

Sir George moved to the decanter, poured out two measures and returned to the fire. "There we are. To what shall we drink? Confusion to the enemy?"

His visitor smiled. "Why not? That's usually been my preference."

The two men drank. The white-haired man lowered his glass. "So, how may I be of service?"

Sir George waited until his visitor had settled into his seat. "I'm in need of your counsel."

"As a friend or in a professional capacity?"

"The latter: as former superintendent."

The visitor's eyebrows rose. "Sounds intriguing, but it's been a while since I held office – fifteen years and then some. Not sure I can remember that far back!"

"I don't believe that for a moment," Prevost said.

The visitor smiled politely and helped himself to another sip.

Sir George rotated the glass in his hand, watching the contents swirl, then looked up. "There's been an incident – a place called Lacolle. Attempted cross-border incursion by our American friends. They failed, fortunately."

His visitor sat back. "I see."

Sir George moved to his desk and returned to the fire bearing papers. "I have here a report from Colonel de Salaberry – you've heard me speak of him. I'd like you to read it and give me your thoughts on how we might proceed."

"Proceed? In what regard?"

"A matter of . . . persuasion. Your experience in fighting alongside our Indian allies is second to none. I would call upon it now. As you'll read in the report, the incursion might well have succeeded if it hadn't been for the assistance of a certain Mohawk war captain. De Salaberry and I believe he has potential, a fellow worth cultivating. He fought for us before, during the Revolution. It's possible you may have knowledge of him.

"Really? His name?"

"It's there in the report. He's called Tewanias."

The grey-haired man had been on the point of taking another drink. His hand paused.

"The name means something?" Prevost said, struck by the expression on his visitor's face.

The grey-haired man did not reply immediately but stared at the papers and shook his head, as if trying to formulate thought. His forehead creased. Then, suddenly, he gave a sharp intake of breath and looked up. "Would his involvement have anything to do with that fellow I saw just now – the one who was leaving as I arrived. Tall, scarred face—"

"What? Ah, yes. . . . why do you ask?"

To Sir George's amazement, his visitor began rifling through the pages of the dispatch. "What's his name?"

Sir George frowned. "Er, Hawkwood. He used to be a soldier; a captain in the Rifles. Tough devils; we could use them here."

"Does he have a forename?"

Sir George looked nonplussed. "Forename? Why . . . yes. It's Matthew, I believe."

His visitor stared down at the dispatch in his hand. "It can't be," he breathed.

Sir George opened his mouth to speak, but was forestalled as his visitor shot to his feet. "My apologies – I must go. This . . . Hawkwood; did he say where he was bound?"

Sir George rose. "Bound? He sails for London on the morning tide."

"Then, there's time! Do you know where he stays tonight?"

"A local hostelry, I believe." Sir George gave a helpless shrug.

"But I'm afraid I don't know which one. Good Lord, man, what ails you? You look as though you've seen a ghost."

His visitor shook his head as he made for the door. "No ghost, my friend. Though I thought he had become one."

And before his host could react, the white-haired man had hurried from the room.

It had taken Hawkwood two wrong turnings to discover the correct set of stairs that led down to the chateau's main lobby, where the clerk who'd directed him to Sir George's office performed a swift interception.

"Would you like me to arrange a carriage, sir?"

Hawkwood thought about the next month and the claustrophobic accommodation he was about to endure on-board ship and shook his head. "I'll walk."

The clerk threw a dubious look through the window to the weather outside. "You're sure, sir? It's no trouble."

"I'm sure. Just steer me on to the shortest path into town."

The clerk duly obliged. Armed with directions, Hawkwood thanked him and set off across the courtyard. The sleet had eased off, but a sharp wind made itself felt as he exited the main gate. He knew he was on the right track when, a short time later, he saw, looming ahead of him, a large stone archway surmounted by a snow-topped wooden guardhouse.

A passage ran beneath the archway and into a street that looked as though it had been blasted out of the rock. Acknowledging the sentry and the soldiers manning the braziers and cannon either side of the gate, he continued on his way.

The street began to narrow. A series of zig-zags led down to a set of wooden stairs. He was about to start his descent when, above his own footsteps, he heard the sound of someone approaching from behind. He tensed.

"Matthew?" a voice said.

He turned. A figure moved out of the shadows and he found himself staring into the questioning face of an elderly man. It took him a moment to recognize the tall, stoop-shouldered, white-haired stranger as the visitor who'd brushed by him in the anteroom to Sir George Prevost's office.

"You seem to have the advantage, sir," Hawkwood said. "Do I know you?"

He waited and watched as the stranger drew closer. Taking a series of calming breaths, the old man offered Hawkwood a rueful smile. "Forgive me, I'm not as fit as I once was."

"You're not alone in that," Hawkwood said.

The old man drew himself up. He took another, deeper breath. "If you're not who I think you are, then I am about to look very foolish."

Hawkwood stared at him. A strange feeling began to stir in his chest.

Then the old man held out his hand and said, "My name is John Johnson. You might not remember me, my boy, but I was a friend of your father . . ."

# HISTORICAL NOTE

Sir John Johnson was a key figure in Loyalist, Quebec and Canadian history. An exceptional soldier and leader of men, his escape through the Adirondack Mountains in the spring of 1776 did take place as described. As did his raid on the Mohawk Valley in May 1780 when, with Captain Thomas Scott of the 53rd Regiment as his second-in-command, he entered the northern part of Johnstown at the head of 528 men – 344 white and 184 native auxiliaries – to rescue Loyalists who were being persecuted by the rebel congress.

It is here, at the beginning of Hawkwood's story, that I deviated from the facts. Contrary to the events in the novel, Sir John achieved his goal – rescuing 143 souls, and escorting them, along with 13 rebel prisoners and the family plate, all the way to the Canadian border in only eleven days – without losing a single man. It was an astonishing feat of logistics, given the difficulties that stood in his way: the number of people travelling with him, the terrain and the distances involved and the fact that he was being hunted by enemy forces.

It was just one of many raids that Johnson carried out throughout the Mohawk and Schoharie Valleys, destroying crops and villages and spreading terror among the Patriot population.

Johnson never returned to New York after the war and his estate was sold by the Americans to help pay off their war debts. He remained in Canada and eventually took over his father's role as Superintendent of Indian affairs. During the War of 1812 he served as Brigadier General for a portion of the Canadian Militia and continued to champion Indian rights up until his death. When he passed away in Montreal in 1830, his funeral was attended by 300 Mohawk.

I'm indebted to author Gavin Watt, whose account of the Johnson raids in his book *The Burning of the Valleys* set me on the right path. Thanks also to Noel Levee, City Historian for Johnstown NY and Bob McBride, Editor of *The Loyalist Gazette*; the national magazine of the United Empire Loyalists' Association of Canada (UELAC), all of whom were immensely helpful. They responded to my requests for information on the Johnson family with both patience and good humour.

While Quade's cross-border raid is fictitious, it was inspired by real events. During the war the Americans launched two strikes against Lacolle, with the intention of capturing Montreal; the first – the Battle of Lacolle Bridge – in November 1812 and the second – the Battle of Lacolle Mill – in March 1814. Both ended in embarrassing failure. On the first occasion, General Dearborn's advance troops, which included cavalry, did reach the blockhouse but such was their state of confusion that in the darkness, the infantry, which attacked in two groups, ended up firing on each other. A counter-attack, led by Lieutenant-Colonel Charles-Michel d'Irumberry de Salaberry at the head of his Voltigeurs, Canadian militia and three hundred Kahnawá:ke Mohawk, forced the Americans to flee back across the border.

In the second attack, melting snow and knee-high mud hindered the advance and the Americans' cannon and mortars were unable to make any impression against the mill's walls. The defenders, a contingent of Royal Marines, retaliated with rocket artillery and the attackers were, once again, forced to withdraw.

After the 1812 raid, General Dearborn ordered his troops into their winter quarters. They had little idea of the hardship and misery that was to follow.

The camp on the Saranac River – also referred to as Pike's Cantonment after its commanding officer – was real; as were the terrible conditions faced by the men who wintered there. More than 200 died during the winter of 1812/13 due to cold, lack of supplies, spoiled food, infection and disease. Only recently have archaeologists managed to verify the location of the site – thought to cover around 100 acres – on land adjacent to Plattsburgh International Airport. At the time of writing, no graves have been discovered but the excavation work continues.

The *Vermont* was the world's second commercial steamer and the first to operate on Lake Champlain. Designed by the Winans brothers, John and James, and commandeered by the military to carry troops and supplies, it survived the war only to sink in the Richelieu River in 1815 when its crankshaft disconnected and punched a hole through the bottom of the hull.

The War of 1812, which was waged both on land and water, has often been described as America's most obscure war. It is probably Great Britain's, too, all things considered. Donald Hickey, in his book *The War of 1812: A Forgotten Conflict*, writes that "the average American is only vaguely aware of why they fought or who the enemy was". The same would probably apply to the average Brit as well.

Hickey puts forward various reasons as to why this should be. There were no great presidents involved and no well-known generals led the charge – either literally or figuratively – in any notable land battles, with the possible exception of Andrew Jackson's defeat of the British at New Orleans in 1814. Neither were there any major naval engagements along the lines of Trafalgar or Aboukir Bay. Plus the causes were complex and are debated to this day.

Many scholars have argued that America went to war over free trade and sailors' rights. Others that it was down to western aims; a new and immature nation's desire to flex its muscles and finally expel the British from the continent – or, at the very least, weaken their influence over Canada and the Indian Nations – in order to secure additional farmland. Others have even put forward the theory that it was a Republican ploy to forge party unity, maintain power, and undermine the Federalists.

As to the consequences of President Madison's declaration of war in the summer of 1812, there is debate over those as well.

Compared to European conflicts of the time, the cost in lives was relatively small. British losses have been put at around 8,600 killed, wounded or missing, while the Americans suffered around 11,500 casualties. When the respective governments signed the Treaty of Ghent on Christmas Eve 1814, the agreement was that all areas of conquest were to be returned to the state that had existed before the war began.

If anyone could claim victory it was Canada. America declaring war on Britain and setting out to make British North America part of the United States led ultimately to the union of the provinces who came together to fight a common foe, thus laying the foundation stones for modern Canada, where the war is commemorated with a great deal of national pride.

But there were losers.

While fighting raged from Canada to the Gulf of Mexico, the main theatre of operations was along the Great Lakes and St Lawrence border which separated the United States from British North America. It was here, according to Carl Benn, in his book *The Iroquois in the War of 1812*, that the opposing armies shed the most blood; in the heartland of the Iroquois Confederacy (Rotinonshón:ni in Mohawk), the affiliation of Indian tribes also known as the Six Nations.

We have only the Iroquois' oral history as a guide, so the confederacy's founding date is difficult to determine. Some academics have put it at around 1450, while others say it could even have been as early as the twelfth century or as late as the beginning of the seventeenth. What is generally held to be fact is that the confederacy's founding father was Tekanawí:ta – the Peacemaker – a shaman and prophet who received a vision from the Great Spirit which set him on the path to bring unity and justice to the various warring tribes.

So successful was he that by the late 1600s the confederacy had become the greatest native polity in North America. Once dubbed the "Romans of the New World", the Iroquois, from their homeland in upstate New York, dispatched raiding parties as far south as the Carolinas, Illinois, Tennessee and Kentucky and as far north as Michigan and Ontario, subjugating every tribe they encountered.

But with the coming of the whites, all that was to change.

The first recorded contact between Iroquois and Europeans took place in 1534 when the French explorer Jacques Cartier met an Indian fishing party. In 1608 Samuel de Champlain built a trading post at Quebec. A year later he led a military expedition up the Richelieu River and into the lake that now bears his name. He and his Huron guides met and defeated a party of Mohawk, killing over fifty and taking several of them prisoner. It was an incident which sealed the Mohawk's hatred of the Huron and sowed their distrust of the French for the next two centuries.

But progress could not be halted. The arrival of the French and later the Dutch and the English led to the opening of the fur trade; the disastrous repercussions that enterprise inflicted upon the lives of the aboriginal population cannot be exaggerated. The demand for beaver pelts had the same effect on the Eastern Woodland Indians that the decimation of the great bison herds had on the Cheyenne and the Sioux during the latter part of the nineteenth century. It changed their way of life for ever. For after the hunters came the missionaries, loggers, settlers, speculators, assorted land agents and, of course, the government, and with the government came the wars.

France, Britain and America all saw the advantages in using Indian forces against their enemies. The Iroquois were superb fighters and they lent their skills to all sides. Of the Six Nations, the most feared were the Kanien'kehá:ka – the Mohawk – the Keepers of the Eastern Door and the first nation to join the Rotinonshón:ni. They supported the British against the French in a series of inter-colonial wars and aided them against the Americans in both the Revolution and the War of 1812.

But after the wars, when the guns fell silent, as has happened so many times over the course of history, the indigenous population and their contribution to the struggle for control of their continent were ignored.

By 1800, after a succession of disastrous treaties and through liberal use of bribery, deception, intimidation and force, Iroquois lands, which had once stretched for more than a thousand miles, covering tens of millions of acres, were reduced in size to a few small reservations in New York State. Home villages were abandoned when their inhabitants moved to new settlements in Canada. Since then, the ownership of the lands they vacated has always been in contention.

In 1974, Mohawk from the Kahnawá:ke Reserve in Canada and the Ahkwesáhsne Reservation, which lies close to the St Lawrence River in New York State, occupied an abandoned 612-acre girl-scout camp at Moss Lake, in the western Adirondacks and declared the re-establishment of the Independent North American Indian State of Kanièn:keh – also called Ganienkeh – on their traditional homeland.

After three years, the occupation ended. In 1977, after nearly 200 sessions of negotiation, the people of Kanièn:keh reached an agreement with the New York State authorities that saw the Mohawk leave their settlement at Moss Lake and move to a new site on Miner Lake, near Altona, New York.

The founding of Kanièn:keh was that rare instance where a native people took back their land from a colonial power. Today, Kanièn:keh claims that it has the right to exist as a sovereign entity under international law and functions under the original Kaianere'kó:wa – The Iroquois Confederacy's Great Law of Peace – without interference from either the United States or Canada.

For many years, historians claimed that the democratic ideals of the Kaianere'kó:wa served as inspiration to Benjamin Franklin and James Madison and the others who framed the United States Constitution.

Their faith was rewarded. In October 1988, the US Congress passed Concurrent Resolution 331 recognizing the influence of the Iroquois Constitution upon both the American Constitution and the US Bill of Rights.

As well as the various books mentioned above, my research was aided by the series of excellent War of 1812 documentaries which are available to view on the PBS website, www.pbs.org. I'm also grateful to Darren Bonaparte (cool name, or what?) who was very generous with his time and advice. His website, wampumchronicles. com, is well worth a visit for anyone who would like to read more about Mohawk history and culture.